Haunted Destiny

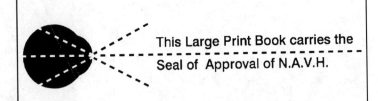

This Large Print Book carries the
Seal of Approval of N.A.V.H.

HAUNTED DESTINY

HEATHER GRAHAM

THORNDIKE PRESS

A part of Gale, Cengage Learning

Farmington Hills, Mich • San Francisco • New York • Waterville, Maine
Meriden, Conn • Mason, Ohio • Chicago

GALE
CENGAGE Learning·

LIBRARY OF CONGRESS CATALOGING-IN-PUBLICATION DATA

Names: Graham, Heather, author.
Title: Haunted destiny / Heather Graham.
Description: Large print edition. | Waterville, Maine : Thorndike Press Large Print, 2016. |Series: Krewe of hunters | Series: Thorndike Press large print core
Identifiers: LCCN 2016015586 | ISBN 9781410490377 (hardback) | ISBN 1410490378 (hardcover)
Subjects: LCSH: Parapsychologists—Fiction. | Large type books. | BISAC: FICTION / Romance / Suspense. | GSAFD: Romantic suspense fiction.
Classification: LCC PS3557.R198 H383 2016 | DDC 813/.54—dc23
LC record available at https://lccn.loc.gov/2016015586

Published in 2016 by arrangement with Harlequin Books S.A.

Printed in Mexico
2 3 4 5 6 7 20 19 18 17 16

For David Curtis Mutter, the best
piano man out there.
(Sorry, David! Yes, I turned you into a
young woman —
quite beautiful, though — for the
purposes of this story!)

And for FRW, surely one of the best
writing groups out there!

CAST OF CHARACTERS

FBI AGENTS:

Jackson Crow (Head of the Krewe of Hunters)

Angela Hawkins (Special Agent and Jackson's wife)

Jude McCoy (Special Agent in the New Orleans field office)

CELTIC AMERICAN CRUISE LINE (ON THE *DESTINY*) IN THE ENTERTAINMENT DIVISION:

Alexi Cromwell, piano bar hostess

Bradley Wilcox, head of entertainment

Clara Avery, soprano, in the ship's presentation of *Les Miz*

Ralph Martini, mature actor

Simon Green, chorus

Larry Hepburn, young heartthrob actor

KEY PERSONNEL ON THE SHIP:

Xavier Thorne, Captain of the *Destiny*
Larry Beach, Head of Security
Johnny Morgan, Security Guard
Jensen Hardy, Cruise Director
Nolan Perkins, Crew Steward

AMONG THE PASSENGERS:

Hank Osprey, brilliant young computer magnate
Roger Antrim, retired executive, and Lorna, his wife
Flora Winters, widow
Ginny Monk, dating Hank Osprey

1

They'd started out on foot that morning — not long after the murder was reported.

The murder that would soon bring the Big Easy to its knees; the eleventh attributed to the man the media had dubbed the "Archangel."

And who had now, apparently, moved into New Orleans.

The perpetrator had already left his mark on other cities. The first two killings had taken place in Charleston, South Carolina, where two women were murdered, their bodies found in churches; the actual crime scenes had never been discovered. That was eight months ago.

After that there'd been a lull. At that time the Archangel hadn't been given his moniker yet and he hadn't been on the nation's radar as a serial killer.

Some people wanted to believe that the killer himself was dead, or that he'd been incarcerated on other charges, the true extent of his crimes never known.

But those first two murders had held a strange signature — both victims displayed in churches with a saint's medallion around their necks. And most investigators expected the killer to strike again.

Which he did, four months later.

The killer had come farther south, taking two lives in Miami, Florida, and quickly followed by two more, just up the coast in Fort Lauderdale.

Then, for another four months, nothing.

Law enforcement worked day and night, certain that he'd strike again — but not knowing where.

He did.

He'd traveled on to Mobile, Alabama. There, he'd killed three young women and a young man — the boyfriend of one of them, by all accounts. He'd arrived too late to save the last female Mobile victim, and was not at all prepared for the homicidal knife-wielder he'd come to meet. An actor returning home after his show, he'd obviously put up a fight. The young woman had been left on church steps, the boyfriend dumped in an alley. They knew this time, however — from various cell phone calls and messages — that the couple had been attacked at the young woman's home, a small bungalow in a wooded area of the city.

But despite the disarray and the traces of blood in the bathtub, the killer had left behind no fingerprints, no fibers — no hint of his identity.

The last four had died in a period of three days, all while local law and the FBI scrambled after the Archangel like ants, certain they were getting close. They'd called out the National Guard in Mobile — only for the killer to refuse to strike again.

The one male victim had been dumped in an alley with no ceremony, while the young women's bodies had been discovered at a church, sometimes on the outside steps, sometimes by the altar. The Archangel had left each female victim laid out as if prepared for burial — arms folded over her chest, a silver saint's medal around her neck, almost covering the ribbon of red where he'd slit her throat.

Jude McCoy had seen the pictures; practically every agent in every city in the country had seen the crime scene photos of the victims.

And they'd all looked just like this young woman he gazed down at now. She lay before the altar of a church on the outskirts of the French Quarter, arms folded over her chest, a medallion of St. Luke around her throat.

Her name was Jean Wilson. She lay there, in front of the altar, a choir robe draped over her naked body, the telltale blood line around her neck — as if it was a chain for the medallion on her chest. She'd been young and beautiful with long, luxurious dark hair and coffee-colored skin.

Seeing her, Jude McCoy felt a mixture of horror, pity, rage — and helplessness.

He knew that no one in law enforcement was to blame. Not the bureau, Homeland Security or any branch of the local police. There were, according to the FBI specialists and scholars at various universities, anywhere between twenty and several hundred serial killers operating in the United States at any given time. This one, however, had been making headlines and had the entire nation on edge.

No one had known where he'd strike next.

Before this morning, Jude and the other members of his division had already been alerted. They'd sat through lectures by the bureau's behavioral sciences professionals. What they learned was that this killer was organized, and he was smart. He was either independently wealthy or had a job that allowed travel. He was aware of the need to wear gloves and leave nothing behind. He also had the ability, in a short span of time, to choose and stalk his victims and silence them quickly, although he never sexually assaulted them. They'd all been found in or near churches; murdered elsewhere, their bodies weren't dumped there, but *displayed*. They hadn't been killed in the churches; two, at least, were murdered in the victim's own home. Under most circumstances, Jude McCoy would have remained with the police and other FBI officers on the scene, since it was apparent that the victim had been moved from the crime scene and that the killer was long gone. He would have walked the church over and over again, making note of any little detail. He would have studied the street and determined just how the killer had traveled there with the body, how he'd brought it into a locked church and displayed it — without being seen.

But not that day.

After the medical examiner had arrived and Jude and Jackson Crow listened to his on-site findings, Jude moved back to the steps of the two-hundred-plus-year-old church to survey the sidewalk and the street.

Not surprisingly, nothing was *usual* that day. Everything felt different. The murder, of course. And maybe it was because he'd been abruptly paired with a stranger. And maybe because he'd heard things about Jackson Crow and his elite Krewe of Hunters unit. The Krewe had been formed right here in NOLA several years ago. Jude had received directions that morning. He would be on special assignment with an agent who knew the area well and had followed the trail of victims from Miami to New Orleans — Assistant Director Jackson Crow. When the body of Jean Wilson had been discovered, Crow had already been on his way in from Mobile, Alabama; he'd made an educated guess that the killer's next strike might well be the city of New Orleans. He'd been on the case for some time, or so Jude understood, and in this situation FBI involvement was expected. Jackson Crow headed up a *paranormal* sector of the FBI — that was the rumor, anyway. They were unofficially known as the Krewe of Hunters — ghostbusters, some people said. Whether that was true or not, Jude didn't know. He'd looked up their records out of curiosity; they did have an uncanny success rate hovering at almost 100 percent.

For Jude, the change of partners was not only an abrupt change, it was also one he wasn't sure he felt comfortable with. His usual partner, Gary Firestone, was at the scene, as well. In fact, with all the law enforcement agencies involved, the greatest danger was that evidence might get lost because of the number of people messing around.

But Crow seemed aware of the danger and quickly organized staff into work units. Somehow, he seemed to manage it all without incurring resentment. He was spare with words, determined, efficient in movement.

Working with him, so far, anyway, was all right; they had an easy rapport, probably since they were both focused on one thing — finding the demon responsible for such heinous deaths.

However . . . Jackson Crow was Krewe of Hunters. And thinking about his own past, particularly a strange event that had haunted him since he'd been in the military, he was a little wary of Jackson Crow. He was intrigued that Crow had sought him out, yet slightly troubled because of it.

He quashed the feeling. He didn't have time for that kind of emotion; they were in pursuit of a killer.

While the medical examiner worked inside the church, he and Crow had stepped outside. Uniformed police were cordoning off the area with yellow tape. A crowd of onlookers had gathered.

"Look," Jude said quietly to Crow.

There was a man lurking on the outskirts of the crowd.

Summer in New Orleans. Hotter than the devil's own seat in hell. And the guy was dressed in a sweatshirt, holding his head down, shuffling his feet, watching. There was something odd about his manner — and his appearance. His face was almost gruesome, and his nose was huge.

"I see him," Crow muttered.

The man might have been a voyeur, the kind who slowed down at the scene of a car accident.

And yet his behavior made him typical of killers who returned to see the aftermath of their work, getting their kicks all over again by seeing the police run around, the crowd gawk — and the relatives break down in tears and denial. Jude carefully started moving toward him.

Just then the man looked up. Jude froze behind one of the columns. It was important, he thought, that the man not see him.

His face was . . . unnatural. Not as if he was wearing a mask, but makeup. Prosthetic makeup, perhaps, giving him a larger nose,

16

a bulbous chin, harder cheek bones. The man turned to run, as if he'd sniffed out the fact that he'd been noticed. Jude shouted to Crow and began to run in pursuit.

Jackson Crow was already beside him. Running.

They tore across Rampart Street and into the Quarter . . . down, all the way down to Bourbon. And there they lost him. By then, of course, there were dozens of officers around.

"Every bar, every damn bar!" Jackson ordered. "The guy in the gray sweatshirt. Black hair."

It was still daytime, around three o'clock, but a summer festival was in full swing. Music of all kinds was blaring, tourists were crowding around and beads were being flung from balconies. There were hawkers on the street, and the sheer flow of people, from the slightly inebriated to the out-and-out drunk did not make for easy movement. Jude thought he saw the man head into a place called Piccolo's. He followed.

A four-piece band was playing a Journey number, and the crowd was gathered by the stage, singing along. Waiters and waitresses worked their way through the revelers.

Police and other agents were bearing

down on the bar, as well.

Jude quickly scanned the bar and the people inside it.

Crow was still right behind him.

"There!" Crow called out.

Their prey had leaped on top of the bar; a girl giggled and started toward him, ready to stuff some dollar bills in his pocket, or so it appeared. But the man jumped down from the bar, a stool crashed over and she went flying back, sending others onto the floor as she did. Chaos erupted to the refrain of "Don't Stop Believing."

"Lost him!" Crow said, swearing under his breath.

Jude was already climbing over the bar himself, past the stunned bartender — standing with his mixer in hand — and through the dingy kitchen to the side street. They were on St. Ann.

From there he saw the man step into the passenger seat of an old Chevy around the corner from the club — and even as Jude raced after him, the car pulled out into the street.

"Hey!" he roared to Crow. His new partner as of the morning was already outside.

"This way!" Crow shouted.

They moved down St. Ann at a run until they reached a bureau sedan. The driver stepped out.

"Assistant Director Crow," the man began, ready to leap into action as driver.

"We'll take it, Hicks," Crow said, accepting the keys and tossing them to Jude. "Drive. You know the streets better than I do."

Jude was surprised but pleased that Crow had the sense to realize that. And it was true. He knew the one-ways and he knew the cutoffs that happened so often when New Orleans was in festival mode.

The man driving the Chevy should have been stopped by the sheer volume of pedestrian traffic. So far, he'd banged on his horn and plowed through. Jude hopped into the driver's seat while Crow got into the passenger side.

Streets were closed; there was no way to traverse them.

Jude shot across to a side street, but the suspect was nowhere to be seen. Moving on instinct, he sped toward Canal, hoping to cut him off.

"Where are you going?" Crow asked.

"We'll catch him on the border of the Vieux Carre," Jude said.

And they did.

There they saw the Chevy surging ahead, and Jude did his best to follow without running over a pedestrian. Even on Canal, people were wandering on and off the road.

"Where's he going? What the hell?" Crow asked, shaking his head. "And who's driving? Are we dealing with a pair of killers?"

The man in the Chevy didn't seem to have a destination. He was driving erratically, avoiding the dozens of cop cars now on the road.

"Airport . . . train station . . ." Crow mused. "Hey! That was him, down Tchoupitoulas!"

"Might be going to the port," Jude said, still trying to follow the Chevy. He wasn't sure, but he thought that the driver was now maneuvering around a one-way street toward the Riverwalk area — and the massive cruise port.

Yes.

The car *was* going to the port!

As Jude drove hard, the siren blasting, Jackson Crow got on the radio, advising all law enforcement in the area to watch out for the car and the two men, giving a description of their suspect's clothing and appearance.

So many ships, so many cruise lines.

"There! Up ahead. The Celtic American line," Crow said. "I see the car."

The Chevy was in front of the entry to

20

the Celtic American line. More chaos was breaking out as last-minute cruisers competed for positions to park or drop off passengers.

Jude jerked the sedan off to the side of the road. Crow was out of the sedan before it was in Park. Seconds later he had the driver standing on the sidewalk beside the old Chevy.

He looked like a man in a trance. He was fifty-five or sixty, a slightly pudgy and balding businessman who seemed completely bewildered — as if he didn't know who he was or why he was there.

"Who were you driving? Why didn't you stop?" Crow demanded.

"I'm Walter Bean. I was supposed to pick up my daughter after her shift at the Red Garter . . . She's a hostess there."

"We need you to tell us about your passenger."

"I'm not even sure he was real, he showed up so fast! I don't know . . . I don't understand . . . Suddenly he was in the car, making me drive, telling me there was a killer after me."

"Where did he go just now?" Jackson asked. "Think. *Where did he go?*"

Walter Bean was very red and sweating profusely. He shook his head. "I don't know.

He said to stop here. I stopped. He got out of the car. I don't know if he . . . if he was a killer. I believed he *would* kill me. He was frantic. He said a killer was after me, and then he said he'd kill me if I didn't drive, didn't get him to the port. Oh, God, oh, God . . ."

The man clutched his chest.

"Heart attack!" Jude warned.

They patted his shirt for aspirin; Jude found the bottle, and Jackson got a pill in the man's mouth. Other agents ran up.

"Get him an ambulance!" Crow yelled, gesturing to a cop in uniform who rushed forward to help.

"Let's move," Jude said. He could hear sirens already. Walter Bean would now receive the medical care he needed.

Once again, he and Crow were running.

Jackson flashed his badge as they moved through the passenger terminal. They were asking questions at a checkpoint when Jude found himself studying a man who had boarded the ship. He'd just crossed the air bridge, and Jude could see him through the window.

No one there had seen a man who fit the description of the man they were chasing.

But Jude did.

He couldn't see him clearly; there were

too many people boarding at the same time.

He turned to Jackson Crow. "He's on the ship. It makes perfect sense. Every city where the Archangel has killed has been a port city — a port where cruise ships depart and return. Some crew members are on for nine months or more at a stint. Some hire on for two, four or six months, especially if they're entertainers or celebrity hosts, that sort of thing. Crow, it's what we've been trying to figure out! How and why the murders happen and then stop. He's either an employee or a passenger on a ship, and I have strong feelings it's that ship."

"Why do you think it's *that* ship?" Jackson asked.

"I think I just saw him. Or at least, I saw the man we were chasing."

"You're not certain?"

"No. Not 100 percent certain."

"McCoy, we don't even know if he's the killer! He could be some gawker jerk who's guilty of some minor crime — and afraid of all the law enforcement. He could also be late for a sailing."

"If he was just late for a sailing, he would've had to go through the line. But he's here on the ship. And no one runs like that because of a parking ticket. He's guilty of something major — *probably these mur-*

ders — and I believe he's on that ship."

Jackson Crow stared at him a moment longer; Jude didn't blame him. They'd met less than three hours ago. Crow had Native American in his heritage, and although Jude wasn't in any way enamored of stereotyping, Crow had the "stoic" attributed to Native Americans down pat. Jude couldn't begin to tell what he was thinking.

"Gut feeling," Jude told him, determined to be honest and equally determined to be convincing. "I have one hell of a gut feeling."

Jackson Crow brought out his credentials and started a rapid-fire discussion with a Celtic American security guard. Within seconds another man came down; some senior person with the cruise line.

When they'd finished speaking, Jude and Jackson were each handed a boarding pass.

"Ever been to Cozumel?" Jackson asked drily.

"Spring break, a thousand years ago."

Jackson shrugged. "Then you should remember it well enough. Anyway, let's hope to hell we're off by then — with him in cuffs. Because if we're not . . ."

"He'll kill again," Jude said quietly. He looked up at the behemoth they were about to board.

24

The *Destiny.*

She wasn't one of the largest ships sailing the seas by far. She was, Jude knew — thanks to the publicity at her most recent relaunch — the pride of the Celtic American line, owned by an Irish American who had come to the States as a college student and gone on to become a billionaire. The ship was old, commissioned in the late 1930s by an English lord who was hoping to give the Queen Mary a run for her money. The timing, for obvious reasons, had been bad. She wound up serving as a hospital ship during World War II, her cruising days curtailed by the devastation facing the world. Following the war, she'd gone through numerous hands until she'd been purchased and completely refurbished by Celtic American. The company specialized in historic ships, making that history part of their charm.

No, she wasn't one of the largest. She still carried about seven hundred crew members.

And over 2,400 passengers.

She was, in essence, a small city.

Jude looked at Crow, then studied the ship again.

"What?" Crow asked.

"He might be feeling the heat's on him now. And that means he just might kill again before we reach our next port."

■ ■ ■ ■

"I really think you should be playing more ballads." Minnie Lawrence said, her painted red lips forming a pretty pout. "This is, after all, a piano bar."

Minnie had draped herself on one of the velvet lounge chairs near the piano. She was beautifully clad in a slinky blue gown with a matching headband around her short blond hair. She managed to smile while maintaining her pout, behaving as the 1930s idol she'd once been. But she was truly sweet and very charming. Alexi could understand why she'd been so beloved in her day.

"I believe she means old ballads," Blake Dalton said, coming behind Minnie to lean rakishly against the chair as they both stared at Alexi Cromwell with their most beguiling smiles. "Well, what *you'd* call old ballads, at any rate!"

Blake definitely had some Valentino mystery-charisma, as well.

"I do my best," Alexi assured the two, sorting through the book she kept for the passengers who wanted to sing. She looked up at them and sighed. "Honestly. I do. But this is the twenty-first century. And I play our passengers' requests. That's my job."

"I'm a passenger, and I'm requesting!" Minnie said.

But you're a dead passenger! Alexi wanted to say.

She refrained.

"I do a smashing version of 'Somewhere Over the Rainbow,' " Minnie said. "And it was in *The Wizard of Oz.* Surely, everyone knows that."

"Or 'In the Mood'!" Blake said. "Minnie sings that very well indeed."

"You do way too much of that new fellow, that Billy Joel man," Minnie said. "I just can't fix on a key with him."

"Most people these days don't consider Billy Joel to be a new fellow and I'm sorry, but I never go a night without someone wanting 'Piano Man.' But a number of people really enjoy older numbers and ask for them, too. How about this? I promise I'll do 'Somewhere Over the Rainbow' tonight. How's that?" Alexi asked.

Before Blake or Minnie could reply, a man came tearing into the Algiers Saloon, racing through the bar area — for employees only — to leap over a neighboring sofa and continue running down the hallway of the St. Charles Deck.

He moved so swiftly that Alexi never saw his face. She had a fleeting impression of

27

his height and appearance — and something a little ghastly. He looked as if he was wearing makeup for a Shakespearean play or a classic Greek drama.

Gray sweatshirt, blue jeans, about six feet, maybe around two hundred pounds.

"Well, I never!" Minnie sniffed.

"How incredibly rude," Blake said, trembling with the indignity of it all.

"We've seen plenty of rude. At least he didn't jump over the sofa where you two are sitting!" Alexi told them, lowering her head so they couldn't see her smile.

Sometimes, guests *sensed* the pair of ghosts. She would see them shiver and look around, remind themselves that they were on a floating island with thousands of people around them. She knew it disturbed both Blake and Minnie when people walked through them. It didn't *hurt* them — they simply didn't like it. Blake once explained to her that it felt as if someone had shoved you carelessly in a crowd. It was rude, just rude. "Some staff member who's late reporting in, maybe," Alexi murmured. "Anyway, my friends, I'm going to my cabin while the stampede of boarding takes place. I'll see you soon."

Alexi rose, scooping up her book, laptop and extra music pages. She smiled at Blake and Minnie. "I promise, we'll start off with Judy Garland," she assured them.

"Lovely!" Minnie called after her.

"Shall we stroll, darling?" she heard Blake ask Minnie.

"We'll find a place high atop and watch as we sail away, watch the city disappear and the beauty of the moon upon the water," Minnie agreed.

Alexi smiled as she hurried on, anxious to get to the elevators and down below where the crew members had their cabins.

She loved having Minnie and Blake on the ship. The *Destiny* had lost many employees to the ghosts they *encountered* on board. People had reported seeing images disappear and things being moved about. Sheet music seemed to do that a lot, according to people who'd worked on the ship. Actually, Alexi owed her position to the fact that the pianist who'd been preferred by the entertainment director had lasted only one cruise. As a result, Alexi had been hired. She was sure that the musician who'd left — disturbed by the way his sheet music constantly moved and keys played when he hadn't touched them — would find a job that made him happy. He was a far better pianist than she was. But he hadn't felt the same need to escape, to live this strange life of fantasy the way she had.

Escape.

She couldn't escape. Her sister, her brother, her parents, her friends — everyone had told her that. Zach was dead. He'd come back from the Middle East in a box. She knew that. She'd never escape the fact that he was dead. But she *could* escape New Orleans, their little Irish Channel duplex and the places they'd frequented for years.

She realized, as she walked, that she'd been on the ship for almost a year. Well, four months on and one off, and then back on, accepting contract after contract with the cruise line. And although she might not have the astounding talent of some piano bar hosts, she did have a way with a crowd. Perhaps equally important, she never complained about ghosts or poltergeists.

She'd been aware of the dead as long as she could remember. Early on, her mom, not in so many words, but by careful suggestion, had let her know *the sense* ran in the family.

And it was best not to share that with others. She was pretty sure her mom didn't actually see or hear ghosts; with her, it really was a *sense.* She felt when they were close, felt the happiness that had existed — and the trauma and tears.

As Alexi walked down the hall to her cabin, she passed Clara Avery, one of the entertainers in the ship's main show, *Les Misérables.*

Clara was supremely talented; she was a soprano with a genuinely impressive voice.

"Hey!" Clara said. "You were back-to-back cruises, too, huh? Did you take some time to get off the ship? Did you see your family?"

"Yes, they came and met me for lunch near the port," Alexi told her.

"Good." Clara hesitated. "It's been a long time, Alexi. I can't imagine having your wedding all planned — and him not coming home. But you can't let your family lose you, too."

"I know. I know that, really. I see them as often as I can. Honestly. I love my folks. I didn't see my brother because he's on tour and Sienna's in Europe. On vacation. Well deserved, I imagine." She grinned. "My poor parents. They're so . . . mathematical and scientific! And they wound up with two entertainers and only one doctor, Sienna!"

"I'm sure they're proud of all of you," Clara said. She grinned. "I think my dad cried when he found out I wanted to go into theater. But he's happy now!"

"And he's a super guy. They came to the

piano bar almost every night they were on the cruise — even when you couldn't. Your mom is lovely, too."

"Your folks haven't taken the cruise yet," Clara noted.

Alexi shrugged. No, her mother would never be on this ship. She didn't see the dead the same way Alexi did, but she knew they were there. She worried not just because Alexi was a piano-playing hostess on a cruise ship; she worried because Alexi was on the *Destiny.*

"The things that happened on that ship!" her mother had warned her. "Terrible! And not just the poor soldiers who died. There were other incidents, too!" The *Destiny,* like most old ships with interesting histories, had the reputation of being haunted.

There'd been incidents aboard, yes. Such as the night in 1939 when Blake and Minnie had died, murdered in cold blood.

But Alexi wished she could explain that none of the ghosts on the ship were malevolent in any way. She'd come across a couple of soldiers who'd died in the infirmary: Privates Jimmy Estes and Frank Marlowe, handsome young men who'd been taken far too soon; Barbara Leon, a nurse who'd died of a fever she'd caught while tending to others; and Captain McPherson,

32

who'd dropped dead of a heart attack at his retirement party, which had been held on the ship in 1967.

He still loved to tell her what the current captain was doing wrong.

All the *Destiny*'s ghosts were pleasant. The soldiers still believed they were convalescing, the captain was still watching over the bridge, and the nurse was still standing duty at the infirmary. They were polite and cheerful, thrilled that Alexi — and more often than not, her friends — could see them.

Her family really didn't need to worry about her. She accepted the fact that Zach was gone. Time didn't heal all wounds, but it allowed memories to offer consolation, to bring smiles instead of tears. She had simply become rather dependent on living on the ship. And she did love the *Destiny,* including all her history and her ghosts. Alexi didn't lie awake at night anymore, the way she had at first.

She'd lain awake and wondered why, when the dead from so many different eras and generations found her, she'd never seen Zachary Wainwright, never had a chance to hold him and be held one last time. Never had a chance to say goodbye . . .

Alexi smiled. "My mom won't be getting on this ship and without my mom — no dad. Mom's convinced the ship is haunted, which of course it is, and she wants nothing to do with that. She's . . . I don't know . . . very Catholic, slightly Wiccan, possibly? She believes that spirits can find her. Don't get me wrong, I adore my mother. But my dad always smiles and tells me that when they were married and moved into our home in the Irish Channel, she called in a priest to bless the house and cleanse it of ghosts."

"She sounds like fun. And, hey, I agree with you that this ship is haunted! I try to say nice things to whatever gives me the chills as I walk by," Clara said, shrugging. "In any event, they leave me alone."

"I'll see you in a little while," Alexi told her. "I'm going to grab some downtime with a pillow."

"And I'm going to pop into the lounge," Clara said. "Come with me and say hi. We have some new people in the entertainment crew."

Alexi didn't particularly want to say hi to anyone at the moment; she wanted to lie down. She'd had lunch with her parents on shore, and much as she loved them, an hour or two in their company could be exhausting.

"Just for a sec!" Clara encouraged.

Alexi followed her into the crew lounge.

They didn't separate crew down here. It was a hallmark for most people who accepted employment with the Celtic American line. Entertainers and officers mingled with room stewards, even though the lounge space was small. But there was a television, a computer, lots of comfortable chairs, plenty of snacks, a refrigerator, coffeepot and a microwave.

And right now the lounge was crowded, mostly with entertainers, those who didn't play or perform as the passengers boarded. "Hey, new guys! This is Alexi Cromwell, for those who haven't met her yet. She runs the piano bar and she loves it when we stop by."

"Hi, Alexi!" Ralph Martini was the first to hail her. She knew Ralph. He'd been on her first contract schedule.

Ralph continued with, "I'm not new. I'm just saying hi first!" Ralph was a friendly, easygoing guy. She thought he was about fifty. He had a great tenor and often did a one-man show. Balding, a little stout — and totally charming. Women on board loved him.

"Alexi. I'm Simon Green," a man said, rising and offering her his hand. He was tall and lean, with a pleasant boy-next-door face. "In the cast, my first go at it. Just a chorus guy."

"No such thing as *just a chorus guy,*" Alexi said. "I'm sure you're very talented. Good to meet you, and please, come by anytime."

Simon Green shrugged, giving her a smile. "I'm a happy guy. I've been on a few cruises with Celtic American as a passenger. So I'm thrilled to be on the *Destiny* and seeing how it all works from the other side!"

She went on to meet Larry Hepburn, early twenties, blond, beach-boy type, out of LA, and Leanne Wilburn, from Des Moines. As they were all greeting one another, Bradley Wilcox, head of entertainment, who'd recently transferred over from the *Dublin,* stuck his head in.

Alexi had met Bradley Wilcox before. He, too, had been on her first run with the ship.

She stayed away from him as much as she could. He organized excellent shows, hired great bands for the various dining spots and bars — and was a complete jerk. He didn't seem capable of compliments.

"Guitar Hero Boys, you're due on the promenade in fifteen minutes. You should be getting in place."

The foursome who made up the group rose and marched out. Alexi heard one mutter as he passed her. "Are you set up? Yes. Ready to go? Yes. Are you an asshole, Brad? Yes!"

She tried not to smile. And when the band had gone by, she left, too, wishing them all well — those who were new and those who'd returned to the *Destiny* or had switched from other ships.

In her cabin, Alexi sank down on the bed and closed her eyes, wishing she could sleep. She found herself thinking about Blake and Minnie.

Their deaths had been tragic. Minnie, a star of stage and screen, had fallen in love with Blake when he'd played Romeo to her Juliet in a touring company in the thirties. The fact that she was taking the *Destiny* for a transatlantic voyage had been huge news at the time; reporters and fans alike had booked onto the voyage.

The fans had included a deranged former lover, convinced that if he removed Blake from the picture, he would have his Minnie back.

Minnie had been singing an impromptu number in the piano bar. Also known as the Algiers Saloon, it was located exactly where it was now. Her previous lover, Allan Snow, had leaped to his feet after one of her numbers and declared his devotion. Minnie had claimed her eternal devotion, as well — to Blake.

So Allan Snow had pulled out a gun and

shot Blake, who'd jumped in front of Minnie to be her protector. Then he'd shot Minnie and himself.

The ghost of Allan Snow didn't seem to be aboard. Minnie told Alexi that she'd never seen him and she'd figured that God had been good, allowing her and Blake a different way to be together. She'd smiled and said their love was eternal.

Alexi figured it was natural that they'd haunt the piano bar.

She turned and hugged her pillow. Since Zach had been in the service and deployed overseas, they'd talked about the possibility of his death. She'd promised that if it happened, she'd always remember him — and she'd go on with her life, be happy.

She wasn't suicidal, never had been. She was willing to find a new purpose, a new role, a new way of being. Just as she'd promised. *Happy* was more difficult.

What worried her now was the fact that he was slipping away. She thought about him often, with love. Sometimes she was happy now. She laughed at the antics of passengers and enjoyed meeting them. She'd even roamed various ports with friends she made aboard. She knew she shouldn't feel guilty, and yet she did.

She reached into the gloomy air of her

cabin, as if she could touch him.

"I just wish I could've said goodbye," she murmured aloud.

Then she was startled out of her reflections when it seemed that something slammed against her door.

She jumped up and hurried to open it.

A man stood there, tall, dark-haired and . . . *bizarre.*

He was wearing a gray sweatshirt and blue jeans and strange prosthetic makeup. The man who'd raced through the piano bar!

He looked at her with beseeching eyes.

"I must speak with you. I must!" he said.

She frowned. Was he new in the entertainment department?

There was a commotion at the aft end of the hallway, and Alexi peered in that direction.

More men were coming along the hallway, men she'd never seen down in the entertainment area before, but they were accompanied by Nolan Perkins, one of the stewards.

"Sir," she began, turning back to the man who had knocked at her door.

He was gone. She thought she saw him disappear around a corner that led to midship. She looked in the other direction.

"Hey, Alexi," Nolan said.

"What's going on?" she asked.

"I'm just showing these gentlemen the ship," Nolan said. He lowered his voice. "They're bigwigs with Celtic American," he told her, then cleared his throat. "Alexi Cromwell, meet Jackson Crow and Jude McCoy."

"How do you do?" the first man said, smiling as he reached for her hand. He was tall, good-looking and obviously had Native American ancestry. His dark hair and light eyes made for a striking contrast.

"Ms. Cromwell," said the other. He was equally tall, broad-shouldered, sandy-haired. His eyes were unusual — blue and green with flecks of brown. His features were clean-cut, his jaw hard and square. Very attractive, in a rugged, austere manner.

He looked at her oddly.

As if he knew her? Or thought he did?

Or worse — thought she was guilty of something!

Both men wore tailored shirts and pants, not the usual tourist apparel. But then, they weren't tourists. They were bigwigs with Celtic American.

"Nice to meet you," Alexi said.

"Have you seen a man?" Nolan asked her.

That made her laugh. "A man? Nolan, I've seen hundreds of men. It's a cruise ship."

She understood exactly what he meant. And yet, for some reason, she was loath to tell him that yes, a man — a strange-looking man — had just gone by. She wondered why company VIPs were so interested in him.

"He's tall, bizarre makeup of some kind, sweat shirt and jeans," Jude McCoy said.

She lifted her shoulders. "I believe I did see him earlier," she admitted, "running through the piano bar when the passengers were boarding."

She *had* seen that same man again, just minutes ago. And she wasn't telling these men. Why? Instinct? Pity?

But there'd been something even more peculiar about him than the prosthetic makeup or whatever it was he had on his face. A sense of anguish, perhaps.

She hesitated. She shouldn't lie to these people. But the young man had seemed so desperate. In her heart, she felt that he'd come to her for help.

Still . . .

"Actually," she said, "I think he was in this hallway. He ran in that direction. But where he is right now, I couldn't say."

That was mostly the truth. She didn't know where he was. He'd run.

"Well, thank you, Ms. Cromwell. If you should see him again, can you report him to us, please? We're in staterooms 312 and 314," Jackson Crow said. "It's imperative that we find him," he added quietly. "But I'm not at liberty to discuss the details."

"Of course," she murmured.

As they walked down the hall, she was more suspicious than ever.

Why were company bigwigs staying down in the bowels of the ship with the crew? The larger rooms — staterooms with balconies, the suites — were on the upper decks.

She was about to return to her cabin when Clara came running down the hallway, leaning against the wall, gasping for breath. "Alexi! Did you have the news on?"

"The news? No, why?"

"Thank God we're leaving! That guy, that horrible killer!" She gasped for more breath. "The Archangel — he murdered a woman in New Orleans!"

2

It wasn't until the *Destiny* was far out into the Gulf of Mexico that Jackson Crow and Jude had a chance to meet with Captain Xavier Thorne and his head of security, David Beach. Their first business on board after walking every deck, including the holds and areas passengers never saw, was to go through the ship's passenger and crew screening. There was a page for every passenger and crew member on board, including a photograph and information regarding citizenship and means of identification. A ship-issued ID was required anytime anyone, passenger or employee, boarded or left the *Destiny.*

In other words, *no one,* including crew, could get on or off the ship without that ID.

Jude and Jackson hadn't seen their man in the thousands of passenger screening documents — but then, even if they'd seen him, they might not have known him.

This suspect could have ditched his makeup anytime after he'd boarded. Or certainly, after he'd been seen by Alexi Cromwell.

It was time to explain to Thorne and Beach just what they were doing there.

Xavier Thorne was fifty-five, according to the information they had, a veteran of many sailings. He'd served in the United States Navy before becoming a civilian employee in the pleasure business; he'd worked as a captain for smaller yachts doing private charters and for a number of the major lines before he'd settled in at Celtic American fifteen years ago. He was a serious man, but still capable of smiling.

Jude had wanted to stop the ship from going out, which had proved to be impossible. Not even the powers that existed behind Jackson Crow had been able to make that happen. Neither he nor Crow knew for sure if the man they'd chased was a killer. And, despite Ms. Cromwell's sighting, they couldn't *verify* that he was on the ship. At least his new partner/supervisor seemed to believe him. He'd not only put Jude on the ship, he'd also accompanied him. So now, at five that afternoon, they met with the captain and Beach.

44

David Beach was an ox of a man, almost six and a half feet tall. Jude, at six-three, felt dwarfed by him. Beach also had stellar credentials, having served with the NYPD and Homeland Security before retiring at fifty to enter the civilian sector and take the job with the Celtic American line.

They knew all this because they'd accessed Jackson Crow's home office to receive dossiers on every member of the crew.

Now they sat in the captain's office to speak and while the space was large enough, it felt small. David Beach, Jude thought, could make just about anyone — short of Shaquille O'Neal, no pun intended — seem small and any space seem close and crowded.

Beach remained quiet after Jackson had spoken, and Captain Thorne frowned as he weighed his response.

"You believe you've chased a serial killer onto my ship?" he finally asked.

"Yes, Captain," Jude replied. "We believe that the killer's been using cruise ports and ships to track and murder his victims — and that we followed him onto the *Destiny.*"

The captain shook his head. "I don't see how you could know this. I heard about that terrible business at the church in the Treme district and I don't think anyone, anywhere in the world, has missed the news about the fear this man is creating, but . . . this was the killer's first strike in New Orleans."

"You don't really even know if the man you followed onto the ship was responsible for the heinous act at the church," David Beach added.

"Captain, we followed a man who behaved suspiciously at the crime scene. I'm aware of both your backgrounds," Crow told them. "Mr. Beach, you've certainly been through seminars on the psychology of killers like this. The man's behavior was the kind we consider exceptionally suspicious."

"So they sent the troops out on a ship because of a man behaving suspiciously at a crime scene?" Captain Thorne asked. "Seems to me it would've made more sense to prowl the streets of New Orleans, tracing hard evidence."

"Trust me, Captain, there are many law enforcement officers doing just that," Jude said.

"Of course. I assume every law enforcement officer in the States is on the lookout, but —"

"We don't intend to be intrusive," Crow assured him.

"Frankly, whether you are or not, I have no real power over this." Thorne glanced over at Beach. "Word's come down from on high at Celtic American. We are to give you every assistance you require. However, I'd hate to put an entire ship full of people into a state of panic because you chased a man for behaving in a manner you describe as suspicious and you *think* he's on this ship."

"We don't want a panic, either," Jude said. "What we *do* want is to advise you that this man may be on board and may be dangerous. I would imagine," he went on, and he could hear his voice harden as he spoke, "that you'd be concerned. You have several thousand passengers, not to mention a large crew, any of whom could be in danger. Granted, most of the so-called Archangel's victims have been women but he's killed at least one man. We'd like you to make a speech warning *everyone* to take extreme care, to lock their cabins and watch out for their personal safety."

"Every cruise company in the world has guidelines warning passengers that while all precautions are taken, crime can still happen," Beach told them.

"I don't usually make announcements like that," Thorne murmured.

"You can make it friendly," Crow said. "As well as serious."

"And of course, you need to alert your

crew, and, most important, Mr. Beach, every one of your security officers," Jude put in. "I doubt this man is still dressed the same. He'd have his own clothing or he'd have stolen a change of clothing by now."

"Can you give me a description of his face?" Beach asked.

"Tragedy," Jude said, recalling the strange prosthetic makeup he'd seen on the man.

"What?"

"He was wearing theatrical makeup when we saw him," Jude explained. "He's probably gotten rid of it, cleaned up, by now."

Thorne raised his salt-and-pepper brows beneath his captain's hat and looked over at Beach. Then he stared hard from Jackson Crow to Jude.

"Gentlemen —"

"Assistant Director Jackson Crow and Special Agent Jude McCoy," Crow interrupted. He smiled, appearing polite, ready to be friendly and helpful, while ensuring that their purpose was noted.

Captain Thorne nodded. "But you need to realize that you're asking me to put a security crew and every one of almost a thousand crew members on guard *and* warn over two thousand passengers — many on the vacation of a lifetime — that there may be a killer on board. 'Enjoy the crystal beauty of the Caribbean! Ah, but be aware. The FBI believes there might be a homicidal maniac on board. Apparently, he was wearing makeup and God knows what he's wearing now. Watch out for him, though!' " He rolled his eyes. "Sorry, Agents. But on this ship I'm like the president, the grand high master, the great pooh-bah, what have you. I can't scare them all half to death."

"We haven't asked you to do that," Jude said flatly. "Captain, don't you want this man caught? Don't you want your passengers safe?"

"Of course!" Thorne replied indignantly.

"Just remind them of safety-precaution tips — and even mention the horror in NOLA without suggesting the killer could be on board," Crow said. "Make sure your officers are advised. Make sure they patrol the bars and clubs and watch out for men who seem to be stalking women."

Beach muttered something under his breath. They all looked at him.

He sighed. "I'd say at least some of the people on this ship are out for more than fun and sun — a chance to get lucky outside their real world. How can I watch everyone in the middle of that kind of behavior?"

"You've been a cop. You know how to observe people, how to judge their moods, how to tell when something's out of whack," Jude said.

Beach nodded grimly. Jude was glad that he'd brought up the man's past; it seemed to remind him of his own sense of self-respect and ability.

"We also have almost limitless resources working on this. Within a few hours, we'll have cleared the majority of people on this vessel. Investigators in our main office will soon learn who has and who hasn't been in the areas of the country where the murders were committed. That will eliminate the majority of people on the ship," Jude said.

Captain Thorne was obviously relieved. "The killer had to have traveled, right? Miami? Fort Lauderdale?"

"And Mobile," Crow said.

"Assuming it's one killer, which we believe it to be," Jude added.

The captain rose. "I must be getting back to my duties," he said. "You'll keep me apprised of what you discover? When do you expect your reports?"

"Soon," Crow assured him. "And thanks for the use of your computers." They'd been given a cabin near the security offices, complete with high-end equipment and systems.

"I'd like the reports as soon as possible.

Naturally, I expect you to be discreet. I don't want people in an uproar because they're afraid a killer could be on board — unless we find it to be true." He paused. "You believe this man might be a frequent traveler or a ship employee? No murder has taken place on the *Destiny*. Well, except for the strictly historical ones," he acknowledged with a grimace. "You might keep my passengers the safest by never indicating that you suspect this killer might be on board. You could cause an out-and-out panic. Some sort of mistaken vigilante justice, that kind of thing."

"We've taken that into consideration, Captain," Jude said.

"Which is why we want you to make your announcement very carefully," Crow told him. "Just mention that, since the ship disembarked from New Orleans, we're all aware of the recent murder. Say that our hearts are with the family and friends of the young woman killed in New Orleans. Emphasize that they should take care at all times, even amidst the warmth and hospitality of the *Destiny*."

"I'll give this some serious thought," the captain said. "Now . . ." He smiled drily. "Enjoy your time aboard the *Destiny*. She's a splendid lady, created when sailing meant grandeur."

They left the captain's office. "That didn't go badly." Jackson Crow gave Jude an awkward half smile. "Not as badly as I expected."

"Could've been worse," Jude agreed. "How soon will we get those reports?"

"In an hour or two. Meanwhile, I'm going to suggest that since the shops on the Promenade Deck are open, we buy more appropriate attire. Once we've done that, I suspect we'll have our reports. Not just names and numbers, but in-depth intel on anyone who might've been in any of those ports at the relevant times."

"You have someone really good on this?" Jude asked.

Crow nodded, his smile growing. "The very best. Angela Hawkins. My wife."

At seven Alexi joined Clara and some of the other performers and crew members in what they affectionately called "the bowels," or the employee cafeteria area, far toward the stern on the second deck. They didn't dine in any of the three main restaurants on the ship, but in a private space that didn't sport linen napkins or elegant wineglasses. It was still fine; Alexi thought the food served belowdecks was just as good as that in the dining rooms and buffets above. She also liked the fact that the Celtic American line considered all "staff" — from prestigious guest performers to the catering and cleaning crews — to be equal. There were no elite employees. Bradley Wilcox was hard to take at times, but aside from that, they were all treated courteously and with respect.

Alexi scooped up tuna and chips and got a salad from the buffet. She saw that Clara was seated with Ralph Martini and Simon Green. Ralph was shaking his head as she sat down with them. "Can't figure it. Can't figure how the police haven't got this guy yet." He shuddered. "Sorry. I'm obsessing. It's just . . . he's in New Orleans!"

"He struck in New Orleans," Simon said. "Doesn't mean he's still in New Orleans. He may be moving north now. Or to Texas."

"How can the cops not catch this bastard?" Ralph asked.

"I'm sure they're doing everything they can," Clara said.

"Hey, there are fibers, fingerprints, blood . . . Forensic science has given the cops all kinds of tools for catching killers," Ralph protested. "I watch all those crime-scene TV shows. This guy has to have left something behind."

"The police use experts and technology and everything," Alexi said, "but crimes aren't always that easily solved. I mean, even if you do have a hair sample, you have to have a suspect to compare it with. And from what I've read, it sounds like the killer must watch all the shows, too — since he *hasn't* left anything behind."

"Not that they're telling us about, anyway!" Ralph said.

Young, blond and sun-drenched handsome in shorts and a tank top, Larry Hepburn made an appearance with his tray, smiling and indicating that he'd like the seat next to Alexi. "You people are being morbid and depressing, and you need to stop," he said as he took his chair. "It's hot and humid, but we're at sea and a breeze is coming in. We have to have faith and let the cops and agents and whoever else worry about it. Who knows? They may have him by the time we're back to port."

"Or he'll have moved on. To Texas, probably," Simon said, obviously still worried. He looked around the table. "I have a sister. And I'm from Galveston. If he does head for Texas, terrible as it may seem, I hope he goes to Houston."

"They'll get him," Larry said. He turned to Alexi. "We have a rehearsal tonight. After

54

that we'll come by the piano bar. Or at least, *I'll* come by the piano bar. They say you're always packed. You must be good."

"I'm good at getting people to sing," Alexi said. "And that's what they want to do at a piano bar." She smiled at him, but suddenly wanted to escape. She was horrified by what had happened in New Orleans and disturbed by the men Nolan had introduced her to, the Celtic American line "bigwigs," and the strange man she'd seen running by. Something was going on.

"And that's why they love you!" someone announced. Jensen Hardy, the cruise director, was beaming down at them from the end of the table.

She'd sailed with Jensen before. He was a nice guy — but so perpetually cheerful that he actually got on her nerves. He was a great cruise director, precisely *because* he never seemed to tire. He had a crew of underlings who managed everything from kids' activities to "naughty" trivia, poolside events and more. Jensen was determined that everyone on board have a good time.

She forced a smile. "Thanks, Jensen."

"Squeeze in, can you?" he asked.

"I have to leave, anyway," she said. "You can have my seat."

"Aw, we have to switch you out for Jensen?" Larry teased.

"Yes, for now," Jensen said, sounding stern. "But don't leave right away. I want to remind you all that many of our passengers have saved for years to get on this ship. We're on the pricier side, as you know. We're here to see that they're entertained. I overheard you talking — murders are happening in the States, not on this ship. Don't go about discussing your fears or ideas, okay? We're not going to ruin lifetime dreams for hundreds of people, are we?"

"Nope, we're not!" Alexi agreed. She stood, a little too wedged in between Clara and Larry, and she smiled apologetically. "Jensen," she told the cruise director, "I will be the embodiment of good cheer. You all have a great rehearsal. The show is the highlight of the cruise for many people. And yes," she added, smiling at the performers, "I'm delighted when you come to the piano bar — especially since, every once in a while, no one wants to sing, so it's great to have your voices."

Larry moved aside but offered her a come-hither smile as he did. He was used to people liking him. He was definitely hot and studly; it was just that his kind of hot and studly was lost on her. She managed a polite smile. "See you later," she said as she tried not to brush against him. She made her way around him, ready to take her tray to deposit at the receptacle.

"You're the best, Alexi!" Jensen called out.

She widened her smile — and escaped them.

Set for the evening in a feminine tuxedo, she went up to the piano bar, passing through the casino, waving or saying hello to some of the hosts and hostesses she'd sailed with before. She crossed the Picture Gallery and one of the night clubs on her way to the piano bar and paused to browse through some of the pictures.

The gallery was always fun to see. Couples smiled and embraced as they were photographed boarding the ship. Large family groups, sometimes all wearing the same T-shirts, grinned and posed for the camera.

Frowning, Alexi went through the first round, the boarding photographs. It wasn't that she really studied every one. But she was pretty sure that at least three travelers had not been captured by the camera.

She didn't see either of the "bigwigs."

Nor did she see the man who'd leaped through the piano bar and shown up at her door.

It was a mystery, but one she didn't intend to pursue at the moment. She went to her piano; seated at the bench, she arranged her music, smiling and telling those who paused to ask that she started at nine.

Her first number would be "Somewhere Over the Rainbow" as she'd promised. That would make Minnie happy.

She actually began a few minutes before nine, welcoming the people already seated at the bar and at the cocktail tables scattered around the room. There were children among them. She idly played melodies while she talked to the guests, asked where they were from and made a point of involving them. Parents usually took their kids up by ten or eleven.

Minnie draped herself over the piano and Blake leaned against it.

"Minnie is ready," Blake told her.

Alexi smiled as she looked down at the keys. "Hey, kids! How many of you have seen *The Wizard of Oz*?"

Some had; some hadn't. A few had seen newer versions of the old classic.

She talked about the original movie and the book, and was glad to see one preteen gazing at her with wide eyes.

She hoped they had the book in the ship's library, because she knew the young girl would be asking for it the next day.

"So this, my young friends," she told

them, "is the song that Judy Garland sang in the original movie — which is even older than I am!" She sang the song. Minnie, of course, was singing, too, in her high, clear soprano. Blake was watching Minnie, enthralled.

It had taken Alexi a while not to be thrown off by Minnie, but now she kept her ghost performer's voice in a compartment in her mind.

She paused to encourage everyone to join in on the chorus.

A cheerful group did so. Even a grouchy-looking old man urged the kids to sing along. When the song ended, she found the piano surrounded by young fans. She asked them what they liked, and pretty soon she'd begun a round of tunes that encompassed most of the animated films produced in the past fifty years. Little girls were fond of princess movies, while little boys seemed to like superheroes of all kinds, pirates and robots. At least, that was the case with her young crowd tonight.

She was glad to see she had two seasoned travelers in the piano bar that evening — Roger Antrim and Hank Osprey. They weren't close friends who took trips together, but retired men who often took Celtic American cruises. Roger had been a

TV network CEO and he and his wife, Lorna, just hopped on a cruise whenever the whim struck them. They preferred the Caribbean, since they were both fond of heat. Hank was some kind of computer programming whiz who'd sold his first multimillion-dollar company before his thirtieth birthday. He wasn't yet forty, although he was retired and rolling in money. Alexi was surprised that he wasn't married and that he usually sailed alone. He was slender but wiry and while not classically handsome, he had warm brown eyes and a pleasant face. He'd told her once that he tended to attract beautiful women — who were usually after his beautiful money. He was looking for a nerdy girl, he'd said. Or a musician, he'd added with a wink, at which point she'd explained that she had a while to go before she was ready to see anyone again.

She'd mused on his comments, thinking that many young women might like the idea of being with someone who had everything — everything material, at least. She liked him just fine; the problem was that she felt absolutely no sense of attraction to him. Hank got on well with kids; he was far easier, more relaxed, with them than he was with adults. So she wasn't surprised that he popped up, asking if he could sing a number from *Song of the South.*

The ice was broken. Roger came up next, wondering if she knew an old cartoon song, which she fudged. The kids sang some more, and then Roger and Hank sang a few tunes. After that she started getting passengers to join her on the choruses, but not performing themselves.

Luckily, Larry Hepburn showed up, just as he'd promised, around ten thirty. She made the kids very happy by doing a few prince/princess duets with him. Then the families began to leave and the more adult crowd moved in. She did some Carole King songs; a regular who was often on the ship sang a couple of Billy Joel numbers and Larry piped in with some Broadway. Someone requested a number by Lady Antebellum, and Larry took a seat at the piano with her to share the song.

Luckily, it was during Larry's part that Alexi noticed the man standing across the hallway from the open bar; he leaned against the clear glass walls to the Banshee Disco.

It was the man she'd seen earlier. But as she watched him, he began to pull the prosthetic makeup from his face. It fell away in clumps; he seemed oblivious.

He just stared at her — and she stared at him.

Larry nudged her. She realized her fingers had moved over the keys by rote, but she was forgetting to sing.

She corrected her mistake quickly, breaking the song to make a joke and tease a woman who was coming in to take a seat. Then she picked up the song again.

When she looked back, the man was gone.

Why hadn't she told the men she'd met that afternoon, the men from Celtic American's headquarters, more about him? What if he was a weird social predator of some kind?

He wasn't, she thought. He was young, in his early twenties. Not particularly tall or well built, but attractive in a wholesome way. She'd seen that once the makeup was gone.

She was grateful that Clara came in then; she asked her friend to do some Kelly Clarkson songs. Clara smiled and agreed.

Alexi searched the area to see if the young guy had headed toward the gallery or even the casino; she didn't see him, but she did note that one of the "bigwigs" was in the lounge.

She froze, quickly looking from him to her piano keys. It was the man who'd been introduced to her as Jude McCoy.

He looked more as if he belonged on the cruise now, wearing denim jeans and a blue polo shirt. Maybe it was because of the shirt, but it seemed as if his eyes were more blue this time than green. A piercing blue. He seemed to be studying her, but for some reason, she didn't believe he was grading her performance or planning to fire her.

He seemed to be looking for something else.

Perhaps he knew she'd been lying to him earlier.

"Let's do the duet from *Wicked*!" Clara said.

Clara was leaning on the piano, dangerously close to Minnie. Minnie could have moved; she didn't. Instead, she glared at Clara — as if she saw her as a rival for Blake's affections.

"Come around here," Alexi suggested, and Clara joined her. Once again, Alexi felt strangely hemmed in, seated between Larry Hepburn and Clara. But she smiled, talked about the fact that they'd started the night with "Somewhere Over the Rainbow," which made it fitting that they should move into the popular Broadway play.

She loved the duet and had done it with Clara many times. They were a hit with the crowd, who applauded loudly. When Alexi looked around again, Jude McCoy was gone.

She didn't understand why she felt so miserable. The night was endless. Other members of different entertainment groups on the ship came by and sang. The crowd grew a little more giddy — the many ship's cocktails no doubt had something to do with that — and was ready to laugh about anything.

Finally, Clara said good-night and left.

Soon after, Larry, tired of being brilliant and handsome, said good-night, too.

Even Minnie and Blake left the piano bar, holding hands, smiling, waving as they headed out for a "constitutional."

By one o'clock, the crowd had dwindled down to about five. Alexi announced the last song, but even after that people stayed. She made a point of picking up her music books; the cocktail waitress made a point of clearing the tables and announcing which lounges were open until two.

At last she was alone. She sat at the piano bench and sighed, closing her eyes, enjoying the moment of peace.

When she opened her eyes, she nearly screamed.

He was back. The man who'd raced

through the lounge today, who'd reappeared in the hallway and then again tonight — standing there, watching her, ripping off his makeup.

There was no one else near her now.

The gallery was closed.

She could hear bells and whistles from the casino, but it seemed far away.

She glanced over to where he'd been standing earlier and began searching the floor. There was nothing there, no refuse from the prosthetic he'd peeled off his face. His makeup was now as ghostly as he was himself.

She turned back to him.

"Please!" he whispered, adding quickly, "Yes, yes, I'm dead. But I need your help. And please believe me — you need mine!"

Jude was tired but he wasn't giving in to his exhaustion until the last of the guests on the *Destiny* had cleared the lounges and gone to bed.

Stupid, maybe. He couldn't be on every deck, and he and Crow had decided they were going to split the time while they waited for the next reports. Crow had gone to his cabin; he'd get up in an hour or so and cruise the decks. They had no idea what time the Archangel struck. No one really

65

knew, since his victims were discovered by day. In every case, the time of death could only be approximated. It was presumed that he killed at night, making use of the darkness and the shadows. If someone meant to attack a guest, this would be the time. Easy to follow an inebriated or tipsy young woman down a quiet hallway . . . and slip up behind her.

The ship, although certainly not mammoth like some sailing the oceans these days, was still big enough. He'd walked from one end to the other, from one deck down to the next, pausing to watch in the various lounges, bars and clubs. He'd enjoyed the piano bar — casual, friendly and engaging. Ms. Alexi Cromwell had deft fingers on the piano keys and she was quick to come up with little routines to entertain the crowd. He'd watched her with professional detachment at first; she was slim and shapely, her hair richly beautiful with its deep mahogany color, and her eyes were the color of amber. Not brown, not green, not hazel, but truly amber. She was both tart and charming and seemed to have no ego. She smiled with delight when her friends joined her and applauded their talent.

And yet, every once in a while when he

looked at her, he thought he saw something infinitely sad. She was a bit of an enigma.

Of course, any real mystery about her would be easily solved. They were in the process of receiving more detailed information on every member of the crew and guest list. They needed to know who to eliminate so they'd know who to focus on. Of course, he didn't really need to study her history, since they didn't suspect the murders had been committed by a woman, although they'd never discounted the possibility that a man and a woman might be working in tandem. God knew it had happened before.

But he was intrigued. He was more than intrigued. He was attracted to her. He'd barely spent any time with her, and yet he wanted to know everything about her. Where she'd come from, where she saw herself going. More than that, he wanted to touch the deep fire of her hair and . . .

Well, more. And he needed to cut his thoughts off right there.

As he'd traveled the decks, he'd found country-western singers, a DJ spinning away in a disco room, a Latin Lovers lounge with salsa, an upper-crust Sky High club where a lone tenor entertained with old big band songs. He'd found the kids' "Rock N Roll Ship Shop," where there'd been games and a dance floor. Then there were the elegant dining rooms, the library, the computer room and more.

He hadn't seen the man they'd followed onto the ship. Or had he? If the man had cleaned his face, they'd never know.

The guy's movements pegged him as young, Jude thought. Between eighteen and thirty.

That left them down with about a fifth of the ship.

As the hour grew later and later, he prowled the hallways. A couple passed him, giddy and laughing as they hurried to their cabin, acknowledging him as they passed.

He decided he'd check out the ship's chapel, which was aft on the Promenade Deck.

It was locked. He was tempted to break it down or call the captain or the chaplain, regardless of the hour. But there was a mullioned glass window to the chapel and he could see through it; there was no one inside.

No young woman lay there, arms crossed over her chest, a circlet of blood around her throat, and a medallion bearing the image of a long-gone saint.

When he moved through the central area again, even the casino was quiet. The Picture

Gallery was closed for the night.

The disco was silent, as was the piano bar.

Except that the piano bar wasn't empty; Alexi Cromwell was there.

And she wasn't alone.

Jude went completely still, staring at the young woman — and the young man who sat beside her. He wasn't in any kind of makeup. His face was boyish, his hair medium length, rakishly tousled. He was talking to Alexi, being very earnest.

He had the same body shape and size as the man he and Crow had witnessed earlier, the man they'd chased, and he was wearing the same hooded sweatshirt and jeans.

Jude made his move, striding down the length of hallway between them, half running by the time he neared the piano.

But he wasn't quick enough. The man at the piano saw him and leaped up — and in a flash he was gone, racing up the steps to the deck above.

Jude glanced at Alexi Cromwell. She watched him with a confused frown. He shook his head as he looked at her, then took off after the man on the stairs. She followed him, calling out, "Mr. McCoy, wait! Please wait!" She was obviously trying not to shout or attract any attention — except, of course, his.

He ignored her, intent on his quarry. But the man was gone by the time he reached the next deck. He hurried halfway down the row of shops there and then ran over to the cabin hallways on either side, first one and then the other.

She kept following him. He came back through the center of the deck with such speed that he plowed right into her.

"Ms. Cromwell!" he snapped, catching her by the shoulders. "Get out of my way!"

"But . . ."

"I have to find that man!"

She grasped his shirt as he held her shoulders, trying to move her aside.

"Wait! You mean you saw him?"

"Of course I saw him. Will you please move!"

"I can move, but you won't find him if he doesn't want to be found."

He stopped, brows knitting furiously as he stared down at her.

"Are you his accomplice?"

"His accomplice in what?"

"You're hiding him," he accused her.

"No!"

"Then what is it?"

She drew in a deep breath, staring up at him, searching his eyes.

"He's . . . he's not — alive," she said.

He knew his jaw must have fallen open.

"*What?* Look, it's imperative that I find him. You don't understand what's at stake."

"No! *You* don't," she said softly. "I realize it sounds crazy, but —"

"Very crazy. You know him? Get him for me. Now," Jude insisted, determined to be stern. He was astounded that this young and charming woman was apparently involved or under the spell of the man who'd been gaping at the church where the last victim was found — and led them to the ship.

"I can't!"

Her voice had risen with exasperation.

A security guard came hurrying down the stairs from whatever rounds he'd been on. He was wearing just a shirt and tie, but Jude knew security when he saw it.

"Is there a problem? Alexi, you okay?" the man asked, eyeing Jude as if he was the worst pervert in the world.

"I'm fine, Johnny, absolutely fine!" she said, running her hands down Jude's chest with a gesture of affection. "Johnny, this man is my friend," she told the guard, and added softly, "Upper echelon, Celtic American!"

"Oh?" The man seemed skeptical. Jude had been ready to whip out his manufactured credentials, but Alexi was continuing as if she'd bought his story about being a Celtic American official. Even if she didn't *really* believe it . . .

"I'm so sorry we disturbed you. We haven't seen each other in a while and I got carried away talking about a movie I saw while I was off!" she said.

Jude decided he'd wait to see what this woman had to say. In any case, she had nowhere to go. But his quarry was definitely gone.

"Well, Alexi, keep it down, huh? Most of the ship's asleep."

"I know, and I'm sorry."

"And just between us, we're on the lookout for men who're acting badly. Bothering women and such."

"Oh?" That really seemed to surprise Alexi. "*Was* someone . . . bothered?"

He shrugged. "We're supposed to be extra-vigilant. So, you're absolutely sure you're okay?"

"Yes, thank you, Johnny." Johnny the security guard nodded at both of them and went back in the direction from which he'd come.

Alexi Cromwell looked at him, her eyes grave and troubled. "We can't talk here. You can . . . you can come to my cabin."

When his day had begun — or when the previous day, actually had begun — the last thing he'd expected was that he'd wind up standing in a deserted hallway on a slumbering ship, a stunning woman in front of him, inviting him to her cabin.

And yet, he knew instantly that it wasn't a sexual overture.

"Ms. Cromwell," he warned her. "You'd better have an explanation."

She stepped away, assessing him. "Right. You're no Celtic American bigwig. I'm assuming you're some kind of law enforcement."

"FBI," he told her.

She nodded. "FBI. Well, you're also what we call a magic man."

"Magic man?"

"You see the dead. *Magic man* — it's an old term in my family. I think it originated with a grandmother who lived on the bayou. Please, just come with me. I'll do my best to explain."

3

Jude McCoy, FBI man, entered Alexi's cabin, not saying a word until they were seated in her tiny quarters. Alexi perched on the bed, McCoy sat in the one chair, which faced the dressing table built into the wall.

"Dead?" McCoy said, turning the chair toward her. "You mean our suspect? And yet he was running around the city of New Orleans and now the ship."

His skepticism was blatant. "Ms. Cromwell, I saw that man at a murder scene in New Orleans. We chased him to this ship. He snagged a ride with some poor bastard on the street who thought he was about to get killed. Oh, by the way, I believe that poor guy's in the hospital with a heart attack. Now the suspect's on the ship. I saw him."

"Yes," she said. "Whether you accept it or not, you see the dead. Trust me."

"You're telling me you're aiding and abetting a *dead* man we chased from the scene of a horrific crime?"

"Yes. I didn't get much of a chance to talk to him. He led you here on purpose."

"A *dead* man led me here?"

He didn't raise his voice. But the sharp look he gave her suggested he'd be good in an interrogation room. If she'd done something, she thought, she'd admit it quickly. He was still, calm, and while his voice had a strange power, he kept it low and intense.

"I didn't get to hear the whole story," she said. "I gather you came after him."

"If he's dead, why is he afraid of me?"

"I don't really know the answer to that," Alexi replied. "I didn't get enough time to talk to him. All I know is that he believes the killer's on this ship. Yes, you saw him at the crime scene. He saw you there — and he saw that you were aware of him. He planned on coming on the ship. Look, I see the dead. It doesn't mean I *understand* them any more than I understand the living."

He leaned toward her. "I saw a man at a crime scene. The older guy driving the car saw him. I'm pretty sure a girl in a bar saw him, and I know my partner on this ship did, too. So, what — we all see the dead? Everybody does?"

75

"No, but more people do than you probably realize." Alexi lowered her head. There was a reason she didn't admit to seeing ghosts on the ship. Sometimes, others saw them, too, but, like this man, they had no idea they were seeing the dead. She assumed that, in the world at large, there were many people with this ability. Some sensed the dead, like her mom. Perhaps their fear kept them from really seeing. Some just didn't understand what they saw.

But judging by the way this man was looking at her . . .

It reinforced her decision to keep silent most of the time. "I can try to find him or I can hope he comes back to find me, and then maybe you can get your answers," Alexi said.

The fact that Agent Jude McCoy was such an *attractive* man didn't make the situation any easier. His presence seemed to fill the tiny space of her cabin. She felt she could almost hear the steady beat of his heart — and feel the waves of ridicule coming from him.

He rose abruptly. "Ms. Cromwell," he said, "Please know that I'll be watching you, and that I'll report our conversation to my partner. And when I find this so-called dead man, if you've helped hide him in any way,

76

I will see that criminal charges are pressed against you."

She stood, as well, suddenly angry. His height was imposing — but then again, she'd stared down David Beach a few times and he was a huge man.

"Knock yourself out, Mr. Agent McCoy, or whatever your title may be. You're chasing a dead man. Period. And therefore, I'm not afraid of your ridiculous threats in the least!"

"We'll see, won't we?" he asked softly.

He barely had to move to open the door to her cabin, but when he did, he turned back. "I hope you're right, actually. I hope this man isn't the killer — and that he isn't baiting you. I've seen one of the Archangel's victims. I'd hate to see you in that condition."

Sincerity at last. Something in his words, something about his voice, caused a cold flash of dread to sweep through her.

She didn't have to reply, because he was already gone.

She made sure that her cabin door was locked behind him.

She hugged her arms around herself, shivering uncontrollably.

She'd been glad the dead man had finally sat down beside her, and that he'd tried to talk to her. She still didn't know his name or exactly who he was or why he was there, but she understood.

He'd *wanted* to lead the FBI men to the ship.

Because he believed there was a killer on board.

The Archangel.

It was ridiculously late, but Jude headed down the hallway straight to Jackson Crow's cabin.

But he hesitated before knocking on the door. He wondered if what he'd read about the paranormal angle to Crow's "elite" unit was true — that agents were hand-selected to work in the "special" department known as the "Krewe."

He was on board with nothing except the few toiletries and articles of clothing he'd purchased at one of the ship's stores. His phone, however, was the next best thing to his computer, and that was in his pocket.

Rumors abounded. But research into the Krewe didn't give him much other than the knowledge that whatever they did, they were damned good at it. Looking up newspaper reports of the cases they'd solved gave him a little more. Jackson Crow was indeed familiar with New Orleans; he'd solved a case in the city that involved the death of a politician's wife in one of the city's "haunted" houses.

As he went on, he even found more information on the Krewe's cases, many speculating that the Krewe of Hunters had an uncanny ability to deal with situations of unusual scope.

He buried his face in his hands for a moment as he stood outside Jackson's door.

Great.

He was on a ship chasing a killer, and he was working with a man who believed they could question a ghost.

Did Crow think they were chasing a dead man? It was all too crazy.

Jude had to assume Crow saw the dead, and he based that on the Krewe's reputation as much as anything.

It was time to confront Jackson Crow with what he'd learned.

Jude tapped at his door. In the silent hallway, the sound reverberated loudly. Or it seemed to.

The door opened immediately. "You've got something?" Jackson asked.

"A ghost," Jude told him.

"Come in." Once again, Jude found himself sitting on a chair in front of a tiny dressing table built into the cabin wall. Crow settled on the narrow bunk.

"You talked to a ghost?" His voice was calm, reserved, and Jude couldn't tell if he was being mocked.

"I didn't," he said. "But the piano bar hostess claims that the man she was talking to — the man we followed on the ship — is dead. And yes, that she was *talking* to him."

Crow took that in. Once more, his expression revealed nothing.

"The man escaped you again?" Crow asked.

Jude leaned forward. "I saw him, clear as day, sitting at the piano bench with her. I saw him — clear as day — jump up and run. I couldn't stop him. Ms. Cromwell stopped me instead and then insisted I come to her cabin so she could tell me that he's a dead man."

"What information did she say she got from him?"

"Not much. Apparently, my arrival interrupted him. She said he wanted us to follow him onto this ship — because he believes the killer's on board."

"What do you think of this young woman?" Jackson asked him.

"What do I think of her? I don't know. She's either delusional — or this guy's as real as you and me, and she's helping him in some way. And if she is, well, then, God help her," Jude said.

"But she seems sane to you?"

"I have to admit, I've been through plenty of behavioral classes, and yet I can't come up with a reliable definition of *sane.* She seems to be sincere. So yeah, maybe she's just delusional. Maybe this guy has her fooled, but she might also come from some crazy family that believes in all kinds of weirdness." He watched Jackson for a moment. "But what the hell. I've read a few strange things about your unit, too."

He thought Jackson gave him the hint of a smile.

"I haven't apprehended a murdering ghost yet," he assured Jude. "But then again, we don't discount anything on heaven or earth or anything in between."

"But . . . ghosts?" Jude asked.

Jackson shrugged. "Let's see if we can find this man. Tomorrow is a day at sea. We have the ship's security forces and we have ourselves. By tomorrow morning I'll have a full manifest of anyone on board who could possibly have committed the murders. We believe — every profiler out there believes — that this is the work of one killer and we assume that he's male. That said, I'll have reports by tomorrow that should tell us who could and couldn't have been in the cities where the other murders took place. Of course," he added with a dry smile, "it would be nice if Ms. Cromwell's ghost happens to know who the killer might be."

"Her damn *ghost* just might be our killer," Jude muttered.

"Since the killer struck in several cities and we're going to learn who, on the *Destiny,* was in those cities at the relevant times, we'll be able to concentrate on those particular people." He looked at Jude, studying him. "Good call on the ship. Makes perfect sense. Ships contract crew and entertainment for specified periods of time. Crew and entertainers might work on other ships, too. A great way to get around port cities — and kill." Jude rose; Jackson hadn't given him any kind of satisfactory answer regarding Alexi Cromwell.

"Stay close to Ms. Cromwell," Jackson told him. "She might be our key."

Key to insanity! Jude thought. But there was no point in saying anything else.

He'd been dismissed.

"Good night, Jackson," he said as he stepped into the deserted hallway.

The ship was quiet for the night, although somewhere, members of the crew were still working.

He prayed that a killer wasn't doing so, as well.

"At least we've narrowed down the possible number of needles in a haystack," Jackson said. He sipped from a steaming mug of coffee. Jude had met him at the café on the Promenade Deck. There were a number of tables, spread out a fair distance apart. It was a great area for people-watching, while carrying on a conversation without being overheard.

That morning they were attired in outfits acquired on board. Jude was in navy blue board shorts and a short-sleeved flower-patterned cotton shirt; Jackson wore khakis and a T-shirt with an image of Janice Joplin on the front. Jude figured they looked like the tourists they were pretending to be — or perhaps "bigwigs" disguised as tourists . . .

Jude nodded as they both studied their phones.

Their task had been made easier than it might have been. Computer programs had allowed tech support workers at the home office to narrow down who, of the several thousand crew and passengers, had been where when. With the majority of the passengers, it must have been pretty straightforward. They'd been in their home states working — until it was time for their vacations. With those who traveled for work, the task was somewhat harder. Their movements had to be traced through hotel and restaurant bills. Same with those who were independently wealthy.

Big Brother might not always be watching — mainly because Big Brother wasn't interested most of the time, Jude thought wryly — but Big Brother was capable of a great deal of research.

"Angela went through every report personally," Jackson explained, perusing the list. "She's meticulous."

"Your wife, right? Unusual that you're in the same unit," Jude said. There was no problem with agents being partners or married, but they were generally required to be in separate units.

Jackson glanced up. "It's different with the Krewe. Angela and I met when the Krewe of Hunters was first formed. The unofficial name is the Krewe because, as I'm sure you've assumed, our first case was in New Orleans."

"Yes, of course. I know about that," Jude said.

Jackson returned to studying the list on his phone.

Jude studied his own list. Jackson Crow didn't act as if he wished he'd managed to have one of his own people on this case.

But neither did he see him as a particularly valuable asset. Or at least that was what Jude sensed.

"So the possible suspects," Jackson began.

"Passengers Roger Antrim and Hank Osprey," Jude said.

"And we have an interesting list of entertainers." Jackson took another sip of his coffee. "Larry Hepburn, Ralph Martini, Simon Green — and head of entertainment, Bradley Wilcox." He nodded at Jude. "Your friend from the piano bar should be able to help us as far as the entertainers go."

For a moment Jude wished he had real printouts — paper he could actually write on, the old-fashioned way — and wasn't working on his cell phone. He refrained from saying so to Jackson.

"Everyone on this list *could* have been in each city where the murders took place," Jackson went on. "These are the entertainers who were between contracts. As far as the two passengers go, both are businessmen with deep pockets. And judging by the number of times they've sailed on Celtic American ships, there's every chance they were in the port cities where the previous

85

victims were killed."

"Wow," Jude murmured, reading. "The list also includes the ship's head of security, our friend, David Beach."

"I'd put him toward the bottom of the list," Jackson said. "The man has an impeccable background."

"Which may or may not mean anything."

"No, but because of his size —"

"He'd be noticed wherever he went," Jackson agreed. "And the last one we have here is the cruise director, Jensen Hardy."

"Two passengers, Roger Antrim and Hank Osprey. One security man, David Beach. No regular crew members — dishwashers, stewards, mechanics. Three entertainers. Ralph Martini, Simon Green and Larry Hepburn. Plus the head of entertainment, Bradley Wilcox. And last, but for the moment we won't say least, one cruise director, Jensen Hardy."

"Eight suspects," Jackson said. "I'll talk to Beach. We'll give him the list — minus his own name, of course. And we'll keep a sharp eye on him, but he and his staff need to be on the lookout. You should go and see Alexi Cromwell again. Actually, I'd like to speak with her, too."

Jude stared down at Angela Hawkins's report, which included pictures of the suspects. "I don't believe any of these men are the one we followed on board," he said.

"No?" Jackson shrugged. "Ghost or not, I haven't really seen his face yet. I don't get it. I don't get what he was wearing. It wasn't a mask. But he *was* disguised."

"A killer would want to disguise himself," Jude said.

"Well, we'll see, won't we? How's your cell working out here?"

"I'm set for international. Should be fine."

"Let's head out. Don't forget, I want to talk to Ms. Cromwell later."

"We can arrange that," Jude said.

"All right. I'll go chase down David Beach. You see what you can do with the entertainer group and we'll send for more info on our two passengers." Jackson rose. Like many law enforcement officers in the field, he'd taken his coffee black and finished two cups.

Jude picked up his own mug of black coffee and finished the last couple of swallows. He rose, too. "I'll find Ms. Cromwell. But all in all, you might do better in dealing with her. I'm not sure she was . . . comfortable with my response to her last night."

He was surprised Jackson smiled at that. "I think you'll do fine."

They parted ways.

Jude used the stairs to reach the crew and entertainment level of the ship. He paused at her door. The entertainers slept late, he assumed, since they worked late.

He raised a hand to knock on the door.

It opened.

Alexi Cromwell seemed very bright and attractive for someone who'd been up until at least 3 a.m. the night before.

She glanced up at him warily — and yet as if she'd expected him.

"Ms. Cromwell, I'd like your help," he began.

"To meet the ghost?"

He didn't answer that. Instead, he asked, "How well do you know your fellow entertainers — and do you ever get to know the passengers?"

"Some of the entertainers I know quite well, but some are here on their first contract with the *Destiny.* Maybe you'd like to meet a few of them yourself?" she suggested.

"I would, thank you," he said.

"Come to the employee cafeteria and lounge with me. I can introduce you to some of the people I know." She looked at him anxiously. "Do you really believe the killer is on the *Destiny?*"

He decided not to lie to her. "Yes," he said.

"Because your man — my ghost — came on the ship?"

"Yes."

"But since you don't believe me and you think this guy is alive . . . Maybe if that's true, he was watching what was going on, and then realized he was late for the sailing."

"No."

"Why do you say that?"

"His behavior."

"It's still just a hunch."

He didn't admit that she was nearly right.

She smiled. "So you believe in gut feelings and not much else."

He shook his head, almost smiling, but he wasn't willing to discuss it. "My partner on this case wants to meet you, by the way. We'll get to that later. Meanwhile, I'd appreciate going to the employee cafeteria with you."

"Follow me," she said. As they left her cabin and walked down the narrow hallway, she added, "You're aware that there are quite a few entertainers on the ship, aren't you?"

"Of course."

"Anyone in particular you want to meet?"

Jude had memorized the names. "Simon Green, Ralph Martini and Larry Hepburn.

And your head of entertainment, Bradley Wilcox."

"Oh!" she said.

"You know them?" he asked her. "Well?"

"Bradley Wilcox was the head on my first contract with Celtic American, too," she said. "He's talented at his job."

"And?"

She shrugged. "To my mind? A jerk. Rude. He seems to think we're all lesser individuals. His servants. But as I said, I have to admit he's good at his job."

"What about the others?"

"This is the first time I've been on the same ship — same contract — with Simon Green and Larry Hepburn. Ralph Martini, I do know. I've worked with him before. He's a nice guy and, again, very talented." She glanced at Jude sideways and he was surprised to realize once more how attractive she was, with her head of sunset-tinged hair and amber eyes.

Just the type the Archangel might choose . . .

"Be careful around these people," he said, his voice gruff.

"They're really suspects? Is there a reason for that?" she asked.

"Proximity," he replied. "They might've been in all the locations where murders took place. And you really *shouldn't* know what we're thinking, and I shouldn't be speaking to you about this at all. At the moment, though, you're about all I've got."

"So, I'm all you've got. Great," she murmured.

But he could tell that she *did* intend to be helpful.

"Grab a tray," she told him, leading him to the buffet. "I see Simon and Ralph — they're over there."

He selected a bagel and a plate of eggs from the buffet and followed her to the table.

Ralph and Simon greeted her with friendly smiles and she introduced them to Jude. "Company bigwig," she said lightly. "Watching us on board."

Ralph stood up to shake Jude's hand. He was a stocky middle-aged man of about six feet. "He's a great tenor!" Alexi said in a cheerful voice.

"And I'm chorus." Simon got up to shake Jude's hand, as well.

"We all start somewhere," Ralph said.

Simon Green was a handsome man, young, classically good-looking. He was lean, and Jude figured he must be a decent dancer if he was in the chorus of a play like *Les Miz.*

Ralph grinned. "Should we be afraid of

you?" he asked. He obviously wasn't.

"No." Jude grinned back. "We're just observing, trying to see what works and where improvements might be made," he lied. "I understand that the entertainment on this ship is excellent."

"That's a relief," Ralph said. "Hey, there's Clara." He waved and Jude turned. A very pretty blonde had come into the room. She looked over at them and waved, frowning curiously as she saw Jude.

"Just getting some food!" she called.

"Clara Avery," Alexi told Jude. "She has a gorgeous soprano voice."

"Part of our *Les Miz* cast," Simon added. "I'll find a chair for her."

Clara joined them a moment later. "You look peaked, girl!" Ralph said to her. "You up all night?"

"Nightmares," Clara said shortly. "Hi," she greeted Jude.

Alexi quickly introduced them.

"Nightmares?" Simon asked her. "On the ship?"

"I shouldn't have, but I stayed up watching the news," Clara replied. "That Archangel killer out there — he was in New Orleans!"

"And he's probably already moved on," Simon said gently. "He goes from city to city. You're safe on this ship. And we're all here with you," he added.

"They don't seem to have anything on this guy, nothing at all! They can't even find some of the actual crime scenes," Clara said, shivering.

Jude considered himself a good judge of character. He believed that the men at the table were as concerned for their friend as they appeared to be. Their empathy and determination to assure her seemed completely genuine. He was as confident of that as he could possibly be.

A good thing, since this young woman, like Alexi, would certainly appeal to the killer.

He lowered his head.

The ship has many beautiful young women aboard. A veritable feast for the so-called Archangel.

Clara shivered again, then managed a smile. "I'm going to stick close to all of you."

"The cops aren't sharing much information," Simon said. "I read somewhere that the women weren't just found in churches, but that they were all posed, with saints' medallions around their necks. What do you suppose it means?"

"I didn't hear about that," Ralph said. "I'll bet the cops weren't supposed to give out

93

that information. I guess some of 'em talk when they're off duty. And once the media gets hold of something . . . well, you know! Of course, I don't think anyone could miss the news that he leaves his victims in churches. Or sometimes on the steps."

Jude was intent on watching their faces and was startled when Alexi Cromwell suddenly rose. Her meal was only half-eaten.

She seemed to notice that everyone was staring at her.

She was thinking fast, Jude thought, looking for a plausible lie. Why, he wasn't sure yet.

"I just saw someone you need to meet," Alexi said, turning to Jude. "Ralph, would you mind returning our trays? Um, Mr. McCoy, would you come with me?"

"No problem," Ralph said, but he watched curiously as Jude excused himself and followed Alexi out of the cafeteria.

Then Jude saw why she'd left so abruptly, why she'd summoned him.

The man in the hooded sweatshirt was moving along the hallway.

"Wait, please!" Alexi called out. The young man who'd tried so hard to speak to her — who'd disappeared at Jude McCoy's arrival last night — had popped his head into the

94

cafeteria.

Now he was hurrying down the hallway.

If nothing else, she somehow had to convince the FBI man that she was telling the truth.

His quarry was a dead man.

"Please!" she called again.

He stopped and glanced back at her and then nervously scanned the hallway.

Alexi realized that Jude McCoy — once again — saw him, too.

"I need to speak with you," the agent said. His voice was calm and even.

The young man remained where he was.

Alexi kept walking toward him, with Jude a few steps behind. There was no one in the hallway just then, but at any minute there could be workers coming through, either to get to their gigs or to eat or return to their cabins if their shifts were during the off-hours.

"My cabin," she whispered.

She reached her door and used her key card to open it. The young man paused, looked at her — and then at Jude McCoy.

Then he stepped into her cabin; McCoy followed.

"Who are you and what's going on?" McCoy asked.

Alexi stared at him. He still didn't know.

He still didn't get it. But the ghost, whose name she didn't know yet, answered him.

"Byron Grant," he said.

The name was vaguely familiar to her; she wasn't sure why.

The FBI agent knew it instantly, though, and his tension and anger were unmistakable.

"Byron Grant is dead, killed in his attempt to save Elizabeth Williams."

"Yes."

Jude McCoy stood completely still, green eyes with their flecks of gold focused on the ghost.

Alexi clutched the edge of the built-in wardrobe as she sank to the foot of her bed. *Now* she knew. Now she understood.

Jude McCoy continued to watch the man in disbelief and anger. She thought, not for the first time, that he knew the truth — he *knew* it — but didn't want to accept it.

Suddenly, his face changed. He reached out as if to place a hand on the ghost's shoulders.

And, of course, he touched nothing.

Ghosts could surprise you. They could learn to make noise, to displace air about, to move objects . . . but they weren't there in substance, as flesh and blood. They were energy, capable of so much — and yet never again would they have bodies that could be touched.

"My God," Jude breathed.

He didn't sag onto the floor. He just stared at the man, almost as though he wished Byron would disappear.

He seemed to hope that the ghost's presence was impossible, a figment of his imagination.

Alexi thought she saw him wince. Saw a slight trembling seize his body.

And then he looked at the ghost again, at Byron Grant, and said, "I don't suppose you're going to be able to tell me who killed you?"

"No," the ghost said. "There's only one thing I can tell you with absolute certainty."

"What's that?" Jude McCoy asked.

"The killer is on this ship."

4

Jude managed to sit, to put aside his own past, his emotions, his disbelief and worse . . .

The fact that he could see the dead —
And speak with a ghost.

The essence, soul or whatever remained of Byron Grant perched next to Alexi on the bed, while Jude took the chair at the dressing table. And he listened as Byron Grant told his story.

"I loved Elizabeth. I'd loved her . . . since high school. We'd been together ever since then," he said. "We were a good couple, a great couple. We would've been married this Christmas." He paused, obviously pained. "She had her wedding dress picked out."

"I'm so sorry you lost her," Alexi said in a whisper. "And I'm sorry about what happened to you."

"I will be with her again. I know I will. I . . ." He paused and gazed at Alexi in obvious distress. "I don't know why I'm here, and she's not. But I have to believe . . ."

"You *will* be with her," Alexi assured him. "Soon."

"You're here right now to help us," Jude said.

Oh, God, that had to be the truth. Otherwise he'd completely lost his mind and entered into some grand delusion with this young woman. "You brought Jackson Crow and me onto this ship," Jude continued.

Damn it! He should have recognized the man immediately. He'd seen pictures of all the victims. And he finally put the facts together.

Byron Grant had been an actor. He'd had stage makeup on when he was killed. Jude berated himself — why hadn't he figured it out, put the facts together more quickly?

"Yes, I knew he'd be on this ship." Byron hesitated once more. "I didn't know he'd kill again before the ship sailed."

"You were playing Cyrano!" Jude said. "My God, I'm an idiot. That was in the police reports. I just didn't connect it with the makeup . . . or realize that the man I was chasing was really one of the victims."

Byron Grant studied him, head at a slight angle. "Yes, I was playing Cyrano de Bergerac." He paused. "I had a hard time getting that makeup off. As a ghost, I mean," he added glumly.

Alexi Cromwell was silent as she watched the exchange.

But Jude could tell she wasn't afraid. She was, if anything, glad that she'd finally managed to get Jude to admit there was a ghost — and the ghost to realize he needed to speak with Jude.

"I suppose," Jude said. *I wouldn't know. I don't really know anything about ghosts.*

"Okay," he went on, "you've got the two of us here — and you have Jackson Crow and me aboard the ship. Now we need *your* help. You must remember something, or you couldn't have known that the Archangel would be on the *Destiny.* You're certain of this?"

Byron Grant nodded. He was, minus the stage makeup, a handsome, fit young man who — *other than being dead!* — seemed somber and sincere. Blue eyes, sandy-blond hair. The boy next door. The kind of guy who'd marry his high school sweetheart.

"I never really saw the killer," Byron admitted. "He took me pretty quickly."

"What made you so sure he'd be on the ship?" Jude demanded. "Tell me what happened, step by step."

Alexi gave Byron an encouraging smile

and he smiled back at her. Then he turned to Jude.

"I was doing the play. Anyway, it ended at around 10 p.m. I usually stayed to take off my makeup at the theater, but I got a call from Elizabeth at around ten twenty. She said the lights were off at the house and thought she'd left them on. I told her to wait for me, said I'd leave right away. I got out of my costume, but didn't bother with the makeup, just grabbed my hoodie and I was out the door." He frowned as he described what had happened that night. "I phoned her back after I left the theater. She didn't answer. I probably should've called the police right away but I drove home as fast as I could. Her car was in the driveway, and the lights were on in the house. I was a little pissed at her, figuring she'd decided to go in but hadn't bothered to call me. I walked up to the door, which was unlocked, and threw it open. I got as far as the entry."

He bit down on his lip and shook his head.

"I saw her. I saw her on the floor," he said. "I ran over to her, but I was just thinking she'd fallen. Then I saw the blood."

Alexi lifted a hand as if she'd reach out to comfort him.

She lowered her hand to her lap, her eyes filled with sympathy.

"I hurried to her, bent down . . . and then he was behind me," Byron said. "He had a knife at my throat, ripping, even as I tried to turn to see his face. I flailed out at him — got him in the jaw. The knife sliced through my arm when I did that. Defensive wound, I guess they call it. But . . . I was bleeding out. And I only saw one thing."

"What?" Jude asked, determined not to let his question sound impatient.

"A ticket. It stuck out from his pocket. He was wearing some kind of suit jacket, pocket on the right. The ticket was for the *Destiny* — out of NOLA. And this sailing date was on it, so I knew. I knew he'd be on this ship."

"I see," Jude murmured. "And then?"

"And then I was dead. I didn't realize it — or have any awareness of it or anything else — until I seemed to rise over my body where the bastard had stuffed it inside a Dumpster in an alley."

They were all quiet for a minute.

Jude suddenly blurted, "But you — you were hovering around the crime scene in NOLA. You jumped on a bar. A drunk girl tried to give you money."

Byron shrugged. "Some people see me. I don't always know who sees me, though. I tried hitchhiking and eventually found someone who saw me and drove me to

NOLA. It's only a couple of hours, and I don't think he ever knew I wasn't . . . alive. And then . . . hey, if I hurt that dude who got me to the ship, man, I'm sorry. I don't want to hurt anyone. I just . . . I just want to stop more people from being killed."

Jude let out a long breath, still unable to grasp that he was sitting in Alexi Cromwell's tiny cabin on the *Destiny* discussing the case with a ghost — a victim of the killer.

And feeling disturbed by the fact that he *did* believe he was talking to a ghost.

"We have a list of people who might've been in the areas where the women were killed," he said. "May I show you the pictures, see if any of them seem familiar?"

Byron Grant nodded. "Of course."

Alexi rose, leaving her perch for Jude. Drawing his phone from his pocket, he slipped by her to sit next to the ghost.

He brushed against her and was startled to feel sparks racing through his system. She was a very attractive woman, and he was feeling a strong physical pull toward her. And that made things more complicated . . . He held his thoughts in check and carefully displayed the photos Angela Hawkins had emailed him and Jackson; one by one he went through them all.

"I wish I knew," Byron said. He hesitated.

"This guy . . ."

"This one? David Beach? He's head of security on the ship."

"Right. No, you can eliminate him. I've seen him. He's huge. The guy who got me was probably about six feet tall."

"Good. That helps," Jude said. He rose and paced the few steps to the cabin door. "Can you think of anything else? A scent — was he wearing aftershave or cologne? Did he smoke? Anything odd about his hands? Did you see his hands?"

He turned back to look at Byron Grant.

But the ghost was gone.

And for a moment he felt absolutely ridiculous, as if he was the butt of a massive joke. He was standing there, talking away, carrying on a conversation with . . . no one.

An illusion.

Alexi Cromwell was still there, leaning against the wardrobe, eyes enormous.

"He was really here," she said softly. "Sometimes . . . well, I think it takes a tremendous amount of energy to appear so . . . completely and to talk and . . . He'll be back."

He didn't say anything.

He should have thanked her. He didn't.

Nodding curtly, he turned and left her room.

There were a few things, *unusual* things, in his past — like the dead appearing to him — and he was going to have to deal with it all, the then and the now.

Cruise ships tended to be happy places.

The cruise line did everything possible to ensure that guests were happy; music played constantly, most of it live. Frenetic tour directors carried on bingo parties, pool parties, disco parties and more.

And in the Caribbean, the sun shone down on sparkling water most of the time, shimmering as if the sea were scattered with diamonds. On the *Destiny,* people seemed to be complying with the cruise "regulation" that they have fun.

Jude needed to go talk to Jackson.

But for a few minutes, he had to be alone, hoping the sweet-salt breeze would wash away the heavy fog of darkness that had settled over his mind.

He left the crew's quarters, mounting the richly carpeted steps from floor to floor until he reached the top deck and walked aft, leaned against the rail and let the sun soak into him while the breeze swept around him. Neither had any effect on the chill that seemed to have crept into his bones.

Once, in the military, he'd believed that

he was experiencing PTSD. Post-traumatic stress disorder. Later in his life he'd used the very situation that sometimes made him think he was crazy to become a crack field officer with the bureau. Only he called it "intuition." Or talked about "hunches" and "gut feelings" to explain his success at solving crimes.

The Caribbean still rippled with that diamond effect, but Jude stared into a haze of dusty darkness. Time seemed to collapse, and he saw himself seven years earlier, moving with his company in the small village where insurgents had taken hold. Felt the way his heart had thundered that day, the way he'd known he couldn't see everything, couldn't see into every home, around every corner.

Some of the soldiers with him had served too long; they shot when something moved — a child, a chicken, a dog, a goat or a pig.

Some still had illusions of morality; they took greater care.

And some, in their desperation to believe in the sanctity of life, died — not firing when they should have.

Corporal Al Bellingham had been one of those men. Hand-to-hand combat, a tiny village, insurgents who lived only to kill . . . and dozens of mothers, children, the aged.

Every corner could mean death, and Jude had turned one of those corners to see Al on the ground, writhing. He'd looked around, then hunkered down by his comrade and friend, the man with whom he'd played cards, baseball, music, enduring the hours in the hostile desert. He'd taken Al by the shoulders and dragged him back behind the small and desolate house that had been his own shield, lying low against the ricochet of stray bullets as he did.

He spoke into his radio, calling the medics, who would do their best. Automatic rifle fire beat a rat-tat-tat just beyond the little enclave where Jude had dragged the wounded man.

Al opened his eyes and gazed up at Jude. He didn't address him as "Lieutenant" the way he usually did, even when the men were doing nothing but whiling away the hours, waiting for their call to action.

He addressed him as "fool."

"Your head was out there, fool," Al said. "Head down at all times!"

"The medics are coming. Don't try to talk. Save your breath," Jude said.

But Al had clutched his arm and looked desperately into his eyes. He rattled off a series of numbers. "Got that? Please, Jude, tell me you got that."

"Al, medics are coming! You have to fight to live."

Al's grip tightened. "Please, Jude. I have a wife. Mellora. Remember? And a baby daughter. You give Mellora that number. Got it?"

He wouldn't be able to keep him alive long enough for the medics to come.

Jude repeated the numbers.

Then suddenly, Al shouted, "Behind you, man, behind you!"

Jude whipped around fast enough to fire first at an insurgent bearing down on him.

He could still picture that moment as if it had been yesterday. The littered courtyard between desert-dusted homes. Al bleeding on the ground; his enemy dead by the corner of the house.

And him — alive — because of Al.

The rat-tat-tat of firepower growing more distant and then fading away, the medics rushing in . . .

Not until they were back at base had he learned from their company physician that he couldn't have spoken with Al Bellingham. Bullets had severed his spinal column and pounded through his skull; the man had died almost instantly.

Somehow Jude had kept it together long enough to get through his tour of duty.

He'd imagined it, he'd told himself. He'd imagined the entire encounter.

And yet he'd felt compelled to speak with Al's wife. He'd called and told her that he'd been with her husband at the end. He told her how much Al had loved her — and what a brave man he'd been, saving others, refusing to let war make him less of a man.

And he'd given her the set of numbers.

A year later, when he was back in the States, Mellora Bellingham had called to thank him. The numbers had been for an insurance policy Al had purchased only days before his death.

She might never have found it without the numbers he'd given her.

It wasn't until he'd applied at the academy that he'd been advised to go into therapy. And he'd gone. He'd thought he understood. PTSD. Sure. Made sense. He'd lived in a world where it was often a case of kill or be killed. Back in North America, he was entering a world where danger often lurked below the surface and the monsters were hidden.

But he wanted that world. Nothing on earth was perfect; he'd seen the good, the bad and the hideous and learned about imperfection. He found he loved his country with an even greater passion, and out of the war zone, he wanted to fight the monsters who lived beneath the civilized veneer.

He had tried to consign Al to the far reaches of memory, although the man had continued to haunt his soul. Especially when they'd lost Lily, and he'd sat with her lifeless body for hours, praying that he would hear her whisper a single word.

The truth was that he'd spoken with a ghost before. He'd spoken with Al.

He was so lost in his thoughts that at first he didn't hear the buzz of his cell phone. He snapped out of his trance and answered.

Good agents did not become lost in the fog of the past, he reminded himself.

It was Jackson Crow, of course.

"I've met with Beach and his men," Jackson told him. "They're on high alert, although it would be nice if they really believed me about a killer being on board. What about Alexi Cromwell?"

"I've talked to her," Jude said. "And Byron Grant."

"Byron Grant?" Jackson Crow's voice was controlled and even. "Byron Grant was the second-last victim of the Archangel — that we know about, at any rate."

"Yes, I'm aware of that," Jude said.

Krewe of Hunters, huh?

"Meet me back at her cabin. With any

110

luck, she's still in," Jackson said, not skipping a beat.

When the ship was first built, tiny peepholes had been set in each cabin door, including those in the crew quarters. No unwary cabin girl or waitress would be taken by surprise on the *Destiny.*

Alexi had never been more grateful for that — even as she realized she'd seldom used it before.

She'd half expected Clara, since she knew how nervous her friend was feeling.

But it was Jude McCoy. He was back, this time with his partner.

She opened the door for them and waited. This man — Jackson Crow — might believe that she was more illusionist or charlatan than pianist and entertainer. She was afraid he'd come to confront her.

He hadn't. He smiled and merely asked if she minded talking to them again. She agreed.

Her cabin seemed entirely too cramped. Jackson Crow sat at the dressing table; Jude McCoy was next to her on the bunk. For a few minutes she found it hard to breathe and wondered if she was having a panic attack. It was impossible not to be aware of the man sitting beside her, of his intensity, which seemed to burn around her — almost as if it held her in a strange grip. She tried to concentrate on Crow, but she was acutely conscious of Jude McCoy. He sat so close to her they were almost touching.

"You've met this man Byron Grant?" Crow asked her. He smiled; he had an intriguing face, his smile both gentle and enigmatic.

She looked at Jude, whose face was impassive. He studied her in return, but she saw no mockery in his eyes. Not anymore.

Because he'd stood there just an hour ago, talking to the ghost himself.

"His fiancée was killed. He came home, and he was killed, as well. He was attacked from behind, so he couldn't tell me much."

Agent Crow nodded. "He and his fiancée, Elizabeth Williams, were murdered in Mobile, a week ago."

"The medallion around her neck was that of St. Bernardino — patron saint of advertising. Elizabeth was a graphic designer with an advertising company."

Alexi hadn't known that.

"The young woman found at the New Orleans church had a St. Luke's medallion around her neck. Patron saint of physicians, among other similar vocations and careers," Jackson said. "But Byron, the only male victim, was left in a Dumpster in an alley. No medal."

Alexi nodded. "He . . . he hasn't re-appeared," she said, and caught herself looking at Jude again. She could tell from his speech that he'd grown up near her, somewhere around New Orleans. Had Jude absorbed enough of the city's mysticism to accept the realities that were beyond any-thing science had yet acknowledged?

Was Crow humoring her? Or had McCoy convinced him? "The thing is," Jackson was saying, "Mr. Grant found you. He saw in you an ability to help him. Helping the dead is necessary and commendable, but it can be dangerous, too."

Alexi almost felt as if something cold and sharp was at her throat.

"I intend to be very careful," she said.

"I just want you to come to us whenever you see the ghost, with any information the ghost can give you."

Alexi nodded toward Jude. "Mr. Grant has spoken with Agent McCoy. He knows you two are FBI and that you're on board."

Crow's smile grew wider. "But he sought *you* out. It's important that you be ex-tremely careful, especially at night. We don't have proof, but the coroners in the different cities where this man has struck believe he kills at night. That doesn't mean you're safe by day. It's just that he's never killed in front of witnesses before."

"Don't worry," Jude McCoy said, and she saw the flicker of a smile on his lips. "I'll be 'haunting' your piano bar. I'll see that you're safely back in your cabin every night."

"We're in Cozumel tomorrow," she reminded them.

"Don't get off the ship without one of us," Crow warned.

"I don't always get off the ship," she told them. "But sometimes a group of us heads over to have lunch at Three Amigos or Señor Frogs."

"Let us know what you're doing," Jackson said. "And let us know anytime Byron Grant is near."

Jackson got to his feet; Jude did the same.

Naturally, she rose, as well.

"You . . . you both seem to believe me. This is strange. It's almost as if I'm becoming friends with a stowaway, but one you happen to know about," she said.

The two men glanced at each other and then back at her. And once again, she thought that Jude McCoy gave her a rueful smile, as if he'd discovered that there'd been a sad joke at his expense.

"He is sort of a stowaway," Jude said. "His

name won't be on the passenger manifest."

"But . . . you . . . Agent Crow, you believe me, too?"

"I do, Ms. Cromwell. Completely. And we're going to do our best to enlist your help — and see that you don't end up in any danger. We need your cooperation on that, too. Let us protect you and don't take any unnecessary risks."

"I'm all for that," she murmured.

Jackson left the cabin and Jude followed him, but turned back at the door. "Stay with friends, at all times. You and Ms. Avery — Clara? — stay close, please."

She nodded.

"We'll be watching over you," he promised.

Then they were both gone.

Alexi sat back on her bed. It was lunchtime; she was hungry.

And she was too unnerved to eat.

Their working conditions were hardly ideal, Jude thought, although David Beach had given them a cabin near his office for meetings, as well as computers, videoconference capability and a printer.

Back in their makeshift office, they sat at the table and stared at each other for a minute. "You haven't blinked an eye," Jude

115

said. "You believe we chased a dead man onto the ship, and that this dead man meant to bring us here. You have no problem accepting that other people might have seen him — without knowing he was dead."

"Correct," Crow told him.

"And it doesn't surprise you that I seem to have accepted this, too?" he asked.

"McCoy," Crow said, "did you think I randomly asked that you be assigned to me in the Quarter yesterday morning?"

Jude felt that sense of creeping frost again.

"You looked me up and, naturally, you have access to all my records. Even the ones with the therapist, which should have been sealed."

"Yes — and those records were sealed. But your history of solving unusual cases was noticed by others. Including Adam Harrison, who established the Krewe."

"I see," Jude said. He wasn't sure he did, not completely. But . . . yes, he did. He was still fighting all of this.

"My service records. You know about them?"

"Yes. I know that you saw your friend, Al Bellingham. According to medical personnel, he was dead at the time. Although you may not have *seen* the dead since then — or at least you believe you haven't — you've got certain abilities . . ."

"I've never been able to explain it," he mumbled, "but sometimes I just *know* things."

"You've been with the bureau for five years, so you must have heard of the Krewe of Hunters," Crow said flatly.

"Yes, of course. But everything on the Krewe is either quiet or speculation."

"We're good at spin," Crow told him, smiling.

Jude digested that. "All right, then, do we have anything more? According to Byron Grant, we can eliminate David Beach, which we'd already guessed."

"Angela is still on the trail of credit card usage and traffic cams."

Jude nodded. As he did, a soft beeping sound came from Jackson's computer. He hit a key, and Jude moved around to watch the screen.

A woman in a powder blue shirt and black jacket appeared, exceptionally pretty with long blond hair and elegant features. "Hey," she said. "Good connection. I see you perfectly, Jackson."

"We've got you, too," Jackson said. "Meet Jude McCoy, Angela. Jude, thanks to the mysteries of the internet and satellites, meet Special Agent Angela Hawkins."

"Hey, Jude!" Angela said, and then winced. "Hmm. Do you get that often? Purely accidental, I swear."

"My folks did love the Beatles," Jude told her. "So do I, for that matter."

She smiled, but then the niceties were over. "I think the killer's been far too smart to leave a credit card trail, so I'm not finding what I'd hoped," she began. "But I can eliminate another suspect for you."

"Which one?" Jude asked.

"The entertainment director. Bradley Wilcox. He was caught by a traffic cam. Yes, he drove out from Texas, but he was west of NOLA at the time the last victim was killed. Not just his car — the cameras got a clear picture of his face."

"One less suspect," Jude said.

"We're researching cameras, hotels, restaurants, you name it. We'll find out more. Sadly, even with computers, it's slow and tedious work." Angela sighed. "Anyway, I'll let you go until I have something else for you. Good to meet you, Jude."

"Good to meet you, too. Virtually, at any rate." He was surprised when Crow said, "Thanks, Angela. Love you."

"Love you, too," she responded.

The connection went dead. Jude couldn't help looking at Jackson, who shrugged. "I told you. She's my wife."

"Okay."

"And a brilliant agent," Jackson assured him, not for the first time.

"I believe you," Jude said, and he did. Turning back to his own screen, he added, "The medallions have to be the key."

Crow frowned. "We know that each medallion was associated with the victim's line of work. For our last victim, Jean Wilson, it was St. Luke — and she was in med school."

"Yes, and St. Luke is the patron saint of doctors. Byron Grant's fiancée, Elizabeth Williams, was found with a medallion of St. Bernardino, patron saint of those in advertising. Have any of our forensic or technical people been able to discover where the medallions came from?" Jude asked.

Crow had geared up his computer. He nodded as he looked at his notes. "It took a while, but we finally have that information. Italy," he said. "An ancient church near the Vatican. These particular medallions could only be bought there."

"And we have people tracing the movements of our suspects — so we'll know who's been in Italy?"

"There's a problem there," Jackson said.

"What's that?"

"The medallions were all manufactured in

the 1940s."

Jude shook his head. "So they came down from a friend, parent or grandparent, to the killer," he said. He leaned forward. "What if they were sold in a collection?"

He swung around, booting into the computer he'd been allotted. He quickly asked Crow the name of the church.

The medallions might not have been created out of gold or silver, but they were historical artifacts and eminently collectible now. There were thirteen in every set; apparently, very few complete sets remained.

"The sets contained medallions for St. Catherine, patron saint of artists. St. Michael, patron saint of police officers. St. Matthew, accountants. St. Barbara, architects and builders. St. Christopher, drivers, travelers and pilots. All of those were found on the previous victims, according to their occupations. With the more recent murders, we have St. Bernardino, advertising, and that was found on Elizabeth Williams. St. Luke, physicians. Jean Wilson." Jude studied the computer screen. "Then we have St. Francis, patron saint of animals. That was left on Debra Harvey, who was a veterinarian, Miami, Florida. St. Joan of Arc — on the second Miami victim, Lauren Macaby, United States Air Force. And St. Thomas

Aquinas, teachers, found on Delores Ramirez, teacher, Fort Lauderdale."

"And the final three medallions," Jackson Crow said, studying his own computer, "are St. Genesius, patron saint of actors. St. Lawrence, patron saint of cooks. And last . . ."

"St. Cecilia," Jude said, his gut tightening. "The patron saint of singers and musicians."

5

"This is all terrifying!" Minnie shivered and cuddled closer to her beloved Blake. "A dastardly killer on this ship!"

"Minnie," Blake said a little awkwardly. "We're already dead. He can't hurt us."

"No, not us! But what about Alexi?"

"I plan to stay safe," Alexi assured her.

"I hear that this . . . this terrible man is attacking young women. And that means you're vulnerable," Minnie said.

"So is every woman aboard this ship." Alexi was a bit distracted, flipping through music sheets, trying to make sure she had a lot of show tunes ready. They tended to be the passenger preference, and the *Les Miz* actors often joined in, so she wanted to be prepared. She looked up; Minnie was staring at her with deep concern.

"Don't worry. No one's going to attack me when we're in one of the busiest bars on the ship."

"By the time you close up, it's late, and most people have gone to bed," Minnie pointed out.

"The dance lounges are still open then." Alexi tried to sound cheerful. "And . . . well, there are people on board, watching over me."

And yet . . .

This was scary as hell.

Was it better or worse that she knew Jackson Crow and Jude McCoy were on the ship? Would she be safer because of it, while others . . .

She hadn't seen Clara since that morning, in the employee cafeteria. She needed to talk to her.

She'd never told Clara that she saw the dead.

She didn't want her best friend on the *Destiny* thinking she was stark raving mad.

How could she tell Clara not to go anywhere alone, to watch herself every time she went to or from her cabin?

Somehow, she had to.

"Minnie, you and Blake will watch out for me, too, right?" They promised fervently that they would.

Alexi glanced at her watch, and then over at the bar. Servers were getting ready to open for the evening. She still had time; it was only eight, and she didn't start until nine.

She stood up, deciding she'd go and see if the cast was rehearsing. But before she could move, she saw that Agent Jude Mc-Coy was approaching her at the piano bar. He nodded politely to Minnie and Blake, and she had to smile.

"You find something humorous, Ms. Cromwell?" he asked.

"Blake and Minnie," she said. "I'd like to introduce you to FBI agent Jude McCoy."

"We know who you are, of course," Minnie said, smiling beautifully.

Always the flirt.

"A pleasure to meet you," Jude McCoy said. Alexi saw that he took note of Minnie's elegant 1930s gown and Blake's tuxedo.

He winced as he looked at Alexi. "Dead?" he asked softly.

"How rude!" Minnie said.

"Darling, we *are* dead," Blake told her.

"Yes, but what a terrible word! Passed, I think, is better. Ethereal, maybe. Or he could say spirits. We *are* on a ship, at a bar, so spirits could refer to more than one thing," Minnie said with a tinkling laugh. "Anyway, sir, the pleasure is ours. As long as you intend to look after Alexi for us."

"I definitely intend to do that," Jude

promised her.

"Well, then, we'll leave you two to chat. There's a bit of time before Alexi's on for the night. Blake, I do believe we should take a romantic stroll out on the deck. What say you, my love?"

"Anything, dearest," Blake said.

The two departed.

Alexi saw that Jude McCoy had changed for the evening. He looked seriously masculine and striking in a dark blue suit.

"What can I do for you now, Agent?" she asked.

"I need to find out if these men come here," he told her, producing his phone and showing her pictures. "Roger Antrim and Hank Osprey?"

She glanced at the photos on his iPhone and nodded. "Yes, I know them both. They're regulars on the Celtic American line. They were in here last night. In fact, I see them practically every night of a voyage. Roger was a TV network CEO and he's in his late fifties. He's married to Lorna, who is lovely. They're retired and they sail whenever they feel like it." She paused. "You don't really consider him a suspect, do you? Like I said, he's *married.* And he's always in here with Lorna."

"I'm sorry, but history's proven that *mar-*

ried doesn't mean much in these situations. But I'm not accusing anyone of anything. I just want to hang around and see them for myself. Now what about Osprey?"

"Hank, as you can tell from his picture, is younger. A brilliant nerd in high school, from what I heard. He sold his first company when he was in his twenties. Very nice guy. You'd never know he was rolling in money."

"Does he ever come in here with a woman?"

Alexi thought about that. "Yes, I've seen him with other people, including women. He brought a bunch of employees on a cruise once. And he was dating a major heiress for a while. Then a B-movie queen. Both of these guys — Hank and Roger — like the Caribbean. And of course, they can sail whenever they want. Honestly, though, you'll see. Neither of them is . . . Well, I can't imagine either of them as a serial killer."

"That's the thing," Jude McCoy warned her. "We're not after a spree killer here. The Archangel spaces out his murders according to some schedule of his own. Going strictly by age, Hank is a more likely suspect, but . . ." He looked at her intently. "It's common knowledge that murderers can be the boy-next-door type. Nice as can be, polite, even charming. Don't trust *any-one*."

That was a nearly impossible directive. She lived on the ship!

A couple entered the room and took a seat at one of the cocktail tables. A family group came in soon afterward, and Dixie, one of the cocktail waitresses, started toward them.

"I need to begin my show," Alexi said.

"Yep, sorry. Your friends come in here, too, right? Fellow entertainers, from the shows and bands and all."

"Yes."

"Did you ever get any — vibes, I guess — from any of them? Particularly Larry Hepburn, Simon Green, Ralph Martini or the head guy, Bradley Wilcox?"

She shook her head. "No, but Ralph's the only one I really know. Wait — not true. Bradley Wilcox is a jerk. I already told you that, but please don't repeat it. He's just curt and rude and treats us all as if we're his personal servants. Ralph — I'd have a hard time believing he's guilty of anything."

"Thanks. Okay. I'll be here. That chair over there okay?" He pointed to one of the comfortable wingback chairs set around some of the cocktail tables.

"Sure." She'd been playing the piano and singing for as long as she could remember.

Yet she suddenly felt a little intimidated. She wished Minnie and Blake weren't still strolling . . . wherever. Minnie would have harassed her about playing a certain song or other, and she would've been busy trying to pretend a ghost wasn't whispering in her ear. All while she was speaking, playing and singing.

She decided to begin with a Carole King number — trying to ignore Agent McCoy. After that a woman wanted to sing another Carole King song and Alexi was happy to pass her the mic.

The lounge had filled up quickly, and she nearly missed a note when she saw that Roger Antrim had arrived with his wife, Lorna. They waved at her with wide smiles, taking a seat at one of the few empty tables left.

She greeted them by name, something she often did, and then teased a couple who'd just arrived, which made everyone laugh. Then she suggested that Roger come up and sing.

He agreed.

He loved anything by Billy Joel, and had a pleasant voice.

Alexi smiled as she played for him.

And wondered if he could be a brutal killer.

Thirty minutes later she'd almost forgotten that Agent McCoy was in the lounge. That was when Clara arrived with Simon Green.

Simon wouldn't be *just chorus* for long, Alexi thought, as the two began a duet from *Jekyll & Hyde.* He was very good. So, of course, was Clara.

Alexi did a Kid Rock and Sheryl Crow number with Simon.

Larry Hepburn — blond, beautiful beach boy — arrived next. He sang a few Beatles tunes. Every woman in the audience seemed to be breathing a little harder.

Then Ralph Martini showed up and graced them with a fantastic version of a Meat Loaf song. In the middle of it, she realized that McCoy had managed to drag his chair over to the table where Roger Antrim and his wife were sitting. In fact, he was engaged in conversation with them.

Hank Osprey didn't make an appearance until almost eleven. He was with a very pretty young woman in a skintight cocktail gown and five-inch heels. They made quite a pair.

He waved to Alexi as he entered, and she waved back.

When the Meat Loaf song had ended and the applause for Ralph subsided, she greeted

Hank, introducing him as a regular who could croon out a great Tony Bennett. Hank flushed, excused himself to the young woman and came up to take the mic.

The night went on without incident. Blake and Minnie didn't reappear. She teased, she joked, kept the passengers singing, and when there was a lull, she sang a few favorite show tunes herself or called on a friend to do so. At one point she saw Bradley Wilcox looking into the room over the small carved wood banister that separated the lounge from the hallway.

Watching her.

Judging her.

Alexi didn't care. The audience was lively and her confidence soared back. She knew she was good at what she did.

She smiled at Jensen Hardy, the cruise director, coming down the hall. He loved the piano bar, loved dropping in. He had a pleasant singing voice, but neither his natural talent nor his training was quite up to par, not compared to performers like Ralph and Clara. In the "quickie" bits of music that were done on board, he was always the announcer.

She assumed he'd come to sing.

But he wasn't going to sing that night. Bradley Wilcox stopped him in the hallway, and although Wilcox didn't move and kept his voice low, Alexi could see that he was reprimanding Jensen Hardy for one thing or another.

Idiot!

At the moment there was nothing she could do to help Jensen. Besides, the eternally cheerful Jensen would probably just shake it off.

Clara sat at the piano bench by Alexi's side and when she could, she whispered, "I'll hang out with you until the bitter end, I promise. And don't tell me I'm being silly. The killer was in New Orleans. *New Orleans!* You're not walking to your cabin alone."

"It's okay. You can leave when you're tired. Get Simon or one of the other guys to take you back, okay?"

"I don't want you alone."

"I won't be alone."

"Oh?" Clara asked.

Alexi indicated Jude McCoy. In his evening apparel, he was extremely presentable. He managed to look casual, and yet a little larger than life.

"Ohhh." Clara grinned. "Hobnobbing with the higher-ups of the company, huh? I'm so glad. You need to hobnob. You haven't . . . hobnobbed in forever. Hobnobbing would be good for you. Hobnobbing is

131

a basic instinct, you know."

Alexi felt a flush cover not only her face, but also her whole body from head to toe.

"It's just business."

Clara laughed at that and Alexi flinched. Yes, her words could have been construed in a different way.

"No, I mean I'm an entertainment liaison, that's all."

Clara studied Jude McCoy and then turned back to Alexi. "It shouldn't be just business. Men like him don't come along every day. And," she added, "I'm talking about more than his looks."

"Hey! I'm working here!" Alexi reminded her. "Right now, as we speak."

Clara smiled. "So is the little beauty on the arm of our billionaire, Hank Osprey." The young woman was, indeed, working it; she leaned against Hank and seemed to be enchanted by his every word.

And despite the fact that Jude McCoy was engaged in conversation with Roger and Lorna, Alexi could tell that he was also aware of Hank and his young woman.

Finally, the crowd began to thin.

When Hank left with his lady friend, Alexi noted that Jude McCoy made a phone call.

Would Jackson Crow now be following the man?

Because it was evident that Jude McCoy meant to keep his word. He'd be seeing her back to her cabin.

Last call was announced.

Roger and Lorna Antrim thanked her for a great evening and left. Three young women traveling together departed arm in arm.

A retired couple, charming, older — and obviously still very much in love — came to the piano to tell her what a wonderful time they'd had. The bar was closed.

Ralph Martini yawned. "Gotta call it a night!" he said.

"We all need to call it a night," Simon agreed. "Hey!" he said cheerfully to Jude. "You didn't sing."

"I thought I'd spare you." Jude gave them a self-deprecating grin, telling the *Les Miz* cast members that he was looking forward to their final night's performance.

He wound up talking theater with them for a while. And then suddenly, he and Ralph were involved in a discussion about sports and New Orleans, and Alexi realized that everyone else was gone, that she was there with Clara, Simon, Ralph — and Agent Jude McCoy.

"You're with the cruise line, right?" Ralph asked Jude.

Jude inclined his head.

"Why'd they stick you guys down in the dinky cabins?"

"If they're good enough for the entertainers, they're good enough for us. Besides, it's a full ship, and we came on at the last minute. I'm sure you know that the reputation this ship has for entertainment is stellar. We're really here to observe what makes it all work so well."

"That's a relief," Ralph said. "Where else would an old hack like me find acting jobs these days? Getting old in the theater is a bitch, you know? Unless you're Sean Connery or Alec Guinness. Which, sadly, I'm not."

"You are a fine, fine actor, Ralph!" Clara insisted.

He sighed. "Thank you. But I have an old friend, Siobhan O'Leary — one of the best voices ever to grace Broadway! She ended up playing a singing Easter bunny on a cruise line and it was downhill from there. Still . . . I need this ship. And at least I haven't been relegated to singing animal roles."

"You're all fine," Jude told them. "We're not here to judge or harass you, just to enjoy your talents." He glanced at his watch. "Damn, it's late." Alexi rose. He wouldn't leave her until she was safe in her cabin. And, she guessed, there was somewhere else he wanted to be.

"Shall we all head down to the bowels of the ship?" Simon Green suggested.

"Let's do it," Clara said.

They walked to the elevators together. Reaching the crew level, they began to break off from the group as they approached their cabins, Simon Green first, then Ralph and then Clara.

"Hey!" Clara asked, before opening her door, "Are we going into Cozumel for lunch tomorrow? We're not on call for the Mexican songfest until five and we dock about eight. I was thinking of around eleven?"

Alexi glanced at Jude McCoy.

"That's great," she said, trying not to make it sound like a question.

"You're welcome to join us," Clara told Jude.

"I just may," Jude responded. "Thanks."

Clara went into her room.

After that the hallway seemed completely still.

The ship listed portside, and Alexi nearly raised a hand to steady herself on Jude McCoy's chest; she managed to place it on the wall instead.

"Did you learn anything?" she asked him.

"No. But at least I met both men and had a chance to observe them."

"Roger and Lorna are such a tight couple . . ." she murmured.

"Mmm."

"You're thinking Hank Osprey?" Alexi asked. "You called your partner, didn't you? And he followed Hank after he and his . . . companion left the lounge."

He nodded.

"And?"

"You'll be glad to know the young lady is alive and well and back in her cabin for the night," he told her quietly.

"Good. But being rich and single doesn't make a man a killer," she said.

"No," he said. "Of course not."

They'd reached her door, and she slid her key card into the lock, then stepped into her cabin. He seemed ridiculously close. And she felt ridiculously . . .

Light-headed. Maybe she was . . .

Attracted to him.

Lord.

She was afraid she'd blush again. Hobnobbing. She hadn't *hobnobbed* in . . .

"However," he went on, "being rich and single doesn't make a man innocent, either, Ms. Cromwell — Alexi," he said. "When I leave you, please lock up, and don't go out

136

again until morning."

He didn't wait for her to agree.

In his line of work, agreement was probably taken for granted.

She didn't even say good-night. He was already turning away.

She locked her door, got ready to go to sleep and crawled into bed.

And lay awake.

Still feeling warm and flushed.

She'd noticed his hands and wondered what it would feel like if he touched her. She lay awake in misery.

In some ways it had been easier to be in mourning.

Easier than feeling this ache and this longing once again.

Jude walked the *Destiny,* deck by deck. He did it swiftly, nodding at the few crew members he passed along the way. In the wee hours, few were up and about.

He passed David Beach on the promenade; he recognized Beach long before he got close. Very few people were Beach's size.

"Agent," Beach acknowledged him. "Like I told your partner, we're on this, so you can get some sleep tonight. I have my men doubling up and adding on to their shifts. We may all be thinking this is a remote possibility, but we're taking that possibility very seriously," Beach said. "I have a man patrolling every deck, and I'll have one on every deck through the day and night, I promise."

"Thank you."

"I need to get some sleep, and you do, too. You won't be much good to anyone without it."

"Of course," Jude agreed. Beach's comment might have been tongue in cheek, mocking him. Except that he didn't think that was the case. There was real pressure on all law enforcement in the States — that pressure had evidently made its way to the ship.

"Good night, then. Glad to know you're out here," Jude said.

"Good night, Agent McCoy."

Jude meant to go straight to his cabin.

He didn't.

Instead, he walked over to the chapel, looking in through the mullioned window.

The chapel was empty.

He turned and went to bed.

Earlier, up in their makeshift office, he and Jackson had thoroughly studied the information they had on the passengers and crew, concentrating on their possible suspects.

But he'd also read up on Alexi Cromwell.

Her university years and professional career were impressive. She'd majored in music and drama and graduated with top marks. Then she'd worked at some of the most prestigious venues in the country. She'd been engaged.

Her fiancé had died overseas. Soon after, she'd headed onto a ship.

Sailing away. One method of escape.

Work. Work was another. She'd done both.

It was the same for him. After his experience in the military and then the tragic loss of his daughter, he, too, had found consolation in work. Soon after that, he'd left the military and been accepted by the academy . . .

No, that wasn't entirely true. He'd always known he wanted to be in law enforcement.

Because of a family heritage dating back to the Battle of New Orleans and relatives still among the military brass, he'd applied to West Point. He'd been in the service when he met Kathy; when they got married, he'd started to ponder resigning. Then Lily had come along.

And the world had changed.

He stared out the one small portal in his tiny cabin. The night was eerie, the ship's lights a weak, yellow glow against the near-black of sea and sky.

Jude loved the ocean. Especially at night, when the horizon seemed to stretch on forever, when the sky appeared to reach infinity and all things seemed possible.

He'd actually slept well in the few hours he'd slept, thanks to the rolling of the ship. Despite the money spent to refurbish and maintain the *Destiny,* she was an old girl, and her stabilizers were nothing compared to those on the new megaliths sailing the seas.

He closed his eyes and remembered that he could never change the past.

And that might be why his obsession with work had grown.

He had, at times, saved lives. That ointment was the balm he needed for the wounds he bore.

He found himself thinking about the medallions again.

Medallions, in sets of thirteen, sold at a tiny church near the Vatican, decades ago. Medallions left on the dead.

Three remaining.

St. Lawrence, patron saint of cooks. St. Genesius, the patron saint of actors.

St. Cecilia, patron saint of singers and musicians.

He tossed and turned.

Alexi Cromwell was just down the hall

from him.

He'd watched her through the night, admired her easy rapport with others, her ability to smile and laugh and tease. She was never hurtful. She just knew how to draw people into her fold. He'd watched her sing a duet with Clara Avery and he'd felt every nerve of awareness, realizing how much these two young women might appeal to the Archangel.

A lovely blonde actress . . .

A beautiful singer . . .

He reminded himself that a cook was still in danger, too, but Jackson had investigated all the kitchen staff that night, warning young women to stay together or with known friends. He and Jackson, *all* law enforcement, were determined to save everyone who might be at risk. To stop the Archangel.

And yet . . .

He knew he'd grown obsessed.

With Alexi. He had to protect her.

Capitan Miguel Suarez of the Cozumel police was a large, fit man. Both Jude and Jackson spoke decent Spanish, but Suarez waved off their attempts. "This is Cozumel, gentlemen," he'd told them. "You'll hear more English spoken here than you will in

141

parts of Florida and Texas, and so on. Please, sit down. We'll speak in English."

Suarez had been briefed ahead of time. John Boulder, an agent assigned to Cozumel out of the Miami office, was with them, as well. Like Suarez, Boulder immediately seemed intelligent and competent.

Suarez was, naturally, most interested in the possibility that the Archangel might kill in Mexico. Boulder was intrigued by the fact that Jackson and Jude might have followed the killer onto a ship.

"There's been no one else killed in the New Orleans area," Boulder told them. "But that doesn't mean anything. The Archangel moves from city to city."

"I want to emphasize," Jude said, "that we have a chance here, the kind of chance we haven't had before with this killer. We believe we've narrowed it down to a small list of suspects, all of them probably on Mexican soil as we speak."

"You're head of the Krewe of Hunters, right?" Boulder asked Jackson Crow.

"I'm field head of the unit," Jackson replied.

"Different kind of unit," Boulder commented.

"One that's solved every single case in

142

which we've been involved," Jackson pointed out.

"I'll take that," Suarez muttered.

Jude leaned forward. "I believe this killer's going to strike here, somewhere in Cozumel." He hesitated. He was terrified by the assumption he was making, but he'd lain awake much of the night going over everything he'd read about the Archangel and his victims. "He'll go after a cook or someone involved in the restaurant industry. We've discovered the history behind the medallions left on the victims. The medallions that remain are associated with the patron saints of musicians, actors and cooks."

"There are beautiful women playing guitars and dancing and singing all over the streets of Cozumel!" Suarez said.

Jackson looked at Jude, nodding, and then turned to the other men. "We're afraid he might have targeted a young actress and a young singer aboard the *Destiny* already. They're known to him and they fit his profile. They might be in his sights for that reason. Which leaves a cook. There's less likelihood that he would've become familiar with one of the cooks on the ship."

"I'll have my officers out in the street on high vigilance throughout the day," Suarez told them.

"We've got officers assigned to watch the men on your list of suspects, as well," Boulder said. He frowned, studying the paper. "I see that David Beach, head of security, was originally on this list. Now, *that's* terrifying. But you've taken him off."

"Yes," Jude said. "A study of his movements seems to eliminate him."

"Hope so," Boulder murmured. "If the head of security might be involved, we're in dangerous territory indeed."

Jude wasn't sure how the territory could get any more dangerous.

Jackson stepped in. "We have a top-notch medical examiner on our Krewe team, Agent Boulder. She's gone over the majority of the bodies. Various cuts and bruising would've been different, had the killer been a man of Beach's size. We're looking for someone between 190 and 225 pounds, between five-nine and, say, six-two."

"Here are the men we're still looking at," Jude said. "Passengers Hank Osprey, late thirties, billionaire, and Roger Antrim, late fifties, billionaire. Entertainers Simon Green and Larry Hepburn, late twenties, Ralph Martini, middle-aged. Also cruise director Jensen Hardy, who's in his early thirties."

"I've sent their photographs out all over the city — and to every tour destination,"

Suarez said. "Your men?" he asked Boulder.

"We're on it, too."

"And David Beach has assigned anyone he can spare," Jackson told them. He stood up and Jude did the same. "Gentlemen, thank you. Let's pray we leave Mexico without incident."

"Amen," Suarez said.

Jude was anxious when they left the office of the police captain.

He was very afraid for an unknown Mexican cook.

And for a beautiful American actress . . .

And the lovely American musician who had somehow managed to creep into his heart.

Alexi had been in Cozumel dozens of times; it was one of the most popular cruise destinations out there.

Some crew members who were at liberty to go into town didn't. They'd been so often and preferred to read, catch up on movies or communicate with those back home.

And sometimes, just sleep!

But it seemed that she and Clara and their little group of friends were ready for a day off the *Destiny.* They met at ten thirty as planned and departed.

No one left the ship without keying in his

or her badge. The *Destiny*'s computer system knew at any given moment whether a passenger or crew member was on board or ashore.

Alexi assumed that Jackson Crow and Jude were already working in Mexico; she hadn't seen Jude since he'd walked her to her cabin, but she'd seen a member of David Beach's staff watching the hallway as she and Clara met the others.

"So many places, so little time," Simon Green said cheerfully.

Larry Hepburn rolled his eyes. "What are you talking about? We're going to a silly restaurant where they put ridiculous hats on your head, make balloon animals and try to get you to drink as much as possible. And, of course, leave big tips."

"Ah, well, some of the passengers will be interacting with dolphins and learning about marine life."

"And on ATV trips! I want to do the ATVs one day," Simon said. "Hey! You guys have been cruising a long time. This is all new to me."

"You could've taken a tour today," Alexi told him.

"Ah, but I wanted to bond with the cool people," he said.

"I just want a cold beer," Ralph muttered.

"So, are we cantina-hopping or picking one place?"

They decided to cantina-hop. Their first stop was The Three Amigos. Ralph loved the nachos there.

Second stop, Señor Frogs. It was Clara's favorite for appetizers.

"Now, for the new place," Ralph announced.

"New place? There's a new place?" Clara asked.

"Right behind that row of kiosks, across the street," Ralph said. "Señora Maria's. It's getting a zillion stars all over those tour sites online."

"You still read up on Cozumel on the tour sites?" Alexi asked him, smiling. "After visiting *how* many times?"

"I know about Señora Maria's — and you don't!" he replied, grinning back at her. "I rest my case."

"Okay! I concede," Alexi said. She glanced at her watch. Despite the tourists from a dozen ships, the local populace and the visitor population, they'd managed to travel quickly. It was barely noon. They'd probably wander back right after eating — which would be the third stage of their meal, after the nachos and appetizers they'd already had. That would give them hours to laze around in their cabins or on the deck chairs before any of them were called to work or rehearsal. "Señora Maria's sounds excellent. *Andiamo!*" she said.

"I think that's Italian. We're in Mexico," Ralph informed her in a mock-officious voice.

"Oh, yes, sorry. *Vamos.*"

"*Sí, señorita!*"

As they headed to the new restaurant, Alexi wondered if she was seeing more uniformed officers in the street than usual or if they'd always been there.

And as she noticed men moving alone through the crowds, she wondered if they were undercover law enforcement.

Or killers.

No, according to Jude and Jackson, she'd know the killer.

He was someone traveling with them, on the *Destiny.*

"See? See?" Roger asked as they stepped into the restaurant.

It really was impressive. The owners had done an excellent job with decor; reproduction Mayan artifacts were displayed in glass cases, while the paneled walls were decorated with objects such as huge Mexican hats, maracas and paintings of blazing suns and majestic mountains. The hostess greeted

148

them and led them to a table; their waiter appeared immediately.

Alexi thanked him after placing her order and he blew her a kiss.

"Americans! I love them. And American dollars, too," he admitted with a grin.

They all laughed at his honesty.

"Seriously," the waiter told them, "you'll be happy to throw your tourist dollars at me. Our cook! She is the best. She is Señora Maria. It's her restaurant. Well, of course, she doesn't do all the cooking, but she is always in the kitchen. And her food . . . You'll find that it is excellent. *Delicioso!*"

Ralph excused himself to go to the restroom. When he returned, grinning, he said, "You guys all gotta go!"

"Um, actually, sorry. I don't," Simon said. Ralph groaned. "No, I mean go see. Coolest restrooms ever. There's a big room with sinks and the doors to the male and female stalls on either side. But in the sink area, you walk by the mirrors, and Aztecs and Mayans and conquistadors all suddenly appear."

They all stood.

"No, no. I'm not going to the bathroom in a group!" Larry protested.

"You go first, and then we'll take turns, one by one," Clara suggested. "Except I don't care if Alexi and I walk in together."

Larry went in while the others explained to the waiter, who delivered their juice and beer, that they were going to check out the restrooms.

"The coolest, huh?" the waiter asked.

That was, apparently, the description in any language.

When Simon came back, Clara and Alexi walked into the large unisex "sink room" and admired the artistry.

"I told you," Ralph said when they returned. "You have to read the tourist sites!"

As they waited for their food, Ralph whined about the fact that he had to be back early for a quickie afternoon songfest, one that encouraged passengers to enjoy the shows and other entertainment.

Clara complained about the way the shows were abridged; there was only so much time that passengers who were especially fond of the casino could be diverted from spending their time and money there.

Alexi listened idly to the conversation around her and then sat up straight. She saw that Jude McCoy was exiting the kitchen — and heading directly for their table.

She also saw him nod to a man in a horrible tourist shirt who'd been sitting near them; she realized that she and her group had been under guard the entire day.

It was a good feeling.

"Hey, look who's here," Larry murmured.

"Mr. Tall, Blond and Handsome!" Simon said.

"What? Is this man an appendage now?" Ralph asked.

"Company bigwig," Clara said lightly. "Be nice, Ralph."

"I'm always nice."

"Hmm. That's debatable," Alexi teased.

"Mind if I join you?" Jude asked, arriving at their table.

He was wearing khaki beach shorts that day. Alexi didn't think, however, that even being in Cozumel could bring the man to wear any kind of bizarre tourist shirt. He had on a green, short-sleeved tailored shirt that seemed to pick up the intense color of his eyes.

He smiled as he joined them, pulling up a chair.

"So," Ralph said. "I saw you coming out of the kitchen. Maria's a celebrity chef, a really big deal around here. How did you manage that?"

Jude shrugged. "I went in and asked if I could see the kitchen and meet Maria. You probably know she has a TV show, too. It recently started on a cooking channel in the US."

"You're a cook?" Simon asked him.

"No, I just like food," Jude said.

"Do you always talk to the cooks or want to see the kitchen?" Simon asked next.

Jude laughed. "I'm going to put the food in my mouth, right? Never hurts to see a kitchen. And like you said, Maria's a celebrity."

After that, he deftly turned the conversation from himself, questioning Ralph about plays he'd been in, talking to Simon about starting out in the theater and complimenting all of them.

As plates of enchiladas and tacos were served, Alexi realized Jude had the ability to smoothly insert himself into a group. The fact that she knew what he was doing didn't exactly make her happy; she didn't believe for a second that anyone in *their* group was a killer. Clara had him pegged, as well.

Clara was ready to give him every bit of assistance. Alexi was, too, of course . . .

And yet, she couldn't help feeling a new sense of tension . . .

She was enjoying the last bite of a nacho when the room was suddenly racked by an explosion.

A burst of fire, like a roar of dragon's

breath, flared out from the kitchen.
And there was chaos.

6

Jude flew to his feet, instinctively throwing the table over, preventing any surge of fire from reaching the group gathered there. He'd accidentally knocked Alexi down, and he reached out a hand to help her up. "Out to the street!" he ordered.

She saw that Clara and Simon were already moving toward the door. Larry looked as if he was in a trance. "Larry!" Alexi snapped, grabbing him by his shoulders. She was strong; she got him to his feet. Ralph was dazed, and Jude reached for him, again ordering, "Get out to the street! Stay close to the police. I'll be back."

He rushed toward the kitchen, clutching a metal tray like a shield. Men and women were staggering out, screaming, as the fire still blazed. A woman caught hold of Jude's shirtsleeve, speaking rapidly in Spanish and pointing. He wasn't sure of everything she'd said, but realized someone had to be in trouble. He nodded and hurried past her.

He found a young woman on the floor, pinned underneath a wooden rack that was burning and about to collapse. The sprinkler system suddenly sprang into action, soaking Jude, but not quenching the fire overhead.

The woman was Señora Maria. He'd been speaking with her just moments before, warning her that he was afraid they might have brought an American killer into her realm — and that she just might be a target.

He dragged her from under the rack, trying to ascertain the extent of her injuries. Thankfully, the Mexican authorities were right there, and medics rushed in.

There were more people in the kitchen.

Jude made two additional trips, finding a man lying in front of a food preparation table and another by the freezer. As he half dragged and half carried them out, one at a time, sirens continued to blare, and more emergency personnel was arriving.

Filthy and smudged with grime, he ran into Capitan Suarez himself on-site. "You warned me about a murder, not an explosion. *Madre de Dios!* The fire inspectors will come and I hope they can tell what caused this mess. An accident, grease . . . a burner . . . gas? Or not *one* murder, but an attempt at mass murder?" Suarez demanded.

"There was an explosion. One explosion. A massive fireball. It seemed to come from the kitchen. That's what I saw. Then people were running out of the kitchen. There were people down in there. I concentrated on getting them out, and others were doing the same," Jude told him. He was quiet for a minute. "I was watching," he said. "I'd just been in the damn kitchen."

"Did you see anyone behaving suspiciously?"

Jude shook his head in disgust. "No. But then, we have no idea what caused this yet. So what would be *suspicious*? Was someone paid to start this? Pour some grease on an open fire, rig a stove — who the hell knows? And why?"

This sure wasn't how the Archangel usually operated. But Jude had been afraid for Señora Maria. She was an attractive woman in her early forties, older than the Archangel's typical victims. She was pleasant and cheerful in the kitchen, and her staff had apparently loved her.

Had she been the target here?

"We will get to the bottom of this," Suarez said, tight-lipped. "I thank you," he added a little stiffly. "My officers told me you were responsible for getting many

156

people out. They owe you their lives."

"Suarez, we do what we're trained to do. No thanks necessary," Jude said. "I have to wonder if this was set to go off to create chaos in the area. To distract from whatever the real plan was. Which may have involved Maria . . ."

"You think this has to do with your murderer?" Suarez asked skeptically.

"One way or another," Jude replied.

"I am completely willing to cooperate, but it's not possible to rush this investigation. Our inspectors will need time. You don't have to worry that we are corrupt or shoddy workers. You may ask your own people. We are the best," Suarez insisted.

"I never suggested you were anything less," Jude began. "But —"

"Accidental. This had to be accidental," Suarez said. "The inspectors will prove it. You have to be wrong. I've studied in your country, studied with your behavioral scientists. This isn't in line with something a man who stalks a woman in the dark and kills her with a knife would do."

"You know what else our behavioral scientists have discovered?" Jude asked.

"What is that?"

"No matter what they know about the stereotypical serial killer, another one will come along and do everything differently."

Alexi never understood how she and her group got separated. They'd tried to exit the restaurant together. In fact, she'd been holding Larry by the sleeve.

But it had felt like being in the middle of a herd of cattle, all trying to get out.

People pushing and shoving and screaming — with the authorities attempting to keep them from stampeding, from trampling one another.

Crime scene tape was strung around the establishment, as ambulance sirens wailed and the injured were carried out.

The police wanted to talk to anyone who'd been in the restaurant. An officer stopped her as she moved along the sidewalk near the entry to the Celtic American terminal. "Miss, you were in there, yes?"

She told him she had been. She gave him her name and produced her employee card, then described what she'd seen — not much. Just the explosion and then the flash of fire, as if a dragon had released a mighty breath.

He let her go.

She combed the area, feeling more and more desperate when she couldn't find Clara. What if she was by herself like Alexi was? What if she, too, had been separated from the group?

Ralph, Simon and Larry would be fine. She had to find Clara!

She headed toward the building filled with shops and restaurants next to the terminal itself. As she did, she barely held back a scream as a man, covered in soot and grime, stepped in front of her.

Then she sighed in relief.

Jude McCoy.

"Alexi!" He whispered her name. "You're safe!" A little shudder swept through her.

She tried to smile, tried to shake off the sizzle of warmth.

"McCoy?" she burst out. "Wow! Wow, you found me. In all this. You're — a mess. God, what am I saying? What difference does it make? Are *you* all right? The people in the kitchen . . . I can't find Clara."

"It's okay," he told her. "Jackson found her."

"I don't understand. We were all together," she explained. "Then people were pushing and shoving, and it's really lucky no one fell. Once I cleared the doorway . . ."

"It's okay," he repeated. She saw him smile beneath the grime. "Clara's fine. Believe me, with everything that happened, I'd say we had a miracle. I just got a report from Jackson. No deaths. A few people, mostly kitchen staff, in serious condition, but no one even critical."

"How the hell did that *happen*?" Alexi asked. She inhaled in a gasp. "Terrorism?"

Jude shook his head. "The Mexican police captain wants it to be an accident. I doubt it, but . . . If it was terrorism, trust me, most of us would be dead. And someone or some group would've taken credit by now."

"Maybe a poorly trained terrorist?"

"I think it was something else," he said. "Anyway, may I escort you back to the ship?"

"Yes, thanks. But where's Clara?"

"On the ship. Jackson took her there himself. He's back at the explosion site now."

"I was with Ralph, Simon and Larry, too," she said. "But you know that."

He nodded. "Will you trust me if I tell you that excellent officers are searching for them now, and that I'm positive they'll return safely?"

She looked at him, raising her eyebrows. "So I can rest assured. Because they're on your suspect list and therefore, you'll find them right away."

He shrugged. "May I see you back to your cabin? I really need a shower. I mean, in my own cabin, of course," he added quickly.

She was absurdly tempted to tell him that he was more than welcome to shower in her cabin. She managed to refrain.

"Let's go in.

They walked by stores selling leather goods and jewelry, liquor, cigarettes and cologne, and they passed mariachi bands that continued to play — or perhaps played harder — against the confusion in the streets.

People all around them were huddled in groups.

Talking.

Speculating.

Alexi and Jude were on the concrete docks that led to the ship. The waters of the Caribbean still glittered like diamonds.

The breeze blew.

There was no residue here of the acrid smell of smoke.

People were staring at Jude, naturally enough. He looked like a walking burnt-out tree. Many asked if he was all right.

Jude told them that he was.

Security at the ship's boarding station stopped them to ask how the fire had started. "They don't know yet," Jude said. "An explosion — and a burst of fire. But the cops are on it," he assured them.

Once they reached Alexi's cabin, he made a point of waiting until she stepped inside. Then he asked politely, "May I escort you to work this evening? Or perhaps for dinner first?" Checking his watch, he said, "It's just four o'clock. We can do whatever you'd like. Whatever your pleasure."

Whatever her pleasure. Nothing suggestive in his tone. She was creating scenes in her mind, and she should've felt guilty — no, of course, she shouldn't feel guilty! She'd lost the man she'd adored, but not a soul in the world believed she should give up on life or love or . . .

Sex.

But Jude wasn't hitting on her. No, she was the one imagining what he'd be like in bed.

"If you're hungry, I'll be happy to go to the employee cafeteria with you," she said. "I don't have to set up before nine. The last tours get back to the docks around seven and port days make things a bit later. I'll just shower and get ready for the evening myself and you can let me know . . . whatever *your* pleasure is," she told him.

Oh, God, did that sound as if I was hitting on him?

If so, he was polite enough not to react. "Thanks. Don't leave until I'm back, okay?

162

Feeling a little skittish."

She nodded and he left.

His presence seemed to linger, and she couldn't help wondering what would've happened if she'd asked him to stay.

Jude checked in with Jackson again before heading into the shower; Jackson was on board, and Agent Boulder was handling things from the American agency sector on land. Jackson reported that there was nothing new. No matter how much they wanted information quickly, the fire marshal still had to do his job.

Jude turned on the water. Then, just as he'd worked up a good lather, he heard his phone ring. He stepped out, dripping, to get it.

Suarez was calling him.

"You've found something?" Jude asked.

"No. Our fire marshal is still investigating. He seems to believe the cause was one of the gas jets or one of their giant ovens and an overflow of grease, which, of course, has greatly relieved Maria Sanchez. It makes the appliance company liable. Not that we sue here in Mexico the way you do in the States — doesn't pay here. But that's another matter. A few of the people in the kitchen received serious burns, as I think you know. Three have been hospitalized," Suarez told him, "but will be released within the week."

"Well, that's good news," Jude said. "We want to thank you for your cooperation in assisting us."

"I cannot say, sir, that I am not pleased you are leaving," Suarez muttered.

"That's understandable."

"Of course, we remain grateful for the lives you saved, Agent McCoy, pulling people out of the kitchen."

"I'm assuming a few of them might be the ones remaining in the hospital?" Jude asked.

Suarez chuckled. "Believe it or not, no. The two men you got out of the kitchen are well. Ricardo Martinez was treated on the scene and went home, and Javier Valiente just returned to his family. Maria Sanchez, too, was simply treated at the scene. She called me when my men had escorted her safely to her home. She lives a quarter mile from the Celtic American dock. A truly lovely woman. She called me from her whirlpool tub, saying she's fine and that you are a wonderful man."

"I'm pleased to hear this," Jude said. "And relieved that she's safe. You'll still —"

"Keep you apprised of the situation, Special Agent McCoy. Yes. It is a vow."

Jude hung up and finished his shower.

He put the final touches on his evening attire — grateful that he and Jackson had managed to outfit themselves at a cost that wouldn't prove a huge burden to the agency, thanks to the "captain's discount" they'd received at the onboard clothing store. Dressed, he decided to go to Jackson's cabin to catch up, but as he opened his door, he saw that Jackson had the same idea and was about to knock on his door.

"I just spoke with Suarez."

Jackson nodded. "I talked with him, as well. Thing is, we don't really know if anything happened here in Mexico or not."

"No, and we won't, not until someone checks the local churches."

"The Archangel has, so far, anyway, displayed the bodies at his leisure."

"But if he killed in Mexico and came aboard the *Destiny* again, he'd have to display his victim quickly," Jude said.

"I'll get hold of Suarez and Boulder and tell them to check all the churches near the cruise terminal," Jackson said. "Because of that explosion, we do have another problem."

"Yeah, we don't know where our suspects were while that was going on."

"I was following Roger Antrim, who came

165

ashore without his wife. I admit I lost him in my efforts to reach the restaurant. Boulder was watching Hank Osprey, who was having a drink with his young companion of last night. They were at a bar across from the restaurant. Her name's Ginny Monk, by the way — part-time student and part-time stripper at a joint on Bourbon."

"And Boulder lost them?"

"Not Ginny, just Hank, who disappeared, according to Boulder, gallantly telling her he had to help when he saw trouble."

"What about Jensen Hardy?" Jude said.

"He slipped away from one of Beach's men the minute he left the ship."

Jude let out an oath of frustration. Six. They still had six suspects — Hank Osprey, Roger Antrim, Jensen Hardy, Ralph Martini, Simon Green and Larry Hepburn. He mentioned that to Jackson, who shrugged.

"Six isn't so bad. We can watch, we can follow. If we get back to New Orleans without an arrest, we'll have resources to stay tight on every one of them. The Archangel may know we're close — which could scare him, make him go into quiet mode for weeks, months, even years. And then strike again."

"He won't go quiet," Jude said. "Not the Archangel. He thinks he's above us all, way better than we are — because we haven't caught him yet. But that's not what'll keep him going."

"What will?"

"The medallions. The saints' medallions. He's on a mission. I don't know what it is. But he won't stop. Not until he has a girl for every medallion in the set."

Jackson nodded thoughtfully. "Beach is posting a guard in the hallway all night. Clara Avery and Alexi Cromwell will be watched, I promise you."

Jude grinned. "I believe you. And whenever possible, I promise *you,* I'll be watching them myself."

Alexi tried to remind herself that she wasn't on a first date.

She wasn't on a date at all. Because she could see ghosts, she was suddenly on the FBI radar.

She hadn't encountered Byron Grant again, and she was surprised. She'd thought he might show up when she was playing. Maybe he'd spent himself trying to reach her and the FBI men and needed time to recoup. Or he was watching them from afar, perhaps convinced he'd already done whatever he could. It occurred to her that the next day, when the ship would be at sea again, she could take him on a tour. He might be interested in meeting a few of the other supernatural denizens of the *Destiny.*

She heard a knock at the door and spun around to open it.

Jude was there.

She recognized the suit and shirt he was wearing. They could be purchased at the Haberdashing Haberdashery on the Promenade Deck.

He grimaced, as if reading her mind. "Honestly, it's better than some of the clothing I own."

"It's a great suit," she told him. "And you wear it well."

"I thank you. And, I might add, you're so lovely in that red gown, the wearing of it should probably be considered illegal."

Alexi laughed.

"Sorry. I'm out of practice. I haven't tried to be charming lately."

She laughed again, and then they both stood there awkwardly. "I'm very sorry," he said after a moment's silence, and she knew somehow that he was referring to Zachary's death in the war zone. "We lost many good men."

"You served?"

He nodded. "Several years. Anyway, now I'm FBI. Glutton for punishment, huh?"

She held her head at an angle, studying him. "You have a distinct advantage, as they say. You have a dossier on me. I know nothing about you. Are you . . . married?"

"Divorced," he said briefly. "Several years now. Anyway, shall we eat? Walk around? Chat with some friends?" He looked at his watch. "It's only five. You have a few hours. Passengers on the shore excursions won't be back for another two hours."

That sounded impossible. The explosion and fire seemed so long ago — almost as if it had all happened days or even weeks ago instead of at lunchtime.

"Let's do all of the above," Alexi responded. "I say we stroll the hallways deck by deck. Okay, not below us, since that's all engine rooms and storage. It actually takes up two decks. This one is called the Atlantic Deck." She gestured around. "Above us is a mixture of crew and entertainment and 'cheaper' rooms, and it's called the American Deck. And above that are some of the little cafés and lounges — such as the Algiers Saloon, where I work — and that's the St. Charles Deck. Next level is the Promenade, and then there's the Main Deck, and above *that,* the Lido Deck. We also have the Bridge Deck and the Sky Deck. And the original infirmary — not in use now, there's

a nice modern one — is aft on the Promenade Deck, near the chapel. The chapel's
never been updated. It's really beautiful
with a stained-glass portal and carved pews
and a lovely plain wood altar. The old
infirmary is, of course, on the tours. I think
you'll like it."

"Because you intend to introduce me to
ghosts there?" he asked flatly.

"If they're around," she replied. "And you
should definitely meet Captain McPherson."

"Still watching over the old ship, eh?"

"Old captains die hard," she said. Jude
apparently wanted to be with her — and yet
he seemed to hold himself at a distance.
She suspected she knew why.

"I'm sorry," she said.

"About what?"

"That you . . . that you're so unhappy with
yourself."

"I'm not unhappy with myself."

"You're unhappy that you see the dead.
It's a gift, really."

"And you've always seen it as a gift?" he
asked her.

She raised her shoulders in a shrug. "I'm
one of those people who had tons of imaginary friends. Most people thought it was
natural for a child. My mother didn't. She

kept telling me I had to ignore my imaginary friends, and if I did, they'd go away. If I didn't, they'd make me crazy, wanting things from me. My grandmother told her once to leave me alone — that I had the 'magic.' Grandpa had been a 'magic man.' And it was prevalent in my family. I love my mother. I know she has whatever extra sense it is to know when she's not alone, but it terrifies her. Don't get me wrong. I love my mom. She's strong and wonderful, but seeing the dead does upset her. Some people are just . . . afraid."

"I'm not afraid," Jude said.

"Of course not. You're FBI. So you aren't afraid of anything."

They'd started out on the Atlantic Deck, casually walking along. They'd passed a security office and were coming to the bank of elevators. He paused there and smiled as he looked down at her.

"Nope. One of the first lessons we learn is that only a fool ignores fear. I just know — or I believe — that the dead won't hurt us. They're trapped in their own form of Purgatory. Yes, I've managed to avoid admitting that I do see them. Except," he added, "once, when I was in the service. A friend of mine was killed. They told me he'd died instantly, that he was dead before he and I talked. But I *know* I saw him, know we spoke. He saved my life by warning me about a sniper. And he had a message for his wife. I gave it to her."

"There, you see! It's a very good thing," Alexi said.

"You accept it so easily."

She shrugged again. "With me, there wasn't much choice. And," she said, smiling, "trust me, there are lots of people out there who sing and play as well as I do. Or better. I'm not putting myself down. It's just that there are more talented people in the world than there are jobs. Anyway, a number of musicians freak out, working in the Algiers Saloon with Blake and Minnie. I don't. So, in a way, my very different 'talent' got me a job when I needed one."

His expression was strange. His eyes were intense — and yet he still seemed distant.

Almost as if he wanted to be close to her, and couldn't quite take that step.

"But you were never able to see your fiancé," he said.

She inhaled. The moment felt strange and painful to her. No. And she'd wanted to see Zach so badly. He'd been deployed for almost three months when he was killed. At first she could see his face clearly in her mind's eye. But with each passing day, she feared that she lost a little more of him. When she felt that way, guilt overwhelmed her, and it didn't matter how many times people told her he'd been dead for more than a year and that to honor him, she should live, pursue her own goals. And be happy. In fact, she'd promised Zach the same thing.

Did Jude fight the same battles?

"No. I've never seen Zach. He was a good guy. I wish you could've known him. He was never pretentious. He was courteous and he had a deep faith, much deeper than mine, I'm afraid, since I questioned his loss and that of so many other good people. I can't see him, but I do have faith that he went to something better, finer. My mother, in one of her strange moments of actually admitting things, said that Zach could go on, that he could leave this earth because he knew we'd all be okay, that I was strong and his family was strong. Anyway . . . we see those we see. I don't pretend to understand it."

He studied her and she was surprised to experience an almost *physical* sensation.

He'd let a barrier fall, she thought.

Well, maybe.

"Shall we continue our stroll?" he asked her.

"That would be lovely, sir, lovely."

"Ah, at the moment I'm feeling like Blake Dalton!" he told her. "With Minnie on his arm."

He offered her his own arm, exactly as Blake would have done with Minnie.

She grinned and accepted it.

Everything seemed to be fine aboard the *Destiny.*

Jude was glad to have Alexi as a tour guide; he'd already walked the ship from the highest deck to the lowest, including the engine rooms, storage area and the bridge.

But it was different, seeing the ship through Alexi's eyes, greeting the people she knew and learning bits and pieces of history.

They passed the exclusive suite, where an Egyptian prince had once stayed, and the "executive" suite, where two different United States presidents had enjoyed vacations.

On the Promenade Deck, Alexi asked, "Have you seen the chapel?

"Oh, yes," she said, answering her own question. "Of course you have. But have you been in it?"

"Locked every time I went by," he replied.

"You must've gone there at night. It's

open during the day, and a lot of the time, you'll find the Reverend Mike in there."

"I'd like to meet the Reverend Mike," he told her. He recognized the name from the ship's list of crew and passengers. Since the Reverend Michael Hudson had not been a "possible suspect," he hadn't continued to investigate him.

As they walked toward the chapel, Alexi explained that the services held there were nondenominational. The Reverend Mike was a great guy — and gave great sermons. "More like casual conversations, really."

Jude expected someone older with graying hair.

The Reverend Mike was about forty, average height and size, with a ready smile and warm brown eyes that seemed to match the shade of his hair. He greeted them enthusiastically. Jude didn't think that Mike believed he was with the cruise lines; he didn't, however, press him about it. Instead, he told him about the chapel.

"Original to the ship. Whether times were good or bad, it was meticulously maintained. The walls are paneled in mahogany and the porthole is Tiffany stained glass. The art on the walls is from various churches worldwide. There — see? *Mother and Son?* The artist's unknown, but it's from Our Lady of Mercy, a church on the outskirts of Istanbul, which was built in 222 AD. The medieval knighting scene is from a Medici holding in Florence. The pews are cherrywood. I'm telling you, sometimes I feel like a curator instead of a minister!"

"You love the ship, I take it."

"I do. I'm signing on for just one more contract, though. I'm planning to get married and settle down. I've been offered a position in a nondenominational church on the outskirts of the French Quarter. Besides, it's time to allow someone else, a new minister, to come aboard the *Destiny*."

"Congratulations," Jude said.

The Reverend Mike laughed. "A bit premature. I haven't found the girl yet, but I figured I won't find her if I don't settle down." He smiled over at Alexi. "I did meet a few exceptional young women on this ship, but alas — not in the same frame of mind. Not looking for marriage just yet. And," he added, "you probably know they're whispering about you and Mr. Crow all over the ship." He turned to Jude. "If you and the other gentleman *are* executives with the company, I should tell you that my time on the *Destiny* has been excellent. Celtic American is definitely a superior cruise line."

"That's gratifying to hear," Jude said. Alexi had wandered over to the side, where a number of holy books were displayed, including beautifully bound versions of the Old Testament, the Bible in Latin and a King James edition of the Bible.

"Are you available every day, Reverend Mike?" Jude asked.

"Yup. All day, every day. And please, call me Mike. There's a buzzer to reach me if I'm not in the chapel or my office. But . . . somehow I'm not getting the feeling that you're looking for spiritual consultation."

"Just asking about the chapel," Jude said. "With all the valuable art here . . . I was thinking that, unfortunately, it might be dangerous to leave it open."

"I keep an eye on the chapel," Mike assured him. "So do our security people. David Beach, our head of security, as I'm sure you know, has a special affinity for the chapel. He had an uncle who served here as chaplain when the *Destiny* was being used as a hospital ship during World War II. But as far as access to the chapel goes, I have a key, David has a key and the captain does. When I'm not nearby — my office is the cabin right next door here — the chapel is locked. And only three people can open it."

"Good to hear," Jude said.

"So, that's really it? You two didn't steal up here in hopes of a whirlwind wedding? An elopement?" Mike asked.

Alexi almost dropped the Bible she'd been holding.

He was astonished to find himself stuttering.

"We — we've actually just met."

"I'm . . . I'm giving him a tour," Alexi murmured.

"I mean, she's wonderful, of course," Jude said quickly.

Mike laughed, raising his hands. "Sorry, sorry! You're an attractive couple and I get the impression you'd be well suited. But I didn't mean to put anyone on the spot. It's the way you seem to communicate . . . Anyway, I'm always around, if you do want me for anything. And it's been a pleasure to meet you."

Mike thrust out a hand, and Jude shook it. "Thank you for your time."

"Absolutely. That's part of the job description. Listen to people, and give them all the time they need," Mike said cheerfully.

Alexi gave him an awkward smile, and Jude realized they were both flustered, a little off.

"The infirmary?" she asked as they left.

"Sure," he said.

"It's just down here, past the Egyptian Room." The Egyptian Room was one of the larger lounges where private functions were held — along with bingo and a few other shipboard offerings. It was a beautiful room, more like an old adventurers' club than anything, with shimmering gold and glass and marble.

Jude hadn't noticed that there was a hallway directly to the side, but that might've been because of a sign hanging from the ceiling that said Staff Only and the velvet rope that served as a barrier.

Alexi had no problem unhooking the rope. "I *am* staff," she told him with a shrug. "Jensen Hardy arranges tours of the ship and he or his people bring guests here. Other than that, it's cordoned off because it's been maintained in its historic state."

"I see."

Down the hall Alexi opened a door that led to a reception area with a nurses' desk and right behind that, a glass-paned room with the word *Triage* on it.

Jude didn't look farther than the desk, though, because it was occupied.

The woman sitting there wore a white nurse's cap over short curly brown hair, and a white nurse's uniform. Jude wasn't much on style, but he knew that the outfit was long outdated, nothing like the hospital attire in different colors or decorated with cute pandas or monkeys that nursing staff seemed to wear in the twenty-first century.

"Alexi!" the woman said, smiling broadly. "How nice." She stared at Jude, obviously curious, and then grinned slowly. "Well, hello, handsome!" she said. The nurse looked back at Alexi.

"He knows I'm here," she said. There was the merest hint of a question in her words.

"Clear as anything," Alexi told her. "Barbara Leon, I'd like you to meet Jude Mc-Coy. People on the ship believe he's a Celtic American executive, masquerading as a tourist, but he's really an FBI agent. Jude, Miss Barbara Leon, one of the finest nurses to serve on this ship, in wartime or anytime."

Jude felt a split second's freeze; Alexi was so comfortable with this. She introduced Barbara Leon with the same ease and warmth she might use when introducing Clara Avery.

The woman was dead! In reality, there was no one sitting at that desk. There was nothing but air . . . and the whispered memory of a life. It was like the scent of perfume on the breeze when someone had already passed by.

He snapped out of it quickly. "Miss Leon," he said. "A pleasure."

"Who's here?"

He heard another voice, the sound raspy.

It wasn't real, either. Not to other people, anyway. Not to most people. It was something that sounded in his head.

A man in a World War II private's uniform had come to lean against the doorway. He looked warily at Jude and said, "Alexi, what are you doing?"

"I brought a friend to meet you. He needs help with . . . a situation. Jimmy, this is Special Agent Jude McCoy of the FBI. A serial killer has been at work in the United States, and we believe he's on board this ship. Jude, this is Private Jimmy Estes."

"Pleased to meet you. I'd offer to shake, but that usually just upsets people," Jimmy said.

"Pleased to meet you, too," Jude responded.

Another man came up behind Jimmy. Alexi introduced him as Private Frank Marlowe.

"I was a cop before I joined the service," Marlowe said. "How can we help?"

"We'd greatly appreciate any observations you can make," Alexi answered.

"Of course," Frank said. "I haven't seen

181

anything suspicious yet, but I'm not sure what we'd be looking for."

Later, Jude would wonder about the fact that he'd taken one of the chairs at the desk and told the three ghosts in the infirmary what he knew. They listened gravely, promising they'd find a way to monitor the suspects.

"Those medallions . . . my dad had a set," Jimmy said. "He was so proud of them. He bought them for me. Said with all those saints, no matter how hard the days were, I could find some comfort. He was right. Unfortunately, I lost them at a camp near Paris."

"Small world," Barbara said.

"Do you think the medallions are objects he uses just to make his kiss-my-ass displays for the cops?" Jimmy asked. He blushed. "Sorry about the language, Barbara, Alexi. It, uh, slipped out."

"That's okay," Alexi said.

Nurse Barbara Leon was shaking her head. "Those medallions have to mean something to this killer." She turned to Jude. "I assume someone is looking into that?"

"The best behavioral scientists in the world," Jude replied. "Plus, we've had our offices working with all the technological resources at our disposal, and law enforcement all over the US and in Mexico — because of the situation in Cozumel — has a hand in it."

"I'd put my money on the medallions," Barbara said thoughtfully. "They have to be the clue you need."

"What else can you tell us about them?" Alexi asked, glancing at Jude. She herself knew almost nothing about them.

And he'd been struggling with whether or not to tell her and Clara that the saints' medallions for musicians and actors hadn't been used by the killer yet. There were, of course, many other singers and actresses aboard the ship, but he happened to know the two of them.

It shouldn't matter.

It wouldn't influence his work ethic, but it *did* matter.

"There's a new fellow on board, by the way," Jimmy said suddenly, swinging around to face Alexi.

"Yes. He was one of the killer's victims," Alexi said.

Barbara appeared perplexed. "And he's here? Does Captain McPherson know?"

Captain McPherson. The captain who'd died at his retirement party on the ship!

"I'm not sure," Alexi said. "His name is

183

Byron Grant. But I haven't seen him since he managed to communicate with Jude and me."

Jimmy nodded. "Ah, a beginner. Yeah, it takes some time. Well, don't worry, we'll be courteous and welcoming. Captain doesn't like new folk aboard, though, unless they pay their respects."

"I'll tell him that when I see him again," Alexi said. "Thank you all."

"We'll be especially vigilant," Barbara promised.

Jude looked back as they left; he felt that he'd entered a time warp. The men lounged against the door frame. Nurse Barbara sat at her station. If he'd had a camera and taken a picture, anyone would've sworn that it was shot in the 1940s.

Except there would've been no one in it. Or maybe there would . . . He'd heard a story — one he'd ignored or chalked up to a prankster — about John Brown, hanged at Charleston, West Virginia, after he was captured at his raid at Harpers Ferry. The long-dead man had apparently shown up in a picture taken there, a photograph that should have been a shot of a tourist couple — and no one else.

Prankster? Park ranger? More than likely.

And yet . . .

He turned to Alexi. "I'll get you back to your cabin."

As he spoke, the ship lurched, at a far greater angle than it had taken before.

Alexi was thrown against him; he was thrown against the wall.

For a moment her eyes met his.

And he wanted to stay where he was, just stay there and feel her body close to his.

The captain's voice came over the ship's loudspeaker. "Sorry, folks, we're hitting a bit of weather. We'll do our best to skirt around it. Seems a storm has whipped up in the Gulf. We're asking that you all take care when you move throughout the ship. Nothing to worry about. The *Destiny* has often weathered harsh wind and pelting rain. Still, take care moving about and I'll keep you informed."

They heard a flurry of voices coming from the hallways and lounges.

"Let me get you back to your cabin," Jude said urgently. They straightened, both flushed — and both, obviously, feeling a bit awkward.

"Sure," she said huskily, and they set off.

The waves continued to be hard; they walked like a pair of drunks.

As he lingered just outside her cabin door, he realized there were many things he wanted to say to her.

None of them came to his lips at the moment.

He smiled. "I'll be back for you later," he said.

She smiled halfheartedly, nodded, then closed and locked her door.

7

Alexi had an hour or so before Jude would come back to escort her to the piano bar. She sat down in front of her computer, determined to research the set of medallions the Archangel was using. She had to type in a few key words before she found what she was looking for, and that was on an auction site. A set had been sold a few years ago to a museum in Texas, and it was still right there, in the institute's Hall of Religion.

She did, however, find information on the various medals.

They'd been manufactured by the Church of the Little Flower just outside the Vatican as a fund-raiser to support the orphans who'd been pouring in from all over Europe. The church had resolved that no child be turned away from their orphanage, but that pledge had been extremely expensive.

Sister Angelina had been the artist behind

the medallions, and she had worked with a parishioner to see to their execution. Five thousand sets had been made. The funds raised had seen to the care and feeding of orphans through the war years and beyond.

Sister Angelina had chosen saints that the working man — and woman — might call upon to intercede.

Alexi found a pad and pen in her desk and started a list.

St. Catherine — patron saint of artists.
St. Michael — patron saint of police officers.
St. Matthew — patron saint of accountants.
St. Barbara — architects and builders.
St. Christopher — drivers, travelers and pilots.
St. Bernardino — advertising.
St. Luke — physicians.
St. Francis — animals.
St. Joan of Arc — soldiers and military.
St. Thomas Aquinas — teachers.
St. Lawrence — cooks.
St. Genesius — actors.
St. Cecilia — singers and musicians.

As Alexi looked at the list, a chill settled over her. Thirteen medallions. A medallion had been found on each of the female victims, but not on Byron Grant.

The ship's security, as well as Jude and Jackson Crow, were protecting her and Clara, she knew that. And the other actors and musicians, of course.

On this ship, performers were plentiful.

So were cooks. She closed her eyes, wincing as she thought of the female cooks she knew who were on board. Lucy Tamarin, Maria Octavia, Brenda Isley . . .

And many more.

Singers . . . Dozens, between the shows and the various lounges. And most of Jensen Hardy's assistant cruise directors had to at least be able to carry a tune.

But Jude had zeroed in on her.

Only because I see ghosts.

Still, as she reminded herself, she wasn't the only potential victim on the *Destiny*.

There was a killer on board. The Archangel. And there were three medallions left. One was that of St. Cecilia, patron saint of singers and musicians.

Yes, she was in serious trouble.

And so was Clara and every woman in the cast of the ship's production of *Les Miz*.

Her breath was coming too quickly. She picked up her cabin phone and called Clara's room number. She felt the pounding of her heart; it sounded like a cacophony in her ears.

One ring, two, three, four, five . . .

A feeling of panic, of fear for Clara, almost overwhelmed her.

And then . . .

"Hello?"

Relief flooded Alexi as her friend answered the phone.

"Clara," she said breathlessly.

"Alexi? You okay?"

"Yes, yes, I just wanted to make sure *you* were okay."

"Hell of a day, right? I was lucky. Jackson Crow found me in the crowd at the restaurant and got me back to the ship. And then we had to delay sailing for an hour. Did you realize that?"

"No, I didn't. I was back on board —"

"I know. I was frantic when we all got separated. But Mr. Crow, Jackson, told me you were fine, that you were with Jude Mc-Coy. I called your cabin and left you a message."

Alexi saw the blinking light on her phone. She hadn't noticed it before.

"I'm sorry."

"No problem. I knew you were okay."

"I'll be going to the piano bar in a few minutes. Want to come with me?"

"Sure. I'm due at rehearsal, but that's down the hall on the St. Charles Deck, too. Meet in the hallway?"

"In a minute. I'll come and get you. *We'll* come get you. Jude McCoy is walking me up."

"Oh," Clara said, a trace of amusement in her voice.

"I've just been showing him around."

Clara laughed softly. "Then you're a fool. There aren't a lot of men like him around."

"He has a different kind of life," Alexi said.

"We all have different kinds of lives," Clara said.

"We'll return to port, he'll get off the ship and —"

"So what if he does? He's here now."

"Well, sorry, but he hasn't come on to me."

He hadn't, had he? No, he had a reserve about him. He kept his distance. Clara laughed. "Come on to him, then."

"Clara, I haven't even flirted in ages. I don't think I remember how."

"Trust me. It's like riding a bike."

Alexi rolled her eyes at the cliché. "Anyway, I'll see you in a few minutes." She hung up the phone.

And she looked at the list she'd written again.

191

Jude hurried to the office David Beach had arranged for him and Jackson.

Jackson, who was at his computer, glanced up when Jude entered the room. "According to the captain, we're in for some bad weather and there's no way he can make a safe docking in time to avoid it."

"Yeah, I heard. But there was nothing coming across from the coast of Africa," Jude said. "My phone has weather conditions and warnings. I checked it earlier."

"Check it now," Jackson told him. "Angela called a few minutes ago. They're monitoring the situation from headquarters. Seems this is one of those wicked Gulf systems that just spins into existence."

"Great," Jude murmured.

"Right now we're bypassing it. But, since no one really knows where this system is going, there isn't much the captain can do, other than get away from Cozumel, where it's forming."

"I'm assuming this ship has weathered her share of storms at sea," Jude said.

"She's a good ship, although her stabilizers aren't on par with those on some of the newer ones. Still, she's made it through some rough weather. I'm not too worried about this storm," Jackson said.

"Jackson," Jude began then hesitated. "I met a few other ghosts today. A couple of WWII servicemen and a nurse."

"And?"

"They got me thinking about Word War II — and about the medallions. We know this guy is using them for some specific reason. But what the hell could the medallions mean to *him*? Are they just for effect? Or is there some connection to the war? Or to the church that sold them?"

Jackson shrugged. "The problem is, there were five thousand sets and there's no way of knowing where they all went. I'm sure they were considered great gifts by servicemen, to send to their loved ones back home. Or, of course, to keep themselves. But over the past decades, the medals that survived might have gone through dozens of hands. People might still find them in forgotten trunks in attics."

"We need more on the history of our suspects," Jude said. "On any relationship to the war in Italy, or to museums and auction houses that bought or sold the medals."

"I'll ask Angela." Jackson typed something into his phone and then looked up. "I believe I'm going to go see a rehearsal for

Les Miz now."

"And I hear Billy Joel calling my name," Jude said.

"We need sharp eyes tonight," Jackson told him. "We may be heading into one hell of a storm."

"In more ways than one," Jude added.

Alexi was still staring at her list when she heard a tap on the door. "It's me, Alexi," Jude said from the hallway.

When she opened the door, he smiled at her. "Showtime?"

"Yes, thank you," she said with a nod. "Clara should be ready, too."

"Jackson's going to the rehearsal with her," Jude told her.

"Oh."

She was glad to hear that Clara was protected; at the same time, she was worried about the fact that both Jackson and Jude seemed to believe she and Clara were intended victims.

"Well, that's good," she said.

"So tonight your friends Ralph, Simon and Larry will all be in rehearsal. That means they won't be at the piano bar?"

"No, they may show up later. And, of course, Clara will go straight back to her cabin, if that's what Jackson suggests," Alexi replied.

"Glad to hear it," Jude said. "Since it's always easier to protect people who want to be protected."

"So, you *do* see Clara and me as the Archangel's targets?"

"We can't know that for sure. There are other entertainers on board and we're doing our best, with David Beach's help, to see that everyone stays safe."

The ship lurched suddenly. This time Alexi steadied herself by clutching at the wall.

"Rocky tonight," she murmured.

"Yes." Jude was quiet for a minute. "Might be rocky the rest of the way, too, and we could be taking a number of detours. No one knows what this system is doing yet."

"We'll be fine. We had to skirt around a hurricane once before. And, actually, Xavier Thorne was the captain during that sailing, too. He's very good."

"Of course he is," Jude agreed. He smiled, and this time she wasn't convinced it was a real smile.

At the Algiers Saloon, he sat with her on the piano bench while she arranged her sheet music for the evening.

She found it disturbing to have him so close.

And exciting at the same time. She hadn't felt like this in years. A little nervous. Breathless — not good when she had to sing.

A little hot; a little flushed.

But as a crowd began to appear, many of them imbibing the spirits available at the bar, he moved to a cocktail table.

Roger Antrim made an appearance — minus his wife that night.

Hank Osprey showed up, as well. He, too, was solo. Alexi didn't know how Jude managed it, but he got both men to join him at his cocktail table.

In the middle of a Patsy Cline number she was doing herself, she felt a presence. Minnie was next to her and began singing along. Blake leaned against one of the support pillars in the lounge, watching her with love and pride. "I Fall to Pieces" wasn't a song from Minnie's era, but she'd picked it up from Alexi's performances.

Alexi tried to remember that she had a large audience; she smiled at her ghosts but paid them no more heed. Next, she began a popular Carrie Underwood song.

Then she saw Byron Grant again. At last. He was standing behind Blake, near the pillar. And he must've said something because Blake turned. He seemed to greet him warmly.

"Alexi, Alexi! Keep going! Finish the country song. I love country!" Hank called out.

She was startled by his remark.

She was accustomed to her ghosts; she never faltered. What was different now? Was it Byron's presence? Or Jude's?

"What, you want more songs about pickup trucks, pit bulls, shotguns and lost love?"

"You bet!" someone else cried.

"Are you a Texan?" Alexi asked.

"A New Yorker . . . who wishes he was a Texan!" the man called back.

"Oh, come on!" she teased, singing a few lines of "New York, New York" and then sliding back into the Carrie Underwood number.

She glanced up. Jude McCoy was watching her. He inclined his head slightly; she knew that meant he'd seen Minnie and Blake — and the ghost of Byron Grant.

He rose after a minute, excusing himself to Hank and Roger, and apparently saying he'd be back soon.

Thankfully, a guest was eager to sing. Alexi played and kept an eye on Jude and the ghost as they moved down the hall.

About ten minutes later he returned.

A couple of people asked if she knew anything about the explosion at the restaurant in Cozumel, and she fended them off easily. "Just that no one was killed. Thank God!" she said seriously.

Someone else asked about the storm as he walked clumsily toward the piano to take the mic for a song.

"Captain Xavier Thorne is the best," she said. "And so is the *Destiny*!"

The young man started to sing, "Oh, they built the ship Titanic . . ."

"Hey, not to worry. You went to your lifeboat drill, right?" she asked. There was laughter in the room.

A woman cried out, "Wuss! I've sailed in much worse."

"Children, children!" Alexi said, and sang some lines from the song "I Think We're Alone Now."

Much of the audience joined in for the rest of it.

Clara arrived with Jackson Crow toward the end of the evening. None of the other players from *Les Miz* came in that night. Finally, the crowd dwindled.

Hank walked to the piano and gave Alexi a kiss on the cheek, thanking her for "another wonderful evening."

Roger Antrim waved. "I'm going to tell Lorna she missed a fun night. I'm meeting her at the casino!" A last table of young men moved on, and Alexi was left with Clara at her side and Jackson and Jude waiting for them.

"Any news from Mexico?" Alexi asked. "About the explosion or . . ."

"Nothing yet. But Cozumel's getting battered pretty hard, which is hampering their investigation," Jackson replied.

Once they reached the hallway, they all went to Clara's door.

Then Jackson and Jude accompanied Alexi to her cabin.

Jackson said good-night. Jude stayed where he was. He didn't speak at all.

After a moment Alexi thanked him and closed her door.

Sitting at her small dressing table, she couldn't help staring at her list again. But as she sat there, she heard footsteps in the hall. And then a door opened — and she heard Clara's voice.

She didn't think; she just reacted.

Jumping to her feet and throwing open her door, she raced the short distance to Clara's cabin.

Larry Hepburn was standing by the open door. Clara stood beside him, frowning.

Jude and Jackson had both left their cabins and were hurrying down the hall to Clara's. Larry looked at them all in complete confusion. "What?" he demanded. "I came to rehearse a scene with Clara!"

"Larry, I said we needed to run through the scene a few times, but not *tonight*!" Clara said.

Larry didn't seem to hear her. Then another door opened, and Ralph Martini stepped out into the hall. He didn't seem to notice the others. Just Larry.

"Larry?" He, too, sounded confused — and hurt.

"Oh, Lord!" Larry said. "What is this? Big Brother spying on me? I heard Clara come in, so I knew she was still awake. We were really rough tonight and she told me she was concerned. Ralph . . . no! It's not what you're thinking!"

Alexi realized then that Ralph and Larry were having an affair. She didn't understand why they'd been hiding it, since all their friends knew they were gay.

"Go ahead!" Larry said, turning to Jackson. "Tell the other muckety-mucks that I'm gay. It's not something I'm ashamed of. I just never considered it anyone else's business."

Jude shrugged. "I don't see why anyone

would care, either. Your personal life should be your own. We came out here simply because we all got a little worried. Too much going on — the Archangel in New Orleans, an explosion in Cozumel, the storm."

"Larry, it's really too late to rehearse. Soon as I wake up, I'll call your room."

Larry smiled, looking around at them. "No one really cares?"

"Why would we? Why would anyone care? If you two are happy, that's great," Alexi said. She'd spoken quickly, but she was sure she spoke for everyone. Their nods and smiles told her she had.

"It's hard for anyone to find the right person and be happy. The best to you both," Jude said. "And now it's late as hell, so —"

The ship suddenly pitched again.

"The storm's growing worse," Jackson muttered.

"Call me in Ralph's cabin," Larry told Alexi, then followed the older, shorter man.

"See you in the morning!" Clara said cheerfully. "I'd have you all over for coffee, but honestly, these cabins aren't big enough."

Alexi grinned and turned away. "Good night, everyone!" She heard Jackson's door close. Jude walked with her and waited until she'd entered her cabin. She knew he'd wait

201

until the door closed and he heard it lock.

She opened her door and he was there. So close . . . She looked at him intently and thought about the way he made her feel — alive again, cherished. But she didn't want to analyze her feelings anymore, or worry about complications or careers.

She wanted to think of some clever comment. "Hey, I'd be safer if you didn't leave at all." Or maybe, "Is there a ghost of a chance you'd want to come in?"

Oh, that was bad! Thank God she hadn't said it out loud.

He was still there, and he smiled slowly, as if he was waiting. Not for the door to lock, but for the invitation. She inhaled a deep breath and stepped forward so they were almost touching. Trembling, she decided that at the very least, she'd place a hand on his chest and thank him for his vigilance.

But when she moved, he moved, too, and once again, his eyes, those beautiful cool green eyes with the brown streaks, were on hers. She moved into his arms. And he kissed her. It was a burst of something wet and hot and sweet, something she'd never expected to feel again. But the past was gone, and this was *now,* and she found herself wanting him with a fever that was new. As they kissed, she forgot that they were standing in the hallway.

It was a beautiful kiss. Long, deep, hungry.

Then he broke away and they both took in several ragged breaths.

They still didn't speak. They both went into the cabin, with Jude locking the door behind him. Then they were in each other's arms again, and although Alexi had thought she'd be awkward and that she wouldn't even know what she was doing anymore . . . Memory brought it all back. More than memory, it was a fusion of the past and the present.

He shed his jacket and holster and gun while their lips were still locked together. And then they paused and gazed into each other's eyes. He kissed her, more slowly this time. She felt his fingers on her back, working the zipper on her red cocktail dress, and she shimmied out of it until it fell in a puddle at her feet. She kicked off her shoes and continued kissing him, her hands on the buckle of his belt.

They were naked before they hit her bunk, heedless of the little towel animal that Nolan Perkins, the crew steward, had left there.

They were touching . . .

And kissing. More and more kissing. Their

lips traveling each other's bodies. He knew where to touch her and when. Instinct kicked in, and she stroked and teased him as he did her, all of it spontaneous, natural . . . and so arousing.

He stopped for a moment, reaching for a condom in the pocket of his discarded pants. "I was hoping . . ." he whispered.

She nodded as he put it on, and was startled seconds later to realize that she'd crawled on top of him, taken him inside her and begun to move. Pure sensation was so strong it seemed to eclipse the world. They moved and rocked with the waves. Every brush of his fingers, every movement he made, seemed to heighten the hunger building in her. When they did climax, his lips were locked with hers, and he held her as if their trembling was some great force that swept around them both. But he was there for her, solid and strong. When he broke the kiss, easing onto his side, pulling her close, she smiled. She should speak; *they* should speak. But for those first moments, she just lay there, grateful for that time with him. Life was fleeting — she knew that all too well.

Times like this needed to be savored.

He stroked her hair. "It might be rude to say so, but . . . I think I've wanted this since

I first set eyes on you."

She laughed softly. "You thought I was a freak, an alarmist, a liar creating fantastic tales."

"That didn't mean that I didn't want to be with you." She curled against him, lifting her head to meet his eyes. "I can't say it was the first thing on my mind. But you do grow on people."

"That's good to hear," he said, and there was humor in his eyes. Then he turned onto his back and stared up at the ceiling. "And bad, maybe. I shouldn't be here. I'm on a case. You're . . . a rather strange witness in that case."

"And I might be a target," she said flatly. "St. Cecilia, you know. Patron saint of musicians and singers."

He nodded slowly.

He still seemed lost in thought, but then she felt him shrug and he turned back to her. "This is an excellent way to keep an eye on you. I know exactly where you are. I don't have to worry about you racing out into the hall. At least, I don't think you run naked into the hall very often."

"Not often, no," she said. "Earlier, it was because I heard Clara. And," she added, "I wasn't naked!"

"Yes, but Jackson and I are just a couple

of doors away from you — and Clara. You have to let *us* be the ones to run out into the hall."

"Stark naked?"

"Hopefully not. Besides, at least I'd have a gun," he told her, pulling her close. "I've seen this killer's handiwork, Alexi. He's quick. You know that from what Byron told us. The Archangel takes his victims by surprise and they're dying before they realize what he's done. He's adept with a knife. Kat Sokolov — our Krewe medical examiner — believes he's used different weapons, depending on what he can get his hands on. We know that Elizabeth Williams was killed with a knife from her own kitchen." He paused. "And yes," he said quietly. "There are three medallions in that set we haven't found on victims yet. Medallions for chefs or cooks, actors — and musicians."

"I don't remember saying that I minded being watched so closely," she whispered.

"That's great. Makes it all much easier."

"Just easier?"

"And much more pleasant."

"Pleasant?"

"Hot and exciting?"

"I think that's better than pleasant," Alexi teased.

He rose up on one elbow and shook his head slightly. "How about, 'more wonderful than I imagined anything could be'?" She should have let it go; lie or not, it was nice. But they weren't lying to each other.

"You were married," she pointed out.

That glaze of pain she'd seen before touched his eyes.

"I'm sorry," she said.

He was quiet for a long time. Then he said, "We lost a child. Lily. She was three."

"Oh, I am so sorry."

"Kathy is a good person. We just drifted apart. Maybe we were drifting before we found out that Lily was sick. She was premature, and then her heart didn't . . . didn't grow the way it should have. We weren't unkind to each other, we just couldn't stay together. Lily had become our only common ground. When we lost our little girl, we had nothing." He stroked her cheek. "And I don't think I've really had anything since."

Alexi couldn't begin to imagine the pain of losing a child. A little girl, just three years old.

"I am so sorry," she said again. There was nothing else to say.

"Thank you. I think I grew cynical about my so-called psychic ability or whatever you want to call it. If I did have a talent, I should've been able to . . . tell her it would be okay. That there was something beautiful she'd go to. I had this terrible helpless feeling. I couldn't protect her. I couldn't protect her from . . . her damaged heart."

Alexi touched his face gently. "You didn't see her *because* you loved her, because she was young and innocent — and there *is* something better and that's where she is."

"I like to believe that," he said. "I have to believe it."

"You know it's true," Alexi said. "You know, because you've met those who aren't ready to go yet. And if they're here . . ."

He sat up suddenly. "Someone in the hall," he said.

He bounded cleanly from the bed, hopping over her.

He did go to the door naked — and with his gun.

But he returned the gun to its holster on her dressing table, then lifted the bedcovers and crawled in beside her.

"Who was it?" she asked.

"One of David Beach's security men. Doing his job," he said. "Enough sadness." He looked as if he wanted to say more.

He didn't.

Instead, he kissed her.
And then . . . they made love again.

8

Just before 8 a.m., Jude entered the office he and Jackson had been assigned. Not many hours' sleep, but he felt as if he could face the world.

He'd left Alexi sleeping peacefully.

He'd been happy just watching her sleep. She was beautiful with her dark red hair curling over the sheets, a slight smile on her face even as she slept. But he knew it was much more that had drawn her to him. She had charm, evident when she worked, but there was something far deeper than that, as well. Maybe it had been her determination in tracking him down to try to convince him he'd been chasing a ghost. She fought for what she believed was right. She had the sense to be afraid — and yet sprang into action — maybe a little too easily when she thought a friend was in danger.

Part of it might have been their shared *talent,* or even the losses they'd experienced in their lives. And then, of course, who knew why, in a world of possibilities, certain people were simply attracted to certain others. He felt he'd been lucky enough to meet an exceptional young woman and that, for these moments at least, he'd been blessed.

He booted up the computer he'd been given for this detail and immediately heard a beeping sound.

Incoming computer call.

He answered it quickly and saw Angela Hawkins, Jackson's lovely coworker and wife, pop onto his screen.

"Good morning," he said. "Jackson should be in shortly."

"That's fine," she told him. "I tried just now. Apparently, weather down in the Caribbean is getting rougher. If you have a chance, look up the 'cones of probability' as to where the storm might go."

"Okay, yeah, haven't had a chance yet," Jude said. "I understand that Captain Thorne is supposed to have led ships through bad storms before, so I think we're okay there."

"Yes, he has an exceptional record," she agreed. "We've investigated him, too, of course."

Jude smiled. "Of course."

"The thing is, they're ordering him to stall

where he is. Those cones I was telling you about are all over the map. One has this system — Dinah, which reached tropical storm status at 5 a.m. — heading straight for Southwest Florida. Another has it moving toward New Orleans, and one had it going at a southwesterly angle toward Belize and Central America. Anyway, communication could get harder, so if I see one of you face-to-face, I'll know all my information's gotten through to you."

"Do you have anything new?"

"Just one significant piece of information that should help you. We've cleared Ralph Martini. He was on a ship that made port in Miami at the time the murders were committed there, but we tracked down the driver who brought him straight from the ship to the airport — and have him on a puddle jumper down to Key West. While it would theoretically have been possible to drive back up to Miami during that time, we have a 'fan cam' video of him performing at a karaoke club there, and we have room service bills and bank and traffic cameras showing him in Key West. The hotel where he stays also has cameras at the entry. In other words, he could not have committed the murders in either Miami or Fort Lauderdale. Oh, we also talked to the driver who picked him up from MIA to bring him back to the port. Ralph's definitely not our man."

"How are you doing with the others?" Jude asked. "In particular, Larry Hepburn."

"We have agents in the Miami office tracking down his friends and acquaintances. He kept his residence on the ship while he was in port there. So far, we know he went to a rock concert, a ball game — Marlins vs. the Phillies — and a party. He was back on the ship soon after each event, and it's highly unlikely he had enough time in Miami to commit the murders there. Not only that, he probably couldn't have attended these events *and* gotten up to Fort Lauderdale."

"It's only about thirty miles, right?"

"Of endless traffic," Angela said. "But, there's a slim possibility that Hepburn could have carried out the murders. *Very* slim."

"And the rest of them?" Jude asked. "How are we doing?"

"It's more difficult to tell with Hank Osprey and Roger Antrim. People with money can whisk themselves away. They both have homes in the Miami area, and they were both there — as well as in the other locations. But their expenses are checking out as regular expenses. Gas stations, restaurants. I've looked into their histories of attending auctions. However, it's quite possible that someone bought those medallions at a flea market and that's painstaking to trace. But we're doing our best."

"You know anything more about Jensen Hardy, our eternally cheerful cruise director?"

"Just that he's eternally cheerful?" Angela said drily. "We're tracking his movements. He was in the ports where the murders took place at the relevant times, but we can't prove or disprove his possible involvement. He was at the ports legitimately, working on two different ships for the Celtic American line."

Jude was writing on his scratch pad as he listened to her. He knew that the teams in the field would be thorough, and he was sure that in Jackson's Krewe of Hunters offices, every method of tracing suspects was being used.

It wasn't part of "seeing ghosts" and had nothing to do with technology, but last night he'd had the gut feeling that Ralph and Larry were just what they appeared to be — entertainers who liked to keep their private lives private. The world might be a more accepting place these days, but he respected their right to privacy regarding their feelings for each other, since prejudice still existed in many forms.

So . . .

Roger Antrim.

Hank Osprey.

Simon Green.

Jensen Hardy.

David Beach, eliminated. Ralph and Larry, eliminated. Bradley Wilcox. A mean bastard and an idiot, but . . . eliminated.

They were down to four men.

"Thank you, Angela," he said.

"I wish I was there with you," she said. "I won't be able to join you, though, not with this storm."

"We're doing all right on our own," he told her. "Well, with your help we are because of the way you're narrowing things down for us. We're watching four people now, and that's a hell of a lot easier than the whole ship at first, and then eight."

Jackson walked into the office and Jude brought him up to speed, informed him that he was going to check out the events at the pool and stepped out of their *office* cabin.

He'd give the two of them a few minutes of privacy, even if it was over the internet.

He stopped by his cabin to change into appropriate poolside attire. After, he knocked lightly on Alexi's cabin door. It opened instantly.

"Hey," he reproved her. "You just opened that door!"

"I knew it was you," she said. "I looked."

"Ah."

"You're going swimming?" she asked.

"Are you allowed — going by the company rules — to be at the pool?"

Alexi nodded. "As long as I'm not taking a lounger a guest might want."

"I don't think the pool area will be full."

"I don't think anything's going to be full, other than the ship's infirmary. I don't usually get seasick, but I'm willing to bet the nurses and doctors are busy today," Alexi said.

He didn't tend to get seasick, either, or suffer any kind of motion sickness. But he was sure a lot of people would be looking a little green today.

"I want to see what's going on poolside. Care to join me?" he asked.

"Okay. Give me a minute to change," Alexi said.

"I'll wait here."

He probably should've been feeling guilt and remorse about their relationship; being with Alexi last night certainly wasn't commendable under the circumstances.

But he didn't feel guilty. He felt *right* —

for the first time in a very long while.

She emerged in a matter of minutes, a lace cover-up over her suit, a straw bag under her arm and sandals on her feet.

"No big-brimmed hat?" he asked her as they walked to the elevators.

"No sun," she told him, grinning. "There's never any sun at the pool. On the *Destiny*, the pool's covered. She was originally an ocean liner and when she traveled the northern Atlantic, the weather would often have been chilly. So . . . they built a pool inside," she said. "And while the ship may be sailing the Caribbean now and not the Atlantic, it's lucky for anyone who wants to swim today that the pool's on an inside deck. Oh, I tried to get more information on the storm. Apparently, it's just sitting over Cozumel. They're in worse shape there than we are on the ship."

"I haven't heard from Capitan Suarez," Jude told her. "They must be battling harsh circumstances while they're trying to investigate. This storm swept up so fast there was no time to prepare."

"Are you from New Orleans?" she asked.

"I am. I grew up a block off Frenchman Street," Jude replied.

"Then you should know that storms can whip up — and despite all the hard work by the world's best meteorologists, they aren't predictable. They can stall, move, stall. And they go wherever they choose. Apparently, the storms aren't always aware of the cones of probability."

"Good point." She searched his eyes. "What are you expecting to hear from Capitan Suarez? There are dozens of possibilities. The explosion and fire might have been an accident. Human error. Faulty equipment. Or maybe someone had a grudge against the owner. What could any of that have to do with the Archangel?"

"Chaos," Jude said.

"Chaos?"

"No one knows where anyone else was during that time. Look at how easily you got separated from your friends. I was certainly distracted by the explosion. All over the area, people were distracted. And every one of our suspects managed to disappear for several hours."

"You think that the explosion was a ploy by the killer — because he knows he's being watched? But I thought you'd heard that Señora Maria made it home fine."

"Yes. I'd like to reach Suarez and find out if she's still fine — and if he's had a chance to search the local churches."

"I'm sure they've been doing that —"

"And I'm equally sure that an American agent asking them to go through the various churches in the midst of being continually pummeled by a tropical storm is not high on their list of things to do."

Alexi nodded solemnly. "No, I guess not."

They'd arrived at the elevators. There was still no one around them, but Jude lowered his voice anyway as he asked her, "How well do you know Jensen Hardy?"

"Ah, so we're watching Jensen today."

"How well do you know him?" he repeated patiently.

"Not that well. He's always nice. I like him but I don't think I could spend a lot of time with him because he's always cheerful."

"How terrible!" Jude said.

She laughed. "No, just exhausting. But I have to admit he's excellent at his job. No matter where the storm goes, Jensen makes sure he keeps everyone on board occupied. You don't have any special information on the storm, do you? Like a bureau insider tip?"

"No. Apparently no one, including the experts in various government agencies, has any real idea where it's going right now," Jude told her. "I do know the captain's holding on the outskirts, waiting for instructions, I assume, from Celtic American head-quarters."

The pool wasn't on the Sun Deck, where it might have been on another ship. Jude actually knew where it was, but he let Alexi lead him. The pool was forward on the Promenade Deck in a special section of the ship entered through a double set of doors. This grand, old-fashioned part of the *Destiny* also offered dressing rooms and a sweeping staircase with carved banners that went up to a second deck of lounge chairs and a bar.

When they got there the ship's pitching had the water in the pool moving as if it was a very modern wave pool.

There were still quite a few people around — pretty girls in bikinis who weren't going to have their Caribbean vacations ruined, families with children and groups of young adults, all of whom had to be entertained, and couples who were ready to relax.

Jude saw that Jensen Hardy was at the shallow end, near the dressing tables. He was busy explaining the rules of a chicken fight in the pool. The lighter person sat on the heavier person's shoulders. There was to be no hair-pulling or punching, but the "supporting" person was supposed to unbalance the other one. Despite the rock and roll of the ship, he had a number of people clamoring around him, eager to enter the contest. The winner earned a hundred dollars in ship credits that could be used in all the shops, cafés, as well as the casino.

In the middle of speaking, Jensen set eyes on Alexi. He beamed.

"Hey! Welcome to our piano bar hostess!" he called out. "For those of you who haven't been to the Algiers Saloon on the St. Charles Deck yet, this is Alexi! She runs a great show. And if she doesn't know your song, she'll find it. Hi, Alexi!"

"Hi, Jensen!" she called back, waving.

"Want to show them all how to play chicken, Alexi?" Jensen asked.

"No!" Alexi's stricken expression brought a roar of laughter from the crowd.

"Alexi!" he said, gesturing at the group of mostly young people who'd gathered around him. "Help me, Alexi!" Her name became a chant, and Jensen left his position to come over to her.

Then he noticed Jude. He'd obviously homed in on Alexi right away — and hadn't seen Jude.

Something flashed in his eyes. *Dislike? Dismay?*

"Oh, sorry. I didn't realize you were together," Jensen said.

By then, the chant had grown louder. "Alexi! Alexi!"

She gave in. "Jude, do you mind?"

"Of course not," he said, glancing at Jensen.

The man's smile was back in place.

Alexi left her bag, sandals and cover-up on a lounge chair. "Okay, let's do this!"

"We got her, folks! We got her!" Jensen cried, and there was a massive round of applause as Alexi took his hand and moved with him to the shallow end.

There were a few catcalls, too. Alexi's bathing suit was a tank-top one-piece thing, not at all provocative.

Still . . .

Maybe, Jude thought, he was in . . . not *love,* surely not love. Too soon. Impossible . . . But perhaps a state of enchantment. She appeared far more sensual to him than the young women barely clad in minibras and string bottoms.

"Okay, folks, we're on. You there, sir, with the lovely redhead. You two — a challenge from Alexi and me. If you dare!"

Jude took a seat on one of the lounge chairs halfway between the entry and the pool. And he watched.

The young man accepted the challenge and came closer to stand beside Jensen, one arm around his red-haired companion. Jensen joked with them briefly. They were Maude and Eric Anderson from Milwaukee.

And then the chicken fight was on. Alexi on Jensen's shoulders, the Milwaukee couple likewise poised to meet them.

Jude could tell that Alexi had helped Jensen out before — and that she knew they were supposed to lose, which they did. Alexi rose from the water, dripping wet and laughing and congratulating the other couple.

Maybe he *was* falling a little bit in love. She seemed to rise out of the water, shimmering, as if she'd been born from the sea. She was not only beautiful, she was also gracious and charming.

He hadn't liked Jensen touching her. Was he just jealous?

Nope.

He hadn't liked the look in Jensen's eyes when the man had realized Alexi wasn't alone — that she was with him. And the guy was a suspect, after all!

The couple won drinks at the pool for a day; to win the big money, they'd have to become the champions, beat all the other contenders. The contest was on.

Alexi climbed out of the pool and stood by Jensen's side, encouraging the contestants in the water.

Jude felt a prickling sensation at the back of his neck, followed by a waft of air. He turned. The double doors to the pool were closing, as if someone had just entered.

Someone had.

For a moment he thought that Captain Xavier Thorne had come to watch the antics at the pool.

But it wasn't Thorne. It was a different man — in a different uniform, a captain's formal attire from a long-gone age.

He was seeing another of the *Destiny*'s resident ghosts — Captain McPherson. He was about to stand up, do what the other ghosts on the vessel would consider right, and introduce himself to the captain.

He never had the chance.

The ghost of the old captain shook his head, as though the antics he witnessed were beyond his understanding.

He turned abruptly and left.

The doors seemed to shudder in his wake.

"So, you don't like Jensen Hardy, either, do you, Captain?" he muttered.

"What?"

He looked up and managed a smile. Alexi, toweling her hair, was standing beside him.

"Seeing ghosts," he said softly. "It's really . . . Well, it's not good for a man's

224

reputation. They make you talk to yourself."

She sat down, her smile wider, and then leaned back on the lounger next to him. "Minnie and Blake think it's hysterical when they try to make me respond to them while I'm working. But you get accustomed to ignoring them when you need to." She closed her eyes for a minute and then opened them again. "So?" she asked him. "Did you learn anything?"

"Yes."

"What?"

"Jensen Hardy is not what he appears to be."

Alexi had just emerged from the shower after their time at the pool when she heard her cabin phone ringing.

She came out in her towel to answer it; Jude had gone to his own cabin to shower and change, and then he planned to meet with Jackson.

Clara was on the line. "Are you doing anything right now?" she asked.

"I'm getting dressed. What are you doing?"

"Thinking about food. I was also thinking I could use some help. I can polish the nails on my left hand myself, but I'm horrible at the right. Want to do it for me?"

Alexi doubted her friend really cared about nail polish.

She suspected Clara didn't want to be alone.

"Sure. You coming here?"

She knew that one of David Beach's men was on guard in the employee corridor here; she'd seen him when she and Jude had gotten off the elevator.

"Yep. Two minutes."

Clara's timing was precise. Alexi had just finished dressing when the knock sounded at her door. Alexi checked through her little peephole before opening it.

"Girls' day in," Clara said. "I spent the morning working with Larry and I think we're doing well with the scene, and now . . . I'm nervous."

"So we'll have a nail polish party. It's a cure for nervousness. With any luck, I won't get it all over your fingers and toes."

"Polishing nails is better than getting drunk, which would probably get me fired," Clara said. She perched on the chair at Alexi's little dressing table, which doubled as her desk. "I wasn't scared when we started this trip, but now I am. There was a murder in New Orleans. Two men introduced as Celtic American executives show up on the ship. They look amazingly like

226

cops or agents to me. What does a cop or agent look like, you ask? It's the way they always seem to be watching, the way they're aware of everything around them. I'm not complaining, mind you — it's reassuring to have them here. But then there's an explosion in a restaurant, and now a terrible storm. We've all weathered bad storms, and this one doesn't scare me. I just have this funny feeling that our new friends are onto something — on this ship."

Alexi couldn't lie to Clara, but she couldn't decide what to say.

"Don't tell me anything. I know it's the truth. And I'm assuming they think they've chased a killer onto the ship. They're obviously law enforcement. My guess is FBI. Let's face it — no average guy just jumps into the fray, saving people the way your Jude McCoy did yesterday. He's had real training in rescue and dangerous situations. And then, in all that chaos, Jackson Crow finds me and I feel as if I've been surrounded by a . . . protective force. Too bad Crow's married. He's a super guy. I'm grateful he's aboard, and grateful to have him as a friend. At least Jude McCoy isn't married — is he?"

"No, he's not married. He's been divorced for several years."

"She must have been an idiot to lose a guy like that."

"They had a little girl who died. After that, the marriage fell apart."

"Oh, I'm sorry to hear that!"

"I know. I can't imagine the pain."

Clara nodded. "I'm so glad you're sleeping with him. Even if it's just for now. You've needed . . . to connect. And," she added, "don't ask how I know! It wasn't hard to figure out."

"He's a good man," Alexi said.

Clara smiled. "And a hot one, too. He *is* government, right? And they do believe there's a murderer on board. And . . . oh, my God!"

Clara had turned, looking down at the desk.

Alexi remembered that she'd left her list of medallions and the saints they represented there.

Clara stared at her, eyes wide with shock.

"Singers and musicians — and actors!" she said.

"And cooks," Alexi pointed out.

"We're in danger. Serious danger," Clara said.

"We don't really know that. But it doesn't hurt to be as careful as possible."

Clara wagged a finger at Alexi. "Don't

stop sleeping with Jude, you hear me?"

"Clara, I didn't say I was sleeping with him."

"For one thing, it's obvious, and for another you didn't deny it."

"Fine. I've slept with him once. *Once.* What that means, whether it means anything, I don't know myself."

"Stay with him or have him stay with you."

Alexi smiled at that. "I can do my best to keep him around, but that's up to him, too."

"You won't have any trouble there," Clara predicted. "And the two of you — stick close to me, okay?" She frowned. "You don't think Ralph and Larry and Simon are dangerous, do you? I mean, I just spent the morning rehearsing with Larry. He's super nice. We had a long talk today. I feel bad for him. I guess there are still people out there who can be really nasty and cruel if you're . . . different. If you're not like them. Apparently, despite his success, his father won't have anything to do with him."

"That's terrible! And we're supposed to be so enlightened today." Alexi picked up the bottle of nail polish Clara had brought with her and shook it. "Give me your hand."

"You didn't answer the question," Clara said, stretching out her hand.

Alexi carefully began to polish her friend's

fingernails, which was no easy task; she was accustomed to the rough movements of the ship, but that did make it difficult for her to be precise with the brush and keep the color on Clara's nails.

"About?"

"My cast mates. Ralph, Simon and Larry."

Alexi shrugged. "Last night Larry honestly seemed bewildered that we were concerned about him. I like Larry. I like Ralph — and we've known him for a while. Simon seems to be great, too," Alexi said.

"But you never know, do you?" Clara asked.

Before Alexi could answer, there was another tap at her door.

"Alexi, it's me, Jude," she heard.

"Don't mess up those nails! I did a good job and it isn't my forte," Alexi said, setting down the bottle of polish and rising to let Jude in.

"Hi, there," he said, greeting Clara.

"Hi to you, too."

"Everything okay?"

"I don't know. Perhaps you could tell me," Clara said.

Jude gave Alexi an accusing look.

"She didn't say a word to me! I'm just not completely blind," Clara said.

"I see," Jude murmured.

230

"I still don't know exactly who or what you are. I mean, what . . . what you are officially. But you're not with Celtic American."

"No," Jude said.

"You're law enforcement."

"Yes."

"What kind of law enforcement?"

"FBI," Jude said.

"That's what I guessed!" she said triumphantly.

"Ms. Avery, Clara, it's important that we maintain a pretense of —"

"You don't think this killer's got any idea that you and Jackson are onto him?" she broke in.

"If only we *were* onto him," Jude muttered.

"But you suspect Ralph and Larry —"

"I don't suspect Ralph or Larry. I believe, because of traffic cams and other evidence, that Ralph and Larry are innocent. I don't know about Simon," Jude said. "That doesn't mean I suspect him. It just means we haven't been able to find out where he was at the times the murders were committed."

"Well, I'm glad about Ralph and Larry. Ralph's an old friend. Larry's new, but working with him is a pleasure. He rehearsed with me this morning, in my cabin — with one of Beach's security guards right outside, so I wasn't worried. But I wasn't really worried to begin with. Gut feeling, you know?"

"Gut feeling, yes, I know," Jude said. "Clara, I've told you more than I probably should have. I need to ask you to keep all of this to yourself."

"I haven't said anything to anyone, except for Alexi," Clara said.

He nodded. "Thank you for that."

"And I don't mind that you and Jackson are our guardians. In fact, I'm very appreciative." She glanced over at Alexi. "What about the cook?" she asked.

Jude turned to Alexi, eyebrows raised.

"There's a cook on Alexi's medallion list," Clara said.

Jude lowered his head, hiding a smile, before he looked up at Alexi again. "You've been doing some investigating?"

"Storm outside, hanging around in my cabin . . ."

"Interesting way to spend your time." Jude turned back to Clara. "I'm still uncomfortable about what happened in Mexico. Right after the blast, Maria, of Señora Maria's, was fine. She let Capitan Suarez know as soon as she could. But was there someone else?" He raised his shoulders in a shrug. "I don't know. I do believe, however, that the explosion was caused by the murderer. No one else seems to think so, but I do. Everyone scattered after that. We're not certain where anyone was. We're out of contact with Cozumel right now. We will be for a while longer." He hesitated. "I want you and Alexi to be more than vigilant. You two are similar in many ways to the victims the Archangel's chosen. You're talented, beautiful — and female. In fact, there are quite a few attractive performers on this ship. I'm afraid for all of you. But the ship's security's on guard, taking nothing for granted."

Clara smiled. "Good. So, anyway . . . I'll forget about polishing the toes. I'm starving. I'd love to have company to go and eat somewhere."

"Are you two required to eat in the employee cafeteria?" Jude asked.

"No." Alexi shook her head. "We can eat at any of the restaurants or cafés — we get a discount."

"Sushi?" Jude suggested.

"Fine with me."

"I *love* sushi," Clara told him. "So you're a sushi fan, too?"

"I'm an any-kind-of-food fan," Jude said. "Shall we go?"

The sushi restaurant, Paradise Koi, was located on the Promenade Deck.

Jude did like sushi, but he hadn't come here for the food.

David Beach and his men had been keeping tabs on the two passengers still on the suspect list, Hank Osprey and Roger Antrim.

They'd received a report from Beach that Osprey was in his cabin and that Roger Antrim and his wife, Lorna, were dining in the sushi restaurant.

Alexi and Clara were greeted by the waitress, who obviously knew them from previous sailings; she was pleasant when she met Jude — especially when Alexi introduced him as an executive with the cruise line.

They chatted with her for a few minutes.

Clara had either genuinely let go of her fears, or she really was an excellent actress; she spoke about the show, and the hostess mentioned a number of songs she'd love to hear Clara and Alexi do together at the piano bar.

The restaurant was only half-full, so they had their choice of table.

Jude was almost sure that Alexi knew they were in the sushi place for a reason, and that seemed to be reinforced for her when they walked by the table where Roger was sitting with Lorna.

Roger came to his feet as he saw them pass by, greeting them all. Lorna had remained seated; she looked pale and he wondered if she was distraught.

"Is the movement of the ship getting to you?" he asked her.

"Poor Lorna!" Roger said. "She's usually a good sailor! But this is pretty rocky, even for us."

"I'm fine, thank you." Lorna smiled weakly at Jude.

"Have you taken anything for it? I know some of the meds are supposed to be taken before you sail, but they could certainly give you something in the infirmary," Alexi said.

"Perhaps I'll go after we eat. Well, after Roger eats," Lorna said. "I'm not so sure raw fish is what I need right now."

"Some crackers, perhaps?" Clara suggested.

"Yes, they're getting me some." Lorna picked up her cup. "And this green tea seems to help."

"Well, take care. And do go to the infirmary," Jude said again.

"I will," she promised.

"I'll walk her there myself!" Roger said. Lorna didn't look at her husband.

With Alexi in the lead, they headed to a table near the back. Jude made a point of taking a chair by the wall so he could watch Roger.

They ordered sushi, sashimi, two shrimp rolls and small salads with an Asian peanut dressing. The food was delicious.

Jude kept an eye on Roger and his wife while making small talk with Clara and Alexi. They discussed the current state of the city of New Orleans, hoping that the storm wouldn't escalate and make landfall. Roger and Lorna were arguing, Jude saw.

They kept their voices low, but the intensity of their words was reflected in their tight, angry expressions.

What was the fight about?

Did Lorna suspect her husband of something?

He wished he could hear.

Lorna suddenly stood and spoke briefly to Roger, then spun around and exited the restaurant.

Roger rose quickly and went after her.

Jude got up, too, and said, "Stay here. Don't go anywhere until I return."

He followed them, aware that one of the

ship's security staff — assigned to watch them — had a large piece of sushi roll in his mouth and was struggling to swallow, dig out his wallet and go after them.

Jude was way ahead of him.

9

"Well," Clara murmured. "What do you suppose *that's* all about? I've never seen those two have a squabble before — and they've been on cruises I've worked at least a dozen times." She looked at Alexi pointedly. "Jude didn't run off to be a marriage counselor, did he? I know he considers Roger a suspect. But it doesn't make sense. He's married. He has a lovely wife, grown children."

"The BTK killer," Alexi said. "His wife had no clue."

"And you think Roger Antrim . . ."

"No, I don't think Roger Antrim. I'm just saying it's possible."

Their waitress, walking to the table next to them with a large sashimi "boat," suddenly veered sharply to the right, thrown by the pitching of the ship.

"It's getting *really* rough," Clara said.

"Yes," Alexi agreed, but she wasn't actually paying attention. Hank Osprey was coming in — accompanied once again by the tiny brunette who seemed very fond of short skirts and high heels.

The ship swayed violently.

The brunette fell against Hank and giggled as he caught her, stopping her fall.

Hank smiled, straightening her.

"Really?" Clara whispered. "Hank?"

Alexi turned to her friend. "Clara! I have no idea. I'm curious about who his friend is. I've never seen her with him before this trip, and apparently she's in her own cabin."

"How do you know that?" Clara asked. Then she waved a hand in the air. "Never mind. I'm going to assume that they're checking up on Hank *and* any woman he's with."

Alexi nodded. "But she got back to her room just fine the other night."

"Was she sailing alone and met Hank? Or did she come aboard with him?"

"I don't know. Jude and Jackson might know, but I certainly don't." She turned from watching the happy couple. "At least they seem to be happy."

"I guess," Clara said with a shrug. "But she definitely seems to be working Hank."

"Maybe she really cares about him."

"Maybe she really cares about his money.

Watch it. They're coming over!"

And they were. Hank had seen Alexi and Clara and was beaming as he came toward them, hand in hand with his young, leggy brunette.

"Hey, you two. I never see you in here."

"I love sushi," Clara told him.

"Well, sure, what's not to love?" Hank drew the brunette forward. "I don't think you've met Ginny yet. Ginny, I'd like to introduce you to Alexi Cromwell and Clara Avery, friends from the many times I've sailed Celtic American. Ladies, Ginny Monk."

"How do you do?" Ginny said to the two of them, smiling. "I saw you both sing at the piano bar. You're so good together."

"Thanks," Alexi said. "Want to join us?" she asked, gesturing at their table. "Be happy to," Hank said. He pulled out a chair for Ginny and started to sit but then frowned when he saw that there was already a third setting.

"We're not interrupting you, are we?" Hank asked. "Someone else here?"

"Jude McCoy," Clara replied. She lowered her voice conspiratorially. "The Celtic American observer!"

She spoke in a natural, relaxed tone, as if she believed her own words. But of course,

Clara was an actress.

Alexi hoped she could be as convincing.

"I'm not sure when he's coming back and we can just pull up an extra chair. Please, do join us."

"Well, I'm already here," Ginny said, grinning at Alexi.

Alexi realized that Hank didn't want to stay. But since Ginny had made herself comfortable, Hank sat down, too. He tried to shrug off his frown. "Are you worried about the storm?" he asked.

"I'm not," Clara said. "I've sailed with Captain Thorne lots of times. He'll get us through."

Ginny turned to Alexi. "What about you? Are you scared?"

"I've been through some rough weather, too," she answered. "It's harder on the passengers than it is the crew. We tend to get lots of experience," she added.

Ginny's eyes widened. "I admit I'm feeling kind of nervous now. I mean, I *have* seen the movie *Titanic*!"

She seemed sweet and innocent enough, Alexi thought. A little on the naive side, but friendly. Needless to say, her innocence could be an act. Alexi couldn't help wondering — considering how brilliant as Hank was reputed to be — why he didn't seek out someone more obviously on his intellectual level. But Hank had also tried, in his usual awkward way, to get involved with her and then Clara. He was rich and pleasant and nerdy. And he wasn't the type of man who easily entered conversations or easily had affairs. He certainly had trouble talking to more sophisticated women.

So Ginny might be just perfect for him.

"The good thing," Alexi assured the young woman, "is that we're not going to run into any icebergs down here in the Caribbean."

"No," Ginny agreed, giggling. "No icebergs here. Well, I hate flying, too. A pilot friend told me once that it's like being in a boat. You know, waves in the water — waves of air when you're up in the sky. Although these seem like really *big* waves."

"The winds are growing stronger," Hank muttered. "The storm's going to reach hurricane force today. It's still just sitting over Cozumel — almost gyrating there, is how the forecasters described it. We should be hightailing our way to port instead of waiting out here."

"They're trying to outrun the storm," Clara said. "They can't tell yet which direction it's going to take."

Hank grunted impatiently. "We could've made it to a safe port by now. But . . . I also understand their hesitation to move us in a specific direction. We could get trapped. Don't worry," he told Ginny. "These ladies are right. Captain Thorne is the best in the business. And I'll do *my* best to make sure you're not frightened!"

Ginny gazed up at him adoringly. Hank flushed with pleasure and turned a look of pride on Clara and Alexi. He seemed to be saying, "See! I got this girl to like me and she's every bit as attractive as either one of you."

Alexi thought that might be why he'd wanted to join them — to let them know he was desirable, even if they'd been foolish enough not to realize it.

"Thank goodness for you!" Ginny breathed.

"Are you two traveling together or did you meet on board?" Alexi asked.

"We met at the craps table in the ship's casino," Ginny said. "I was rolling the dice, I looked up, and there he was!"

Alexi glanced at Clara. She could tell they were both wondering if Ginny hadn't known exactly who Hank Osprey was from the beginning — and if she hadn't planned to be at the craps table at exactly the right time.

But if she made Hank happy, what did it matter?

"That sounds very romantic," she told them both.

"Eyes meeting across a crowded room," Clara murmured.

"Yes!" Ginny said.

Suddenly, they all realized a waitress was standing there.

Hank quickly ordered for himself and Ginny. Ginny allowed him to, gazing at him with tender, approving eyes all the while.

Alexi wondered if Jude was coming back soon.

"How do you like sailing on the *Destiny,* Ginny?" Clara asked politely.

Ginny giggled again and turned to Hank. "I couldn't help but love it, could I?" she asked.

"I guess not," Clara murmured, meeting Alexi's eyes.

Silence fell. Neither Hank nor Ginny seemed to notice.

"Um, what do you do for a living, Ginny?" Alexi asked.

"Pardon?" Apparently, Ginny had to tear her gaze away from Hank in order to hear.

"What do you do? Where are you from?" Alexi repeated.

"Inquiring minds want to know," Clara

244

said lightly.

"Oh, well . . . I'm a student," Ginny said.

"Where are you going to school?" Alexi asked.

"Oh, I'm originally from Baton Rouge. I go to school in New Orleans. Loyola."

"Great school," Clara said, nodding.

"You went there, too?"

"No, I went to Carnegie Mellon," Clara told her. "But I'm from New Orleans. And I know Loyola well."

"Ginny's in hospitality management," Hank explained proudly. "She could probably tell your Celtic American execs a thing or two about how to run a ship!"

"Oh," Clara said. "What would you say to the executives at Celtic American, Ginny? What do you think could be improved?"

Ginny laughed. "The infirmary — and that would be it. I went to get some Dramamine, and it took forever. Naturally, that was after we started getting the horrible weather. And I guess most cruise ships have one doctor and one nurse, so . . . oh, well. If I ran a cruise ship, I'd make sure there was more than one doctor on board."

"Poor Ginny was so sick! It was terrible. That's why she wasn't with me at the piano bar last night," Hank said.

"I begged him to go ahead without me,"

Ginny said hastily. Maybe something in Clara's and Alexi's expressions told her they were thinking he shouldn't have left her if she was that sick. She winced and grinned, almost at once. "I don't . . . I really didn't want Hank seeing me — Well, there's no delicate way to put it. I didn't want him to see me puking all over the place! It's hideous. So ugly."

"You could never be ugly to me!" Hank vowed.

Clara glanced at Alexi.

"I wonder what's taking Jude so long?" Clara murmured.

Lorna Antrim had gone straight to the infirmary, which was on the Promenade Deck, wedged between a perfume store and a cupcake shop and not far from the historic infirmary.

She'd walked in immediately.

Roger had followed her.

Jude was twenty feet from the entrance, ready to follow them both, deciding to ask for a motion sickness remedy himself as an excuse — when the door opened and Roger stepped back into the hallway.

He was scowling; he didn't see Jude.

For a long moment he stood staring at the display in the window of the cupcake store.

He seemed to have blanked out.

Then he walked over to the infirmary again and started to open the door.

He didn't.

Instead, he walked into the hallway again and stood in front of the perfume store window.

Jude waited a few minutes, then casually sauntered by.

"Roger, is everything all right?" he asked.

Roger turned and seemed to need a minute to focus. "What? Oh, yes. Well, you know, Lorna's in the infirmary. I'm just hoping they can help her."

"I'm sure they will."

"I hope so. I asked about arranging for a helicopter to get us off the ship, but that's a no-go. They're not sending anything out in this weather. And . . . I offered a great deal of money."

"It's going to be rough," Jude said. "I'll bet Lorna will be fine after they've given her something for the motion sickness. She's a seasoned traveler."

"Yes, she is." Roger was quiet for a minute. He shrugged. "At the moment, though, and I hate to say it, but I feel a bit like we're on the *Titanic.* The ship's rocking and rolling as if we were on an amusement park ride — zero to sixty in no time — and we're all walking around, people shopping, eating, drinking, gambling as though nothing's wrong. They don't seem to notice that they walk down hallways — and then crash into them."

"We're going to be fine," Jude said in a comforting voice.

"Well, I guess you *would* say that. You're a CEO with Celtic American, right? But think of the liability if everything's *not* fine," Roger said.

Frankly, Jude didn't know a hell of a lot about being any kind of a CEO.

He smiled. "Act of God," he said with a shrug.

"Oh, come on!"

"Everything's going to be fine," Jude repeated. "We're on a ship that's survived war, mammoth storms and much more. We're with a seasoned captain who knows the Caribbean better than a computer mapping program."

Roger studied him. "Of course, I'm not really frightened. I love sailing. I don't mind a little pitch and sway. I guess I'm just worried about Lorna."

"I'll see if I can hurry things along for her in the infirmary," Jude said.

He could see that David Beach's security guard, assigned to keep an eye on Roger, was now in front of the cupcake shop.

He walked into the infirmary.

It was different from most of the ship; the nurses' station and the triage area were all chrome and glass, and the floor was tiled, as it was in any modern hospital.

About twenty people were crowded into the waiting room, some of them filling out papers.

A sign on the nurses' desk read, "If you're seasick and you feel you need the doctor, please fill out your paperwork."

A harried nurse was reassuring the passengers and answering their questions, disappearing behind a door, then bustling back out again.

Lorna sat in one of the waiting room chairs, her head resting against the wall. The woman next to her stood up as the nurse called her name, and Jude quickly slid into her seat.

Lorna opened her eyes; after a second, she smiled. "Don't worry. We're not going to have our attorneys sue you," she told him.

She meant the Celtic American line, of course.

"I'm not worried about being sued," he said. "I'm worried about you."

"It's just a little queasiness," she said.

"It's more than that, isn't it?" She closed

her eyes again. He found himself admiring her. She kept herself fit; she was a very attractive woman who was embracing her age. He wasn't an expert, but there were no telltale plastic surgery signs on her face. She looked over at him. "Are you married, Mr. McCoy?"

"I was," he replied. "I'm divorced."

"I'm sorry," she said.

"So am I. But under the circumstances, it was the best thing. For both of us. And I wish my ex every bit of happiness she can find."

"You're a nice man," Lorna said. She let out a sigh. "We've been married a very long time. Three children. Five grandchildren."

"A life well lived," Jude said.

She glanced at him, a slight smile curving her lips. "I'm hoping I still have a few years left, young man."

Jude laughed and apologized. "I just mean you two have used your years well. You both seem to have accomplished a lot."

"You'd think so, right?" Lorna remarked. "I didn't make any millions, but . . . I do have beautiful children."

"I'm sure you do."

"And they're good people, too."

"That's wonderful."

He waited. There was no reason for her to

trust him or confide in him. They'd only met a day ago; he'd spent time talking to her and Roger in the piano bar. And yet she seemed to trust him.

"I just wonder if I haven't become old hat," she said.

"Old hat?"

"Tired, rusty, worn-out!" she said with a smile. "Of course, I'm a woman, so I see things a certain way. But it's still a man's world — I don't care how many female rulers there've been. I'm talking about biology. Men might be able to procreate forever, while women have a set number of years during which they can have children. As the cliché has it, women get old, while men become distinguished."

"And bald, sometimes," Jude reminded her.

At least he'd made her smile.

"Isn't that supposed to prove a man has extra testosterone or something like that?" she asked, grinning.

The nurse called her name. "Mrs. Antrim, if you'll come with me . . ."

Lorna turned back to Jude, who'd risen along with her. "Thank you, Mr. McCoy. Thank you for listening to me." She hesitated briefly. "Did Roger send you in here?"

"No. But I talked to him. He's waiting for

you outside. I came in to see how you're doing, because *I* wanted to know."

He felt a tinge of guilt.

I came to talk to you because your husband's on a short list that might include the name of a serial killer.

"Thank you," she said, smiling again.

"My pleasure. If you need anything, please let me know."

"Because you're an exec?"

"Because I like you."

She studied him for a second. "You mean that, don't you? You mean you like *me* — and not my husband's money. Thank you for that."

She went in to see the ship's doctor. Jude opened the door for a woman and a little girl who were just leaving, and followed them out.

Roger Antrim was nowhere to be seen.

"I'm just lucky, I guess," Ginny said humbly.

Hank had been going on and on, describing Ginny's natural grace and her ability to dance. "My family originally came from Virginia and West Virginia. They did all those reels and square dances and stuff. Maybe that's why I love to dance, whatever kind of dancing it is."

Alexi smiled — wondering if her smile had

gone completely plastic.

"You're lucky," Clara said. "I have to work at every step."

"Isn't she wonderful?" Hank asked, looking besotted.

"Lovely," Alexi agreed.

"Absolutely!" Clara chimed in.

To Alexi's relief, Jude was coming back into the sushi restaurant. He smiled at the hostess and exchanged a few words with her.

The ship rolled heavily portside, but Jude didn't appear to notice; he seemed to balance instinctively and continued to walk toward them.

"Hello," he said to Hank and Ginny, pulling up an extra chair.

"Hello, Mr. McCoy." Hank stood up to shake his hand.

"It's just Jude."

"And I'm just Hank. This is Ginny. I'm not sure if you two have officially met."

"Jude," Ginny said sweetly, offering him her hand.

"Hi, Ginny."

To Alexi's mind, Ginny had offered that hand as a queen might — expecting her royal subject to kiss it.

Jude didn't.

He shook it briefly, taking his seat. "So, how are you two faring?" he asked.

"Ginny was a little ill," Hank said.

"I'm fine now."

"The fact is, she was *very* ill. But she's fine now," Hank said. "My poor girl! Ah, well, good to spend time with all of you — and we'll see you at the piano bar tonight, Alexi." He stood up and Ginny did, too. "We'll leave you to your privacy," he said and then inclined his head, grinning. "That sounded polite, didn't it? Actually, I'm itching to go into the casino. Ginny brings me luck!"

"So he says. He plays craps. I hardly know what's going on," Ginny said. "But I like standing there with him."

"May the fortunes of the sea be with you," Jude said.

"Lots of luck!" Alexi added.

"Ditto," Clara said.

When they were gone, Alexi moaned, "Oh, my God!"

"What?" Jude asked.

"Not to be crass, but . . . yuck!" Clara said. "If I had to listen to one more word about the wonders of Ginny . . ."

Alexi laughed. "If we had to watch them mooning over each other one more minute . . ."

"They just met, didn't they?" Jude asked.

"Yeah, on the ship," Alexi replied.

Clara smirked. "Their eyes met — across a crowded craps table."

"She's beautiful, she's oh, so perfect," Alexi said.

"And he, of course, is the studliest, most macho man she's ever seen," Clara said. "Now, I have to say I hope he's not being taken, but —"

"Well, wait," Alexi broke in. "If she's taking him, so to speak, and intends to keep him, that's great. Hank needs someone."

"She's making him pay for her," Clara said softly.

"Pardon?" Jude asked, frowning.

"She's a very pretty girl," Alexi said, stating the obvious. "Hank is nice and he's brilliant — but he's not firemen-calendar or NFL-quarterback good-looking. Plus, he's awkward with women."

"In other words," Clara said. "We believe she found his eyes so fascinating because she knew exactly who he is."

Jude grinned at them. "Well, that hadn't missed my attention, either. She is indeed a very pretty girl, but he's not such a pretty man."

"What I'm saying is this. If Hank wants to buy happiness and she wants to provide it, then that's a fair exchange," Alexi said.

Clara looked at her watch. "I have to be

in the theater for a sound check. Want to walk me there?" she asked Jude.

"Will do," he said, rising. "Let me go take care of what we owe."

Alexi set a hand on his arm, stopping him for a moment. "What about Roger? And Lorna?"

"I don't know," he said. "Midlife crisis on someone's part? Or something worse? I don't really know yet."

He left to pay the check, then returned to Alexi and Clara, looking somewhat stumped. "We have no check. Hank Osprey paid it," he said.

"Well, that was — nice?" Clara suggested.

"I don't like other people picking up my bills."

"Hmm," Alexi said to Clara. "I'm willing to bet he was trying to pick up the check for all the sushi we ordered — and he's annoyed because Hank beat him to it!"

"All right, all right, point taken," Jude muttered. "Except that . . .'

"What?" Alexi asked.

"I'm not a suspect in a series of murders — which he still is at the moment, making it very uncomfortable that he picked up the check," he said. "Shall we go? It's time to get Clara to her rehearsal."

"Why does even that sound ominous?"

Clara asked.

Jude dropped Clara off at rehearsal and brought Alexi back to her room; she promised she'd wait for him there, and he promised he'd be back in plenty of time so she could settle in and get organized for the night ahead.

He told Jackson about the scene between Roger and Lorna, and how Hank and Ginny had been with them at the sushi table.

"What do you think? Is Ginny in trouble — or is she taking advantage of Hank Osprey?" Jackson asked. "I'll get Angela on it, see what she can find out regarding Ginny Monk."

Jude shrugged in response and found himself studying Jackson curiously.

"What is it?"

"None of my business, probably," Jude murmured.

"Well, whatever it is, I'd rather you spoke than stared at me."

"Okay. How exactly did you end up on this case?" Jude asked. "I understood from the beginning that you're with a special unit of the bureau. But your special unit comes in when there's something unusual about a case. When there's an unexplained element. Or a special request. Not that this case isn't top priority right now, but still . . . you're from this 'special' unit in the Quantico office. There are excellent agents all over the country — not to mention profilers and behavioral scientists — studying the case. So . . . why the Krewe of Hunters?"

Jackson Crow had been focused on his computer screen. Now he gave Jude his full attention. Jude wondered about his background. Had Crow spoken to someone he'd later discovered was dead? Or had his relationship with the lingering souls of the dead begun as it had for Alexi, something he had somehow known and accepted from the time he was a child?

"Angela and I were away for a weekend vacation eight months ago," he began. "In Charleston, South Carolina. We were staying at a bed-and-breakfast with a charming courtyard. Our room opened onto the courtyard, and I went outside in the morning, just to see the sunrise. The courtyard started to fill with light — and that's when Peggy Carlyle came to me."

"Peggy Carlyle, the first victim," Jude said.

"As we later learned. She appeared suddenly, as if she was part of the light. She wore a beautiful white dress."

"But, of course, she was dead."

Jackson nodded slowly. "She was fragile,

barely noticeable, like dust motes on the air. I was almost afraid to speak, in case she just disappeared. The doors to our room opened and Angela came out, smiling, happy, excited. She loves Charleston and that particular B and B. But she stopped, seeing what I saw. And she whispered to the young woman, asking if we could help her. Peggy looked lost, entirely lost. And then she disappeared. The next week we were back at our offices in Northern Virginia when we heard that the body of a young woman, draped with a saint's medallion, had been found in a church near the bed-and-breakfast. I knew it was her. Peggy was a graphic artist and the medallion around her neck was St. Catherine's. Patron saint of artists, as you'll recall . . . The police were on it, and naturally they wanted the case to be under local jurisdiction, but I was able to obtain the crime scene photos — and then those of the next murder, also in Charleston. I knew I had to get myself assigned to the case. Then, while we were investigating leads, the killer moved on. Four women were killed in South Florida, and while we were following leads there, he struck in Mobile. I believed the Archangel was speeding up, and that he might well hit New Orleans next. It just seemed to fit his pattern. And you know the rest."

"So," Jude said, "it was a Krewe case from the beginning."

Jackson shrugged. "As far as I was concerned, yes. Now we're officially in. We've had Krewe members working in the cities where he's already struck. And we have one of the finest medical examiners around, Kat Sokolov. She's seen the bodies, determined how the killer manipulates his weapons, the way he displays his victims. Which has helped us conclude that we're looking for one man — and not copycats."

"Did you ever see Peggy Carlyle again?" Jude asked.

Jackson shook his head. "No. Just that one moment. I found out that she liked to come to the courtyard where I was sitting. The B and B had a little café, and she'd buy a coffee and bring it to the courtyard."

Jude digested that information. "And you investigated me before you reached New Orleans?"

Jackson smiled at that. "As we've discussed, you had a reputation for solving difficult cases because of your uncanny hunches — or what you called hunches. And your military record was interesting. Yes, I had access. You managed to cover it all really well, and you were smart to agree to therapy. I doubt it answered your question — whether or not you'd talked to a dead man. At least it helped you live with yourself more easily."

"Maybe we all need therapy," Jude said.

"Maybe you've finally discovered the therapy that's right for you," Jackson said.

Naturally, the man knew that he and Alexi had become close, that the relationship had gone beyond agent and — what? Witness?

He raised his hands; he couldn't tell if he was being reprimanded. If he was supposed to have an excuse for being in a situation he shouldn't be.

"It's not easy for people like us to find the right partners," Jackson went on. "Our best therapy seems to be the fact that we can speak freely to one another."

"Magic men," Jude said.

"Is that what you call it?"

Jude smiled. "That's what Alexi calls it. Seems the ability is genetic or inherited. In her family, anyway."

"Magic men," Jackson murmured. He looked at Jude. "I'm praying *we* can pull off some magic. The storm's been upgraded. It's a hurricane now. We're going to need all the magic we have to make it through the next day or so."

10

That night even the piano bar was slow.

The storm had put a damper on everything by then.

People who didn't normally get seasick were seasick.

The infirmary was the busiest place on board.

Captain Thorne had done a good job advising his passengers, giving them all the information the meteorologist and the executives at Celtic American were giving him.

He'd been told to head toward the port of Galveston; as soon as they'd made a slight turn in that direction, the storm had taken another turn in a *different* direction. Now the cruise line's management was asking him to wait once again. Everyone hoped the vicious weather would leave Cozumel — which was being pummeled — and travel in yet another direction. That would allow the ship to make a speedy turn toward a safe port.

At first, people seemed to be okay. But since the storm had actually followed them, or so it seemed, they were now getting worried.

Bradley Wilcox had actually been very decent to the employees in his sector, reminding them how important they were to shipboard morale. The *Les Miz* cast would still plan for the show, but further rehearsals would be cut short so they could entertain at other venues on the ship.

Alexi and other employees involved in individual or group entertainment would also be called upon. In Alexi's case, she'd be asked to do impromptu music the next morning with children and others waiting for assistance at the infirmary.

That was fine; she didn't mind being busy.

But as for that night . . .

They'd all been asked to "play on," even if only one passenger showed up at their venues.

It wasn't quite that bad for Alexi.

For one thing, since the rehearsal for *Les Miz* had ended early, she started her performance with the able assistance of Clara, Ralph, Simon and Larry and a few other members of the cast. Regulars, including

Roger Antrim and Hank Osprey, were there.

So was Jude McCoy.

Couples with older children seemed to opt for the piano bar as a way for the family to stay together.

The Algiers Saloon filled to capacity, many people standing to enjoy her crowd-teasing or to sing along.

Blake and Minnie appeared after a few minutes.

They seemed subdued, as if they were watching over her like anxious parents. It bothered her that her ghosts were acting so worried. The storm hadn't bothered her, but the fact that the two of them were so uneasy made *her* uneasy, too. Except, of course, she had to hide it from the audience.

"All I can think of is the *Titanic*," Clara whispered to her at the piano bench.

"There are some great stories about our ship," Alexi reminded her. "Like the one about that huge storm off Dover during the 1940s. The *Destiny* — laden with injured men! — made it safely to shore."

"I know, I know. I'm feeling a little frantic. This storm, and possibly a homicidal maniac on the ship, who might be after an actress and a musician."

"And a cook or a chef," Alexi pointed out.

"But we have two FBI agents here on board with us."

"It *is* good to have Jude nearby," Clara murmured. "And the way he's watching over us . . . He's even ignoring that couple beside him."

Alexi frowned.

Blake and Minnie had moved closer to Jude.

"The pretty woman in the old-fashioned dress — and the nice-looking guy she's with?"

"Yeah. He's such a solid guy. I'm surprised he's not trying to reassure them. They seem kind of nervous."

Alexi had been playing a medley of tunes, but she stopped, managed to jokingly welcome some parents and children just joining them, and started again. She tried not to gawk at Clara.

But it was difficult not to stand up and ask Clara if she was *sure* she saw those two — and to explain that they didn't need reassuring for themselves.

They were already dead.

"How about some Disney tunes?" a woman with a girl of about ten called out.

Alexi realized it had to be hard for parents to stay calm themselves — and to keep their children feeling secure.

"You got it!" she said happily. "And look! I have an 'Aurora' right by my side. Clara, how about 'Once Upon a Dream'?"

"I'll help her out," Larry Hepburn offered, coming up to join them. "Every Sleeping Beauty needs a prince!"

The kids seemed to love it, especially when, in the middle of the song, Larry went to the ten-year-old and danced her around the chairs. Larry caught her and helped her back into her chair just as the ship made one of its pitching movements and might have sent them both sprawling.

Alexi went on to do "Let it Go" from *Frozen.* Simon sang his favorite song from *Hercules,* and Ralph and Clara did a duet from *Aladdin.*

Around midnight the parents who'd allowed their children to stay up late, no doubt hoping they'd become sleepy, finally decided to call it quits.

The crowd was mainly an adult crowd then.

"They're both alone tonight. Did you notice that?" Clara asked Alexi.

Alexi had. Roger was there without Lorna.

And Hank was there without the woman he'd fallen in lust or love or enchantment with.

"Do you think . . ." Alexi began.

"What?"

"Okay, so Roger's wife was behaving a little strangely, but they've been married for years. An argument here and there is bound to happen. And as for Ginny Monk — maybe she doesn't like piano bars," Alexi said. "Maybe she only claimed that she did to be polite. Or to please Hank."

"Speaking of Hank . . . Here he comes now," Clara said, forcing a smile. "I don't know how she feels about piano bars, but I do get the impression that Ms. Ginny Monk is very fond of our geek's money."

"Cynical, cynical!"

"And probably right!" Clara retorted.

"Hey!" Hank Osprey had reached them. He was smiling, apparently undisturbed by the fact that his drink had nearly slid off the table when he stood up. "Will one of you do 'Picture' with me?"

" 'Picture,' " Clara repeated. "Kid Rock and Sheryl Crow. That's you, Alexi. You do a wicked Sheryl Crow!"

"Of course, Hank," Alexi said, handing him one of the mics.

She played and sang, studying Hank as she did. Yes, he was a geek. Yes, he was a multimillionaire. Not muscled, but not flabby. Not tall, but not short. Not handsome — but not ugly, either.

Tomorrow, she decided, she'd find out more about Ginny Monk.

What if Ginny *was* just after Hank's money?

What if Hank was a serial killer?

She looked over at Jude. He was studying Hank, as well. And, she realized, she could ask him about Ginny.

The FBI must be researching her already. Hank was on their radar, which meant that anyone with him would be, too.

The night wore on, and soon it was after one. She saw that Blake and Minnie remained in the room, still peering anxiously around. They didn't come up to tease her or ask her to do any numbers.

Minnie didn't even want to sing.

As the time to close the Algiers Saloon for the night approached, she noticed that Bradley Wilcox was standing in the hallway, watching her.

To her surprise, he gave her a thumbs-up and mouthed the words, "Thank you."

And while Bradley apparently wanted to be pleasant, she had to force herself to smile in return.

Bradley was off the list, she reminded herself. He was off the list of suspects.

And yet, as he stood there, she saw someone slipping around behind him. It was

Byron Grant.

And the way Byron studied Bradley . . .

Alexi was suddenly getting chills.

She had to keep playing.

And the band played on . . . As the *Titanic* sank.

Her sheet music suddenly went flying as the ship heaved and swayed.

Clara hopped up quickly to retrieve the pages.

Someone in the audience giggled.

"Why don't you play the theme song from *Titanic*!" someone else called out.

"Uh, that might be in bad taste at the moment," Alexi replied. "How about something fast and light?"

She began a Billy Joel song, and Roger jumped up to sing.

Jude just sat there until the night came to a close.

Watching all the while.

Jude noticed everything that went on and everyone who came in.

And yet . . .

He still knew nothing.

He saw how interested Byron Grant had been in the entertainment manager, Bradley Wilcox.

But Bradley was in Texas when the New

Orleans murders took place.

Every profiler in the FBI had been asked for an opinion. Each one seemed convinced that the murders were the work of one man. So was the Krewe's ME, Kat Sokolov.

The ghost of Byron Grant was equally convinced that the killer was on the ship.

There were medallions left in the Archangel's collection for a cook, a musician and an actor.

There were many cooks, musicians and actors aboard the *Destiny.*

Then again, the killer had always struck on land. Or so far he had. That didn't mean he wouldn't strike on the ship. While timetables — and Byron Grant — suggested that the killer was likely a habitual passenger or a crew member, they still really had no actual proof that he was even aboard. Byron claimed he'd seen a ticket in his killer's pocket. But maybe the killer had missed the sailing.

He might've been in the crowd outside the historic church in New Orleans. Someone they'd missed in their determination to follow Byron Grant.

Jude was frustrated; the Krewe and other agents in the home offices had been eliminating suspects, but he didn't seem to be getting anywhere.

He couldn't just barge into Roger and Lorna's stateroom and demand to know what was going on between them. And even if Ginny Monk *was* a gold digger stepping into some very dangerous territory, he couldn't stop Hank Osprey from seeing her.

And if she wanted to be with Hank, he could only warn her to be careful. He doubted she'd worry about the fact that Hank might be a murderer. *Might.* They had no proof; he didn't know if Hank was guilty of anything. To Ginny, the prospect of an affair — or perhaps marriage — with a man of his means might be worth the risk.

It wasn't until the bartender announced last call that Jensen Hardy made an appearance. He took a seat recently abandoned by a burly businessman and ordered a drink.

Jude admitted to himself that he just didn't like Jensen Hardy. He didn't like him because of the look in his eyes that morning when he'd realized Alexi was with Jude.

He had a thing for Alexi, or so it seemed.

But that didn't mean anything; Jude was sure that lots of men had *a thing* for Alexi Cromwell.

There was something about Hardy, though, something that disturbed him. And that predatory gleam in his eyes . . .

Jude rose and walked to the bar. Hardy

glanced over and didn't seem thrilled to see him. Still, he was cordial.

"Long day," he said to Jude.

"Must be hard for you right now," Jude commiserated.

"Oh, very. I'm good at my job. I like people, I like doing fun and crazy things. But trying to keep morale up when so many of the passengers are terrified — wow." He took the glass of scotch the bartender had poured for him and downed it in a swallow. "Sorry, but if this is going to get me fired, fire away," he muttered.

"I'm not here to fire anyone," Jude told him.

"Good. I'll have another," Hardy said.

"I'll be happy to buy you a drink." Jude signaled the bartender.

"Well, thank you! I accept. Then I'm going to try to sleep. Gotta be up and at 'em first thing tomorrow!"

The bartender brought his drink; Jude signed the tab.

Hardy turned and leaned against the bar, lifting his glass toward the piano where Alexi and Clara sat, now doing a Broadway song together.

"Gorgeous, huh? Simply gorgeous."

"Yes, they are."

Hardy turned back and studied Jude and

raised the glass to him next. "Well, kudos to you, sir. Kudos. I tried to become . . . friends with Alexi many times. I guess she seemed all the more beautiful because she was so untouchable, so tragic. I guess you've managed to break through that wall of ice."

"She's been helping me," Jude said.

Hardy broke into laughter. "Helping you, huh? That's what you call it?"

Jude smiled. "I need to know people on the ship. She's introduced me, taken me around, shown me how things work."

"They work well for you, huh?" Hardy asked, sounding bitter. Then he shrugged. "Sorry. Sour grapes. Anyway, sir, once again, kudos to you. I guess Clara is *helping* you, too?"

Jude pictured himself giving the man a sharp blow to the jaw.

Instead, he smiled again. He'd long ago learned that his job required him to maintain his temper — and he learned that he could.

"You've tried to *befriend* Clara, too, huh?" he asked.

Jensen Hardy flushed a dark shade of red. "She's another ice queen. Apparently, she joined the cast after a bad breakup. She's primarily interested in her career. Her friends are all the actors and performers on board. I could be an actor, you know. I was an actor. Hell, I *am* an actor. Acting pleasant all the time is worthy of an Emmy, I can tell you that." He winced. "Sorry, don't take offense. I need my job. And I'm an idiot, talking to you like this. Because you can get me fired, right?"

"You're not going to be fired," Jude told him again. "Not through me, anyway."

"Well, here's hoping!" Hardy said. He stared at the piano bench and the two young women smiling as they sang another duet. He gulped the rest of his drink, set down his glass and said, "Thanks for the drink . . . Jude."

Then he left the piano bar.

Jude saw the ghost of Byron Grant following him . . .

Hank asked for a final number; Alexi obliged. Then, with effusive thanks, he turned to leave. Jude cut him off when he would've headed into the hall.

He frowned at Jude before managing a smile.

"What can I do for you, Mr. McCoy?"

"Just wanted to ask about your friend Ginny. Is she okay?"

"Sure. She wasn't feeling well. Lots of people are down with seasickness, you know?" Hank held his head at an angle.

"What? The two beauties at the bench aren't enough for you, sir? You're trying to corner every cutie on the ship?"

He asked it lightly, as if he and Jude were just two guys discussing the merits of certain women.

"I was making sure she's doing okay. And that you are, too," he added.

"Ah," Hank Osprey said, assessing Jude. "She's fine. And so am I. She's in her own cabin, by the way. You don't rush a good thing. Well, maybe *you* do. Maybe you can. I can't — I'm rich. That's my asset. I guess you've got a few others. Anyway, like I said, she's fine. And I intend to see she stays that way — and stays in love with me. I know what you're thinking. You're thinking that she's using me. But I don't believe it. Not this time."

"I hope you both continue to do well throughout the voyage," Jude said. "And afterward."

"You'd have to say that, huh? Being with Celtic American and all."

"No. I'm saying it because I mean it."

"Well, I hope you do okay, too. And . . . hey. Look after Alexi. Everyone knows there's something going on between you. She's special. I guess I always hoped that one day she'd see me, *really* see me. Not just be kind to me because it's her job and part of her nature, but . . ." He paused and shrugged. "I'd have married her in a wink. She might've changed everything for me."

"But you're in love with Ginny."

"That's right, I am! But you have a woman I lusted after for many a long night."

"I wish you and Ginny the best," Jude said simply, ready to wrap up the conversation.

"I wish the best for all of us. This storm is really bad. They say Cozumel is a mess. Some ships were smashed to pieces. They couldn't get out. They're expecting a high death toll once the hurricane moves on. Guess we got out just in time. Makes that explosion seem like nothing, right?"

"As far as the storm goes, we'll be fine."

"Well, then, good night. I'm sure I'll see you tomorrow. You ought to sing, Mr. McCoy. This is a piano bar, after all."

"I'll think about it," Jude said, then watched as Hank Osprey walked out of the saloon and down the hall to the elevators.

"Mr. McCoy?"

He turned. Roger Antrim was just behind him. Smiling.

"Roger," Jude said, nodding.

"I shouldn't have stayed out so long. Poor Lorna . . . But being like this has made her pretty cranky. I was trying not to be a terrible husband, *and* trying not to get on her nerves. See you tomorrow, I guess."

"Yes, see you then. Is Lorna doing any better? Was the ship's doctor able to give her anything that helped?"

"Yes, I think so. She was doing better, just very tired. Well, I'm going to go back up to see her. Maybe she'll be asleep," he said, sounding — to Jude's ears — rather hopeful.

When Jude returned to his seat, he saw that Alexi, Clara, Ralph, Larry and Simon were all singing together. The number was "Closing Time."

As they sang, Jackson Crow came along and waited in the hallway.

When Alexi finished, Jackson entered the Algiers.

"Time for all good little boys and girls to go to bed, I take it," Ralph Martini said.

"So it is," Jackson said, greeting them with a casual salute.

"And we appreciate having two G-men — or should that be *he*-men? — walking us to our rooms," Simon said. "Alexi, you need any help?"

"Nope, just throwing the music in the bench and the cover over the piano," Alexi said. "Let's go down." Easily said, but not as easily done. As they reached the elevators, the ship pitched severely. Ralph crashed into Jackson; Simon fell against the wall, and Alexi and Simon almost tumbled onto the ground.

They all laughed, regaining their balance.

"This is getting serious," Ralph murmured.

"Hopefully, if it gets any worse, they'll ask us all to stay in our cabins — and be ready to climb into our lifeboats," Larry said.

"Hopefully, it *won't* get any worse," Clara said mildly. "Anyone for taking the stairs? I'd just as soon not be stuck in an elevator."

"I say we take the stairs," Jude agreed.

"And I'll add that everyone should use the banisters," Jackson said.

So, they proceeded down the stairs. And Jude and Jackson made sure that, one by one, they all got into their rooms until only Jackson, Alexi and Jude stood in the hall.

"I'll see you in the office in the morning?" Jackson asked Jude.

"Anything new?"

Jackson shook his head, glancing at Alexi. Even to Jackson, Jude thought, she was one of them.

After all, she'd been the one to bring them Byron Grant.

"I've asked Angela to check into Ms. Virginia 'Ginny' Monk," he said. "We're still trying to regain contact with the police in Cozumel. Then we'll be able to learn if they found . . . anything in the churches. So for now, good night."

Alexi opened the door to her cabin, and Jude closed and locked it. As he did, the ship rolled again. He wasn't quick enough, and they both tumbled backward.

Luckily, they wound up on her bed together, laughing.

"We could be in real trouble, like we were saying, and here we are, laughing."

"Yes." Jude was careful to lift his weight off her. "But worrying about the storm isn't going to change the weather.

"I hope they'll ask everyone to stick to their cabins," Alexi said.

"Maybe they will." Jude looked at her as she lay there beside him, eyes wide, hair floating around her. He stroked her arm, marveling at the softness of her skin. She reached out and touched his cheek.

"I wouldn't mind staying here," she said, and added softly, "with you."

He kissed her. She tasted sweetly of mint. At first his kiss was gentle and then it deepened and, as it did, he felt his muscles tighten. His fingers found the zipper to her gown. She stood up to remove it and fell back on the bed. He helped her take it off

279

before awkwardly struggling to remove his own jacket, holster and gun.

They managed to get their shoes off.

He unclasped her bra and nuzzled her breasts. Then he felt her fingers at his belt buckle. Felt his erection swell. Felt her touch.

Their lips met again. Bit by bit, they threw off the rest of their clothing.

The ship continued its wild pitching and swaying.

And somehow, that seemed to enhance every brush of their fingers, every kiss, every caress.

Desire became overwhelming. After a moment's pause to deal with protection, he quickly slid inside her, embraced by her warmth, Alexi meeting his every movement with a writhing motion that drove them both to climax. They were barely breathing regularly before they were moving again, touching . . .

More slowly this time. Each of them seemed determined to know the other completely. Jude felt that she was part of life itself; that her scent was part of breathing, her warmth part of his existence.

They made love, accepting the rise and fall of the waves beyond the porthole, clutching each other as if it was the two of them against the world.

At last they lay together, naked, panting, still holding on.

"I'm pretty sure that by tomorrow, Captain Thorne will ask for limited movement around the ship," she said. "He'll batten down the hatches, so to speak. And he'll get us to the closest safe port as fast as possible."

"And you mean we won't catch our killer on board?" he asked.

"I just pray that the killer won't have a chance to strike again."

"We'll stay on it — with greater resources," Jude said. "We've eliminated a number of suspects. And we're watching everyone still on our list. We've also got the help of agents back in the offices who are researching the histories and recent movements of —"

"What if they don't believe that the killer is actually on the ship?" Alexi broke in. "We're going on the word of a ghost. Will the powers that be even believe you?"

He could see her eyes in the ship's dim light.

And all he wanted was to make port.

For her to be safe.

And yet, when they left the ship . . .

"Jackson will stay on it, with his Krewe of

281

Hunters. Because, in his unit, the bosses believe in the words of a ghost."

She settled closely against him. "And what about you?" she whispered.

I just want to keep holding you.

"I imagine I'll stay on the case. It's Crow's case now and I think he wants me to continue."

She nodded. "I hope we reach port soon," she said, echoing his own thought. "And I hope they cancel the next sailing. They'll probably need some repairs, anyway."

"Yes," he said simply, and he held her even tighter, wanting to feel her next to him. Making love with her was beyond the physical; lying here with her felt . . .

Peaceful. It gave him a sense of peace. Something he hadn't felt in years.

He moved her gently so that they were face-to-face.

"Other than the fact that I want you all safely off this ship, I don't ever want to leave this bed, this cabin," he said.

He loved the look that appeared on her face, the smile that was so subtle on her lips, so full as it touched her eyes.

"If only," she said, grinning.

And so they lay together.

They finally slept.

When morning came he would've risen

and quietly slipped back to his own cabin to shower and change, but she moved against him, half awake and half asleep, and yet . . .

Seductive.

Moving against him and then touching him, her fingers trailing down his chest and past his hips . . .

They made love again. When he finally got out of bed, she was smiling and her hair was like a glorious sunset all around her. Her eyes were closed. She might fall back to sleep.

"Don't leave without me," he whispered.

"I wouldn't dream of it," she whispered back.

When he left her, he made certain that her door was locked.

It was time to meet with Jackson Crow. Time to begin the day.

And while he prayed that no one on the *Destiny* would be murdered, and that they'd weather the storm and did make port, he also prayed they'd catch the killer before that.

Because if they didn't . . .

More were destined to die.

11

It probably wasn't the best idea to be reading about serial killers when there might be one on board, Alexi thought.

Reading about men who'd terrified the world was unsettling, to say the least.

There'd been far too many. From Ted Bundy to John Wayne Gacy, BTK and Jeffrey Dahmer and many more.

And there were some who'd never been caught, like Jack the Ripper. There were also other names Alexi didn't know; crimes committed by those who might never be named.

She sat back from her computer.

What did the medallions have to do with the murders? Could the killer have been alive during World War II? She doubted that, although it was possible. Had he been traumatized as a child? Was he fighting his own views of religion?

Or was it all just a ploy — something to confuse the police?

She thought about their remaining suspects. She couldn't imagine Simon Green was the killer, and yet, based on what she'd learned from Jude and Jackson, Simon hadn't been cleared yet. Their perky cruise director, Jensen Hardy, was still on the list, too. And her piano bar regulars, Roger Antrim and Hank Osprey. Three of the four were too young to have had fathers or mothers who'd served in World War II. Perhaps, in Roger's case, he'd grown up knowing about the medallions and perhaps he'd even been to the little Italian church where they'd been crafted.

But did World War II have anything to do with it? Or was it just the medallions? And if so, what was their purpose?

Were any of the men religious?

Maybe she could draw them out, persuade them to speak about it. Once again she looked at photographs of the saints' medallions online.

She heard a sound at her door; it wasn't exactly a knock. Then she heard a voice — at least, she heard the words in her head.

"Alexi, it's me. Byron."

She stood up to open the door, wondering if she needed to do that for a ghost.

She didn't; he said, "I can come in. I'd like your permission, that's all."

A very polite ghost.

"Yes, of course, Byron."

A moment later he'd entered her cabin and had begun to take on form. "How are you doing?" she asked as he reappeared, now in his entirety.

Stupid question! How was he doing? How *could* he be doing? He was dead!

But he responded cheerfully. "Very well, Alexi. I'm learning to find form when I need to. I've met some of your friends. Blake and Minnie are great. What a lovely couple. I've been up to the infirmary, too. I've met Barbara Leon, the nurse, and the servicemen, Jimmy and Frank, and they've all been helpful and nothing but kind. Oh, by the way, your friend sees me. She walks by me and always says hello. I don't think she knows I'm dead."

"She may not," Alexi said. "I assume you're talking about Clara. Clara Avery, the blonde singer? She's with the cast of *Les Miz*."

"Yes, that's who I mean."

"Maybe . . ." Alexi murmured, wondering if she should try to tell Clara that she was seeing ghosts. Clara seemed very intuitive. And she'd certainly pegged Jude and Jackson pretty fast.

"Anyway, I thought I'd tell you what I'd seen."

"Thanks, Byron. But you should tell Jude and Jackson, too."

He gave her an awkward smile. "I'm becoming a better ghost, but not a perfect one. Not yet. I can reach you fairly easily, it seems, so . . ."

"Okay, that's great. You know you're more than welcome to talk to me, and I sincerely appreciate your coming to me, helping us."

"I want — oh, hell, it's not justice. I want *revenge*. They took my love and my life."

"I understand."

He shrugged. "Anyway, I still don't know *who* did it. But this is what I've observed. Roger Antrim and his wife are having problems. I figure it's because Roger was with a woman in Mexico, hanging out with her at a bar about half a block from Señora Maria's restaurant, while Mrs. Antrim was shopping. The woman's a passenger. Her stateroom is on the St. Charles Deck, and she's often at the bar in the Algiers Saloon when you're playing. An affair? I don't know. I realize security men have been watching Roger, but I believe that Mrs. Antrim might *think* it's an affair."

"We can look into that," Alexi told him, smiling inwardly, mocking herself for the way she'd said *we.*

She wasn't with the FBI. But in a sense, on this ship, she was.

"There's more," he said. "Well, there's an observation I've made that might help."

"What's that?"

"Jensen Hardy has a crush on you."

"What makes you say that?"

"It's the way he watches you. The way a man watches something he wants. Almost like a great cat stalks, not leaping idiotically, but watching — and then, when the time is right, making that lethal pounce."

She'd never thought of Jensen Hardy as a pouncing tiger, that was for sure.

Maybe a smitten kitten . . . but a pouncing tiger?

"Thank you," Alexi said, determined to take Byron's words as a serious warning.

How well did she really know Jensen, anyway?

Byron seemed pleased with himself. Casual and happy. He leaned against her door and shut his eyes. "We're getting close. I can feel it. We're going to catch this bastard."

The ship swayed again, and Alexi fell backward, onto her bed.

Byron's eyes flew open and he appeared to bounce away from the door. He seemed to fade, reappear and fade again.

"I'm watching, Alexi, I swear, always watching. I will *not* let him get near you."

"You mean Jensen Hardy?"

"Him — or any of the others. Whoever the killer turns out to be."

She smiled, righting herself.

She was grateful to have Byron watching over her.

In their *office,* Jude and Jackson were able to make contact with Angela for five minutes or so before the satellite went down. Angela told them that their investigation still hadn't proved — or disproved — anything about the suspects' movements at the various "murder ports."

They were trying to figure out what the medallions might signify.

"I don't think what the medallions themselves mean really matters," Angela said. "I think it's what they mean to the Archangel. We're working on that angle, tracing family histories, schooling and so on, for each of the men who were in the cities at the times the murders occurred.

"How are you doing there?" she asked when Jude and Jackson had thanked her.

"We're noticing some interesting behavior. Trouble in rich folks' paradise, between

Roger and Lorna Antrim," Jackson said.

"And we also need to know if you've learned anything about Virginia Monk," Jude added.

"She's currently a student at Loyola. She's been working on a bachelor's for several years and we're not clear on where her money's coming from. She makes a lot of cash deposits on her bank account."

"Stripper, I understand?" Jude asked.

"Could be," Angela replied. "Which means there might not be any traceable income. We've learned she has an apartment in Metairie and lives alone. She doesn't have a criminal record. She hasn't sailed before, as far as we can tell. She booked through a travel agent and we're checking on that agent now. Thing is, when you deal strictly in cash, you make it hard for anyone to follow your movements. If she *has* been working as a stripper or even a prostitute, someone has to have seen her. As soon as —"

Angela never got the rest out. The connection turned to static.

"Interesting," Jackson murmured.

"You bet," Jude agreed. "I'm not sure yet whether to be afraid for Ginny Monk — or for our dot-com millionaire."

"So far, according to ship security, she

goes back to her own cabin every night."

"You said we've got a meeting with Beach and some of his people?"

Jackson glanced at his watch. "We do," he said. "They're due here right about now."

During the meeting a few minutes later, Beach's security men confirmed that there was, indeed, trouble in mega-rich paradise.

"Mrs. Antrim has spent a great deal of time in the infirmary and in their cabin by herself. On the other hand, quite a few passengers are staying in their cabins. The captain hasn't closed down the ship's activities yet, although he's stopped the functions at the pool and assigned Jensen Hardy to create more bingo contests and the like in the main ballroom. As you requested, we've followed Roger Antrim religiously and discovered that he's been seeing a lot of a Mrs. Flora Winters, cabin 615, on the Promenade Deck."

Beach kept his face straight as he spoke.

"He's been *seeing* her? Doing what?" Jackson asked.

"Nothing overt," Beach said. Three of his men who weren't following a suspect at the moment were in the meeting, as well. They all nodded.

"Is he especially . . . friendly?" Jackson asked.

"He's not holding her hand or anything like that. He *is* signing her drinks to his tab and they've engaged in what looks like deep conversation," Beach said. "None of us knows what they've been talking about."

"We'll see if we can get a little closer," Jude said. "Anything to report on anyone else?"

"Simon Green's spent most of his free time in his cabin. When he's not there, he's at rehearsals or in the employee cafeteria. We've kept a tight watch on the employee cabins. Nothing unusual," Beach said and cleared his throat. He turned to Jude. "If we were just going by behavior, Special Agent McCoy, you'd be the most suspicious."

Jude nodded. "Yes. I suppose I would be."

"We've seen all the suspects return to their own rooms. Oh, except for one instance," he said, checking his notes. "Jensen Hardy's room is more toward the forward section of the cabins, and he was seen walking down to the central area where you and a number of the actors and musicians are staying."

"What did he do there?" Jackson asked.

One of Beach's men stepped forward and introduced himself. "Ben Eckles, sir." Then he described what he'd seen. "Hardy just stood there and looked at the doors, and then . . . nothing. Oh, we also followed him late one evening. He went up to the chapel. He tried the door but it was locked."

"We need you to keep a close eye on him," Jude said.

"Yes, sir." Eckles nodded vigorously. "Mark Naughton is following him, but Hardy's running a bingo game in the Egyptian Room."

"Is that it?" Beach asked, turning back to the agents.

"Yes. Thank you," Jackson replied. "We all know you're not convinced that we're right about this. We want you all to know how much we appreciate your diligence."

Beach acknowledged Jackson's words.

Beach and his men trailed out of the office cabin, and Jackson glanced at Jude.

"Well?"

Jude sat there thoughtfully for a moment. "I don't like Jensen Hardy," he finally said. "I'm trying to discount that. But I've seen the way he looks at Alexi, and that scares me. And Roger Antrim — is he just going through a middle-age crisis and flirting to feel better about himself? Or is he lining up a victim?"

"When we get hold of Angela again, we'll have to find out what we can about the woman he's seeing."

"What do you think about Ginny Monk?" Jude asked.

"She may have planned this trip in order to meet Osprey," Jackson said.

"If she did some research on him, she might have found out that he usually sails alone, without a bevy of assistants or advisers. And, if so, she might've realized that this would be a prime opportunity to get to know the man — and seduce him."

"I agree," Jackson said. He gestured at the computer screen with disgust. "The ship's going onto emergency status pretty soon," he said. "May be good, may be bad. If everyone's in his or her cabin except for the necessary crew, at least the women aboard will be safe."

"Let's hope." Jude got to his feet. "I'm going to see what I can find out from Lorna. I went in to see how she was doing at the infirmary yesterday. I've got a bit of a connection with her — I think. I'll see what she can tell me."

Jackson nodded. "And I'll see if I can engage Ginny in a discussion while you're at it." He opened the desk and produced a square black object. "Walkie-talkie," he told Jude. "Computers are down, and that means the cell phones will be out. These are clunky and awkward, but they'll work."

Alexi grew restless.

She couldn't work on her computer; nothing was coming in.

She tried calling Jude; there was no cell phone reception.

She bathed, washed and dried her hair and paced the cabin.

Byron Grant was gone, and she doubted he'd reappear for a while.

Clara hadn't come to Alexi's room, because they were supposed to stay in their own, orders of Jude McCoy. The captain hadn't put the ship in lockdown yet, but Alexi felt as though it had already happened.

Finally, so much time had passed and Alexi was so on edge that she cracked open the door to her cabin. She looked both ways down the hall and saw no one.

Just when she was about to step out, Jude came walking down the hallway.

He was frowning at her. "Alexi, I told you not to open the door!" he said.

"I'm sorry, but you didn't come back. And I'm worried about Clara. And isn't there supposed to be a security man assigned to this hall? That means I should be safe enough checking on Clara!"

"Don't you understand the risks?" he shouted. "Death. You might face a terrible bloody death!"

"I do understand that, but if you expect me not to worry about a friend in the same situation, you're flat-out crazy," she told him angrily. "Have some faith in me! I was just stepping into the hall — where there should be a security man! — to check on my friend."

He was equally frustrated and angry, Alexi realized. But when she thought that he'd blow up again, he went silent.

"Stay there!" he snapped.

"Hey!" she protested as he walked down the hall.

It was a very long hallway. He walked the entire distance; she could see him retreating, and then coming back, eventually striding in the opposite direction, all the way to the stern.

He returned, looking perplexed.

Before she could say anything, he pulled out a black box that had to be a walkie-talkie. It was. He sounded terse as he spoke to someone, presumably Jackson, on the other end.

"I'm telling you, there's no one down here," he said. "I've been up and down the length of the ship." He listened to whatever Jackson was saying.

Then he turned to her. "You want to get out of the cabin? Fine, let's go pick up Clara. You two can play bingo."

"*Bingo?*" she said with dismay.

"And keep an eye on Jensen Hardy while you're there."

"Really?" Alexi demanded. "If Jensen's leading a bingo game, I imagine an awful lot of people will have their eyes on him."

"Alexi, damn it, will you just play bingo?"

She crossed her arms. "Do you realize, Jude, that I know all these people better than you do? And that if they need to be drawn out, if someone needs to speak with them, it should be me?"

He lowered his head and she guessed he was fighting for control. Either that, or maybe he was actually considering her words.

He looked at her again. "Alexi, I have no idea where the security man is, the guy who was supposed to be watching this floor. If he's disappeared . . ."

"Could he be in the men's room?"

"Then he would've reappeared by now, don't you think?"

"Check the hall again," she suggested.

He stepped back outside; she did, too.

It was easy to see forward.

And aft.

And, as he'd said, there was no one.

"Hold on a minute," he told her.

As she watched, he knocked on Ralph Martini's door. A minute later Ralph answered sleepily, still wearing his robe.

"Yeah?" he asked, puzzled.

"Just making sure you're okay," Jude said.

"I was. I was sleeping," Ralph said. He frowned. "Anything new? Anything with the storm?"

"We'll be battening down soon," Jude said. "That's all."

"Keep us informed, huh?"

"Absolutely," Jude promised. "Is Larry in there with you?"

"No, he's in his own room," Ralph said. "He's fine. He, uh, left here a little while ago."

Alexi waved to Ralph, who rolled his eyes and smiled. Apparently, he — and the others — knew exactly where Jude was sleeping.

Jude went on, knocking at select doors. Simon Green was next, and he seemed perfectly okay. He was playing show tunes on an iPod or other sound system; "Oklahoma!" sounded from his cabin as he opened his door. Alexi saw him nod, then go back inside.

It took Larry a few minutes to come to his door. He must've been in the shower, since he was draped in a towel. Larry seemed bewildered, but in the end, he, too, nodded — and seemed to appreciate Jude's visit.

Jude returned to Alexi's door and said, "Let's go get Clara. Will the two of you play bingo? Please?" he added quietly. "I know you'll be safe while you're in a crowd — and that way you can observe Hardy for us, too."

"All right, all right," she said, feeling aggrieved. "Bingo. Great."

They went over to Clara's cabin and tapped on her door. She threw it open, saying, "I checked. I checked the peephole. I knew the two of you were the ones at the door."

"Excellent," Jude said.

"He wants us to play *bingo,*" Alexi told her.

"Oh," Clara responded, looking from Alexi to Jude. She grimaced. "We're not actually allowed to play bingo. Ship's rules."

She hadn't known that, since the question had never come up for her. She wasn't much of a gambler, period. The only time she'd ever played bingo was at a church charity.

"There!" Alexi smiled at Jude, relieved. "We can't play bingo."

"Yes, you can, when a ship's executive says he's sending you in to help out with passenger entertainment due to the storm," he said pleasantly.

Alexi realized she was going to play bingo, whether she liked it or not. And she didn't.

"Bingo. Can't wait," she said with a sigh of resignation.

They took the elevator up to the ballroom, where a large crowd had gathered. Shelly Moore, one of Jensen's crew, was assisting him, but she seemed a little overwhelmed.

Jensen was speaking to the group, some ready to play, and some still in line buying cards.

"We'll be going for a straight line down the middle this time around," he announced. "Remember, not just any old bingo — a straight line down the center. Now, this is the Celtic American line, the *Destiny*!" he said. "If we don't make our stop in Belize, everyone on the ship will be getting a free cruise to replace this one, even though we're not responsible for acts of God. That's the Celtic American way! But whoever wins this game gets an upgrade to a suite on their next voyage!"

He stopped speaking, aware that Jude, Clara and Alexi had entered the ballroom. He looked at the three of them with annoyance.

Jude walked between the rows of tables to reach Jensen first. "I've brought a couple of the entertainers to help out."

"Clara and Alexi?" Jensen asked warily.

"Yes."

"You're, uh, leaving the two of them with me?"

"Yes."

"And you . . ."

"I have other business," Jude said.

"Oh." Jensen's expression was blank at first. Then he grinned. "I can certainly use the help. I have my other people running around, going from cabin to cabin with news sheets for the passengers. Everything's topsy-turvy because of the storm."

"Of course. And Celtic American understands," Jude said agreeably.

"Can one of you give me a hand with the game sheet sales and the other one check the winners, confirm that the cards match the letters?"

"I'll do sales," Clara said.

"I guess I'm the checker," Alexi chimed in.

"See you all after bingo," Jude told them.

She watched as he left. He definitely had his sea legs.

And that was impressive because the *Destiny* was rolling even more heavily than it had been before.

Jude got hold of Jackson as he walked down the hall, taking the stairs to the higher decks.

There was something very wrong with the fact that their assigned security guard wasn't on duty in the employee sector — where one of their three suspects and at least two potential victims were staying.

"I'll talk to David Beach and we'll start a search," Jackson said.

"I have a bad feeling about this."

"Yeah, I do, too," Jackson said. "Over and out."

"Over and out."

Jude shut down his walkie-talkie.

He wasn't sure how to separate Roger and Lorna Antrim, since he needed to speak with Lorna alone. He'd try their cabin first, see what kind of arrangement he could make.

Cabin? Suite!

When he knocked on the door, Roger answered. "Mr. McCoy."

"It's Jude, please."

"Jude. Come on in. Have you seen a salon like this? Oh, but you must have, being with Celtic American."

"Actually, I've never seen this particular salon," Jude said politely.

It was one hell of a salon.

Roger, dapper in a velvet-and-silk dressing gown, his gray hair still damp from the shower, made a sweeping gesture and gave him a tour of the lower level. "Piano here — hey, it would be fun to get Alexi Cromwell up here for a private party sometime, huh? Anyway, mini-kitchen there, meeting room in there, parlor area, games table — and all that balcony space over there is mine. Two bedrooms upstairs."

Jude could hardly imagine what accommodations like this would cost on a ship.

"Very nice," Jude murmured. "We're delighted that you're pleased with it."

"There aren't many ships as grand as this," Roger said. "With such old-world elegance. The *Destiny* is a special ship, indeed. We've always loved sailing on her. Well, except for this trip, but that's not the ship's fault, eh? No one can predict nature. Other than Lorna being so sick, I rather like the fact that nature is still stronger than any of us — any politician, any government, even our most advanced technology."

"That's nature, all right," Jude said. "How is Lorna? Is she in bed?"

"She was awake when I was in the shower. Let me go see if she's up. She'll be happy that you've stopped by."

Roger ran up the stairs to the bedrooms on the upper level.

A minute later he came back downstairs, frowning.

"She's not up there, but I never saw her go out."

"Maybe she was feeling poorly and went back to the infirmary. Listen, I'll head out and find her. I'll keep in touch."

"I should be looking for her, too," Roger said worriedly.

"Why don't you stay here? I'll inform security and we'll search for her. You wait here — be here if she comes back."

Roger didn't seem too pleased with that idea, but he agreed. "I'll get some clothes on. I can at least keep watch out in the hallway."

Jude nodded and pulled out the walkie-talkie to reach Jackson again. Jackson told him he'd alert Beach and his staff.

Jude went to the infirmary first, but she wasn't there and hadn't been in that morning.

When he left, there was a nurse standing

outside. For a moment her appearance didn't register with Jude; he was so focused on finding Lorna.

His heart was pounding. He didn't like this one bit. A security man gone, disappeared.

And now . . .

Lorna Antrim was missing.

As the nurse approached him, his mind suddenly clicked into gear.

Dead. Dead nurse. Barbara Leon, from the historic infirmary that was no longer used in its old capacity but maintained as a museum.

"Agent!" Nurse Leon called to him.

"Miss Leon."

"You're looking for Mrs. Antrim?"

He didn't understand how a ghost from a distant past could know that, but he didn't ask.

"Yes."

"Schooner Bar, just down the way," she said, bustling forward to show him.

There weren't many people out, although as of now, the shops, bars and the casino were still open.

Once Barbara Leon had led him to the Schooner, she simply faded away.

But she'd been right.

Lorna was seated at the bar, sipping a blue-colored drink.

Jude quickly called Jackson on his walkie-talkie to tell him she'd been found; Jackson said he'd get one of the security men to tell Roger.

"Hi," Jude said, taking the chair beside hers. "If you're still feeling seasick, that might not be the best thing for you at the moment." He pointed to her glass.

She smiled at him. "Should be straight scotch, huh?"

"You're feeling better?"

"I'm trying to feel like a man," she said.

"A man?"

"I'm not all that seasick, I've discovered. I'm . . . old-age sick, heartsick and maybe even angry sick. So, I want to see what it's like just to take off and drink — oh, and find a good-looking, unattached man about my age with whom I'd like to flirt."

"Ah." Jude couldn't quite figure out *what* to say to that.

She studied him, an attractive woman, he thought, at any age. She had a great smile. "Mr. McCoy, a storm is raging. Who knows? We may not even make it back to port. Then again, this is my third drink. I suppose that's why I'm speaking frankly to you. Besides," she said, still studying him intently. "You seem like a tough man. I would've said law enforcement if I didn't know you worked for the cruise line. But under that tough exterior, you're damned decent. So, what the hell."

She wasn't making much sense, and yet he understood what she meant.

"You think your husband is cheating on you?"

"What I *know* is that he disappears a lot," she said. "The day of the explosion, I was supposed to meet him at a bar in Cozumel — and I find him with a lovely woman. A woman from the ship. They were just talking . . . but how do I know what's really going on?" She was quiet for a minute. "He went wandering while I was out shopping. We agreed to meet at the bar, so he knew I was coming. And he introduced me to her, of course. We all sat and chatted and . . . then there was the explosion. We weren't at the restaurant, but we could see the chaos. Roger told us both to get safely back to the ship. He said he was going to see if he could help. Then he was gone. And when I finally found him again, it was on the ship. At a bar. With — with that same woman. Flora Winters."

"It may not mean he's cheating on you," Jude said.

It may mean that he's a killer, that he set the explosion.

But if so . . . why?

It bothered him not to have spoken to Capitan Suarez in nearly two days.

He didn't know if they'd found anything in any of their churches!

"I realize that," Lorna said, raising her glass to him. "May I buy you a drink, Mr. McCoy?"

"I'd love a glass of water."

"Of course. You're not the kind who'd drink on the job, are you?" she asked. "You want your attention completely focused."

"I also happen to like water," he told her, smiling.

So, her husband could have rigged the explosion at the restaurant. He hadn't been with her; he might've been anywhere.

But he could just be a man with a wandering eye.

Or a nice guy being kind to someone else.

"Crazy, huh? Me drinking like this — and confiding in a stranger!" Lorna said.

"It's all right. Sometimes it's a good thing to talk to someone who isn't involved."

"I don't even know what he's doing right now," she went on. "The cells aren't working, and the computers are down. And I left the suite. Think he headed straight to her cabin, Mr. McCoy?"

"No, I just got in touch with my coworker,

Jackson, a few minutes ago to ask him to call off security. Before that I was at your suite. Your husband's worried."

She lowered her head. "I'm grateful you were all worried about me," she said. "Embarrassed, too. But . . . I'm actually glad that I gave Roger a few moments of worry. Now he'll know how *I* feel," she said softly.

"Want me to see you back to your cabin?"

"Sure," she said. She set down her drink and stared at it. "I don't even like these sugary things."

"Shall we go?"

He hoped he wasn't bringing her back to a serial killer — to the Archangel himself.

But even if Roger *was* the Archangel, statistically Lorna was safe.

Most serial killers didn't strike at or near home. They used their standing as family men and good neighbors to protect their secret identities.

Besides, at this point Jude had no reason — and certainly no actual evidence — to think that Roger was the Archangel.

He offered Lorna an arm; she took it with a smile. "Well, I am feeling a bit wobbly. And the ship is . . . well, quite wobbly, too."

He escorted her from the bar, to the elevator and up to her suite.

Roger was waiting anxiously in the hallway. "Lorna!" he said, rushing forward to embrace her. "Oh, my God, I was so worried!"

"Were you really?" she asked, pulling back to study his face.

"I was scared silly. You just — you just disappeared!"

"I went out for a drink."

"But you always tell me when you're going somewhere!"

"But you don't always tell *me.*"

He drew her into his arms. "I'm sorry," he said in a low voice.

Jude slipped quietly away.

It might have been an act.

If so, it was a damned good one.

One way to find out; he would pay a visit to Roger's friend, Mrs. Flora Winters, in cabin number 615.

12

Bingo was over.

There was, as yet, no sign of Jude.

But as the winners came forward and giddily collected their certificates, she and Clara sat at one of the rear tables in the now-empty back room, exhausted.

This was her chance to talk to Jensen Hardy.

After he'd thanked her and Clara, she found her opening. "It's okay. I don't know if we'll be working tonight."

"Right now you're on the entertainment schedule, but that may change. Probably *will* change. We're still just staying put, waiting on forecasts. But I happen to believe the captain suspects more than he's telling us. Tropical storm Dinah was upgraded to Hurricane Dinah over Cozumel. They thought she'd advance to the Gulf, so they ordered us to sail 'cautiously' south. Now Dinah's changing her mind."

"What makes you think that?"

"We haven't been ordered to any port," he said. "If they'd had a good handle on the storm, they'd have gotten us out of harm's way by now. Maybe they should've taken a chance! Everybody figured Dinah had to move. Instead, she pummeled Cozumel!"

"So . . . ?" Clara asked slowly.

"In another few hours, I bet Captain Thorne will announce that we're closing down all our entertainment facilities. He'll have to tell everyone what's going on. But we're trying to maintain calm and in my opinion we've done it really well!" he said.

"You're very good at what you do," Alexi told him sweetly.

He smiled, and she realized that he did look at her as if . . . as if he wished they were more than friends.

"Thanks," he said huskily. He reached across the table and placed his hand on hers. "And we're going to be fine," he insisted.

She drew back, trying not to appear obvious about it.

Fortunately, Clara interrupted whatever Jensen had been about to say next. "Alexi and I aren't afraid of the storm," she said quickly.

Alexi laughed. "I do miss my computer,

though! I started playing around on one of those ancestry sites. My dad was a vet, and both my grandfathers were in World War II. I was trying to find out more about them."

"Too bad the computers are down. Makes people anxious. And bored. That's why we have to keep them entertained. As long as it's safe for us," Jensen said.

"I want to do more research on my ancestors, too," Clara said. "I know one of my grandfathers was in World War II. Oh, and it was sad. He was my mom's father. His parents were Italian, so he was second-generation American. The army sent him to fight in Italy because he knew the language. He'd been born in the States, but his first language was Italian."

"Where was the family from?" Alexi asked.

"Rome, I believe," Clara replied.

"I think I had ancestors who were Italian, too — on my mom's side. I haven't gotten that far yet. I think they lived somewhere near the Vatican. My folks loved to travel to Italy. And rosaries! My mom had a huge thing for rosaries. She brought them back all the time and, of course, when I went to Italy, I brought *her* a rosary."

"Catholic, huh?" Jensen said.

"Much of my family," Alexi said. Everything she'd told him was the truth.

She hadn't been completely open with Clara, but Clara seemed to know exactly where she wanted to go with Jensen.

"How about your family?" she asked him.

"What? Pardon?" he said. "You mean, religion?"

She shook her head. "Alexi was saying that her family had liked collecting rosaries. With my mom, it was those miniature religious paintings — of the Virgin Mary and the Christ Child and so on. What about your family? Did they do anything like that?"

"My . . . my parents weren't big travelers."

"They must've gone somewhere!" Clara said.

"They went to France a few times. And they brought me back those T-shirts that say things like 'My dad went to Paris and all I got was this lousy T-shirt!' "

Alexi actually managed to laugh at that.

"Parents and grandparents didn't have to travel to give us interesting presents," Clara said next. "When I was a teenager, my father gave me a collection of foreign coins."

"I was given my mom's doll collection," Alexi said. "She had a Shirley Temple doll, for one. It's made out of porcelain. I love it."

Clara smiled. "I'll bet she's worth a

314

bundle now."

"I'd never sell her, unless I was down to desperate," Alexi said.

"I can't imagine either of you being down to desperate," Jensen told them. "You're both so talented."

"Thanks," Alexi murmured.

"You're making us feel good," Clara added.

"Nothing but the truth, ladies. Nothing but the truth."

"Well, thanks, Jensen." Clara paused for a few seconds. "What about you? Did *you* ever get anything really cool from your family?" Clara asked.

Jensen grinned. "Yeah, T-shirts! Like I said." He frowned, staring at the large carved doors that led into the ballroom.

Alexi's back was to the door. "Is something wrong?" she asked.

He shrugged in response. "Besides being trapped in an old ocean liner while a major storm sweeps in? No. There's just some guy who keeps looking in here."

"Someone you don't know?" Alexi asked. "I mean, you know almost all the crew and performers on the ship."

"I can't see him properly. I keep wanting to tell him to come in, but he's always gone before I can do that." Jensen shrugged again. "I'm going to have to get ready for Name that Tune," he told them. "You two helping with that, as well?"

Where the hell was Jude?

"I guess we'll go wherever the big bosses tell us to," she said.

She turned toward the door.

Someone had been standing there, someone who managed to be a fleeting shadow every time they tried to see who it was.

"That's it!" she said, hurrying toward the door — where she saw her friend, security officer Johnny Morgan. He'd also been there when she'd chased after Jude, before she'd realized just who Jude and Jackson were.

The night she'd tried to catch Jude — to tell him *he* was trying to catch a ghost.

"Johnny!" she said.

"I'm on guard duty, assigned to you and Clara. I'm just trying to keep an eye on you."

"We appreciate that, Johnny! Why don't you come in?"

"Best that I don't. I'm just watching over you, and I'm not twenty feet away, if you need me for any reason at all."

"Thanks, again. You haven't seen Jude McCoy or Jackson Crow, have you?"

"Not recently. And all I know is that I'm

not to leave you or Clara." It looked as if she and Clara were going to be playing Name that Tune!

And so far, she'd gotten nowhere. Guilty or not, Jensen Hardy wasn't interested in holy relics. He apparently hadn't received any as presents.

He'd gotten nothing but T-shirts.

Unless he was a better liar than he seemed.

Flora Winters of cabin number 615 answered her door after Jude's second knock.

She was an attractive woman, nearly as fit as Lorna Antrim. Unlike Lorna, though, she'd clearly had work done and from a distance might look even younger.

Up close . . . Jude observed that her expression seemed a little pinched.

But she had an appealing smile and didn't behave as if she was concerned about opening the door.

"Can I help you?" she asked.

He introduced himself, using his current "identity." "I'm Jude McCoy, Ms. Winters, with Celtic American lines."

"Nice to meet you, sir."

"We're trying to speak with all our passengers. To apologize for the weather — not that we can do anything about it! And to say that we're doing the best we can to make everything as easy as possible."

"I haven't been too disturbed by it yet, Mr. McCoy. I was in the service — with the United States Navy — way back when. I've been on a few rough voyages."

"Really? Well, thank you for your service to our country."

"Hard to say it was always a pleasure, but I'm glad I did my duty," she said. "What about you? Were you ever in the military?"

"Yes, ma'am," he told her.

She nodded approvingly. "Not that it's for everyone — and I'm so glad the days of the draft are gone! But for those who choose to serve, it's a very good thing. Were you navy?"

"No, ma'am. Marines."

"Commendable!" she said. "Well . . . do you want to come in? This may not be the grandest suite, but it's comfy and I do have a coffeemaker."

"Actually, that would be great. Trying to keep people calm during storm conditions isn't easy," Jude said.

Not that he'd really kept anyone calm.

"I can imagine. How do you like your coffee?"

"Black is fine," he told her.

Her suite wasn't as sumptuous and elegant as Roger and Lorna's; it was, however, quite elegant. She had a little living room and a mini-kitchen with a coffeepot/wet bar/ refrigerator area. The place also featured a small sofa and dining table. He sat down on the sofa.

"What's the latest news on our girl?" Flora asked as she prepared his coffee.

"Our girl? Which girl?"

"The storm. Dinah."

"Oh, *that* girl. Well, they're keeping pretty quiet," Jude said. "So far, Dinah's ignoring all the cones of probability the meteorologists have made for her. Basically, she isn't moving. She's done this back-and-forth thing just outside Cozumel."

Flora seemed amused as she brought him a cup of coffee and sat beside him on the sofa. "They're keeping quiet?" she repeated. "Who are *they*? Aren't you in the upper echelon of the company?"

"It's a big company," he said. "There's an echelon above me. But I don't think it's the company so much as the fact that storms don't necessarily do what the meteorologists predict. I do know that Captain Thorne is doing his best to keep us on the outskirts — the problem being that the *outskirts* seem to be growing."

"Well, I suppose for most people the wait-and-see is excruciating," Flora said. "For me, hoping a torpedo wasn't going to hit our ship was a far greater fear. I haven't sailed with Captain Thorne before, but I'm often on a Celtic American ship and I've heard that he has an excellent reputation. We'll be fine."

"What made you choose the *Destiny,* Ms. Winters?" he asked. He kept his words light. He planned to move gradually into asking about her friendship with Roger Antrim.

"Call me Flora," she said. And she smiled. "Oh, that's easy to answer. I met Roger Antrim on another cruise with the line. I took this one specifically because he was going to be on it."

"Oh," he said, hoping he didn't sound too surprised.

"We're doing business together," she said.

"What kind of business?"

"Nothing bad by any means, young man," she told him and laughed, shaking her head. "Roger loves his wife very much. And I can understand why. Lorna's delightful."

Jude wasn't sure Lorna felt the same way about her!

"She is, yes," Jude said. "Well, if I implied anything by word or tone, I certainly didn't mean to. No implication intended at all. Except that now I'm curious. What is your business?"

"My dear departed Sam's business,

really," she said. "Sam and I had a wonderful marriage for forty-three years. We were
high school sweethearts who married immediately after graduation. Then we spent a
decade learning what a mistake we'd made
— not in loving each other, but in failing to
obtain higher degrees while we were still
home with our parents! Anyway, Sam and I
both joined the navy, and when we got out,
he began accumulating little collectibles,
and went on to big ones. He knew how to
buy and he learned how to sell. I lost Sam
last year. I don't have his knowledge of
what's valuable and what isn't, so I'm
liquidating. Roger suggested this cruise. He
said he wanted certain things that Sam
would've had up for auction soon and also
that he'd help set me up with one of the
major auction houses to finish closing out
the business."

"I'm sorry that Sam passed away."

"A year ago. Don't be sorry. Few people
have so many beautiful years together! I
cherish my memories. Oh, I have my children and grandchildren to fill my days, and
I love to cruise. I'm doing it on my own
now, but Sam and I used to take cruises
whenever we could. It's a nice way to keep
my independence and meet new friends."

Flora Winters seemed to be sincere. He

found himself liking her very much.

He also found himself wondering about the *collectibles.*

"What sort of things is Roger interested in buying?" he asked her.

"Estate jewelry. Gifts for his wife. Unusual pieces rather than pieces with massive diamonds or the like," Flora said.

"Yes, I'd think Lorna's tastes run to the unique. She doesn't seem the type of woman who'd need to flash a large diamond."

"No."

He started to rise; he still didn't *know* anything, not for sure, but his gut instinct said Flora was telling the truth.

And that Roger wasn't having an affair. He just wanted to buy his wife some nice jewelry.

"Then, of course," Flora went on, "there are the religious artifacts."

Jude eased back into his seat. "Religious artifacts?"

"Oh, some gorgeous things! A marble cross, a stained-glass window from an ancient church in Rome, parish Bibles from England. I'd keep them myself, but I'm selling the house and moving into a condo in New York City. My son works on Wall Street and my daughter is in fashion design. They're in the city, so of course, I want to be nearby."

"Of course," he murmured. "Tell me something. Since your husband must've known about collecting such things . . . Did you ever handle a set of saints' medallions that were created right before World War II?"

"Why, yes, I believe Sam did have a set. Italian, I think. I'm not sure which church they came from, but I recall that they were created to help provide for orphaned children. I vaguely remember seeing the set. The medallions were silver-plated — exquisite but not very expensive!"

"Did he happen to sell those to Roger?" Jude asked.

"Oh, no, Mr. McCoy — Jude," she amended quickly. "I didn't meet Roger until after Sam died. I'm afraid I don't know who the medallions were sold to. But the buyer would be on record with my husband's accountant. Sam's bookkeeping was meticulous. Were you looking for a set of medallions? Perhaps Myles Barton could help you. He was Sam's assistant."

"Yes, I've been looking for exactly this set," Jude said. "Flora, as soon as we're able to make contact with the outside world again, I'd appreciate it if you'd speak to your bookkeeper and find out who bought

323

that set from Sam." To make his interest in the medals seem straightforward — merely a collector's obsession — he added, "I've wanted these for years, ever since I, uh, first read about them."

"I'll be happy to look into it," she told him.

After a few more pleasantries, he left.

There had originally been five thousand sets. Just because Flora's husband, Sam Winters, had sold a set, that certainly didn't mean he'd been the one to sell it to the Archangel.

But being this close to learning about one of the sets — and, more than that, learning there'd been a connection between the seller and one of the suspects . . .

It seemed like more than a coincidence.

He wasn't much of a believer in co-incidence.

Ghosts, yes, he told himself drily.

Coincidence? No.

Jude did not come to rescue Alexi and Clara.

They stayed with Jensen Hardy through an afternoon of contests and games.

By five o'clock, Alexi was pretty sure she hated Jude McCoy.

Hank poked his head in, Ginny Monk on

his arm, just as Jensen was teasing that they'd make one of their last games of the day a wet T-shirt contest.

During the final trivia game, the ballroom had begun to fill up with older teens and young adults. They cheered him on.

Alexi could see Hank entering the ballroom with Ginny. The bar had been open for a long time; maybe that was why Jensen's suggestion of a wet T-shirt contest brought enthusiasm and laughter — and a surge of people heading to the bar.

"Sales!" he told Alexi and Clara happily.

"Sales," they murmured to each other.

"How can we have a wet T-shirt contest?" one young woman called out.

"Well, now that you ask . . ." Jensen grinned and searched the shelves of the large trunk, on rollers, that often went with him from venue to venue on the ship. "Aha!" he cried, producing spray bottles of water. "Ten. We can have ten entries. And to make it lots of fun, each young lady willing to have a wet T-shirt is welcome to have her man — her friend, her sister, broker, companion, whoever — wield the spray bottles!"

"What if a young man wants to enter the contest?"

"I know that voice," Clara whispered to Alexi.

"Simon?"

"It's the singer!" someone else said.

"I say let him join!"

Simon walked through the crowd, smiling, his hands up. "Just kidding, folks. However, the winner is welcome to wet down my T-shirt!"

"That's a deal," a girl called out, drawing a round of laughter from the crowd.

"Ah, now, if my lovely assistants will select ten young ladies — only those with their hands raised, we take no prisoners on this ship! — we'll get it going," Jensen said.

"I am really going to kill Jude," Alexi muttered to Clara.

"I'd kill him, too — except that I'm happy to be alive!" Clara said.

So am I! Alexi thought. *Still . . . how could he just leave us here?*

Guarded by Johnny, a security man she liked, she reminded herself.

But with Jensen? For bingo and all these games — and a wet T-shirt contest.

"Hey!" someone shouted. "Personally, I'd like to see the lovely assistants in the wet T-shirt contest."

"Not a prayer, buddy!" Clara said under her breath.

326

"We can't," Alexi said. "But for those of you who are eager and willing . . ."

In fact it was easy for Alexi and Clara to come up with the right number of contestants. First rule for volunteers — to enter the wet T-shirt contest, you had to be wearing a T-shirt. And then you needed a companion or friend.

She was standing near the bar when she heard Ginny and Hank talking. "It'll be fun! Oh, come on, Hank. We'll have a good time!"

"I don't want everyone seeing my girl in a wet T-shirt," Hank said stubbornly.

"Actually," Alexi said, walking toward them quickly, "the T-shirts aren't going to get that wet. They're just little spray bottles."

"See?" Ginny said.

"If you're set on it, be my guest. But I don't want to be involved," Hank said.

"Okay, don't worry about it," Ginny told him. "We'll just watch."

"I'm happy just to watch, too," Alexi said, moving on.

One girl joined with her brother, who was mortified. Jensen had a great deal of fun teasing the two of them. Alexi discovered that, in some ways, this event was similar to her evenings in the piano bar — minus the singing and the piano, of course.

It all had to do with engaging the crowd.

And Jensen Hardy was very good at that.

Each team had a cheering section. And despite what Alexi had seen as a distinctly uncomfortable activity, the contest was fun. It had nowhere near the sexual edge it might have had poolside.

The brother kept wetting his sister's arm, drawing all kinds of criticism and laughter from the crowd.

And everyone involved got a ten-dollar credit for drinks or the casino — with no expiration date, in case the weather got worse and they were unable to use them during this cruise.

Casino credits certainly didn't represent a loss to the ship; most people used up their ten dollars and perhaps even won. Only to put their winnings — and more — back into the machines and in the hands of the dealers.

Simon allowed a group of girls to soak his T-shirt with their bottles when the contest was over. He was more the lean ascetic type than the brawny he-man, but the girls still enjoyed themselves and Simon was entertaining.

"You're just chorus?" she teased, bringing him a towel after he'd been drenched.

He grinned at her. "Ah, but I don't intend

to stay just chorus!"

"And I'm sure you won't."

Guests were trailing out now. Hank and Ginny were having an intense discussion at the bar. Clara, she saw, was staring at the door. She started walking toward it, and Alexi hurried after her as she stepped out into the hall. And there was the ghost of Byron Grant, leaning against a wall. He'd probably been there, watching all the while. But Clara was still staring at him, and he was staring back.

"Who are you?" she demanded in a whisper.

"Clara!"

Alexi caught her by the shoulders, turning her so they were facing each other. People were walking by, giving them curious looks, since Clara seemed to be talking to herself.

"Clara, please don't!"

"Who the hell is he? He's watching all the time. He could be —"

The killer.

"He's not!" Alexi responded quickly to the words Clara didn't quite say. "He's not! Look at me, listen to me. Let all these people get out of here."

Jensen was inside the ballroom, cleaning up.

"Jensen, we have to leave. See you later!"

she called. She set an arm around Clara's shoulders and led her down the hall, glancing at Johnny, who was waiting for them, so he'd follow them down the hall to the elevators.

"Don't talk yet. I'll explain in my room."

"Everyone just ignores him," Clara said. "And I see him all the time. It's creepy!"

"Clara, we have to get to my cabin before we talk about this."

She smiled weakly as they passed people they knew, or had met while entertaining on the ship. Finally, they reached the employee cabins. Alexi waved her thanks to Johnny and urged Clara into her room.

"Out with it!" Clara insisted. "Who *is* that man? Why are you defending him? He looks suspicious. He sometimes follows me!"

"Clara, he's not going to hurt you," Alexi said.

There was a soft knock at the cabin door. "Alexi, it's me, Byron."

"That's him, isn't it?" Clara demanded. "Let him in. I'm going to tell him a thing or two. Is he with the FBI? Someone should've told me."

She didn't open the door.

But a second later Byron appeared inside.

Clara looked at him, and then at Alexi.

And then she collapsed — luckily, close

330

enough to Alexi's bed so she could guide her friend onto it.

Every inch of the *Destiny,* with the exception of the guest cabins and employee quarters, had been searched.

The security guard who'd been assigned to the employee hallway that morning was gone. He was Nathan Freeman, veteran of many a voyage. He'd been a Dallas cop before he'd joined the Celtic American group over a decade ago, and he was one of David Beach's most dependable men.

But he was nowhere to be found. He seemed to have vanished into thin air.

Engine rooms and storage areas, every lifeboat, every nook and cranny, had been exhaustively searched. Various members of the staff had taken part and, after his visit with Flora Winters, Jude had joined in, as well.

Regular announcements had been made over the PA system, asking Nathan Freeman to report to Security. Nathan had not appeared.

Once again, Jude and Jackson met with David Beach and his security men in their small office. This time, Captain Thorne was present, too.

"The only places we haven't searched, of

course, are the cabins," David Beach said. "Captain, do you want us to start checking out guest and employee cabins?"

"If he is in a cabin somewhere, I'm going to assume it's with a friend, a crew member. Perhaps he was suddenly taken ill," Captain Thorne said.

He didn't believe it. None of them believed it.

"At least we haven't found his body," Beach said, a catch in his voice.

Jackson had been silent, listening to Beach and his men go through their reports.

Now he spoke up. "I'm afraid we're not going to find Mr. Freeman's body. We're all aware that we're sailing in very rough seas."

"You think Nathan deserted his post — and fell off the ship?" Beach demanded indignantly.

"No, I do not," Jackson said. "I do suggest another intense search for him. Knock on cabin doors. Honest people will understand that we're in a difficult situation. Anyone who won't cooperate will give us reason to take a second look. Captain, aren't there maritime laws that can be invoked?" He paused as Thorne nodded grimly. "However, I'm afraid we won't find him."

There was silence.

"But we'll try every possible approach,"

Beach said.

"Yes," the captain agreed.

Beach struggled to speak for a moment before he said, "You and Agent McCoy believe that the Archangel is on board. But the Archangel is a man who kills women. I'm not suggesting all women are weak and vulnerable, not at all, but Nathan is a big guy — broad shoulders, lots of muscle. If I've understood anything about the psychopathic killers, which I'm assuming the Archangel must be, it's that they're often weaklings, cowed by greater strength. How could a man like that have taken my officer?"

"By surprise," Jackson told him. "We'll keep searching, of course. None of us will stop searching. But I'm afraid that we're not going to like the outcome."

Again there was silence.

"We don't even know that this man is really on the ship!" Captain Thorne protested.

"We have reason to believe he is," Jude said flatly.

Captain Thorne turned red. "No, *we* don't," he retorted. "I have to be in the main dining room. Tonight's the captain's dinner, and, after this, I may well be declaring a state of emergency. The *Destiny* is one of the most elegant ships sailing the seas, and we will not make a mockery of her tonight. We will continue to cooperate in every way with the FBI, but we'll also assume the best — and not the worst! — regarding Nathan Freeman. Is that understood?"

"Captain," Jackson said, "it's your ship."

"Yes, and at sea, I am the ultimate law."

"Of course, and we appreciate the cooperation," Jackson said.

Captain Thorne spun around and marched out of the room.

When he'd left, Beach looked at Jackson and Jude, his expression pained. "This part of *we* believes you, Agents," he said. He spoke to his men. "During the captain's dinner tonight, we have to be more vigilant than ever, stay in closer contact with one another." He looked back at Jude and Jackson again.

"And God help us, the weather's only going to get worse."

13

Clara seemed to be in shock at first. Disbelieving.

That was the initial response most people had to seeing — and speaking with — the dead.

But Byron must've been a decent man. He and his Elizabeth had surely been a loving couple, the kind of people who were bound to make the world a better place, Alexi thought sadly, watching him talk to Clara. She admired his earnestness, the way he assured Clara that he was doing everything he could to see that the murderer was brought to justice.

And by the time Byron had gone through whatever reserves of strength or will or whatever allowed him to appear, Clara in turn was watching him as he vanished before her eyes.

"I see the dead." Clara was staring straight ahead. She looked at Alexi. "I see the dead.

You see the dead. You take it so . . . calmly."

"I've known for years that I see them," she said in a quiet voice. "It's . . . it's in my family."

"Sure." Clara shrugged with a hint of humor. "Some people inherit blue eyes. Some people inherit the ability to see the dead," Clara said. "And now, now when I'm terrified of a serial killer, I get to see the dead, too. Wow. What a voyage."

"You've been seeing them all along," Alexi told her.

"What?"

"Blake and Minnie. They're always at the piano bar."

Clara flopped back on the bed and closed her eyes. "This isn't real. It can't be. We're getting cabin fever because of the storm. And because . . . there's a serial killer aboard."

"Clara, seeing the dead is a good thing," Alexi reassured her.

"Why? Is the ghost going to catch the serial killer?"

"Well, no, but he *is* looking after us."

"And if he sees someone about to attack us, what's he going to do? Scream for help?"

"Maybe," Alexi said. "Others see him, too."

Clara bolted into a sitting position.

"You're going to tell me the FBI men see ghosts?"

"Uh, yes," Alexi mumbled. "These two, anyway."

"No. Oh, no! This can't be true. It can't be."

There was a knock at her cabin door and Alexi hurried over, hoping it was going to be Jude.

It wasn't.

It was Jensen Hardy.

She hesitated, not wanting to open the door. She'd had enough of him that day.

And she wasn't supposed to open her door — except for Jude or Jackson.

"Yes?" she called.

"Hey, all entertainment on deck, dressed and ready to go. Captain Thorne wants all singers and dancers ready for impromptu performances. Captain's dinner!" Jensen announced.

Glancing through the peephole again, Alexi saw that Johnny was still on duty, watching over them. He stood just beyond Jensen.

She opened the door. "Why?" she asked.

"I have the feeling Thorne just wants to get through the dinner," Jensen said. "We'll probably go into emergency mode after that. He'll be asking passengers to stay in their cabins and listen to the PA system. So, we're going to entertain at dinner."

"With no plan?" Clara asked, rising. "No rehearsals or anything?"

"Hey, this came down to me from Bradley Wilcox," Jensen said. "A few minutes ago."

"And we have to do it?"

"Only if you want to keep your employment with Celtic American," Jensen said. "Report to the main dining room in an hour, all prettied up and ready to go. Come on. I know you guys helped me out today, but I'm as tired as you are. Think of it this way. You can sleep all day tomorrow if we go into emergency mode. Great sleeping," he added sarcastically, "tossing and turning like we're on a roller coaster."

"Okay, okay! We'll be there," Alexi said, closing the door. Clara wasn't in her usual state of self-control; she seemed ready to throw a pillow or something harder at Jensen.

"Dickhead!" she muttered.

"It not Jensen's fault," Alexi pointed out.

"I meant Bradley Wilcox. But they're both dickheads." She stood. "I'd better go clean up and get dressed."

"Are you okay?" Alexi asked, afraid her tone was more anxious than she wanted it to be. If she was going to convince Clara

338

that it was actually a good thing to talk to ghosts, she had to make sure she projected her own comfort with the phenomenon.

"No, I'm feeling pissed off, but . . ." Clara squared her shoulders. "Yeah, I'm okay. I'm not religious, although I've always believed in something beyond this life — and I guess that could include ghosts. Seeing them, hearing them, talking to them. All the philosophical ramifications of this . . . well, I hope I'll be able to take them in when there isn't a serial killer aboard the ship I'm on. Not to mention a storm named Dinah bearing down on us."

She headed for the cabin door, then turned back.

"They don't just pop in on you unexpectedly, do they?" she asked, sounding worried.

"Byron is very polite," Alexi replied. "he knocks when he comes to visit."

"But you said he's not the only ghost on this ship."

"All our ghosts are very circumspect," Alexi said.

Clara sighed. "Courteous ghosts. What next?" She set her hand on the cabin door.

"Wait!" Alexi said. "Careful. Let me check that Johnny's still out there."

She looked through the peephole. They

were safe. Johnny was there, standing guard. Alexi opened the door and smiled at him. "Could you walk Clara across the hall?"

"Of course," Johnny said with a nod. "My pleasure." Clara had barely been gone two minutes when Alexi heard another tap at her door. She assumed it was Clara coming back for some reason.

She almost forgot about safety and was on the verge of throwing open her door. But she heard Jude's voice, identifying himself.

Grateful that she hadn't just opened her door, she let him in.

"Where have you *been*?" she demanded. "Jude, it went from bingo to trivia. And on to a wet T-shirt contest." She rolled her eyes. "I really tried to draw people out. I had a few minutes with Jensen, who doesn't seem to be the least interested in collectible religious objects. And I saw Hank Osprey. He was there with Ginny, and she wanted to enter the wet T-shirt contest, but he wouldn't let her. Or at least he discouraged her in no uncertain terms. Is that overly possessive? Or is that how a guy might naturally feel? Oh, and I've discovered that Clara sees the dead, too. I'd suspected it, but now I know. I think she's okay with it." Alexi stopped speaking; she felt as though she was babbling. Maybe she was getting tired. Or maybe she was so glad to see Jude she was afraid she was becoming dependent on him.

Maybe she was even wondering what would happen if they survived this journey . . . She was afraid that her flustered state of mind might repel him.

But it didn't seem to. Although he'd been tense, he smiled and took her gently into his arms.

"I'm sorry," he said softly. "I'm sorry you were brought into this."

"Nothing to be sorry about," she insisted. She pulled away from him, meeting his eyes, then laid her cheek against his chest. "Byron came to me because he needed help. And, apparently, my life is at risk. I *have* to be in on this. And despite the geyser of words with which I greeted you, I'm fine."

"Very fine," he whispered.

"Jude, it's so hard! When you're dealing with people who seem to be so normal, how do you begin to figure out who could be a brutal killer?"

He drew in a breath, and she knew he was thinking that there were cases when a killer hadn't been caught, when he terrorized others for years — and perhaps died of natural causes without ever being discovered. And some serial killers had preyed on the unwary for years before being brought to justice.

"We keep engaging them, as you did today, with Jensen and Hank. We wait for them to give themselves away. Sometimes all it takes is a word or mannerism. Sometimes, we can eliminate people if we can determine where they were or weren't at a certain time. And occasionally you talk to someone, and you somehow *know*. You sense that he's guilty — and then you have to prove it. But in this situation we have to narrow down the possibilities."

"When the computers were still working, I was trying to gather whatever information I could on the saints' medallions," Alexi said.

"Which, as we've all agreed, could be the key." Jude hesitated. "I may have tracked down a set of the medallions."

Alexi sat on the bed and listened while he told about his day, about speaking with Lorna, and then Flora Winters — and learning that her husband had sold a set of the collectible medallions.

She felt there was something he wasn't telling her, though.

"Jude? What is it?"

He shook his head unhappily. "A man's gone missing," he explained. "Nathan Freeman, one of David Beach's security crew.

He was scheduled to be in the hallway this morning. He's missing. We've searched the ship for him. Searched everywhere."

"You think . . . the killer got him?"

"I think it's possible." He changed the subject abruptly. "I'm going to dress for dinner. You're staying with me, and I don't care whether or not we're following staff policy."

"I have to be in the dining room," she told him. "I'm one of the entertainers giving an impromptu performance for the captain's dinner."

"I won't be far away," he promised. "I won't be far from you — at any time."

The tension among the passengers on the *Destiny* seemed palpable.

The ship now had a constant sway, although it seemed to be riding the waves well.

To reach their tables, people had to hold on to the backs of chairs. Once they were seated, waiters took more time than usual delivering drinks; they carried fewer glasses on a tray in case they lost their balance.

Alexi observed that not everyone had made it down to the captain's dinner.

Clara was with her at the piano. Alexi had been given the task of playing "mood" music while the passengers found their seats.

Jude stood near the piano, which was situated on a little dais. It had the added advantage of providing a good view of the dining room.

Hank and Ginny, as well as Roger and Lorna were at the captain's table; Jackson Crow had also secured himself a seat there. So had Flora Winters. The table seated ten, but Jude wasn't familiar with the other four people there. He wasn't surprised to see two of his suspects at the head table, since they were among the richest men in the country and had taken the ship's most expensive suites.

Simon Green was with a group of the performers.

Jude didn't see Jensen Hardy at first and stepped to the side to ask one of the security men to take a look around.

It wasn't long until the man returned; apparently, Jensen was preparing to come out and make announcements when Captain Thorne finished his speech.

Soup and salads were served, and then the main courses.

Alexi played throughout the meal. Jude watched her, admiring her. Her fingers moved with pure elegance over the keys. He loved the ease with which she played, and the way she could speak without missing a beat, sing and harmonize, and do it all as naturally as breathing. He studied her face and her expressions, and he felt a slow tightening in his muscles, wondering how one human being had become the world to him in just a few days.

Because she was ready to risk everything when it mattered?

Because she saw the dead?

Because, somehow, she seemed to reach his soul?

He saw Jensen approaching the captain's table with a microphone.

Captain Thorne rose, and Alexi stopped playing.

"Ladies and gentlemen!" he said, addressing the dinner guests. "I'm Xavier Thorne, your captain on the *Destiny*. I believe that all of you are on this ship because you've chosen to sail with history. Many of you have taken the tours we give of the ship, and have learned about her role as a hospital ship. You sail with her through time, and you sail with the ghosts of the past."

They sure did! Jude thought.

"This is proving to be one of our more unusual cruises," Thorne continued. "Our guests who are from certain areas of the

345

country are well aware of tropical storms. We here, on the *Destiny,* also know them well. I want to welcome you aboard to reassure you that no matter how hard the winds blow, the *Destiny* will prevail. She's made it through wind and rain and fire. She will do so again." He cleared his throat. "I'd like to ask you to pay attention to our PA system. Announcements will be coming to you regarding our position at sea. We may ask that our nonessential personnel — that is, anyone not engaged in actually operating the ship — stay in their cabins for a spell. I ask our passengers, entertainers and staff to be expert sailors along with me and my crew, and to cooperate at all times. I invite you to speak about your voyage, and when we've returned to port, to brag that you were aboard the *Destiny* when she ran circles around Hurricane Dinah. I won't confine anyone to their cabins unless it becomes necessary. If it should, I ask that you obey my directives. Other than that, enjoy your time aboard, just as I always enjoy mine. And thank you sincerely for sailing with Celtic American!"

A round of applause followed his words.

But then someone called out, "Captain, exactly when will we be reaching port?"

Another asked, "Why haven't you found a

346

safe harbor yet?"

"What are the cruise line officials doing? There has to be someplace to go!"

"Hey, Cozumel was nearly flattened!" someone else shouted angrily.

And then . . .

"Captain! I heard that a man went missing today. Is that true? Was he swept overboard?"

"Oh, my God!" several other people shouted.

Captain Thorne raised his hand, his expression betraying no reaction at all. "You are safe aboard the *Destiny.* Obviously, we ask you not to hang over your balconies! As to our travels, we're doing everything suggested by the United States government and the national weather experts. That is all."

He nodded toward Alexi.

She began to play. Clara rose and sang. She had a crystal clear soprano that was distinct and captivating, and the room quickly became enthralled. When they took a break, several *Les Miz* performers — including Ralph, Larry and Simon — came to the dais and launched into a sketch of waiters on a cruise ship that was very funny.

The diners began to talk again. They laughed and chatted at their tables.

Jude's walkie-talkie went off. He answered

immediately. It was Jackson.

"We've heard from Mexico," Jackson told him. "From Capitan Suarez. Meet me in Communications as soon as possible."

Nothing was going to happen in the main dining room, Alexi told herself.

There were far too many people.

Despite Jude's assurances that Johnny and other security men were right there, Alexi knew he was unhappy about leaving her.

It made her unhappy, too. But she forced a smile, then swept one arm toward the room, showing him how crowded it was, even though some tables were only half-occupied. The captain was still in attendance and there were dozens of security personnel lining the walls, many of whom she knew.

She promised to stay with Clara and Johnny. And she smiled as she watched him walk away.

Truth be told, though, she felt uneasy. Especially when she noticed that the captain was called away at the same time.

Jude wouldn't have left if something major hadn't happened.

The captain wouldn't have left — unless something major had happened.

She was supposed to continue playing. She did. She sang duets with Clara, keeping it light and lively.

Finally, the last of the guests wandered out of the dining room. Jensen came over to thank all the entertainment crew for their help in making it the best captain's dinner yet, despite the difficult circumstances.

"So, what does that mean? Are we all off for the night? No rehearsal?" Ralph asked. "If we go into emergency mode, there obviously won't be a show."

"The captain hasn't declared an emergency yet," Jensen said. "Our fearless leader, Bradley Wilcox, has ordered all entertainment tonight to go on as usual."

Alexi and Clara looked at each other.

"This is ridiculous," Clara murmured to Alexi. "Half our cast has done *Les Miz* before. We're rehearsing ourselves to death."

Apparently, Jensen heard her. "Ms. Avery, do you have a problem with working?"

"I never have a problem with working, Mr. Hardy. I just hope we're not becoming so comfortable with the material that we forget to make it spontaneous and exciting."

Jensen gave her his typical perky grin. "Ah! Yes, well, you'll have to take that up with management."

Johnny approached Alexi and told her, "It's all right. Eckles is assigned to Clara. I'm with you, and Eckles will see that she gets to the piano bar as soon as rehearsal is over."

Much as she loved music, she was tired. In some ways, she wished they were in emergency mode now. In fact, she wished they were down to minimal crew, that all passengers and staff would be ordered to their staterooms, and that Jude and she could weather the storm alone in her tiny cabin. There was so much she wanted to know about him. She reminded herself that she'd been in mourning, that she'd loved Zachary truly and deeply. Yet Jude had come into her life under such strange circumstances and changed it completely.

She would never forget Zach. But maybe the way they'd felt toward each other had allowed her this — the ability to love again.

She couldn't really *love* Jude, could she? So quickly? And where would it all lead? What would happen when they made port?

"Onward!" Clara said, grimacing as she went off with the other *Les Miz* cast members, with Ben Eckles trailing behind them.

Alexi gave her and the others a wave, collected her tote bag and headed for the Algiers Saloon with Johnny.

People were already filling the tables.

For the most part, it seemed that even the passengers had gotten accustomed to the

350

rough seas. They'd learned to walk, sit and chat with the water rolling beneath them.

She greeted everyone, then sat down at the piano bench. As usual, Roger came in, finding a seat close to the piano. And Hank came in, as well, taking a chair at the same table.

Neither of the men had come with their ladies.

Alexi couldn't help wondering what, if anything, that meant.

"We could lose connection with him at any time, so I've taken notes while I was waiting for you."

Tom Vance was First Communications Officer for the ship; he'd been the one to finally make contact with Capitan Suarez in Cozumel.

"We are doing our best to follow through on your request, but you must understand the conditions under which we have been working," Suarez said, once Jude, Jackson, Captain Thorne and David Beach were gathered in the control room. The amount of static made him difficult to hear. "We had a number of emergencies to cope with first."

"I've been in storms," Jackson said. "I understand."

"But we did find her," Suarez said, and he sounded ill as he spoke. "We found her, Maria Sanchez. In San Jose's, a small church not far from the docks. It took some doing. The church was heavily battered and damaged by the storm. She . . . she was beneath a piece of fallen timber and rescue workers did not find her right away because the padre had been injured in the rectory and . . ."

Jude wasn't sure at first if the man's voice had faded away or been overpowered by the static on the line.

Then Suarez spoke again.

"She was laid out, her arms folded over her chest. She looked as though she was asleep, except that her throat had been slit. And there was a medallion on her chest, just as you said there might be. It has been identified for us as representing St. Lawrence."

Jude nodded. "Patron saint of chefs," he murmured.

"Yes." Suarez went on. "I don't know how or when she was taken. She returned home after the explosion. You may recall that I spoke with her. The morgue is overcrowded right now, but our medical examiner is working on her remains. We don't know if she was killed soon after the explosion or if the ship had already left the dock. I'm sorry. It is impossible for me to tell whether your Archangel remains in Mexico or has created a copycat killer here. Or perhaps he has sailed with you and is on the *Destiny* now. I did not really believe you gentlemen when you claimed that the killer would be in Cozumel. It is a mistake I will not forget for the rest of my days. Maria was . . . she was so important to us. She was a shining light . . ."

Jude remembered the woman he had met so briefly; he remembered the way she'd looked at him, doubting that this killer would have come on a cruise ship from America — and that he could have been after her. He understood how Capitan Suarez felt about this tragic loss. "Capitan Suarez," Jude said, "we cannot tell you how very sorry we are."

"As Americans, we can't convey our apologies enough," Jackson added.

"No country is responsible," Suarez said. "We do not blame the government or the police forces of our northern neighbor. You made every effort. I blame myself. I should have gone to her house and I should have stayed there until the ship sailed." He paused briefly, and Jude could hear the crackling on the line. "We are picking up the pieces now. You can imagine the damage from the storm. We lost several people, some because they were poor, some because they did not heed the warnings. We are all scurrying here, trying to find others who may have survived and need rescuing, but this . . . Do you believe that this man has left with you? Is there any reason to suspect that a copycat might exist? That such a killer may still be here, in Mexico?"

"We have no guarantees, Capitan," Jude said. "But it is my sincere belief that there is just one killer — and that he's now back on the *Destiny.*"

The radio suddenly went dead.

Jude felt a deep anger as the sense of loss swept through him. He turned to Captain Thorne. "Sir, you didn't want to believe us. There *is* a killer on this ship. He has now killed in Mexico. It's time to warn the passengers."

"I can't have a panic!" Thorne responded.

"We're in the middle of a major storm, one I know you will navigate to the best of your ability — but panic? You're afraid of warning your female passengers when it's now evident that a killer is almost certainly aboard?" Jackson set a hand on Jude's shoulder.

"Captain, you do need to communicate

the truth to your passengers and staff," Jude said.

"The government does not own the *Destiny*!" Thorne protested. "Have you ever seen panic on a cruise ship? I have, and it's not pretty. It results in multiple injuries — and sometimes death."

"Captain Thorne," Jude said, carefully keeping his temper under control and his voice level. "You *have* to tell people what's happened. You have to warn the women on this ship not to go off with men they don't know and not to be alone on this vessel. You have your security staff in place. You've lost one, probably to this killer. We can only assume he was thrown overboard. If you don't do something now, your actions will be the height of irresponsibility, and any more deaths on this ship will be on your head."

"Damn it, Captain Thorne!" David Beach suddenly exploded. "Will you listen to them? I've lost one of my men and now we know that a Mexican woman is dead. I'm good at my job — damned good! But it's impossible for us to watch every person on this ship *and* to keep an eye on the suspects, especially with this storm. For the love of God, listen to them!"

Thorne inhaled on a long breath and then

exhaled. "If there's a panic when I make this announcement, it's on you," he said, staring at Jude and then Jackson.

"Really? Then let me do the speaking," Jude said.

"Of course not! That's preposterous!" the captain thundered.

"Not at all," Jude told him. "You want to avoid a panic, so I'll do the talking. You see, your very fear of a panic might cause one. Since I don't intend to create a panic — and I do intend to make sure people are extremely careful, I'll manage the task better than you will."

"Hank!" Alexi said, her fingers idle over the keys. She figured she might as well speak to Hank and to Roger as she normally did. "Where is that lovely young lady you've been seeing?"

"Asleep!" he replied, grinning. "But you know me. I can't stay away from the piano bar."

"That's because you have a great singing voice, my friend," Alexi said. "So, what are you in the mood for tonight? Broadway, classics, blues?"

Minnie and Blake lounged against the piano, watching the crowd.

"His voice isn't *that* good," Minnie said.

"And if he's so in love with that girl, why is he leaving her by herself? Blake would never leave me," she added, giving Blake a smile and an adoring look.

"Never," Blake agreed passionately.

"Alexi," Minnie wheedled, "I realize they're going to do whatever they do these days, but throw in some Billie Holiday for me, please?"

Alexi ignored her ghosts and handed the mic to Hank Osprey. "Whatever your pleasure, Mr. Osprey."

" 'Smoke Gets in Your Eyes'!" Hank suggested.

Despite Minnie's comment on Hank's voice, Alexi thought he did a nice job with the number. "Thank you, thank you!" she said, leading the applause that followed. "What a smooth voice," she commented. She turned quickly to Roger next. "Another guys' night out, huh? Where's the lovely Lorna?"

"Sleeping, too," Roger said, taking the mic. "She sends you her best, by the way."

"Thank you, sir. Now what will you be doing for us this evening? Folks, another brilliant man who ruled the business world for years, all the while hiding a fantastic tenor voice!" she said, calling for applause as Roger stood to sing, smiling and pleased.

Maybe he's always wanted to do nothing but sing!

He graced them with a Tom Petty number, done very well. But it was while Roger was singing that Alexi saw the ghost of Byron Grant standing just near the tables at the far end of the Algiers Saloon. At first, she thought he wanted to talk to her, but then she realized that he wasn't watching her; he was studying the men who surrounded the piano bar.

She found herself wishing the night would end.

Thankfully, within the next ten minutes, Clara arrived, along with other members of the *Les Miz* cast. They began singing, and despite the pitch and roll of the *Destiny,* it seemed that everyone in the piano bar was having a good time.

Then the little bell sounded, announcing that someone was going to come on the PA system.

Alexi stopped playing; everyone waited. She expected the captain to speak.

But the voice that came over on the loudspeaker wasn't the captain's; it was Jude's.

"Good evening, everyone. This is Jude McCoy for Celtic American Cruise Lines. It's time for everyone except essential personnel to return to their cabins and remain there. This is a safety measure. And while we feel that we have some of the best security officers on the face of the earth, we also believe it's critical that we report all news regarding our ports of call. Because of our strong belief in communication, we feel we need to advise you that a murder took place in Cozumel at the time our ship was docked there. Authorities believe it might be connected to the explosion at Señora Maria's restaurant. Sadly, the victim was the owner, Señora Maria. While we don't want to cause our passengers undue stress, we do want everyone to be on the alert, which is something most of us don't think about on a beautiful vacation. Let's face it, the weather's put a damper on this cruise to begin with — no pun intended. Cozumel is struggling to deal with the damage caused by Dinah, so the police haven't been able to investigate this incident, and the Mexican authorities are warning all ships that were in port on the day of the murder. Therefore, we're going to ask all our female passengers in particular — especially those traveling on their own — to be careful. We have security officers available on every deck, watching doorways. But if you're walking to your cabin alone and would like an escort, don't hesitate to ask. Now, back to the storm . . . As you all know, Dinah has been completely unpredictable. She moved south, preventing us from moving north. She's just taken a southward turn. We're still ahead of her, and tomorrow, we'll make an announcement about the safety of venturing out of your cabins. You're sailing with one of the most capable and experienced captains anywhere, and I have no doubt that all will be well. Still, any security measures we take are for your safety. Thank you. I know it's a bit early, but we're asking all our passengers to call it a night."

Alexi sat at the piano, stunned.

Clara looked at her and shivered. "We were *there,*" she whispered. "We were at Señora Maria's restaurant."

Alexi nodded. She was surprised that Jude hadn't told her about the murder.

But then she realized he hadn't known — until recently. That was why he'd been called away.

"Okay, folks! Last call. Feel free to take your drinks to your rooms," the bartender said.

Voices rose as everyone began to discuss the announcement; some people were obviously afraid.

Some were annoyed.

"Well, what do you think of that?" Roger wondered aloud, looking at Alexi and Clara where they sat at the piano.

Alexi didn't want to answer. She smiled at Roger and spoke into the mic. "Well, you heard the powers that be, people. Thank you so much, as always, for being with me. And whether I like it or not, I'm afraid I'm not considered essential crew."

There were a few good-natured protests, and she smiled.

She went into the song "Closing Time," and everyone joined in.

By the time she'd finished, most of the passengers had gotten their last drinks.

"Hope to see you all tomorrow!" Hank said, waving good-night.

"Ladies and gentlemen, shall we?" She turned in surprise. Johnny was there — to see the crew members down to their cabins.

Especially her and Clara.

Alexi covered the piano, and her group gathered together to head down the stairs.

"We were at the restaurant. I'm the one who said we should go there," Ralph said, shaking his head. "I never met Señora Maria, but . . . how terrible."

"So," Simon said, "someone was out to get the poor woman. That must be why there was that explosion."

"They tried to blow her up!" Larry shuddered. "Scary! Hey, do you think they're making us go to our cabins because of the storm — or because that woman was murdered?"

Clara shrugged. "I just hope we get tomorrow off."

"Oh, I doubt we'll be off," Ralph said. "They can't keep people in their cabins all day. Everyone has to eat."

Simon laughed. "Maybe they'll have us delivering food."

"Ouch! So much for fame and fortune," Ralph murmured.

"Do you know what's going on?" Larry asked Alexi. "I mean, you're McCoy's . . . *liaison*, right?"

Alexi let his tone — and the word *liaison* — go without comment. Apparently, they still believed Jude was with the cruise lines. And that she was sleeping with a bigwig.

Well, she *was* sleeping with him.

"I don't know," she said. "I really don't. I wish I did."

"Should we all hang together?" Simon asked.

"Oh, guys, I'm exhausted!" Clara said. "I'm going to lock myself in and sleep — and worry about the storm and everything else tomorrow morning."

"And I'm betting Alexi will have company at some point," Simon put in.

"I have a bottle of single malt scotch and I'm willing to share," Ralph offered. "The three of us can whine about our careers for a while."

"Everyone inside," said Johnny, who'd been following them.

"You got somewhere to go, Johnny?" Ralph asked.

"Oh, no, sir, I'll be here all night."

Clara glanced at Alexi and said softly, "I'll be in my cabin. Sleeping, I hope."

Alexi knew that Clara would wait until she and Jude knocked on her door in the morning before she left her cabin again.

"Well, then, good night, all," Alexi said, and escaped into her cabin.

She waited. She showered. She paced.

At last, she went to bed. She was tired, so tired that even with her mind flying, she eventually drifted off.

Then Jude knocked on the door and called her name. When she let him in, he pulled her into his arms and just held her.

She knew he was tired and tense and worried. He opened his mouth to talk and then shook his head. "I would've told you," he said. "Suarez finally managed to reach us.

He's the Mexican police captain in Cozumel."

"I heard," she said. She swallowed painfully. "That means the killer really is on the ship, doesn't it? The Archangel is on our ship."

"I'm convinced he's one of our four suspects. We have officers on them constantly, but . . . well, the missing security guard is still missing."

"You're exhausted. You have to get some rest," she insisted.

He nodded, stripping down to his briefs. She crawled into her bed, and he crawled in beside her. He was distracted, but it seemed that he needed to hold her.

They just lay together. She wasn't sure if he drifted off or if they both did. She wasn't sure if he touched her and instigated their lovemaking, or if she'd touched him first.

There were moments of bliss. As they held each other, Alexi felt she'd found an island of strength in a tempestuous sea.

And she never wanted to leave.

14

While most communication was down, the cabin-to-cabin phone service was working fine.

Jude woke very early to the ringing of Alexi's cabin phone. She was still asleep so he grabbed it quickly. "Hello?"

It was Jackson. "Security's in place," he said, "and the captain's staying ahead of the storm. He's moving north now, around the edge of Dinah. If we're lucky, by the end of today we'll be heading for port, either in the central Gulf or along the Florida coast. He's allowing passengers access to shops and restaurants during the day. All ship-run activities will be in the Egyptian Room, dinner served as usual — but there'll be a ten o'clock curfew this evening. I'm in our office, reviewing the information we have, working on the Mexican angle. The explosion, which I'm now positive was planned and somehow executed by the Archangel, created a lot of confusion. And of course that meant we lost visual contact with the suspects."

"Yeah," Jude said. "And if we had access to computers or even some way of getting in touch with the home office, we'd have a better handle on who could have rigged the kitchen to explode like that."

"In such a way that the experts couldn't ascertain with any assurance whether it was accidental or deliberate," Jackson added. "At any rate, David Beach has just rotated his people. They're working twelve-hour shifts until we get to port. The best solution for the day, I believe, is probably to arrange for Clara and Alexi to get involved in whatever activities are going on in the Egyptian Room. That'll put them in a public place, with lots of protection — and witnesses — around. If you can see to that and then join me here, we can go over what we do know and try to figure out who might've been able to rig the explosion and then get to Maria Sanchez, kill her and deposit her body in the church before we left port."

"I'll make the arrangements with Clara and Alexi. I'll join you after that," Jude told him.

Alexi was stirring, but Jude knew he had to get up, even though he didn't want to.

Alexi looked like an artist's dream, sheet pulled down below the base of her spine, the curve of her body elegant, the sweep of her hair vivid against the white of the sheets.

He climbed out of bed. "I'm going to shower, then get to work," he said briskly.

When he emerged, she was in a terry-cloth robe, sitting at her little desk. She glanced up at him, her expression bleak.

"It seems to me that any of our current suspects could've rigged something in the kitchen — and then gotten away with the murder of Maria Sanchez. Every one of them — Roger, Hank, Jensen and Simon — might've had the opportunity. Neither the ship's security nor the Mexican police believed you and Jackson. *No one* in authority believed the killer could be on this ship until Maria Sanchez turned up dead in that Mexican church," she said. "If only . . ."

"If only?" Jude echoed.

"If only we knew what the medallions meant to the killer."

He leaned down to kiss her neck. "Go shower," he said huskily. "I'm escorting you and Clara to the Egyptian Room."

He dressed as he waited for Alexi.

They were in a battle with time; they had to reach port with Alexi, Clara and every other entertainer safe. All the women on board were in danger. And if they didn't determine who the killer was by the time they docked, he might strike again elsewhere.

At least once they were on land, the FBI and local authorities would have the personnel to watch each of their suspects, follow in their footsteps, research their comings and goings.

But they'd known who their suspects were from the start of the voyage. They'd known when they were in Mexico. And yet the killer had still managed to elude them and rig the explosion. Which had given him the opportunity to kill Maria . . .

When Alexi had emerged and dressed, she called Clara to tell her they were on the way to pick her up.

Jude could hear Clara's response. "More bingo!" she said loudly and with feigned enthusiasm.

"People love bingo," Alexi reminded her.

"I wish I was one of those people," Clara muttered.

As Alexi hung up, there was a knock at her door. Jude looked out and saw Jensen Hardy.

He opened the door, and it was immediately clear that Jensen hadn't expected him there, judging by the way the man scowled at him.

"Morning," Jude said cheerfully.

"Good morning," Jensen said, just as cheerfully. He thrust a paper at Jude. "Notices for day duty to the entertainment crew. Alexi has the Egyptian Room again."

"Yes, I know," Jude said pleasantly.

"Of course you do." Jensen smiled grimly. "Bingo."

"Bingo," Jude agreed. He took the paper and closed the door.

"You really don't like him, do you?" Alexi asked.

"He's fake. His smile is fake," Jude said.

Alexi shrugged. "Well, he has to have that enthusiasm going all the time. No human can be that constantly happy."

"Ah, yes, but have you seen the way he looks at me? His eyes become daggers!"

"Hmm. Maybe he doesn't like you."

Jude laughed. "Hmm. You think?"

She grinned, but then her expression grew somber. "That doesn't make him a murderer, though," she said. "I can't really see it."

"Which of these four men do you see as a murderer?" he asked her. "Simon, Mr. Song and Dance? Hank, the awkward wizard, just lookin' for love? Roger Antrim, married

369

father and grandfather?"

"No, I don't see how it could be any of them."

"Serial killer Ted Bundy worked at a help line," Jude told her. "If he'd looked like some kind of monster, people might have suspected him sooner. That's just it. We never want to accept that the boy next door could actually be a killer."

Alexi nodded. "I have a hard time believing *any* of these men could be monsters — but I know that one of them must be. And . . ." She paused for a moment.

Jude waited, curious.

"And I want to stay alive!"

So did he, Jude thought. He recalled the pain he'd felt when they'd lost Lily. Nothing could have been worse. Yet, even then, he had never contemplated suicide.

Now he knew, more than he ever had before — he didn't want to survive just to catch the bad guys.

He wanted to *live*. Maybe now, for the first time in years, he could really live.

"We're going to get through this," he told her.

"Of course we are."

She kissed him. A quick kiss.

He smiled, thinking that neither of them dared to go any further. Out in the hallway,

Jude saw another of Beach's men dutifully watching over his section of the ship. As Alexi tapped on Clara's door, Ralph and Larry stepped out of Ralph's cabin.

"Egyptian Room?" Ralph asked.

"That's where we're heading," Jude replied.

Simon left his cabin. "Egyptian Room?" he, too, asked.

"On our way," Alexi murmured.

"Bingo, yay!" Clara said.

"Well, if we could win the big bucks," Simon said, "it might be fun. But since all we do is look at the cards . . ."

"Cheer up. Maybe there'll be another wet T-shirt contest," Alexi told him.

Simon grinned. "A bunch of cute girls squirting me with water? Not so bad."

He started singing "Master of the House" from *Les Miz* as he led them down the hall.

Alexi found it difficult to maintain a smile and an air of casual pleasure while working that day.

She couldn't help being acutely aware that every man on the suspect list was in the Egyptian Room.

Hank was there with Ginny, the two of them sitting at the bar. While Hank might not want the girl of his obsessions and dreams involved in a wet T-shirt contest, he wasn't at all averse to bingo. In fact, they had dozens of cards between them.

Roger was there with his wife — and with Flora Winters, the woman whose husband had owned a collectibles business. Alexi made a point of going over to chat. Flora was happy to meet her; she'd never been to the piano bar on the ship, she said, but since Roger and Lorna thought it was so wonderful, she'd decided to come by.

Flora seemed very nice, and she and Lorna seemed to get along well, Alexi observed after she'd talked with them. The two women engaged in conversation and laughter, some of it — or so it appeared — at the expense of Roger, who just smiled and shrugged.

Happy. Domestic. Friendly.

Alexi looked around the room whenever she could, trying to keep an eye on everyone.

It seemed ridiculous that a killer, the Archangel, could be among them.

They were all so . . . normal.

Simon appeared to be having fun.

Jensen was a little beleaguered, possibly because Bradley was in the room as they began their storm-swept day, arms crossed over his chest as he watched.

Alexi didn't care that Bradley was there. She realized she didn't care about his opinion of her work that day. She was a good employee, and if he didn't appreciate her, well . . .

Well, *what* she wasn't sure. But she knew this cruise had changed her.

She didn't need to escape anymore. Whatever happened in the future, she prayed Jude would be part of it.

She didn't believe she was just a diversion to him — or just someone he needed to keep safe.

But everything, even having a future, seemed to hinge on these last few days on the ship.

The bingo games went on. She and the others ran around, checking cards, helping out, improvising interactions with the guests.

After bingo Jensen announced a break before the trivia games.

First prize for trivia would be from Artiste, the ship's jewelry store.

Alexi considered their break a great opportunity to have a conversation with Hank Osprey and Ginny.

There was no empty bar stool near the two of them so she pretended she needed a glass of water and slipped by them to ask the bartender to hand her a glass.

She turned to them and shook her head sadly. "All those cards — and no bingo!" Hank laughed. "We didn't care. The challenge was keeping track of all the cards."

"Actually," Ginny said, "I think we did have bingo once. There were so many cards, we must've missed it."

"Ah, well. Next up is the game I'd like to be on."

"Ah, yes, jewels! The way to a woman's heart, right?" Hank teased.

"The main prize is a diamond necklace," Alexi said. "Although — and you may not believe this — I prefer funky jewelry to diamonds. I like unusual designs. Or things that have some meaning. I inherited a pewter coat of arms from my mom's family. It's Italian. And an old cross that meant a great deal to my grandmother. Oh, and some weird dragon pieces I bought at a Ren faire."

"I know what you mean!" Ginny said. "I have some spider stuff a lot of people might think of as nothing but Halloween costume attire, and yet I love it."

Hank had risen, offering Alexi his seat. She shook her head. "Thanks, but I have to be back on the floor in a second. What do you think about jewelry? If you were trying to impress a woman, I mean. Are diamonds the way to go or would you opt for something else?"

Hank was thoughtful. "I'd consider the woman. I'd try to know her — and know exactly what kind of jewelry she'd like. Now, Ginny —"

"Trivia!" Jensen Hardy boomed over the microphone, interrupting whatever Hank had been about to say. "If my lovely singing and dancing assistants will please join me down here?"

Alexi set her glass on the bar and hurried down to the stage.

So much for her attempt at subtle interrogation.

But as she walked across the room, she saw that the ghost of Byron Grant was in the room, as well, leaning against the far wall.

Just watching.

He seemed confused, and Alexi quickly realized why.

Simon and Hank remained in the room, ready to play whatever game Jensen announced.

But Roger was on his way out, accompanied by his wife — and Flora Winters.

"There's nothing like working with charts,"

Jackson was saying. "Physical charts, that is."

"Actually," Jude told him, "there'd be nothing like it — if we had some more information to put on our charts."

They'd written their list of suspects on one side of an eraser board.

The list of medallions and the known dead was on the other side.

Jude stared at the two, thinking of the conversations he'd had with the men on the list. Something, some idea, was forming in his mind. Something to do with the medallions. As if reading his mind, Jackson said, "The medallions are the key. We know which saints they represent, and we know that they were made prewar in a small church in Italy."

"I'm not sure that where they were made really matters. What they mean to the murderer is what's important," Jude responded. "Now, we know that Flora Winters's husband sold a set of the medallions but that, too, could mean nothing."

"It would be a big help to have our communications up and running," Jackson murmured. "Angela always works like this — everything on a chart. But usually, our researchers are available to answer any questions that might arise from looking at the lists!"

"If those medallions were bought at auction or from an antiquities dealer like Flora's husband, that would indicate someone with money," Jude said. "Hank Osprey or Roger Antrim, in other words."

"But if the buyer of the medallions sold by Sam Winters turns out to be John Smith or David Jones or someone entirely unrelated, the Archangel might have inherited his — or even found them at a flea market," Jackson said. "Or, who knows, stolen them . . ."

"But what do they *mean* to the killer? Are they just a way to taunt the police, or do they mean something personal to him? He obviously chose his victims, one for each of the medallions. He had to know who they were. He had to know about their lives and their work."

"As far as we can tell, the victims had never met one another. We couldn't find anything in common among them. The only connection was through the medallions. Each woman who was killed had a profession that correlated with the medallion left on her body," Jackson said.

"Maybe it has to do with the fact that they were professional women," Jude suggested.

"Maybe this guy has something against working women."

"That's possible. Could be he was spurned at some time in his life by a professional woman — and the medallions somehow emphasized the fact that, in his mind, women shouldn't be working," Jackson said.

"Because — in his mind — they should be giving their attention to the men in their lives?"

"One would think that would leave our Roger Antrim out of the equation, since he's been married to the same woman for almost thirty years," Jackson mused.

"You've had profilers in Quantico on this. Remind me what you've got from them so far."

"He's between the ages of twenty-five and thirty-five, male, white, heterosexual. They believe the killer is either wealthy or someone with reason to travel frequently. This pretty much fits all our suspects, except for Roger, of course, who's a little older than the other men."

Jude didn't get a chance to respond because there was a tap at the door, and David Beach poked his head in. "Agents, the Reverend Mike has asked to see you, down in the chapel."

Jude and Jackson looked at each other and

quickly rose. Beach nodded solemnly as they thanked him. He was ready to help them now, in whatever way they might require. Sad, Jude thought, that it had taken the death of Maria Sanchez to make everyone so willing to cooperate fully.

"You coming with us?" Jude asked him.

"I'm checking in with my staff regularly. That's a lot of people," Beach said. "But . . ."

His words trailed off. They knew he was thinking about Nathan Freeman.

They didn't know for a fact that he was dead; his body hadn't appeared anywhere.

But none of them expected to find his body. It was somewhere in the vastness of the sea.

The Reverend Mike was sitting in one of the rows of cushioned chairs in front of the altar. He jumped to his feet when they entered.

"Thanks for coming. I don't like to be away from the chapel right now. People are coming in here every few hours. They're praying that we make it through the storm," he told them. "And praying that they stay safe . . ."

"Only natural," Jackson said. "But you wanted to see us? Has something happened?"

"Someone was in here. And I'm not sure how that person got in. I definitely didn't leave the door unlocked last night and security officers have been patrolling the ship. But someone *was* in here. Someone looking through the Bibles."

"How can you be sure?" Jude asked.

"It might mean nothing, but one Bible was open to what I thought was an unusual reference for someone to be seeking out these days. It referred to the role of women. Titus 2:5. 'To be self-controlled, pure, working at home, kind, submissive to their own husbands, that the word of God may not be reviled.' "

Jude and Jackson exchanged glances. " 'Submissive,' " Jackson said.

" 'Working at home,' " Jude quoted.

"Reverend, you have no idea who was here?" Jackson asked. "Based on any previous conversations or anyone you might have seen hanging around?"

"Nothing that I recall. I must've been in my office or perhaps sleeping when this person got in. I have no idea who, how or when. All I can tell you is that the Bibles were moved. And that, as I said, the King James Bible was open to the page I just told you about. I thought you should know. Especially because of what happened the day we left NOLA — and in Cozumel." He studied Jackson and Jude. "And you're not with the Celtic American line, are you? You're investigators of some kind. There's a reason you were on this ship when we left New Orleans. That's obvious."

"Yes," Jackson said. "You're right. We're FBI."

"Figures." Mike nodded. "This guy, whoever he is, this so-called Archangel — he's down on women. Hates women. He attacks successful, professional women. And he was in my chapel last night. Gentlemen, I will not be leaving my chapel again. If he comes back, I will know it."

"Reverend," Jude said urgently. "If he comes back, remember he's an adept killer. Don't confront him yourself. He's killed a man, as well."

"That young man was unsuspecting. I intend to be ready for him," the Reverend Mike said.

"If he comes —" Jackson began.

"There's an alarm button on the wall there, below the painting," the Reverend Mike interrupted him. "Trust me, I will hit that alarm."

"I believe my colleague was about to ask that you not try to take him down yourself," Jude said. "We're not doubting your capabilities. It's that we're just closing in on this killer and we know he's dangerous. And chances are you won't recognize him as the killer when you see him."

"If I suspect anything, like I said, I'll hit that alarm," the Reverend Mike vowed. "Now, you have suspects on this ship. So, I'd appreciate knowing who they are."

"Reverend, this is an ongoing investigation," Jackson said.

"And you, sir, should remember that I answer to a higher authority than the law. What you tell me will stay with me. I swear I will keep your information to myself."

Jackson nodded thoughtfully. "Then I'll trust you. There are four men we're looking at. Two are employees of the cruise line, and two are passengers. A new man in the entertainment department, Simon Green. The cruise director, Jensen Hardy. And passengers Roger Antrim and Hank Osprey."

"Roger Antrim?" Mike sounded shocked. "That can't be."

"Why?" Jude asked sharply.

"Well, he and his wife are on this ship quite frequently. Nice man. Always courteous, which you might not expect, seeing what a powerhouse he was in business. And his wife! She's lovely."

"Yes," Jude murmured.

382

"And Jensen! He's a ball of fire. People love him."

Not all people, Jude thought. But he knew he couldn't let his personal feelings influence his search for a killer.

Still, he couldn't forget the way Jensen had looked at him when he'd realized that Alexi hadn't been alone — that she'd been with Jude.

"Hank Osprey," Mike went on. "I don't really know him. And I've never met Simon Green."

"I have pictures on my phone. It's worthless for communication right now, but I can show you some shots of these men," Jackson said, and proceeded to do so. "If you see any of them here, let us know immediately."

"Immediately," Mike echoed. "And your list is safe with me." He smiled. "I swear to God. And coming from me, that's a real vow."

Jude and Jackson left the chapel and strode down the Promenade Deck. Some people were out and about; the shops were open, but doing little business. A few people were in the cafés.

"I'd give my eyeteeth to speak with Angela," Jackson muttered.

"You think this supports our theory?" Jude asked.

Jackson glanced over at him. "Either that, or the killer wants us to pursue that angle. I do actually think we're on the right track. This killer is organized. Careful. He stalks his victims and is familiar with their routines, their habits. He knows how to hide their bodies — until he's ready to display them. The only time he's ever made a mistake was when Byron Grant returned home too quickly."

"And even then, he killed Byron. Dumped his body and displayed Elizabeth's."

Jackson nodded.

"Do you think the killer might have known his victims personally? That some or all of them were women who snubbed him? Perhaps they even used their work as a way to turn him down."

"It's possible. The evidence shows that killers like this often prey on women who remind them of someone they want to hurt. Some kill their mothers over and over again — and some repeatedly kill the girl who got away."

"Yeah, I know, but that doesn't really narrow anything down for us," Jude said. "Every one of these suspects has been to Cozumel before. And every one of them had opportunity in the cities where the killings took place."

"Roger, though," Jackson murmured. "He's been in the news quite a bit over the last few years. If he'd been spotted in the vicinity of any of these murders, there's a good chance he would've been identified."

"It's interesting," Jude added, "that he's always portrayed as a family man in the media." He paused. "Nevertheless, his wife suspected him of having an affair — with Flora Winters. But of course, it turns out that Flora's someone he met with for business reasons." He sighed. "Yeah, we could really use some communication with the mainland right about now. For one thing, we'd find out who bought those medallions from her husband."

"It won't be long," Jackson said. "By tomorrow we'll reach port. At least there, we'll have agents and internet access again. We'll get this guy, whether it's on the ship or on shore. He must realize that."

Jude felt suddenly chilled. "He must realize that," he repeated slowly.

"And yet the Archangel seems to believe he's invincible."

"I hope so," Jude said. "Because he has two medallions left. And he's probably growing impatient, maybe desperate. He might start taking too many chances."

"Which might help us catch him — but could also make him all the more dangerous," Jackson agreed. "Maybe we should see how the day is going in the Egyptian Room."

Musical chairs.

Alexi could tell that even Jensen was running out of things to do.

But she had to hand it to him; the passengers did seem to be having fun.

The game was actually enhanced by the movement of the ship, since the players had to try harder to reach their marks. There was a lot of laughter and good-natured hysteria.

It didn't hurt that the bar had done a booming business.

Hank wasn't playing musical chairs. He and Ginny had left after Jensen had introduced a game of Twister.

There'd been too many people touching too many people, she was certain, for Hank to want his Ginny playing such a game.

She was relieved to see Jude and Jackson walk into the room and saunter over to the bar to watch the activity. She was sure that they'd both noticed exactly who was — and wasn't — in the room.

"And . . . sit!" Jensen said.

People scrambled for chairs.

Jensen swung around to see who was out. Before he could say anything else, the bell of the PA system sounded. Captain Thorne's voice came on over the speaker.

"Good evening, ladies and gentlemen!" he boomed. "I'm happy to announce that we're drawing ahead of the storm. Tonight, however, we're going to be passing through rough waters. We won't be returning to New Orleans. Rather, we'll round the tip of Florida and reach the Port of Miami. Now, no one should worry about that. The Celtic American will arrange to fly you back to New Orleans as soon as we're assured you won't be facing evacuation lines out of the city. They still aren't sure. Dinah may head for Cuba or Florida, but we'll be getting to Miami in time to see that you're all safe. By early tomorrow evening, we'll have you docked. Now, of course, we'll try to work our Celtic American magic to make this up to you — even if the storm is an act of God. As for this evening, folks, we're going to have one dinner sitting in the main dining room. That will be at seven o'clock. We'll let you enjoy the pursuits of your choice, including the casino, until ten. At that time, we'll ask everyone to return to their cabins.

The crew will be very busy through this last patch of rough sailing. As I said, we want all of you safe. We'll be closing our restaurants, cafés, bars and other venues at ten, to ensure our staff's safety, too. Thank you all, and see you at dinner!"

The PA system went silent.

"Well!" Jensen said. "I proclaim everyone still by the chairs a winner! Yes, even you, Ms. Starbridge, although you did lose on that last go-round. My gorgeous assistants — including you, Simon! — will be handing out the bottles of champagne you've just won. I'll let you get back to your cabins in case you want to dress for dinner, and if you don't . . . well, the bars are open from now until ten."

Alexi distributed champagne as quickly as she could.

She kept a smile on her face, even though she couldn't wait to be out of the Egyptian Room. She didn't need Jensen bounding over to tell her cheerfully that she'd be playing through dinner again, and that she'd still have to spend the hour from nine to ten in the piano bar.

At last, the champagne had been handed out — and Jensen thanked them all for their aid and assistance in keeping the passenger fun *rolling,* right along with the ship.

A few of his people were just returning from the task of circulating out the ship's instructional sheets — just in case anyone had somehow missed the PA announcement, heard all over the ship — and they laughed at the feeble joke.

The entertainers who'd been brought in barely managed a smile.

After that they were free. Simon nudged Alexi and shook his head. "You're a trouper. They're going to have you playing piano for hours again. After all the fun and games that kept things *rolling* along today."

"It's not exactly heavy labor," she said. "I'd rather be off tonight, but I can play if I have to. I was looking forward to seeing *Les Miz* on our final night."

"All that rehearsal and no show." Simon groaned. "Hopefully, they'll keep the cast together and open the show on another voyage."

"It'll depend on how many of the cast are on the same contracts with Celtic American," Alexi told him. "People sign up for different lengths of time with the company. Anyway, who knows? We could wake up tomorrow to beautiful clear blue skies. I'm going to take advantage of my two free hours, Simon. You coming back to your cabin? I think a bunch of us are heading down together."

"Yeah, of course."

They walked across the room to join the agents, as well as Clara, Ralph and Larry.

"Alexi!" Jensen called, stopping her. She turned around as he trotted toward her.

"You understood all that, right?" he asked her. "You play through dinner. Then you'll open the piano bar, but only for an hour. At some point I may need everyone again tomorrow. If we're far enough ahead of the storm by morning, we'll entertain until we make dock."

"Yes, I understand, Jensen."

He gave her a strange smile. "It's almost at an end, Alexi. Almost at an end."

He kept looking at her, waiting for her reply. Something about the way he smiled seemed to create a shiver in her blood.

"Yes, thanks, Jensen," she said, and hurried on past him.

She wanted to throw herself in Jude's arms; at that moment she didn't care about appropriate behavior — or about her own job.

She refrained, though. Jude was an FBI agent, so *his* could be at stake if she did something as public and as obvious as that.

Somehow, she forced herself to behave with decorum as she approached the group.

"Everything okay?" Jude asked.

"Other than a killer being on board and a raging storm?" she returned softly. "Just great."

When he frowned, she said, "Really. I'm okay. Except for the obvious, everything's fine."

"Yeah, wonderful," Clara muttered, grimacing. "I love this impromptu business. I'm glad you've got a hell of a repertoire, Alexi. We've had so many of these events, I don't even remember if I know any more songs."

"Of course you do!" Ralph insisted. "Just on Celtic American cruises, you've done *Phantom, Chicago, Chitty Chitty Bang Bang* and *Rent.* We are *actors*!" he declared with a dramatic sweep of his arms. "The show must go on!"

"Oh, rot," Larry said, passing by him. "The show isn't going on. We'll perform whatever silly songs, chorus numbers and dance routines we can manage. And tomorrow, thank God, we'll be off this floating pile of sticks. I, for one, am grateful."

When he walked ahead, Ralph glanced at the others worriedly, then chased after him. It didn't take long to catch up. They were both waiting for the elevator as the rest of the group arrived. Alexi lowered her head and smiled.

"Two hours," Simon grumbled. "Two hours until whatever we're doing — and after that I can go to bed and sleep until we reach port! Ladies and gentlemen, it's been fun, but forgive me if I can't wait until it's over."

"Forgiven," Clara assured him. "I think we're all feeling that way."

"Not Jensen. He's thriving on being in charge, enjoying his time in the spotlight," Alexi said.

The elevator finally came and they all crowded in; everyone was silent as they rode down.

Alexi thought there was a heightened aura of tension around them.

Simon was still a suspect.

Stepping off the elevator, Alexi saw one of the security officers. He nodded at Jackson and Jude, and smiled at the others. He was in a good location, Alexi thought. From where he stood near the bank of elevators he could look down the length of the hallway.

All seemed well.

Together the group walked to each of their cabins.

Simon waved as he went into his and closed his door. Then Ralph and Larry marched arm in arm into Larry's cabin, heedless of who was around them.

"You'll come for me later?" Clara asked when they reached her door.

"Yes," Jude replied. "Don't worry."

When she'd entered her cabin, Jackson said goodbye to Alexi and Jude and headed into his own.

Alexi opened her door. She was afraid she'd act like a nervous schoolgirl, desperate to be in his arms.

He pulled her to him and held her close. Then he drew away.

"Have any of the men on our list ever wanted to date you?" he asked.

"Not Roger Antrim, although he's never been anything but nice," she said. "The others? Not really. I just met Simon on this cruise. He hasn't asked me out. Jensen's been flirtatious and he seems harmless, but . . ." She paused. "In some ways, he's kind of —"

"Kind of what?" Jude pressed.

"Creepy."

Jude nodded. "And Hank?"

"Oh, he's always a gentleman. I used to feel sorry for him. There's nothing wrong with Hank. He — Well, I'm happy he seems to like Ginny so much. I hope she didn't get involved with him just for his money, because I think he really cares about her. Why? What's happened? No one else is missing, right?"

"No, no, but the Reverend Mike called us down to the chapel. Someone had been there — moving the Bibles around and leaving one of them, the King James Version, open at a certain page. A certain verse. One that talks about how women should serve their husbands and work in their homes."

"The . . . Archangel did that?"

"We don't know for sure. We're very concerned about it, though. Here's the thing. It's possible that the killer knew his victims. If he moved from port to port on business or leisure, he could have met them. They *might* have been women who turned him down. And, instead of being cruel or blunt, we think they might've used their busy work schedules as an excuse. A way to tell him politely that they weren't interested. Even if he hadn't met his victims, he stalked them and knew who they were. He was certainly familiar with their patterns. We're also considering the possibility that they were stand-ins for a certain woman who did turn him down at some point in his life," Jude explained.

"I wonder . . . We need to find Byron Grant. Maybe he can tell you more. Fill in some details."

"Byron Grant was in love with his fiancée, Elizabeth, and it sounded as if she was deeply committed to him, too. Unlikely that she would've been seeing anyone else."

"Yes," Alexi said, "but what if someone had asked her out — when she was at work, when she was having lunch, picking up her dry cleaning, whatever! She would've told Byron."

"Even if we go with your premise, I doubt Byron would have seen the guy. And if he recognized someone on the ship, wouldn't he have pointed that someone out to us?"

"Yes. But what if he and Elizabeth were talking and she casually said that he should appreciate her, that she'd had another offer? You know, in sort of a joking way. He wouldn't have been jealous or angry. At least, I don't think so. They were in love. So Byron might've said something like, 'Teasing me, huh? Who was this guy?' And Elizabeth might've answered with something that could potentially narrow it down. Like, 'Oh, just some rich dude,' or 'some guy who works on a ship. Not to worry, I told him I was too busy with work.' " Alexi shrugged. "Can you imagine that kind of scenario?"

Jude studied her. "Maybe. But whenever he crosses paths with Jackson and me, he shakes his head sadly and moves on."

"He's a ghost. In theory, he can be anywhere and see anything," Alexi murmured.
"But he didn't see what happened in Cozumel. I know he's still trying to help you,
though."

"Yes, I believe that, too," Jude said. "And
I agree it's worth talking to him again."

She searched Jude's face, trying to read
his expression. "Just one more night on the
ship," she whispered.

He smiled at her, smoothing the hair from
her forehead. "I'll be glad to have you safely
on land," he told her. "I'll be glad to have a
nice large field office and every cop in
NOLA on this. I want computer tech
help . . . and I want you safe!" he repeated.

"My home's in NOLA, too, remember?"
she said, her arms locked around his neck.

He grinned. "Oh, yeah, I remember."

"It'll be a relief to get home. I certainly
don't need to be sailing for a while," she
told him huskily.

He pulled her close again. "Good," he
said. "Because this Archangel mess isn't
over yet. You need to be extra cautious. And
I need to watch out for you and — Oh!"

"What?"

"Do you live with your family?"

She laughed. "No, I have a really cool

396

apartment. Supposedly," she added, "Andrew Jackson slept there."

"I can deal with him. Or his ghost. I'm just glad you don't live with your parents. I'm sure I'm going to love them, but I'd feel a bit awkward introducing myself and sleeping with their daughter."

"So, we'll stay at my place when we get back to the city?"

"Or mine. I'm in the lower Garden District," he said. "Nice place. Pretty big, with a backyard. Perfect for a dog. No dog yet, I'm afraid. Maybe we'll get one. Dogs are great guardians."

"And great pets." She smiled. The ship pitched and they fell together, catching each other.

She moved away from him, saying, "I'm going to take a quick shower and dress for dinner. You're welcome to join me."

"I am fond of cleanliness," he joked. "I'll be with you in a minute. I'm just going to check in with Jackson."

Alexi went into the shower, shedding her clothing as she walked. With a teasing little movement, she tossed her dress up and then let it fall to the floor, kicking it aside with her foot — still clad in its elegant strappy sandal.

Jude laughed and said, "Be right there."

She stepped into the water. A moment later the bathroom door opened.

She waited, anticipating his arrival with the soap in her hands, the water crashing down all around her, steam rising.

"Alexi!" Jude called.

"Yes?"

"I'm on my way out. Get hold of Clara and the two of you meet in the hall. Johnny will be there, and he'll stay with you. I have to head out. Something's happened. I'll explain as soon as I see you. Don't leave the dining room, you understand? Don't leave until Jackson and I are back!"

Her throat constricted and she couldn't talk, couldn't respond.

Finally, she managed to croak, "Okay!"

She heard her cabin door close. She stood with the soap in her hand for another minute, then finished her shower and got dressed. She chose a blue velvet gown that was simple and classic.

Alexi was about to put on her makeup when she saw a piece of paper stuck under the threshold of her cabin door.

She bent down to retrieve it and a wave of cold fear washed over her as she realized she'd have to open the door.

She did, looking nervously up and down the hallway. There was no one there. Including Johnny. He must be on his way to meet her and Clara, to take them to the dining room for the final dinner of the cruise.

She picked up the scrap of paper. It had been ripped from one of the ship's daily fliers.

The words had been printed in thick black ink. *The end, Alexi. It's the end for you.*

15

"And you don't think she's just at another bar?" Jackson asked Roger Antrim.

Roger was pacing the ground floor of his suite. He shook his head. "I asked her not to go off without me. Or, at least not without telling me." He stopped pacing and turned to stare at Jackson, Jude and David Beach — who had all come running when he'd sent a summons through one of the security guards.

"You two were together most of the day, correct?" Jude asked.

"We were. I'd wanted to surprise Lorna with the presents I was buying from Flora Winters, but . . . well, it seemed prudent to explain the situation, since Lorna thought I was trying to see Flora in — you know — in *that* way. How she could think that, I don't know! But we had a great day on the ship and then we came back here. I went into the shower. I was puttering around for a while before I realized she wasn't here. My Lorna wasn't here!"

"But maybe she did go out," David said.

Roger stopped pacing and frowned at him. "Why don't you communicate with your security men and find out? I asked the guy I sent to find you. He said he didn't know anything. Said he'd just come on for the night!"

David had a pile of notes he drew from his pocket. "He relieved Clarence Murton," he uttered. "Clarence is probably sleeping. I'll wake him up and see if he has any idea what's going on."

"You'd better!" Roger said angrily. "By God, a woman was murdered in New Orleans, and another woman was murdered in Cozumel! Not to mention the women killed before that and the young man . . . Yes, you'd better find out what's going on!"

"I'll put out an alert right away," Beach vowed, turning on his heel.

"I'll check the Promenade," Jackson said.

"I'll try the bars on the St. Charles Deck," Jude told him. "Roger, hang tight." He didn't tell him not to worry, but added, "Wait here."

On his way down the St. Charles hallway, he suddenly reversed his steps and headed for the smaller suite Flora Winters had taken.

Flora and Lorna had become friendly. Lorna must have been very relieved, learning that her husband wasn't *seeing* the widow; he was merely friendly with her as he looked into buying something special for his wife. The scenario Jude was creating in his mind was certainly possible. Jude wondered if she'd left to visit Flora and had called out to Roger to tell him that, and Roger, beneath a thundering spray of water, might not have heard her.

But Jude's vision of a happy ending began to fade.

A greater tension gripped him as he neared Flora's suite; he didn't see any of the security officers standing guard in the hallway.

And when he reached Flora's cabin door . . .

It was open.

The captain was at his table, which was half-empty.

Playing a medley of Broadway tunes, Alexi couldn't help noticing that the esteemed Captain Thorne seemed a little disturbed. An invitation to the captain's table was, of course, an honor bestowed only on certain passengers.

Ralph and Lorna weren't at the table.

Neither was Flora Winters.

Alexi thought that situation probably disturbed her more than it did Captain Thorne, even though he seemed indignant.

Alexi wasn't indignant.

She was scared.

She hadn't told Clara or Johnny or anyone else about the note under her door; she intended to wait until she saw Jude. Clara was nervous enough, and Alexi didn't want to put any more of a burden on her. While Alexi could sit at the piano, Clara was required to sing and occasionally dance — and look happy all the while.

Jensen stood near the dais, directing the performers. He'd exchanged a few words with Bradley Wilcox first — Bradley, who watched from the back of the dining room, arms crossed over his chest. Simon was there. He seemed exceptionally energetic, ready to give his all to his last performance on the voyage.

Larry, Ralph, the others . . .

The show must go on, she thought drily.

Jensen stopped by the piano. " 'One Day More!' " he whispered. "They won't get to see *Les Miz.* So, we'll give them a great chorus number from it."

Alexi nodded, wishing he wasn't standing so close.

She remembered what Jude had told her.

The Archangel hated women. He wanted the man in the relationship to be superior. He didn't want women working out of the home. He'd probably been turned down . . .

The end, Alexi. It's the end for you, her note had read.

She couldn't stop herself from snapping at Jensen. "Please! Could you move back? I can't play."

He stiffened. She heard him mutter beneath his breath, a single word. "Bitch!"

She ignored him and resumed playing. The cast of *Les Miz* went into an excellent rendition of the song, along with some dance movements, definitely a challenge on the small dais, especially when half the space was taken up by the piano.

Minnie and Blake hadn't been in evidence tonight, but toward the end of the number she finally saw Byron Grant. He was by the door looking in, and she waved at him. Anyone who saw her would no doubt assume that she was waving at someone in the room.

Byron saw her and nodded.

A minute later she felt him arrive and sit next to her on the piano bench. He seemed weary and frustrated.

He's dead, she reminded herself.

"Can you talk while you play?" he asked.

She kept her head down; thankfully, the song was loud.

"Byron," she said in a low voice, "I know you and Elizabeth were going to be married. I know how much you loved her. But did she ever mention whether someone had asked her out?"

"One day more!" the cast sang.

"Men always asked her out. She always said no."

"But did she tell you about anyone in particular? Say, in the last several months?"

He shrugged. Suddenly, his eyes widened. "Yeah! Actually, I think it might've been about six months ago. She came home tired and aggravated. Said some guy at a lunch place told her she was inventing a fiancé — and that even if a fiancé or boyfriend existed, she was with the wrong guy. If she gave him a chance, she'd never have to work again. She told him she loved her work — and thank you, but she really did have a great fiancé who wasn't a chauvinist and was proud of how well she did. Oh, God, what an idiot I am! The medallions. They weren't just associated with the woman, with their jobs — they were a reprimand!

They were there to mock all those poor women for loving what they did." He looked at her in horror. "For thinking work was more important than a guy. That's it, isn't it?"

"Maybe," Alexi said. "Think, Byron, please! Did she say anything more specific? Did she tell you if he was young or old, or if he wore a certain cologne or anything at all?"

They were coming to the end of "One Day More."

"He wasn't old," Byron said thoughtfully. "Elizabeth would've mentioned that, because once, one of her bosses — an older guy, about fifty — wanted her to go out with him. Elizabeth told me he was a jerk, he'd had a wife, and he'd left her to chase after younger women." He shook his head. "She would've said if this guy — the . . . the Archangel — was older."

Did that help? Did that clear Roger Antrim?

And leave just three suspects?

"I guess they've more or less had him pegged from the beginning," Byron murmured. "Archangel! Pathetic loser's more like it. Killing because he couldn't get a date. I'll bet he really thought that he'd punish all the women who hadn't fallen for him. And Elizabeth would've been so nice to

him. She would've tried not to hurt his feelings."

Alexi played the last notes of the song.

Applause filled the room and she glanced
over at the cast. Clara sweeping a bow to
the crowd. She saw Ralph . . . Larry . . .

Simon. Simon?

At her side, Byron faded away.

Alexi didn't know if he'd just lost
strength . . .

Or if he was furious and as intensely on
the hunt as a dead man could be.

Jude shouted Flora's name and entered the
suite.

It didn't take more than a few seconds to
see that there was a body on the bed.

He rushed over, his heart racing. The
woman might be asleep; she might be
unaware that her cabin door had been left
open.

But . . . she wasn't just sleeping.

And she wasn't Flora Winters. It was
Lorna Antrim who lay on the bed, cold and
lifeless, and yet . . .

"She has a pulse."

Jude almost jumped; the ghost of Nurse
Barbara Leon was at his side.

"You need to get help for her immediately.
She's been given something — a massive

overdose of some kind of drug. Maybe a prescription drug belonging to Flora Winters. One that's lethal in large doses."

There were vials on the bedside table. And a needle.

"Yes," she said, bending down to check. "Someone's used Flora's medication. She's diabetic, I see."

"Insulin?" Jude asked.

"Yes, an overdose. She needs the doctor fast. Tell him what happened."

Jude nodded and dug out his walkie-talkie to reach Jackson.

Why had the cabin door been open? Was the killer taunting them — showing them that even when he made it easy for them, they couldn't catch him?

Jackson had the doctor there in a few minutes. He had an antidote called glucagon with him to raise her dangerously low blood sugar. Jude didn't know how severe Lorna's condition could become; she seemed to be comatose. But the doctor had come prepared.

By the time he arrived, Barbara was gone.

The ship's doctor quickly gave her a shot. Lorna didn't open her eyes.

The doctor glanced at him. "Her pulse is picking up. I wish to God we had a hospital close. I'll have to get her to the infirmary and watch her through the night."

"Is she going to make it?"

"If you're a praying man, pray. But she's got a chance. We might have saved her life. *You* might have saved her life," he added.

Jude lowered his head. *No. Barbara Leon, dead for decades, was still aboard the ship.*

Still saving lives.

Lorna was in the capable hands of the ship's physician now. Before he could respond, Jackson appeared in the cabin doorway. "We've found Lorna Antrim," he said. "So where the hell is Flora Winters?"

Captain Thorne stood up to speak, holding a mic passed to him by Jensen Hardy.

"Ladies and gentlemen!" he began.

But just as he spoke, the ship was plunged into darkness.

Pitch-black darkness.

It lasted less than five seconds; the auxiliary lights, pale and eerie in comparison to the brilliance that had flooded the dining room moments before, came on.

"Well, ladies and gentlemen," Captain Thorne said. "Sorry about that. Instructions will be coming from the bridge. As you're all aware, our main power has shut down. Don't panic. You'll be able to see the way to your cabins with the guide lights along the floor. I don't know what's caused this, but rest assured, I'll be on the bridge dealing with the situation in a few minutes. For now, I'm going to ask you all to return to your cabins. Room-to-room phones are working, but please, at this time, use them only in an emergency."

He winced; he'd still been speaking when the PA system came back on. His first mate was addressing the loss of power and, like Thorne, he assured the passengers that the auxiliary lighting would see them to safety. All guests were asked to go to their cabins and stay there. If the ship was in any danger whatsoever, they'd be alerted and could change course as instructed.

"Folks, the *Destiny* is sailing on smoothly — okay, maybe not smoothly," he said, trying to make a joke. "But she's sailing on safely. Head to your cabins. Relax, and just pay attention to our announcements. Hopefully, we'll be telling you about fun events that'll take place as we reach calmer waters and the port of Miami."

"You heard the instructions, people. Please, don't panic. Please, just be safe!" Captain Thorne said.

People began to rise, ready to return to their cabins.

Alexi stayed at the piano, listening to the

410

passengers as they left the dining room.

They were chattering, many of them worried. "Lightning? Were we struck by lightning?" she heard.

"I didn't see any lightning," someone else said.

"The ship is pitching like crazy."

"The ship's been pitching like crazy for days."

"It's worse."

"No, it's not. They say we're ahead of the storm, and no one on this ship has lied to us. We'll be safe in port tomorrow!"

"Did you go to the lifeboat drill?"

"He went, all right — drunk as a skunk!"

"We can't get in the lifeboats! We'll drown!"

"The ship isn't sinking," another person said calmly. "It's perfectly sound." Some people seemed to be panicking, despite their instructions.

Clara came and sat next to Alexi. "What do you think?" she asked, wide-eyed and obviously trying to keep the fear from her voice.

"I think we lost power for some reason," Alexi replied. "The ship's movement isn't any rockier. Celtic American's put a fortune into this ship, but it *is* old. We've lost power. We'll get it back. And in the meanwhile, we

411

do have auxiliary."

Clara grinned at her. "You've been hanging around the FBI too long. Trying to be logical. I want to go down to my cabin. Lock myself in and stay there until we get to Miami. I'm not holding this against Celtic American, but . . . I need some land time!"

"I agree," Alexi murmured.

"Who were you talking to earlier? At the piano?" Clara asked.

Alexi looked directly at her and Clara shuddered visibly. "Never mind! Dead man, right? Did he . . . did he know anything?"

Alexi surveyed the room. No one was paying attention to them. She didn't see Jensen; Bradley was talking to the rest of Clara's crew.

She lowered her voice. "Clara, which of the guys on this cruise have asked you out? Or come on to you? I'm going to mention some names."

Clara raised her brows. "I don't mean this to sound like bragging, but we're on a ship. Just about every guy who's straight and available has made some kind of innuendo."

"Simon?"

She shrugged. "Yeah. Either that or he wanted to let me know that even though he loves his gay friends, he's heterosexual himself."

"Roger Antrim, by any chance?"

"Antrim?" She shook her head. "He's always with Lorna when I see him and he behaves just as a married man should."

"Jensen."

"Hell, yeah. He's a jerk."

"Hank Osprey?"

Clara laughed. "Not in ages. I'm happy for him. He seems to have found true love. Hey, we don't know very much about Ginny. She might be telling the truth about being a student, but maybe she's a Bourbon Street hooker, on the side. But if they're making each other happy, who cares?"

"I agree." Alexi saw that the group on the dais was beginning to disperse.

Bradley came to the piano. "You get a night off, Alexi. And no rehearsal, Clara."

"Thanks." Clara looked downward and then sideways at Alexi. "Greatly appreciated. It was a really long day."

Their boss ignored her reference to the fact that he'd called on them for many more hours than they were contractually obligated to provide.

"You're probably going to be on tomorrow. They'll get this lighting thing solved and we'll be done with the storm. We'll try to give the passengers good memories of their trip, right?"

"Only the best!" Alexi said cheerfully.

"You're free to go now," he told them.

Simon and a few others had turned to leave and were already on their way out.

"Wait!" Wilcox snapped. "We let the guests go first. Show some courtesy!"

A few cast members hadn't heard him — or pretended not to. With a grunt of irritation, Wilcox moved away from the piano and toward the door.

"Nice of him to thank us!" Alexi said sarcastically.

"Yes, I'm sure our efforts will make all the difference," Clara retorted.

"Yeah, these passengers will have the best of memories — a massive explosion and a murder in Cozumel, stormy seas . . . a killer on board. Great memories, all right."

Clara shivered. "The room's clearing out. I don't even see Bradley anymore. Let's get to our cabins."

"We're supposed to wait for Jude," Alexi began, but Clara nudged her. "The government men aren't here, but we're covered."

Clara indicated the big man waiting for the two of them and their entertainment group. "Johnny's over there. I'm betting he's been assigned to see us safely to our cabins. I've changed my mind about staying by myself. I'm going to put on some flannel pajamas, get cuddly and warm and come stay in your cabin. Okay?"

"Sounds good to me," Alexi said.

Most of the performers had moved out by now, ignoring Wilcox. The dining room was empty except for a few of the waitstaff, who were doing their best in the gloomy light to get things cleaned up.

Johnny was a great security officer — and a friend. He linked arms with the two women. "It's my pleasure to be your escort!" he told them.

Alexi smiled at him. She wished Jude was with her.

Johnny was the next best thing.

"Thank you," Alexi said fervently, and Clara echoed the words.

The hallways outside the dining room had almost emptied out. "Elevators were set to work using the auxiliary power on this ship, but they might be slow and busy. Shall we take the stairs?" Johnny suggested.

"Stairs work for me," Alexi said.

"Love stairs," Clara chimed in.

A woman walking in front of them tripped; Johnny released Clara and Alexi, ready to help her.

But a passenger by her side was there before Johnny could move. "You okay?" Johnny asked the woman, taking her other arm and guiding her to her feet.

"Fine, thank you both," the woman said. "Embarrassed, but fine!"

"If you're hurt," Johnny told her, "I can take you to the infirmary. You're sure you can walk?"

"Yes," the woman said. "I'm mortified but otherwise okay."

Johnny thanked the passenger who'd assisted her, and the two of them went on. "Trying times," he murmured. "They can bring out the best in us — and they can bring out the worst."

They reached the landing of the next deck; the woman and the man who'd helped her walked to the cabin hallways. Alexi saw that two security officers were on duty, watching both sides of the hall.

Except that was going to be more difficult now. The auxiliary lights created a strange yellow glow.

And a realm of shadows.

"Hard for you guys to see, huh?" Alexi asked.

"Don't you worry. I have great eyesight," Johnny assured her.

Alexi smiled at his response but still felt uneasy.

She doubted he could see the entire length of the hallways, not in the meager light that shone with such an eerie glimmer, and that pale illumination so close to the floor.

They came to Clara's cabin, and she went inside.

"I'll be with you in a few minutes, Alexi."

"Okay, see you then."

Alexi knew she wouldn't be a very effective buffer against any danger that threatened them, but Jude would be coming back to her cabin. And that was a comforting thought.

And in the meantime, it was better to be scared together than to sit in the dim light and be scared alone.

Johnny stopped at her doorway and waited for her to step inside.

For a moment Alexi felt sheer panic.

What if they'd all been wrong? What if they'd missed something?

What if Johnny was a serial killer, and somehow, his records had been disguised to hide his past?

"Here we are. Now, lock yourself in, safe and sound," he said firmly.

She smiled, the tension leaving her.

"Johnny, you haven't heard if something else has happened, have you?"

"All I can tell you is that the lights went out. Who knows why? It's a bad storm. The *Destiny*'s undergone millions of dollars in restoration, but it's still an old ship."

She nodded, searching his face.

Something *had* happened, even if Johnny didn't know what it was. That was why Jude wasn't with her.

She wished she could run through the ship looking for him.

But that would be stupid, almost akin to suicidal stupidity. She was a target, and she'd been told to lock herself in her cabin. If she did that, the killer couldn't reach her. "Johnny, you're a sweetheart. Thank you and good night." She stepped into her cabin and leaned against the door, looking around. She knew her tiny space so well. This same cabin had been her home several times now. Her desk — with the list of medallions still on it. Her bed . . .

Where she'd learned to live again, love again — with Jude.

She wished the electricity hadn't gone out, that there was more than the pale auxiliary lighting. The thought of brushing her teeth and getting ready for bed in the semi-dark wasn't one she relished.

She wasn't sure why, but she was suddenly afraid of her bathroom.

And that was ridiculous! There was no way she'd be able to avoid going into her bathroom.

She sighed, prepared to push away and open the bathroom door so she could wash her face, brush her teeth, get ready for bed. Clara would be there soon. And then she saw a change in the strange yellowish haze pervading the small cabin; it was a form, a shadow, something taking shape.

Her heart seemed to leap into her throat.

Then she realized it was Byron.

"Run, Alexi! Run!" She frowned; she could barely hear him, barely see him . . .

"Run!" he shouted again.

And she saw that her bathroom door was opening.

Someone was in there!

Someone . . .

Was waiting for her.

Byron threw himself ineffectually at the door.

Alexi turned and yanked open the door to her cabin, then stepped out into the hallway and pulled it shut. Johnny was there; he was somewhere down at the end, near the elevators.

She couldn't see him! The cabin door opened behind her.

She was being pursued!

She screamed as loudly as she could.

And she ran.

Great.

The ship being plunged into darkness was only causing more problems, even when the auxiliary lights were on.

But they all moved as efficiently as possible.

Radio communication with the bridge assured Jude that the dining room was being shut down and all personnel were being directed to their rooms.

David Beach called Jude to tell him that Alexi and Clara were fine. He said Johnny was with them. Then he hesitated. "I'm missing another man. The guard who was watching Roger and Lorna Antrim. We can't find him."

Jude swore softly. "If he's found, let us know right away. Let's hope he's all right."

At least Alexi and Clara were safe, which was a relief.

He and Jackson were on their way to the Antrims' suite to escort Roger to the infirmary when they received another call from Beach.

"It's the reverend," Beach told them. "He sounds hysterical. He wants us in the chapel. Now."

Jude knew — long before they'd reached the chapel — what they were going to find.

He was right. Flora Winters was there.

She'd had her head bashed in; that was evident, from the blood dripping down her forehead and matting her hair.

Then her throat had been slit. She was missing a shoe. She'd been left in front of the altar, but she hadn't been posed like the Archangel's other victims had been. She'd just been dumped there. "No medallion," Jackson said, hunkered down by the body.

"No, she isn't one of the victims the Archangel wants," Jude said. "Somehow, she and Lorna got in the way, or else . . ."

"Or else the killer is Roger Antrim."

"But that doesn't make sense," Jude argued. "He'd have to move pretty damn fast. Getting to Flora's cabin, knocking her out, then injecting Lorna with the insulin and leaving her to die. Getting Flora here. And after all that, going back to take a shower and call security to say his wife is missing. It doesn't add up."

"Flora knew," Jackson said. "She knew we'd find out who her husband sold the medallions to."

"Well, we'll get that information once we hit Miami," Jude said, thinking it through. "Unless . . ."

"Unless?"

"He doesn't care anymore. He wants to finish his task, find his actress and his musician and kill them right now. And then . . . give himself up," Jude said grimly. "Or kill himself." He turned to Beach and to the Reverend Mike. "How long were you away from the chapel?" he asked.

"I was asked to visit a sick guest," Mike said. "That was just after five. She said she'd been in the Egyptian Room, playing the games until they ended. But then she felt sick and she called me. I went from there straight to dinner. However, I guarantee that I left the chapel locked."

"Someone has the keys," Beach said. "Someone's accessed all the *Destiny*'s keys."

Someone had accessed all the Destiny*'s keys?* How the hell?

Beach cursed angrily. "There's a master key . . . hangs on a hook just inside the captain's cabin. Wonder if we'll find out it's gone?"

"Call the captain," Jude said.

Beach did so, then nodded grimly. "Gone."

Jude had expected as much. "Get the doctor up here. Help him move the body into the infirmary. We can't wait for the proper medical authorities because of the time it'll take to reach port. I know I don't need to tell you this, but please —"

"Watch for any possible trace evidence on the body," Beach said.

"Yeah," Jude agreed. He closed his eyes for a moment. He'd really liked Flora Winters.

But he couldn't mourn her now. "Beach, close the infirmary and put two guards up here. I'm convinced this killer is going to try to finish up tonight. Jackson —"

"Yes," Jackson said. "Alexi and Clara. They're in serious danger."

Jude was on his way out, running for the stairs while Jackson was still speaking.

Alexi couldn't see Johnny. She couldn't see anyone at all.

Suddenly, a door in the employee hallway burst open.

"Alexi!"

She blinked. It was Jensen Hardy. "Alexi, come on! Into my cabin."

He grabbed for her, and in raw panic, she jerked back, away from him.

She half turned. And saw, in the strange light, that someone was still chasing her. Someone who'd been in her room.

Alexi started to run again. She hoped Jensen had locked himself back in his cabin.

Johnny had to be there, had to be at the elevators.

She heard a scream — a scream of surprise, horror and pain.

She paused, turning back. There was a body on the floor, writhing and crying out.

And, in the weird, murky yellow light, she saw that someone was stepping over the body. Someone holding something.

A knife.

And now it dripped blood.

16

The door to Alexi's cabin gaped open. Jude knew she wasn't going to be there.

Still, he looked as Jackson rushed ahead to knock on Clara's door, identifying himself.

Jude hadn't made it all the way in when he heard moaning. He ran out to the hallway. Doors were opening all along the hall; entertainers were coming out, speaking in panicked voices.

"There was a scream, a terrible scream," Ralph said, clinging to Larry's arm.

"I tried to go out," Larry said. "To see what was wrong."

"I stopped him!" Ralph shrieked. "There was a killer out there."

Jude ignored them all, racing down the hall. He dropped to his knees beside the moaning body.

He recognized one of the security guards. There was blood all around him, but he was struggling to sit up, tears in his eyes. "Alexi . . . killer . . ."

"Don't try to speak," Jude said.

He turned to see Jackson coming down the hallway with Clara. Jude felt something like a waft of air against his cheek.

Barbara Leon had come to this injured person, too.

"It's not a mortal wound," she said. "The killer was in too big a hurry to catch Alexi. Wrap his throat. At least the bastard didn't hit an artery or a vein."

Simon had come out of his cabin and stood nearby; he pulled off his nightshirt and handed it to Jude, who swiftly tore it into strips. He made a bandage, stopping the flow of blood from the area just above the guard's collarbone.

Jackson had placed Clara into the safe-keeping of another security officer, who'd just arrived on the scene. Jude leaped to his feet and dashed down the hallway to the elevators and the exit to the stairs, Jackson close behind.

Johnny? Where the hell was Johnny? He would've stayed with Alexi unless . . .

Jude found him, on the floor, trying to get up.

"Johnny!" he said, crouching beside him.

"Arm broken . . . concussion . . . I'm okay,

go!" Johnny said.

"Where?"

Johnny shook his head. "She . . . ran to me . . . for help. I went over to her and he was on me . . . She stopped to come back, to help me. He only left me alive to chase her. Go!"

Jude stood. "Where, Johnny? Which way did she run?"

"To the stairs! Up . . . She ran up the stairs. Go, Jude, go, for the love of God . . ."

Jude didn't need his directive.

He was already taking the stairs, two at a time.

The vast ship was oddly empty.

Alexi made it up to the Promenade Deck; no one was there. She wondered what had happened to security here.

Yet, how could security help? The killer was on the officers the second she ran to them. The guard in the hallway. And Johnny . . . Johnny . . . her fault. She prayed that the killer had been too intent on her to finish Johnny off.

On the Promenade Deck, she looked desperately for a hiding space.

The shops were closed.

Cafés closed . . .

The Picture Gallery was farther down the

length of the ship.

The ghost ship! Oh, God, it seemed like a ghost ship now!

And it was!

She glanced to her left and nearly screamed, but managed to stop herself. She wasn't alone. Private Jimmy Estes was running with her.

"He knows the ship, Alexi, but you do, too. This way . . . There are rows of pictures in the gallery. You can get lost in them and listen, listen for him. I'll be with you . . . I'll do what I can."

"I'm here, too, Alexi," Private Frank Marlowe said, running on her other side. "We'll do whatever we can."

The Picture Gallery was just ahead and Alexi raced toward it.

There were false walls set up in rows and at different angles to display the photographs of passengers, smiling as they boarded the ship.

There was also a section of pictures taken as passengers left the ship, preparing to spend the day in Cozumel. Pictures with local Mexican women in colorful garb, pictures with parrots and with people dressed in ancient Mayan attire.

Alexi ran past them all.

She dove behind a wall filled with photographs of elegantly dressed people ready for the captain's dinner. She paused, doubled over, gasping for breath.

Then she heard him.

He was running — until he reached the Picture Gallery. She listened intently. He's stopped near the entrance, trying to hear her.

She hardly dared to breathe.

"Alexi! I know you're here. And I'm sorry, but it's time for you to go. It'll be quick, I promise. I don't want to hurt you. I'm afraid that you . . . well, you're among the women who have to pay for their crimes. You told me you were engaged once. And he died, a poor soldier died. And you weren't even waiting for him. You were working, working, working. Your music was more important to you than his love — or mine. Oh, Alexi. I gave you a chance! But . . . it's your time. In another world, you'll learn."

She listened, thinking that a week ago, even days ago, she would've been shocked to recognize the voice now speaking to her.

He was calm. His tone was well modulated.

"Alexi, don't add to your pain! I will find you. I knew that this medallion was just for you. There could be no other."

She wanted to scream and shout. She wanted to tell him that he was a sad, pathetic man — and his beliefs and his behavior would keep any woman from desiring him.

She wanted to tell him he'd be caught. She wanted to confront him, hurt him for all the pain he'd caused.

But she knew she had to keep silent. Absolutely silent.

She'd run screaming through the ship; now it was time for silence. But someone — Jude, Jackson, the ship's security officers — had to be after him. He was just one man. He could be stopped. He *would* be stopped.

She prayed it was while she was still alive!

"I'm coming for you, Alexi."

She held still, closing her eyes to better listen.

He was moving toward her, moving around the walls and walls of pictures.

Suddenly, Jimmy was in front of her, handsome in his uniform, beckoning to her. She realized she had to move; the Archangel was coming around the false wall where she'd taken refuge.

Private Frank Marlowe was behind her. He slammed a wall with all his ethereal strength.

And made a noise.

The killer turned, moving backward.

Alexi ran again, ran for her life.

Heading down the stairs to the St. Charles Deck, she was stunned to crash into Simon Green.

For a moment she was paralyzed, riddled by confusion. What the hell was Simon doing out here? He should've been back in his cabin . . .

"Simon," she began. "Why are you —"

Could he be with the killer? Could the two of them be working in tandem? No, the murders had been committed by one man. That was what Jude had said.

"Simon," she repeated.

The killer had been behind her in the gallery. She'd known the voice.

But there was no way he could've gotten ahead of her, so Simon really was trying to save her.

She could hear the footsteps coming now . . . coming closer.

Simon frowned. "He's here, right? The guy who killed the woman in Mexico? Oh, my God, it's the Archangel! I don't know where the hell everyone else is, but I'll protect you!" Simon vowed.

"Simon, why are you here? What made you come here?" she demanded, still wary.

Simon caught her arms, shaking his head

in confusion. "Alexi! You were screaming. I've been trying to find you. Oh, my God, what's going on? There's a guy on the ground in our hallway . . . a security officer. I don't know if he's dead or alive. I don't know what's going on, but I'm going to help you —"

No, he couldn't help her.

"Run!" she told him. "Simon, I'm begging you, run. Please!"

"Alexi, I may be a chorus guy, but I'm not a coward! We can take him. I'll —"

"No, please run! We have to run! We can't beat him. Simon, damn it, he has one big-ass knife. Come on. Simon, listen to me, it's going to take more than two of us to overpower him. You have to believe me!" They'd been talking, talking too loudly. The killer knew exactly where they were. And she knew exactly where he was, from the telltale sound of his footsteps. He was still above them in the Picture Gallery, but he was making his way to the stairs. She understood, far too late to save herself, that she'd known the Archangel for some time. She hadn't suspected him, but she — like the other victims he'd targeted — had turned him down.

"Simon, follow me! We have to get to security, to someone who can stop him!"

she said, trying to drag him with her.

He shook her off. "Alexi, whoever the hell this bastard is, *I* will stop him!"

"No!" She pulled fiercely on his arm. "Simon, let's go!"

He looked at her solemnly. "Chorus, Alexi — not coward."

"It has nothing to do with courage!" she cried.

But Simon slipped from her grasp and headed back up the stairs.

"No, no!" she breathed.

He didn't heed her warning; she heard him confront the killer.

And then she heard his scream as he came tumbling down the stairs, thrown by the killer who was pursuing her again.

She'd looked frantically around the St. Charles Deck. She prayed that Simon wouldn't be killed — that the Archangel wouldn't stop and make sure he was dead.

She paused briefly to listen.

Judging by his footsteps, the Archangel didn't check to see if Simon was dead; he was hurrying after her, stalking her with single-minded intensity.

"Alexi . . . Alexi . . . I'll find you. You're beginning to get on my nerves now, you know. Kind of like that stupid Flora Winters. Couldn't leave well enough alone. Oh, she suspected me, suspected that I had the medallions. Even figured out how I got them. They'll find out, of course, who bought them for me. I knew about them before. My grandmother had purchased a set for my grandfather before the war. It was during their honeymoon in Italy, you know. She wanted him to be safe, no matter what the service asked of him. She was a good woman. She stayed home. She looked after his children. She cleaned his house. She cooked. She knew what it was to be a wife."

Alexi realized she was making her way to the piano bar.

Why? Where would I hide there?

"Alexi, I have to finish this task tonight. Damn it, Alexi! I still have to go back and track down Clara. There's one more medallion that must find its place — after I've finished with you."

Jude reached the Promenade Deck, which was eerily silent.

He wanted to yell at the top of his lungs. Scream at the Archangel, tell him he was a dead man.

But he forced himself to silence. If he called out, he'd warn the killer — who might have Alexi. Jude had to reach them.

He had to reach them before . . .

He didn't dare think. Refused to imagine what the Archangel might do to the woman he loved.

As quietly as he could, he moved along the Promenade. Past locked shops, cafés with the grating closed, elegant facades and an Irish pub.

He neared the end of the row and arrived at the Picture Gallery. The walls of photos seemed to provide a never-ending array of hiding places. He started to go from row to row, moving as silently as possible, Glock drawn and ready.

But he found no one.

Then, he heard moans coming from the stairway.

Jude rushed to the stairs and then tore down them.

He discovered Simon Green stretched out awkwardly on the bottom step. When he bent down, Simon opened his eyes — and they widened with horror as he saw Jude and the Glock in his hand.

"No, no . . ."

"Simon, I'm not going to hurt you! Are you bleeding? Are you . . ."

He couldn't ask the man if he was dying.

Simon answered his unspoken question. "No . . . not dying. Jude, quick, go . . . That way . . . down to the St. Charles Deck." Simon gasped, his face constricted with pain.

Jude nodded. "All right. Thank you."

He should've stayed with Simon; at the very least, he should have pulled out the walkie-talkie and called for help. But Simon grabbed his arm and whispered, "No time! No time, go. Me — it's just my leg. Broken. He's got a knife . . . It's Hank! Hank Osprey. He hardly even saw me. I was just . . . just something in his way."

How long could Alexi run?

Jude nodded again. He stood and started down the length of the St. Charles. Then he stopped.

There were so many places on this deck where they might have gone. He hesitated for a few seconds, praying. He couldn't make a mistake.

Alexi might be out of time.

"Someone!" he whispered. "Please . . . help."

And then he saw a soldier. The man materialized slowly, but he seemed anxious. Jude had never seen him before. He hadn't met him at the infirmary.

This soldier hadn't fought in World War II.

But he was urging Jude onward.

It was Zachary Wainwright. Alexi's fiancé. Jude was sure of it.

And followed him.

Alexi knew that Hank was directly behind her. If he caught up with her, no matter how hard she struggled, she was going to die. He was wielding a knife.

At the entrance to the Algiers Saloon, she paused for a split second.

Then she ran over to the piano bench and sat down. She began to play, hoping that if a security officer was anywhere nearby, he'd hear.

And he'd come to her rescue . . .

Someone would come.

Blake and Minnie appeared, Minnie on her right side, Blake on her left.

"You must keep him talking," Minnie said.

"Yes . . . talk, play — and keep the piano between you and him, Alexi," Blake told her. "This is his favorite place. He's always loved being here. Maybe he became rich and famous as a computer genius but always wanted to be a singer? Make him talk to you. Even beg him to explain."

She played a Chopin piece.

And stared at Hank Osprey across the piano.

He seemed disconcerted, she thought.

He'd expected to find her cowering and cringing behind a wall somewhere.

"Want to sing, Hank?" she asked. "Perhaps you could sing me a song about all this. Why the hell would someone with your money and success decide to kill people? Kill women? If nothing else, you could've bought the kind of woman you wanted. Someone who'd stay home, who'd cook, clean and have a dozen children for you?"

"Alexi, you can't buy love." He sighed. "Surely, you know that."

"No, Hank, sometimes, love is something that just comes along. And sometimes, just by living, you earn love," she said. "You earn it with your actions, with laughter, with kindness."

"Oh, Alexi!" He rested one hand on the opposite side of the piano. "I never had a chance to earn it. I tried to earn *your* love. You gave me that line about honoring the memory of your fiancé! Oh, he was a soldier, killed in action. Boo hoo. But that was a lie. You didn't care about him. You needed this, your *career.* You wanted to be a musician when you should've been home, mourning his loss. If he even existed. Women are great at making up boyfriends and lovers when they're trying to give a man the cold shoulder. And their supposedly great love for those men is a lie, too."

"Zachary existed, and my love for him was real, nothing I made up, Hank, which should be easy enough for a *computer* genius to find out. He existed and I loved him with all my heart. I still do."

"Okay, so yeah, I knew he existed. You got me there. But what about your great love for him? You still love him? That's why you're sleeping with the bastard you just met on this cruise? Oh, Alexi. Really? Did the man even take you to dinner? No, you're a whore, like the rest of them. No real respect for the men doing everything they can to please and support a woman!"

Alexi pretended to give his remarks serious thought. She considered mentioning Ginny, and then wondered if that would just set him off, make things worse.

"Zach's been dead longer now, Hank. You asked me out too soon," she said at last.

"Oh, yeah? If I'd asked you out now, would you have gone with me? No, you'd have slept with that cruise line guy, anyway. You'd see nothing but quick gratification — and someone who wouldn't stop you from doing *this*. Ah, yes! Entertaining, playing, singing. Bringing in your talented and beautiful friends, loving your precious work — more than you could ever love a man.

Lying to me now isn't going to help, Alexi. I know you."

"Hank, some of us *have* to work. It's an expensive world for those of us who aren't computer geniuses."

"You women look at me and think 'gawky nerd.' A guy to use, to take money from."

"I never took money from you, Hank!"

"Okay, I'll give you that. You wouldn't even let me buy you a drink! But you used me all the same. You used me, teased me, in this room. Oh, Alexi, you're another one of those terrible women, and that's so sad. You're lovely. And you play the piano so beautifully . . . I even thought about finding someone else to be my musician, but it had to be you. No other woman was truly worthy of St. Cecilia's medallion. St. Cecilia, patron of musicians. The medallions needed — no, demanded! — sacrifices. Women who loved working more than they'd ever love a man. Ah, Alexi. You're implying you might have dated me, loved me, if the timing was different. You're such a desperate liar. I might have *earned* love? No, you wouldn't have bothered to know me. And Clara! Oh, she's something else. No dead serviceman for her, huh, real or not? Or is she like you, hiding behind the wall of mourning? Let's see, what did you

440

tell me once?" He spoke in a falsetto. " 'Oh, Hank. I can't . . . I still can't see anyone. Zach is still there, so close, in my heart.' "

"Zach was real. And I was in love with him in ways you'll never understand," she said.

"Right. You were in love with muscles and a tan, Alexi. And now you're going to tell me you're in love with Jude McCoy?"

"I might be," she said quietly.

"You disgust me! You're not in love. You're in lust."

"And what about you, Hank? Were you ever in love? Or just in lust?"

"I'm saving you, Alexi. From a life like this. And I'll save Clara, too. She'll be forever remembered, forever young. Forever a bitch — but a dead one."

"You'll never get to Clara," she told him. "You seem to believe you're so smart. That you're invincible. But I can promise you won't have a chance with Clara. They'll know it's you. They know now. You were clever. Of course, you *are* a computer genius. You killed and you plotted the disposal of the bodies and you kept moving on and . . . Really, who would suspect a man like you? Plus, you've been on this ship so many times. How did you do it? Befriend someone and figure out how to steal a master key? Everyone on this ship knew you — and trusted you. But it's over now. They'll trace how you bought the medallions. By now they'll have a mountain of evidence against you. Because guess what? You really weren't that smart. What a waste!"

He ignored her scornful comments about him. "The master key. Yeah, piece of cake. Even the captain sucks up to a guy like me! I've been on the bridge, in his cabin, at his desk. Where he kept his copy of the master. So easy to slip into a pocket."

"And Mexico? The explosion?"

"Women who worship work and the almighty dollar come in every nationality, and everyone's for sale. You carefully pay a dozen different people for a dozen different services — and voilà! Explosion. But no one can trace you because you've paid different people who have nothing to do with one another. And you create chaos by causing an explosion." He smirked. "I am *very* good."

"They'll know it's you."

"How? They'll never trace the medallions. Like I said, my grandmother bought them for my grandfather. That original set disappeared years ago . . ." He frowned. "But I bought another set from old Sam Winters. I paid an employee, now sadly gone, to be my go-between." His frown had turned into a grin. "And every single one of them went to the right woman. There are just two left. Yours — and Clara's."

"You perverted the meaning of those medallions," Alexi said. "You dishonored those saints."

"No! They wanted me to do it!"

She shook her head. "What a waste!" she murmured again.

"Waste? What *waste* are you talking about?"

"Of yourself!" she said softly. He seemed to be growing disjointed and irrational in his speech. "You will die or rot in prison."

She had to keep him talking. Help would come.

"You're wrong. I'll walk away. They don't know it's me. They'll never know."

"Hank! People aren't blind. You've been *seen*. When they . . . when they find me, they'll catch you red-handed." She flinched at the term and then swallowed a gasp when she saw his fingers tightening on the hilt of a knife. It was more of a cleaver, she thought, looking more closely at the weapon he carried. He must've stolen it from one of the kitchens. Just as easily as he'd visited the captain, he could've had access to any of the kitchens. Everyone loved Hank. He was a frequent and popular passenger on Celtic American ships.

"He's getting agitated," Blake murmured.

"Play that Billy Joel guy," Minnie suggested. "Throw him off!"

"He's not going to sing now, Minnie," Alexi said.

"Who are you talking to?" Hank demanded as he looked around.

"I'm talking to Minnie," she replied. "I can't believe you don't know Minnie — or any of the other ghosts on the *Destiny,*" she said. "Since you're so familiar with the ship."

"Ghosts! Bull," Hank spat, his fingers moving and the knife twitching in his hand.

Blake stood, staring at Hank.

The murderer.

"Minnie sings beautifully," Alexi said.

"She's dead. She was a whore, too, who wanted to sing instead of caring for a husband and children?" Hank asked, his lips curling in a wry smile. "Too bad she's dead. Or I could've killed her, too."

Blake was shaking with ghostly fury. "Minnie is gone, as am I, and we are together. But this is beyond madness and I'll not watch a covetous ass like you kill again. If you touch Alexi, I'll . . . somehow, sir, I will see you dead!" he announced.

Needless to say, there was no response from Hank.

"Blake, it doesn't work like that," Alexi said. "He can't hear you. Or see you."

"Stop that! There's no one here," Hank insisted.

"Blake *is* here, with Minnie," Alexi said. "He wants to kill you. Believe me, he's here," she told Hank. She kept playing, and her fingers moved smoothly on the keys as she switched into a Billy Joel number. "Blake and Minnie!" she said. "You know the history of this ship, Hank. It's filled with ghosts."

It was; that much was true.

And another ghost had just arrived. Byron Grant.

"Hank, I see someone else coming, someone you met — briefly. Very briefly. He never sailed on this ship alive. You dumped his body in an alley. You killed the love of his life before slicing him to shreds. His name is Byron Grant, and he's joining us now."

Byron Grant was there. He walked over to Hank, slamming a fist into his jaw.

Hank jumped as if he'd felt something.

"Stop it, stop it now!" Hank roared. "You're going to die, Alexi. You can join your precious ghosts here on the *Destiny*. Ghosts! Alexi, you're a liar."

"I'm not a liar, and you know it. You may not see the dead or speak to them the way I can, Hank, but you *feel* them. I know you can feel them. Byron just slugged you. I saw you jump when it happened. The ghosts are all here — and they really hate you."

She'd definitely said the wrong thing.

He started to move; before she could jump up and clear her bench, he came around the piano at an ungodly speed.

She made it to her feet, but he caught her by the arm. She twisted around, staring into his eyes. "Kill me, then, Hank. I hope they put you up on federal charges. I hope you rot to death in solitary, eating prison food. No more riches for you, Hank. No fine food, no music. No piano bars. Not where you'll be. I promise you that . . . Oh!"

She suddenly stopped speaking — and her furious rant ended on one startled breath.

She was looking down the hall.

Hank was looking at her, his back to the hall.

And saw what he did not, what he *couldn't* see. Someone was coming quickly down the hallway . . . running, even floating, and he was almost at the Algiers Saloon.

446

A soldier. A ghost soldier, who led a living man.

Alexi gasped, so shocked by the image that she was heedless of the serial killer who held her in his grip. The Archangel, who stood ready with his bloody knife to end her days.

The soldier wasn't from World War II. She'd never seen him on the *Destiny* before.

But she *knew* him. She knew him with everything in her heart and soul.

Zach.

She whispered his name. "My God," she breathed. "Zach. Zach . . ."

"Stop it!" Hank bellowed. But he didn't bring the knife down on her. He spun her around, dragging her roughly so he could see down the hallway, see what she saw.

And then Alexi heard a voice. The voice of a living man.

"Osprey, let her go. Let her go *now.* I have a gun on you, and I will take you down without blinking."

Jude.

He stood just outside the realm of the yellow-glowing auxiliary lights, staring at her, his expression hard and strained.

And strong, she thought. Strong enough to risk danger. And strong enough to admit when he was vulnerable, how he lived with pain . . .

And to admit that he hadn't wanted to see the dead — and yet he was strong enough to know the truth in his heart.

Like Zach. Willing to fight for what he believed in. Even if that fight took his life.

They stood together, the two men she loved, and she had to wonder if she'd soon be joining the dead herself. Or staying among the living . . .

"McCoy!" Hank suddenly raged. His anger and his jerking movement drove the blade closer to Alexi's throat. Against her skin.

It was sharp, so sharp. She didn't know if he'd drawn blood yet.

And then she felt it . . . a trickle down her throat.

She thought Jude was going to fire, but Zach put a hand on his arm in time to stop him.

He would have to have perfect aim. If not, he risked hitting Alexi.

"Where the hell are you, Jude McCoy? Show yourself — and bullshit you have a gun," Hank shouted. He dragged Alexi to the right and then the left, his movements so fevered that he sent the ghosts of Blake and Minnie back several inches.

"Bastard!" Minnie exclaimed angrily.

Hank jerked again, as if he could hear a

distant whisper of her word.

Jude came walking out of the shadows, absurdly calm — and definitely holding a gun.

"You can't have a gun," Hank said. "You're on a ship. Even if you're an executive. Security would have stopped you." He seemed to be smiling, and his hold on Alexi eased just a fraction. "The world is full of terrorists and murderers, you know. And homegrown crazies of all kinds."

Jude seemed exceptionally, absurdly, calm. He shook his head. "Osprey, for a so-called genius, you're not that impressive. You haven't figured out what several others on this ship got pretty quickly. I'm FBI, Hank, and we followed you onto this ship, and yes, I'm armed. I'm carrying this gun legally. Actually, we need a chance to talk, so it may be a good thing that we're at a standstill right now. I need to know about the security officers."

Hank laughed softly. "What do you need to know?"

"Where they are, Hank, the security guards you killed? We've assumed, of course, that you threw their bodies into the ocean."

"Well, of course. But prove something like that! It's a big ocean. And I can't tell you how ridiculously easy it was to get them out on deck, even in the storm. I mean, I'm Hank Osprey. I come up to a security man begging for help and the idiot follows me like a puppy — right over the guardrail and into the drink. They didn't matter. They weren't important."

"But Flora Winters. No medallion, but you still left her in the chapel?"

"She could've had a medallion, I suppose. I just didn't have one for her. The medallions were special, anyway — intended for certain people. Flora was . . . well, she was a traitor. She would've gotten the name of Tony Cass when she talked to her husband's accountant. In fact, I'm afraid she might already have known. Or guessed. She certainly asked me enough questions that weren't any of her business. Tony, unfortunately, died in a hit-and-run car accident. How sad," he said with mock sorrow. "Still, I felt it was best to see her meet up with her husband. I do admit I couldn't quite throw her overboard. I should have, though."

"I told you, Hank. Even geniuses make mistakes. What about Ginny? Ginny Monk? Did you kill her? Will we find her body?"

"Ginny is a good girl," Hank said.

"So she's alive," Jude murmured.

"She's sleeping. She knows how to love a

man, stay with him, do what he says at all times."

"She's a part-time stripper in a club on Bourbon Street," Jude said bluntly.

"No!" Hank shouted.

"And if you were to find out that what I'm saying is the truth, would you kill her? If she *is* a stripper — but she's ready to obey you in exchange for all that money? Because, if she's with you for the money, Hank, she won't stay forever."

"And she would've died if she left me!" Hank snapped.

"Hank, you have no remorse at all, do you? You had a plan, sick and crazy though it was. And if other people happened to get in your way, well . . . they just didn't matter."

"No one matters," Hank told Jude quietly but with conviction. "I'm a genius. I'm a rare human being. Others . . . well, seriously. How much could those fools matter?"

"Every human life is special, Hank."

"To you, maybe," Hank said with a shrug. "I'll agree that in her way, Alexi is special. She gets a medallion."

"No." Jude shook his head. "Alexi doesn't get a medallion. Now, it's your choice. You let her go and step away, and I take you in

— or I shoot you right here."

Hank was growing more and more agitated.

But he hadn't killed her yet!

And yet, she felt the blade of his knife against her throat. She thought she smelled something tinny. The scent of her own blood.

"I'll kill her before you can shoot me," Hank said.

"No, I don't think so," Jude said calmly. "I don't think *they'll* let you."

"You freaks!" Hank screamed. "Who the hell do you believe is here? Some loser guy I killed in Alabama when he interrupted my work? An old whore and her whoremaster? What, and they'd fucking call *me* crazy? You're the sick bastards! You two are trying to tell me a dead man led you onto this ship — and that he and his ghost buddies are going to kill me now?"

"That's not exactly what I'm saying," Jude told him. "You see, *I'm* going to kill you now. They're just going to help."

"You're sick!" Hank roared again. "The dead are . . . dead!"

"You know they're not, Hank. You know they've been watching you. You've felt them. You've felt Byron. He really hates you," Jude said. "Frankly, he didn't learn until now that you're the one who killed him. All Byron knew was that his killer had a ticket to board this ship. But you see, Hank, there were only so many people on this ship who might've been in all the cities where you killed. Odd, huh? You like to travel on the Celtic American line, and a Celtic American ship happened to be in the port cities where the women were killed just before their bodies were discovered. The killer had to have a job that allowed him to be in a number of places — or he had to be a very rich man, one who could afford to go wherever he wanted. Everyone slips up, Hank. And you slipped up here, on the *Destiny*. Although I will admit killing that poor woman in Mexico — and getting her into that church! — took some planning. But now you've finally messed up. You thought you were so smart. Either that, or you didn't plan to get away. Either way, I don't give a damn. It's over for you."

"Not until I kill Alexi," Hank snarled.

"What was it with the medallions, Hank? I'm just not seeing you as a religious man," Jude said.

Hank gave Jude a crooked smile. "You want to know about the medallions? I've already told your *girlfriend* and now I'll tell you. My grandfather originally had a set.

He fought in World War II. Don't know exactly what happened to those, but he told me what they meant. He warned me that there are bad women out there, women who don't deserve to live. He said I'd see the difference and that the bad ones . . . I shouldn't fall for them, that they were the kind who stripped a man of his soul and everything else. Not like my grandmother or my mother. So, you see, I realized when he died that he wanted the medallions around the necks of women who need to be punished." Hank took a deep breath. "I managed to get hold of another set from Flora's husband."

"It's interesting that your grandfather never said anything about murder being a bad thing," Jude said drily. "And he must not have known that sometimes, those who were murdered come back. And some of them are here — ready and waiting for you to join them."

Hank stared at Jude in shock. "You're fucking crazy! I already told you that. Get away from me now. Buy Alexi some time. Because every extra second is precious. Tell him, Alexi. Tell him to drop his gun. Then I'll let you live for a few more minutes."

"She's not going to die, Hank," Jude said. "Don't you see Zach? He was her fiancé.

He loved her, Hank. And she loved him. He lost his life, but you know something about him? He earned a Purple Heart. He died saving children. I guarantee you he's not going to let Alexi die."

Alexi looked from Zach to Jude. She managed to smile.

"Maybe I'm supposed to go now," she said softly.

"No," Zach said, his spirit walking closer to where she stood. He was just across the piano from her.

For a moment she saw him clearly. Saw the kindness and gentleness in his eyes, and she remembered how much she'd loved him, and how they'd learned what it meant to love.

She'd seen ghosts all her life.

She'd never been able to see him before; she'd never been able to say goodbye.

And now he was here.

He smiled at her, unafraid for her — despite the man with a knife at her throat.

"No, Alexi," he said again. "I do love you. I always will. But you have to live. That's why I'm here. You have to live."

She would have shaken her head; she couldn't. Tears stung her eyes, tears that had nothing to do with fear.

She couldn't move at all. The knife was

too close to her throat.

She looked at Zach, feeling the blade as she spoke. "I won't buy time, Hank. I don't need to. I think Jude will shoot you, and you will die. Maybe I will, too. I don't think so. But if you don't release me this second, *you* will."

"Alexi," Jude warned her.

"Now?" Zach asked, turning to look at Jude.

Jude nodded. "Now," he said.

"What? What the hell . . ." Hank began.

Zach made a leap and a roll that took him over the piano. Blake, Minnie and Byron Grant went swiftly into action, all of them hurtling themselves at Hank. Alexi felt the knife at her throat, but she also felt as if the powerful storm raging outside swept onto the ship.

What happened was uncanny.

Hank's head seemed to be pulled back.

Just enough from her to give Jude a clear target.

He took aim.

And fired.

Alexi let out a long primal scream as Hank was ripped cleanly away from her. His head exploded in a spray of blood and he dropped to the floor.

The knife clattered at her feet.

She collapsed to her knees, stunned, her ears ringing, her body covered in blood. She was aware that people were shouting, that the St. Charles Deck had come alive with the sound of footsteps and security officers rushing around.

And she was aware that the Archangel was dead.

There'd been no other choice; it had been his life or hers.

She wanted to feel grief and horror at a life that was lost . . .

But all she could feel was relief for herself, and for others who might have died.

And to be grateful for Jude and for the dead — the ghosts of the *Destiny,* and from her own life — who'd come to save her from a killer's knife.

EPILOGUE

The next day as storm conditions abated and the *Destiny* made for a safe port, Jude was finally able to be with Alexi.

Of course, with Hank dead and the danger gone, he'd run to her and fallen on his knees, taking her in his arms. He'd held her until Jackson and David Beach had arrived with a slew of security men. He had to give Jackson a report, as the ship's doctor had come and tried to tend to Alexi — who hadn't wanted tending to. She was worried about the people she'd seen on the ground. Johnny, Simon . . . Were there others?

Simon and Johnny were going to be fine; the ship's doctor had reassured her of that. Simon, however, wouldn't be dancing for a while. He had a broken leg. The other ship's security guard who'd been injured, Marty Holm, was going to be all right, too. He'd been taken to what was now a fully occupied infirmary. The doctor would not be sleeping that night, nor would the four nurses who staffed the place.

They'd be very busy throughout the final hours of this sailing.

The Reverend Mike had come to the St. Charles Deck, to comfort Alexi. And then Clara and Roger and Jackson . . . Finally Jackson had said they had the entire situation mapped and reported, and Alexi was free to leave with Clara.

Jude knew that Alexi couldn't wait to shower — perhaps for hours — to cleanse herself of the blood.

He also knew it was more than blood that she needed to wash away.

There'd still been truly tragic events to deal with that night — the murders of Flora Winters and David Beach's two security guards.

Jude had been sad to tell Beach that, yes, Hank Osprey had confessed to the killings. He hated that they'd never find the bodies of the men who had been lost; the sea was unforgiving.

The ghosts of the *Destiny* had gone, fading into the ethereal glow of the auxiliary lights as the others raced onto the deck. Jude hadn't been able to even think about them.

Everything had been too chaotic, too busy.

At least by then, he'd known Alexi was safe.

And so was Clara.

The Archangel's killing spree was over now, and they could all mourn the dead.

He was beyond exhausted at eight the next morning when he knocked on Clara's cabin door, anxious to see Alexi. He was rumpled and his hair was tousled and he was, frankly, a mess.

Alexi didn't seem to care. She opened the door and threw her arms around him. She didn't speak; they held each other close for several minutes. He breathed in the scent of her shampoo and soap, and for the first time, he began to shake.

"Oh . . . please, get a room," Clara murmured. "I mean cabin. Oh, wait you have one. Before you go, I need a minute, Alexi."

Alexi stepped back, and Clara threw herself at Jude, giving him a big hug.

"Thank you!" she said huskily. Then she pulled back. "I could've been the one he went for first — and I don't know if I could've done what Alexi did. Making him talk, distracting him . . . Thank you both. From me. From everyone."

Jude shook his head. "Don't thank me for doing what we're supposed to be doing. I wish we'd learned the killer's identity before we lost others to him — Maria Sanchez, the security men, Flora. There's still . . . still a lot to deal with. I don't think Hank was the primary suspect in anyone's mind. Ah, here's a good note, though. Ginny Monk is fine — and, by the way, she does earn her living at a club on Bourbon Street. She wasn't lying about being a student, a part-time one, and plans to enroll full-time in the fall. However, she thought she might escape a life of difficult financial circumstances by following Hank Osprey. She's grateful to be going back to that life now."

Clara pushed back a lock of blond hair. "And Simon? He's okay?"

Jude smiled. "We'll make him look like a true hero when we speak to the press. He'll have a chance to feel that he's a lot more than *just chorus.*"

Clara nodded. "Get out of here, you two. I heard that we've finally outrun the weather. Ralph and Larry were here earlier, and they've been out on deck. The sun is shining. There's still a breeze, but —"

"I'd like to go out on deck," Alexi broke in.

"Me, too," Jude agreed. "Let's do it."

There were quite a few people on the Promenade Deck, sitting in lounge chairs and enjoying the day. Alexi generally liked the company of others but Jude realized that, just then, she didn't want to see anyone else. So he found a private place for them, a little nook between a storage area and a lifeboat. From there, they could gaze out over the sea. The waves were still white-tipped, the breeze was blowing quite fiercely.

But they could feel the sun and bask in its radiant light.

As Alexi stood by the rail, Jude slipped an arm around her shoulders. He didn't speak; he didn't tell her they'd get past it all. You never forgot events like this, but you learned to live with what had happened. He believed, with his whole heart, that they'd manage it together.

"You're part of the Krewe of Hunters now," she eventually said. He nodded; Jackson had made the official invitation this morning.

"And I got to see Zach," she went on. "I'd wanted to see him so badly. He was there, and then he was gone." She turned to Jude. "You saw him, right? And you know they're there to help us."

"I met Zach. He led me to you," Jude told her.

"I still never really said goodbye."

"Say goodbye now," came a voice.

They both turned, toward the sun.

He was there, the man in the contemporary soldier's uniform who'd been there last night. The man without whom Jude might not have been able to save her life.

"Zach!" Alexi walked toward him and Zach reached out a hand.

Jude thought the ghost held her, and then he seemed to smile. "Goodbye, Alexi, I love you." Inclining his head to the side, he said, "You know how I hate clichés, but . . . be happy. You've found a man who's worthy of you." Jude smiled. He would've liked this man very much.

Zach looked past Alexi at Jude. "Say goodbye, too," he said very softly.

And Jude realized that Zach wasn't alone. His breath caught; a sob tore from his throat as he looked down.

Because there was Lily, beautiful in the blue church dress in which she'd been buried, golden curls ringing her head beneath her blue-ribboned Sunday hat.

He dropped to his knees and felt Lily rush into his arms. Felt her little hands on his face, her kiss on his cheek. A moment later she drew back, smiling, and said, "I love you, Daddy. Be happy." Imitating Zach's words. Exactly the *right* words to say.

"I love you. Oh, Lily, I love you so much, so very, very much . . ."

He felt one more kiss; then he briefly saw

her standing with Zachary Wainwright, who had a gentle hand on her shoulder. The sun was pouring down on them both, and they seemed to become one with it. And then they were gone.

Alexi reached for him, helping him to his feet. He was a little unsteady.

They didn't speak.

They stayed on deck until the sun began to set.

Finally, arm in arm, they returned to Alexi's cabin.

They both knew they'd been very lucky. Their pasts had been laid to rest. The future was theirs, and it would be filled with love and hope, no matter what it might bring.

ABOUT THE AUTHOR

New York Times and *USA Today* bestselling author **Heather Graham** has written more than a hundred novels. She's a winner of the RWA's Lifetime Achievement Award, and the Thriller Writers' Silver Bullet. She is an active member of International Thriller Writers and Mystery Writers of America. For more information, check out her websites: TheOriginalHeatherGraham.com, eHeatherGraham.com, and HeatherGraham.tv. You can also find Heather on Facebook.